"I want to hear you say it."

"I want to hear you say that you loved me when you made it clear that you didn't." Jack tried to tell himself that Ava coming to find him didn't matter, that what she said now wouldn't change how he felt. It couldn't. But maybe it would heal the wound that had refused to close up for ten long years.

They were near soaked at this point, but neither seemed to care. The only thing that mattered was what she said next.

She didn't hesitate to answer.

"I loved you, Jack. I loved you *every* day we were together, and I'm pretty sure I'd fall for the man you've become if I had the chance to."

His scrambled brain decided to take a rest, and before he knew what he was doing, his mouth was on hers, his hands cupping her cheeks, skin slick with rain and tears. She kissed him back, and despite the chill in the air he felt heat beneath his palms. Ten years of loss and ache and longing for something he hadn't known still existed poured from his lips. Her tongue plunged into his mouth, and he knew whatever it was he was giving to her he received in turn.

PRAISE FOR A.J. PINE

"Both new and returning readers will be pleased."
            —*Publishers Weekly* on *Make Mine a Cowboy*

"A sweet...love story."
            —*Publishers Weekly* on *My One and Only Cowboy*

"*My One and Only Cowboy* was an entertaining romance
that was woven with wit and warmth."
            —GuiltyPleasuresBookReviews.com

"A steamy cowboy romance novel that is sure to warm your
heart!"
            —LovelyLoveday.com on *Hard Loving Cowboy*

"*Hard Loving Cowboy* was a delightfully sexy read that
made me want to go in search of a cowboy of my own."
            —KimberlyFayeReads.com

"Sweet and engrossing."
            —*Publishers Weekly* on *Tough Luck Cowboy*

"Light and witty."
            —*Library Journal* on *Saved by the Cowboy*

"A fabulous storyteller who will keep you turning pages
and wishing for just one more chapter at the end."
        —Carolyn Brown, *New York Times* bestselling author, on
                                    Second Chance Cowboy

SECOND
CHANCE
COWBOY

ALSO BY A.J. PINE

CROSSROADS RANCH SERIES

Saved by the Cowboy (novella)

Tough Luck Cowboy

Hard Loving Cowboy

MEADOW VALLEY SERIES

Cowboy to the Rescue (novella)

My One and Only Cowboy

Make Mine a Cowboy

A Christmas Cowboy at Heart (novella)

Only a Cowboy Will Do

ALSO BY A.J. PINE WRITING AS AMY PINE

The Bloom Girls

SECOND CHANCE COWBOY

A.J. PINE

A Crossroads Ranch Novel

FOREVER

New York

Copyright © 2018 by A.J. Pine
Excerpt from *Rocky Mountain Wedding* copyright © 2016 by Sara Richardson

Cover copyright © 2022 by Hachette Book Group, Inc.

Forever
Hachette Book Group
1290 Avenue of the Americas, New York, NY 10104
forever-romance.com
twitter.com/foreverromance

First edition: February 2018
Reissue: August 2022

Forever is an imprint of Grand Central Publishing. The Forever name and logo are trademarks of Hachette Book Group, Inc.

The publisher is not responsible for websites (or their content) that are not owned by the publisher.

The Hachette Speakers Bureau provides a wide range of authors for speaking events. To find out more, go to www.hachettespeakersbureau.com or call (866) 376-6591.

ISBNs: 978-1-5387-2388-3 (mass market), 978-1-5387-2705-8 (ebook), 978-1-5491-4665-7 (audio download)

Printed in the United States of America

OPM

10 9 8 7 6 5 4 3 2 1

ACKNOWLEDGMENTS

Thank you, first and foremost, to you—the reader. To those of you who followed me from my romantic comedies to my foray into the wonderful world of cowboys, I'm so grateful for your continued support. And welcome, new readers. I've got two more sexy stories coming your way for Luke and Walker!

A huge thanks to my fabulous editor, Madeleine, for your excellent guidance on Jack and Ava's story. Can't wait to work on Luke next.

Thank you, Courtney, for finding the Everett brothers a great home.

To my wonderful critique partners and friends—Lia Riley, Chanel Cleeton, Jennifer Blackwood, Megan Erickson, and Natalie Blitt—I love you all to pieces. Your friendship and support are everything—as are our daily conversations that usually leave me laughing until I'm crying.

Jennifer Ryan, I cannot thank you enough not only for reading and giving Jack and Ava your stamp of approval but for being a fabulous friend and mentor. You are truly the best.

Thank you, S and C, for being the best fans even though you're not old enough to read my books yet. I love you to infinity.

SECOND
CHANCE
COWBOY

PROLOGUE

Ten Years Ago

Ava snaked her fingers through Jack's and squeezed.

"Come on," she said. "It's going to be fun."

His head fell back against the seat as he put the truck in park. Parties weren't his thing, especially here. He'd only been at Los Olivos High School for five months, so celebrating graduation as the odd man out wasn't exactly top on his list.

But it was top on Ava's list, and there was nothing he wouldn't do for the girl who'd made those months bearable.

No. That wasn't fair. Time with Ava was more than bearable. It was everything that got him out of bed in the morning and kept him from cutting class when he would have been fine taking the GED, even if it meant losing his baseball scholarship. It's how he endured not being able to play his senior year. And it was the reason that maybe— after college and getting some distance from this place— he'd be able to come back and see it differently.

"I love you," she said softly, her pale cheeks turning pink as she leaned across the center console and kissed the corner of his mouth.

He blew out a breath and skimmed his fingers through her thick, auburn waves.

"And I know you're leaving soon for summer training, but I think we should tell my parents about us. Unless—I mean if this *is* only a senior year thing."

He tugged her closer, his palm cradling the back of her neck as he brushed his lips over hers. "You're it for me, Red," he whispered against her. "But I thought they were still getting over you and Golden Boy breaking up."

She groaned. "I know you know Derek's name."

The corner of his mouth quirked into a crooked grin. "Doesn't mean I have to say it."

"You wanted to wait, remember?" she reminded him. "Because my dad is way overprotective."

Jack laughed, the sound bitter, and his smile faded. "And thinks I'm gonna be like *my* father. I got it then, and I get it now."

It didn't matter that Los Olivos was an hour away from Oak Bluff, Jack's hometown. News traveled fast when three new students transferred into a school second semester. And a drunk almost killing his oldest son was the best sort of gossip for a small California wine country town.

It wasn't as if he didn't have the same fears. The apple usually didn't fall too far from the tree.

He hadn't planned on anything more in Los Olivos than biding his time and getting the hell out of town when summer came.

He hadn't planned on *her*. So when he'd suggested they keep the relationship quiet—that he didn't want to make waves in her seemingly perfect life—she hadn't argued.

She cupped his cheeks in her palms and tilted his forehead to hers. "He doesn't *know* you. Plus I'm not good at secrets. Or lying. As soon as he sees how amazing you are, he'll know there's nothing to worry about."

He closed his eyes as she kissed him. Maybe this could

be him now, the guy a girl brought home to her parents instead of the one people whispered about when they thought he couldn't hear.

"I love you, too," he finally said. "In case you didn't know."

He felt her lips part into a smile against his.

"Oh, I know," she teased. "But I like to hear you say it."

Both of them startled at the sound of the passenger side window rattling.

"Party's out back!" someone yelled as another graduate drummed against the glass again.

Ava giggled. "One hour," she said. "If it sucks after an hour, then we leave. Promise."

He pressed a soft kiss against her neck and she shivered.

"Anything for you, Red."

He leaned across her and opened her door. Then he hopped out of his own and met her at the passenger side.

Maybe this was what it had been like for his parents before it all went to hell—when his mom was alive and his dad sober. He couldn't remember anymore. The past five years couldn't be erased, but maybe whatever the future held could cushion the blow.

Ava swayed when her feet hit the ground outside the truck, and Jack caught her by the elbow.

"Hey there," he said. "You okay?"

She forced a smile even as her stomach roiled.

"Yeah," she said. "I'm fine. It's just so hot out tonight." Thankfully, that was the truth—even if it wasn't *her* truth. "I need to splash some cool water on my face. That's all. Head out to the bonfire, and I'll be right back."

He hesitated, but she needed to get inside—quick.

"Go." She nudged his shoulder. "I'll meet you out back."

"I'll come with you," he said insistently, and she could see the worry in those blue eyes.

"Ava!"

They both turned to where a group of girls were coming up the street toward Jack's truck, her friend Rachel heading up the pack.

"Ohmygod," Rachel said in one breath. "Please tell me you know where the bathroom is and that you can get me there safely."

Saved by the drunk friend.

"See?" Ava said to Jack, grabbing Rachel's hand. "I'm not alone. See you in five minutes."

He ran a hand through his overgrown blond waves, then kissed her on the cheek.

"Five minutes," he relented. "You're sure you're okay?"

She nodded, afraid if she opened her mouth again her lie would be exposed. Instead she and Rachel ran for the front door of the house up the drive.

Once in the bathroom, she dropped to her knees in front of the toilet and emptied her stomach.

"Damn," Rachel said. "I thought *we* prepartied too much."

But Ava hadn't had one drink that night. And this was the fourth time this had happened in the span of a week.

She grabbed a wad of toilet paper and wiped her mouth, then flushed and turned toward the sink.

"Yeah," she said absently. "Too much prepartying." She cupped cold water in her palms and drank, then thankfully found a tube of toothpaste in the medicine cabinet. "I'll see you out there."

She slipped out of the bathroom and into the small hallway off the foyer, heart hammering in her chest.

She pressed a palm against her flat belly. She would

have to take a test to confirm, but she was already over a week late. It looked like she had something to tell Jack before they broke the news to her parents that they were dating.

"There you are," a voice crooned from the end of the hall.

Ava rolled her eyes. "Not now, Derek," she said, attempting to push past him as he came nearer. Instead he backed her into the corner where the wall met the doorframe to the guest bedroom.

"Not funny," she said, trying to slip out from where his arm palmed the wall above her shoulder.

"I miss you," he said, his breath tinged with the scent of liquor.

"You're drunk. You always miss me when you're drunk."

His free hand cupped her breast and she swatted it away. "What the hell do you think you're doing?"

But he wasn't deterred. This time he pressed the length of his body against hers. "Come on, babe. I know how much you like taking in strays, but enough is enough. Two years, and you never gave it up for me, but you give it up for that trash from Oak Bluff?"

He ground against her pelvis, pressed his fingers hard against the base of her throat. He was too close for her to knee him in the balls—too big to push away.

"Stop it, Derek."

Golden Boy. Right. Nothing could be further from the truth.

She pushed her palms into his chest, but he wouldn't budge. It only made his weight against her feel heavier, his fingertips on her skin pressing harder.

Over his shoulder she saw Rachel step out of the bathroom. The girl caught Ava's eye and grinned, then pressed her fingers to her lips in a promise to keep quiet as she started backing away. After all, Ava and Derek Wilkes had been the couple most likely to—well—*everything* just before the holidays. Until she wouldn't give him what he wanted for Christmas. To Rachel this probably looked like reconciliation.

"Rach—" she started, but Derek shut her up by pressing his lips to hers.

This wasn't happening. Except it was. So she bit down on his lip.

"Shit!" he growled, backing away and swiping the back of his hand across his mouth, his skin smeared with blood. "You little—"

He reached for her again, but his hand never made contact. In a blur, someone slammed Derek up against the adjacent wall.

"She said *stop*, asshole."

Jack was seething, something dark and dangerous in his eyes.

"Thanks for breaking her in for me," Derek said with a sneer. "But I think I can take it from here."

Jack slammed him against the wall again.

Derek laughed.

Ava yelped, and Jack's eyes met hers.

"I'm okay," she said. "Let's just go."

But then his gaze dipped to her collarbone. She ran her fingers over the skin, wincing when she felt the beginnings of bruises.

That was all it took for Jack to lose his focus—and for Derek to throw the first punch.

Ava watched in slow motion as Jack's head snapped to the side and blood trickled from the corner of his mouth.

And then before she knew it, Derek's head crashed into the wall as Jack's fist collided with his face again and again until blood poured from Derek's nose and a group of guys Ava hadn't seen arrive were pulling Jack from his limp human punching bag.

She hadn't even known she was screaming until the commotion settled and one of the guys let go of Jack to keep Derek—now unconscious—from crashing to the floor.

Jack stared down at his bloodied knuckles, then up at her, his eyes wide with horror.

"I'm *him*," he said softly—like he hadn't meant anyone else to hear but himself—as sirens wailed in the distance.

CHAPTER ONE

Jack glanced down at his rumpled shirt, then ran a hand through his perpetually overgrown hair. Despite a sleepless night, he had somehow made the five-plus hour drive from San Diego to the outskirts of San Luis Obispo County—and the blip on the map that was Oak Bluff—without killing himself. A shit night of sleep was the norm. Spending the entire morning on the 101 with only the two cups of coffee he'd bought on his way out of town and thoughts he'd rather not have the time to *think*? That was another story. A man alone with his thoughts for too long was a dangerous combination. It was one of the reasons he rarely came home. Another one of those reasons was about to make his way six feet underground.

His vision blurred, and he shook his head, swerving to avoid a blown-out tire in the middle of the road right before the entrance to the cemetery. The coffee wasn't exactly doing its job.

He let out a bitter laugh as his truck rolled to a stop on the narrow lane along the gravesites. "Would you have appreciated the irony?" he asked aloud. His voice was deep and hoarse after the hours of silence, hands white-knuckled on the steering wheel of his now-parked truck.

"Me kicking the goddamn bucket the day I come to see you laid to rest?"

No one answered, of course. He glanced at the cattleman hat on the passenger seat, still not sure why he'd kept it all these years in San Diego, or why he'd felt the need to bring it with him for the drive back. As soon as he made sure Luke and Walker—and even his aunt Jenna—were taken care of, he had another life to get back to.

Because *home* wasn't here anymore. Hadn't been for years. He wasn't sure any place fit that definition these days, but it sure as hell wasn't the small, ranching town of Oak Bluff. Boxed in amongst vineyards and only miles from the ocean, tourists who wanted a quaint, off-the-beaten-path segue from wine country kept the place on the map. But Jack hadn't taken *that* segue in a decade. Until now.

He hopped out of his truck and grabbed his suit jacket from its hanger in the back of the cab and the fresh bouquet of flowers from the floor. In the distance he could see the distinct figures of his younger brothers, his aunt, and a fourth body—most likely some funeral officiant—standing at the grave.

That was it. The four of them and a stranger to preside over the burial of a man he wasn't sure deserved even that much. Yet here he was.

As he approached, his aunt Jenna was the first to look up. Not even ten years his senior, she'd always felt more like a sister, and a pang of unexpected longing for the family he'd left behind socked him square in the gut. It had been over a year since he'd seen her—since he'd seen any of them. God, she looked more like his mother now than ever, her short blond hair having grown to her shoulders since the last time they'd met. At thirty-six, Jenna, the baby sister, had now seen more years than his mother ever would.

He stopped at the grave next to his father's and knelt down, laying the small arrangement of white and purple orchids on the grass in front of the headstone that read CLARE OWENS-EVERETT, BELOVED WIFE, MOTHER, SISTER, AND DAUGHTER.

"Hey, Ma," he said softly. "Still miss you. Brought you your favorite."

"Has it really been fifteen years?"

He heard Jenna behind him, the lilt of her Texas twang that never left, much like his mother's—but he lingered several more seconds with the orchids and his memories. He silently wished for his mom to send him some sort of sign that she was at peace. Had she known what happened to her husband after he lost her? What he'd become and what he'd done to her boys?

"I tried," he said under his breath, not wanting Jenna to hear. "I tried to fix him. But he didn't want to be fixed."

He stood then, towering over the woman who'd taken them in when she was barely done being a kid herself.

"You're huge," she said as he pulled her into a hug. "Were you always this tall?" He laughed, and she pushed far enough away to rest her palms on his lapels. "Look at you, Jack. Christ on a cracker, you're all grown up. You bring home any of your fancy lawyer friends for your aunt? Maybe on the other side of thirty, though."

She winked at him. Still the same Jenna.

"Not this trip," he mused. "Maybe next time."

She hooked her arm through his and pulled him the last several feet to their destination, where his father's casket sat suspended over the rectangular hole in the ground.

"Nice suit," Walker sneered. Jack could barely see his

brother's eyes under the brim of his hat, but he knew they were narrowed.

"Aren't you supposed to remove your hat to show respect for the dead?" he countered.

Jack thought he heard his youngest brother growl.

"Is that what that getup is?" Walker asked, taking a step closer. Jack was sure he smelled liquor on his brother's breath and decided to let any sort of comment about drinking before noon slide. He'd give him a free pass for today. "A sign of *respect*?" Walker continued. "Since when do you respect the man who almost killed you? And since when do you have a fucking say? This ain't your home anymore, pretty boy."

Jenna gasped.

The funeral officiant cleared his throat.

Luke, taking his role as middle brother literally, stepped between the other two men, removing his own hat and holding it against his chest.

"All right, boys. Let's save this twisted pissing contest until later and shove our dicks back in our pants. Shall we?"

Jack caught sight of the laceration across Luke's cheek, the few stitches holding it together. "What the hell is that?" he asked.

"Here we go," Walker said, turning away. He'd either lost interest in pushing Jack's buttons or was happy to let the attention fall on Luke.

"Tried my first bull," Luke said with an easy grin. "He didn't like me much."

"You're riding bulls now? I thought this rodeo stuff was a hobby. When the hell are you gonna take life seriously?"

Luke's ever-present smile fell. "You mean like running the ranch *you* left? Hell, I know you send money, Jack. Helping in your own way. But I take life plenty seriously when I need to. When there isn't need, I think I'm entitled to a little fun."

Jack spun to Jenna, who had conveniently backed away from the conversation. "You knew about this?"

She shrugged. "Y'all are big, grown men now. You can make your own decisions." Then she laughed. "Though I hate to see him mess up that pretty face of his."

Luke threw his hat back on his head. "If it's any consolation, Jenna, the ladies do *not* complain."

His aunt shook her head and squeezed her eyes shut. "Sometimes I think it was easier when you were teenagers."

Jack gritted his teeth and fisted his hands at his sides. It didn't matter how long he'd been gone. After their mother died, their father had been far from a model parent. Jack had practically raised his brothers himself through their teen years, but he wasn't going to lecture Luke, not now. Instead all he muttered was "It's dangerous."

Luke threw an arm over his big brother's shoulder. "It's *fun*, asshole. Thought by now you'd have figured out what that word meant."

Again, the sound of a throat clearing interrupted their reunion, and all four of them looked up to find the funeral officiant, a small man with a gray comb-over in a suit one size too big, fidgeting as he stood at the head of the grave.

"Sorry, folks," he said. "But I have another service in an hour. I don't want to rush you, but—"

"Good," Walker said, joining the fray again. "Let's get this over with."

The officiant swallowed. "Does anyone have something they'd like to say about Mr. Everett before interment?"

Jack's stomach twisted. He wouldn't speak ill of the dead, but he sure as hell wouldn't say anything of import for the man who only knew how to speak with the back of his hand. He remembered standing here for his mom's burial, the space crowded with family and friends—their local pastor leading the small ceremony. Jack had been thirteen, Luke twelve, and Walker ten. They'd watched the cancer *and* treatment ravage her body for a year. That was all they'd had from diagnosis until the end. When they'd lowered her into the ground, tears had streamed down both his brothers' cheeks, but Jack decided then and there he had to be strong—for his brothers and his father. It hadn't taken him long to realize he'd failed at the latter, but as for Luke and Walker, he was still trying, even if they ended up hating him for it.

"If no one says anything," Jack finally said, "does that mean it's over?"

The man raised his shoulders. "I work for the funeral home, so this is not a religious ceremony," he said. "Usually the way it works is a family member or friend reads something. Or—or gives *me* something to read. If you have something prepared—"

Jack shook his head and looked at his brothers, who both studied their boots.

"Well, then…" The officiant wrung his hands. "If no one has any words…"

"I do!" Jenna said, a little too loudly for the small gathering. "I mean, someone should say something, and if y'all don't want to, that's okay. But—but someone *should.*"

She strode up to the head of the grave, and the man stepped aside. In her floral dress and cardigan, she really did look like their mother. Jack was so used to Jenna in a tank top and denim shorts—rain boots up to her knees as she stepped inside her chicken coop or chased rabbits from her garden. If this was a new look for her, it would take some getting used to.

She squared her shoulders, and the Everett boys all gave her their attention.

"Hi," she said. "Um, yeah. Okay." She took in a long breath and blew it out. "Jackson Everett Senior was my brother-in-law and the love of my big sister's life. When we moved here from Houston, I was a scrappy seven-year-old who knew nothing more about love other than crying when our baby chick died. We lost our daddy when I was too young to remember him, and though I loved our mama—like I said, I was all about the chickens when we came here."

She swiped at a tear under her eye, and Jack thought he should go to her, hold her hand or something. But the thought of standing there while she paid her respects to a man he'd lost all faith in years ago only made him clench his teeth harder, so he dug his heels into the soft ground and decided to stay put.

"When Clare, my sister, came home from her first day at her new high school, she told me she had met the boy she was going to marry, and when Clare Owens said something, it was the truth. Always. When she and Jackson were only eighteen and got pregnant with you, Jack?" Her eyes glistened when she looked at him. "Well, he practically married her on the spot. His dreams were always your mama and Crossroads Ranch. You boys were his legacy—the second generation of Everetts on that piece of land." She took a breath, the tremor in it audible amidst the silence. "They built the place up with the little savings they both had, filled the house with boys born to be ranchers, but—" Another pause as Jenna seemed to relive the loss of her sister—their mother.

Jack noticed Walker was holding his hat at his side now. Bitter as he was toward Jack Senior, his baby brother would never disrespect his mother, no matter how many years she'd been gone.

Jenna choked on a sob. "He broke when he lost Clare. We *all* did. I know that. But something in your daddy broke real deep. And I'm so sorry I didn't know—" A hiccupping breath stole her words. "I'm so sorry—"

Jack was at her side now, his arm around his aunt. No way in hell was he going to let her fall down the rabbit hole of guilt. He'd spent enough time there to know it wouldn't do her an ounce of good.

"Jenna, don't," he said as he led her from the grave. "You didn't know," he added. "No one knew."

He'd made sure of that. Because despite the verbal attacks—and the physical ones—Jack Senior was all he'd thought they had. He'd cut his boys off from any other family. Jack had always believed he could wait it out until he was eighteen. Because what was the alternative? Report his father and risk him and his brothers getting separated in the foster system?

Instead Luke and Walker had almost lost him completely.

She wrapped her arms around him and buried her head in his chest.

"I'm sorry," she said again.

All he could do was whisper "shhh." She might have been eight years his senior, but she felt like a child in his arms, clinging to him to keep steady.

He knew her tears weren't for his father. And as much as Jenna missed her sister, the choking sobs weren't for her, either. They were for what Jackson Everett Sr. had hidden from everyone for five years—until that 911 call and the last words his father ever spoke in his presence:

Help. I think I killed my boy.

* * *

Ava Ellis stood in the open doorway of the empty bedroom—empty but for the countless portraits lining the floor—the ones filled with still lifes of fruit or images of the dog in various states of play—and the easel in the corner, the one holding the blank canvas waiting for another attempt at the one thing she still hadn't captured. She could make a million and one excuses not to walk in there.

I should really catch up on laundry.

I haven't put in enough hours at the vineyard this week.

It's almost noon. I should start prepping dinner.

It's Saturday. It would make more sense to try again on Monday.

Ah, yes. That last excuse was her favorite. Everything seemed possible on a Monday—until Monday actually came around and the week got away from her again.

The sun peeked through the curtains, dappled light and shadow cutting across the blank canvas—the silhouette of the olive tree outside the window.

"Don't tease me, tree," she warned before huffing out a breath and reaching behind her neck to tie her auburn mane into a loose bun. "I'm just—*preparing*." She laughed quietly. "Preparing and talking to a tree."

She'd been intending to paint it since she'd moved into the house several years ago. The hulking yet beautiful tree had been what drew her to the property in the first place, a reminder of something she'd lost and was still trying to find.

She pulled the small case of charcoals from the back pocket of her jeans.

"It's only drawing," she said to no one in particular as she crossed the threshold into the room. She certainly wasn't still talking to a tree, trying to trick it into acquiescence. "We're not ready to paint, yet." *We're.* Shit. She *was* still talking to the tree. "Fine," she added. "If we're going to be spending the weekend together, I guess we both better get used to the talking. I don't do quiet."

Yet here she was, in her quaint split-level, alone in what many would consider blissful silence compared to the whirlwind that was her life, and she was ready to go mad.

She opened the case and set it on the table beside the easel, eying the different widths of the charcoal sticks before settling on a short, stubby one that fit comfortably between her thumb and fingers. She rolled it there for a minute, getting the feel for it as it smudged the ridges of her skin. And then, as if it was the most natural thing to do, she drew a leaf. One, simple, perfect, lonely leaf. It barely took a minute—barely took any space up on what now felt like a colossal piece of canvas.

"Shit," she said. "It's too goddamn quiet."

She dropped the charcoal onto the table, not bothering to fit it back into the case. What would be the point? She was coming back. Eventually. Another day or two meant nothing in the grand scheme of years—except that now she actually had a deadline. If she wanted to apply for late admission to Cal Poly's art program, she needed to produce a piece of meaningful art. Soon. *Still Life of Labrador Catching a Frisbee* wasn't exactly meaningful.

She *would* succeed. Just—not today.

Famous last words.

Barely touching the six steps to the lower level, she grabbed her sunglasses off the kitchen table, raced toward the back door and out to the shed. It was the weekend, after all, and the grass wasn't going to cut itself. And hell, she needed *noise.*

With the mower on, maybe she could ignore the stupid,

taunting tree. Maybe she could forget walking past the room with a wistful glance for the past six years, always aware of what lay beyond the curtained window. And maybe, if she kept at it, straight through to the front yard, she could convince herself that a tree—a freaking *tree*—had not been getting the best of her for each of those six years.

She yanked the starter on the mower, smelled the familiar odor of gasoline, and then there it was—noise.

But it didn't matter if she wouldn't admit it out loud, not when her own inner monologue refused to shut up.

The first place she'd seen him had been under an olive tree more than ten years ago, across the street from Los Olivos High School. She couldn't hear what he was saying but knew by the way the other two boys listened to him so intently that it must have been important. There was no mistaking that they were brothers; each boasted a similar mop of golden, California waves. But he was the oldest, patriarchal in his care for the younger ones. She could see it in the way he tousled the youngest one's hair even though the boy responded by slapping his big brother's hand away, in how he gave the other that all-knowing single nod of the head. All this while he balanced easily on his left leg, keeping his weight off the right, the one wrapped in plaster from the knee down.

That was where she'd first laid eyes on Jack Everett, and it was where, six months later, she'd broken both their hearts.

She pushed the mower across the lawn, her jaw clenched and heart seeming to constrict with each beat. Breaking up hadn't been her intent when she'd asked him to meet her there one late summer night, even after what had happened at the graduation party. She'd had other news to tell him.

But instead she'd told the boy she loved with all her heart that she didn't love him at all. Ava had *freed* him under that very same tree—and then she'd gone and bought a house with its doppelgänger looming in the backyard. She'd thought if she could paint it—draw it at least—that would mean she was over it. Over him finding happiness in a life that didn't include her. But she hadn't been able to finish a single attempt. Today's leaf was the furthest she'd gotten in months.

Ava knew the truth of that tree, why she'd wanted to be so close to it. Whether or not she'd ever gotten over her first love didn't matter when she couldn't forgive herself for what she'd done. *That* was why she was an artist who couldn't create anything more than a replica of fruit or the dog. It was the real reason she needed the tree. Because why let guilt eat you from the inside out when it could stare at you every day?

"Good question," she said aloud, over the roar of the mower. The tree didn't answer. Not that it ever did.

Then she bumped straight into said tree.

"Damn it!" She yelled as the handle jammed into her ribs. She turned the mower off and growled at the ugly beast of a plant. "Enough," she said, a small weight lifting with the word. *"Enough,"* she repeated, and her next breath came even easier. "I don't need your approval," she snapped at the tree, and for the first time she actually believed it.

There was plenty of meaning in her life. Maybe not the dog catching a Frisbee, but there was so much inspiration to draw from. She'd pick a new subject to paint, complete her application, and turn it in by the end of the month. *It's time to stand on my own two feet*, she thought. She'd given up her independence for her son, and she wouldn't trade the experience for what she'd thought was her carefully constructed life plan. But she didn't want to rely on her parents anymore for financial stability. She didn't want a job at the family vineyard. She wanted a career. A passion. Something just for her. And nothing—not even a tree—was going to get in the way of that.

CHAPTER TWO

Jack stood for several long seconds outside the modest two-story house, the living quarters of what was commercially known as Crossroads Ranch. The rich wood of the shingled siding had paled in some areas, so that now patches of weathered tan mottled against the dark brown looked like fading bruises. The wraparound porch was still intact, but he could tell on first glance it needed to be refinished and stained. He'd add that to his to-do list. He was sure that after they'd gone through Jack Senior's things there'd be repairs here and there to make, but he also knew Luke and Walker had kept an eye on the ranch, so he wasn't worried about having to stay too long. He'd need to check the stables and the herd, meet with the accountant to ensure they could continue paying the hired hands. All this, of course, following today's visit from his father's estate attorney.

It wasn't as if he'd forgotten the place and all the work it took to run it. That was why he sent money each month to help keep the place afloat—to make sure the mortgage got paid. Luke and Walker were plenty capable. They'd proved that well enough. But the money only did so much to ease the guilt of his absence—not from the ranch but from his brothers' lives. Now that Jack Senior was gone, he could be the positive physical presence he hadn't been all those years ago. At least until he up and left again.

"You gonna take a fuckin' picture?" Walker asked as he strode past him and up the porch steps.

Luke approached next. "That's *asshole* speak for 'Come on in and grab a beer,'" he said with a grin.

"When you're ready," Jenna added, standing next to him now. "And maybe when you need a break, you can drive me home. Walker picked me up but..."

She trailed off, only confirming what he'd suspected when he'd smelled the liquor on his brother's breath. Walker would be in no shape to drive anyone anywhere in the immediate future.

"He's been pissed at me for a lot of years, hasn't he?" he asked. "I left. I own that."

But his brothers had understood. Hadn't they? He'd *had* to go. After what he'd done to Derek Wilkes, he was lucky the guy's family hadn't pressed charges. He'd only meant to be gone through college. But plans had changed, thanks to the fiery redhead he'd never quite forgotten.

Jenna lifted a hand to his shoulder, giving him a gentle squeeze. "Did you ever think that maybe it's not *you* he's pissed at?"

She didn't wait for him to answer but instead followed her other two nephews into the house.

He squinted at what used to be his home, trying to see what it had been prior to fifteen years ago, but the well of his memory came up dry. He knew there had been happiness behind those doors. There had been a family. But he couldn't picture it. The only thing he saw in his mind's eye now was Walker getting backhanded across the face—or a dazed Jack Senior at the top of the stairs, staring down at his oldest son's broken form. Losing their mother would have been enough to reshape their history. But instead it had been so much worse.

"You must be Jack Junior."

The voice came from behind him, which meant the man couldn't see him grit his teeth. He'd never truly escape the connection to his father, not when he was his namesake. And that one little thread that kept them bound also kept that tiny voice in his head questioning how alike they were other than a shared name. The loss of Jack's mother had sent Jack Senior over the edge. What would it take for him to do the same?

Jack spun to face the man.

"Mr. Miranda, I assume," Jack said, and held out his hand.

The guy didn't seem much older than he was, maybe early thirties. He wore a plaid shirt with the sleeves rolled to his elbows and dark jeans, and it finally hit Jack that although this man was a stranger to him, it was *he* who was the odd man out on the front lawn of his own childhood home.

"Please," he said as he shook Jack's hand. "Call me Thomas. And damn if you don't look just like him—or like I bet he looked before the drinking." Thomas ran a hand through his wavy, dark hair. "Damn it. That was out of line. I apologize."

Jack loosened his tie, feeling overdressed and misplaced. He shook his head. "No apology necessary, not when it's the truth."

Thomas gave him a nervous smile. "I don't normally do this on the weekends," he said. "But your aunt told me this was the only day she could be certain you'd all be in the same place at the same time. Do you mind if I come in?"

"Not at all," Jack said as he moved toward the porch steps.

Thomas followed closely behind, and the two of them—both strangers to this place now—entered a house Jack hadn't stepped foot in for ten years. Now it was simply a reminder of a father who'd lost himself in his grief and taken it out on his boys—of a past he'd been trying to outrun for a decade. Before today, he thought he'd gotten past what this place could do to him.

Now he wasn't so sure anymore.

"Grapes?" Walker asked, tipping back his third bottle of beer since they'd all sat down at the wooden table in the kitchen. It hadn't been there growing up, and Jack wondered what would have possessed Jack Senior to buy new furniture when all he'd ever seemed to spend his money on was whiskey. "He left us fucking grapes?"

"A small vineyard," Thomas clarified. "He left you three equal shares in the ranch—which he mortgaged to buy the vineyard."

Walker scoffed, slamming his empty bottle down in front of him. "So—*grapes.*" His cheeks were flushed and his eyes a steely gray as he pushed back from the table and headed to the fridge, undoubtedly for another beer.

Yeah, after six hours in the car this morning, Jack knew he'd be driving his aunt the hour ride back to Los Olivos.

"We can sell it, though, right?" Luke asked. "I mean, Walker and I have enough on our hands working the ranch, and we don't know shit about wine."

Walker nodded as he opened the fridge. "Bet our big brother knows plenty, though. All those fancy restaurants he goes to on the bay in San Diego."

Christ. Was that really what they thought of him? It wasn't as if he'd fallen off the face of the earth in the past decade. He'd come back to Jenna's for at least half the Christmases he'd been gone, but it hadn't been easy, not when he knew Ava Ellis lived nearby and wanted nothing to do with him.

A weight pressed firm on his chest.

He hadn't run from *her*.

Shit. He had a goddamn useless piece of land to worry about. He couldn't afford to let his mind wander down that destructive path.

"Look, asshole," Jack said to Walker. "It's not like Oak Bluff is the ends of the earth. We may have our tiny pocket of cattle land here, but shit. You've experienced a restaurant once or twice before. We *are* smack-dab in the middle of fucking wine country."

Walker opened his mouth to lob a comeback at him, but Jack ignored his brother and turned to Thomas. "Can we?" he asked. "Can we just turn around and sell it?"

Thomas blew out a breath. "That's where things get tricky."

Walker was back at the table now with the rest of his six-pack—and he wasn't offering to share.

"The vineyard's not thriving," Thomas continued. "Your neighbor—the one your father bought it from—let it go once he decided to sell. And, well, Jack Senior wasn't exactly in the best shape to get it going himself."

"How long's he had this thing?" Walker asked, popping the top off another bottle.

"Six months," Thomas said. "I know it's hard to believe, but he had his moments of lucidity. He knew he was sick and needed to get his affairs in order. I can assure you he couldn't have bought the vineyard without being sober, and the same goes for his will. I helped him finalize everything and—he knew what he was doing, boys."

Luke shook his head like he was trying to wrap his brain around it all. "Six months?" he asked. "Six months and he never said shit about it to us?"

Jack narrowed his eyes. "When would he have said something?" He knew his brothers had been keeping the ranch running, that Jack Senior was drunk and incoherent for most of his waking hours, but he hadn't suspected much in the way of interaction between his father and his brothers.

Luke blew out a breath. "We weren't going to say anything because we knew it'd piss you off, but c'mon, Jack. Jenna got us through the years we needed looking after when we were still minors, but after a while an hour drive twice a day gets to be too much. The days got longer. Jack Senior got sicker. It seemed like the right thing to do, moving back and all."

The right thing to do?

"Is this some sort of joke?" Jack pressed the heels of his hands into his eyes. "It didn't cross your mind to tell me you've been living with the man who lost his right to even speak to you before you turned eighteen?" He gritted his teeth and looked from brother, to brother, to aunt. "How long?" he asked. His pulse raced, and he recognized the feeling—the anticipation of the back of his father's hand or a fist to the ribs. The fight or flight as the wind was about to get knocked out of him. "How damned *long* have you been back?"

Tears pooled in Jenna's eyes as she waited for one of her nephews to answer. It was Walker who finally did.

"Two years," he said softly, for once with no hint of anger or resentment in his voice.

Two years? Christ.

"So you all flat-out lied to me about what's been going on around here?"

Luke shrugged. "You didn't ask, and we figured it wasn't something you'd want to know. Judging by your reaction, I'd say we were right."

Jack's jaw tightened, and he could feel his pulse throbbing in his neck.

"It's their *home*," Jenna added. "Their livelihood and their home. I never would have let them talk me into it if I thought they were in any danger, but look at them, Jack. Look at your brothers. They are strong, smart, grown men who knew what they were doing when they decided to come home." She opened her mouth to continue but must have thought better of it and said nothing more.

He knew what would have come next: that it was his home, too.

But it wasn't. Not anymore, no matter how much he missed the open land with nothing looking down on him but the sky above.

There had been physical distance between him and his brothers when he left, but it hadn't registered until now how far he'd really gone—how great the divide was between him and his only family.

"I'm going out for a ride," he said, pushing back from the table and standing, relieved that he'd changed into jeans and a thermal before beginning their little meeting. "Check out the herd—the grapes too. Leave whatever needs to be signed, Mr. Miranda. I'll drop it by your office later this week."

Thomas stood to shake his hand, and in seconds Jack was out the door and headed toward the stables. Just because he no longer lived on the ranch didn't mean he'd forgotten how to ride.

The horse whinnied when he threw open the stall door, but when her eyes met his, she steadied as if she'd been reacquainted with a long-lost friend. She made no protest as he saddled and readied her to leave.

"Hey, girl," he said, running a hand along her silky, caramel-colored coat. "Hey there, Cleo." And without another thought, he led her out of the stable, mounted the saddle, and took off for the hills.

They rode past the herd, which did little more than glance in his direction as he sped by until nothing but green pasture rolled out ahead of him, stopping only where he could see the hint of grapevines—rows and rows of them.

He steeled himself against the memory of a vintner's daughter, his last good memory of home—and also one of his most painful.

He breathed deep as he tapped his boots against the horse's flanks, urging her faster and farther toward the oak trees in the distance, welcoming the burn of the leather reins against the flesh of his palms.

This, he thought, *is the only part of the ranch that feels like home.*

CHAPTER THREE

Jack woke to the sound of a buzz saw in the kitchen. At least, that's what the noise *felt* like after however many shots he'd thrown back the night before. But when he managed to open one eye and peel his half-naked body from the leather couch, he realized—thank God—that what he'd heard was coffee beans grinding.

"You look like shit," Walker said as he leaned against the counter. Jack couldn't tell if that was his brother's norm or if he did it for balance. He guessed it was a little of both.

"You seen a mirror lately?" Jack asked. "What the hell was in that bottle last night, by the way?"

Shot glasses still lined the table. He vaguely remembered getting back from his ride and Jenna sitting him and his brothers down at the table with a takeout pizza and a direct order that they bond. Apparently bonding meant getting shitfaced and not remembering when or how he'd ended up on the couch.

"Where's Jenna?" he asked.

Walker squinted as if he was searching for the answer, but after a few seconds he shrugged. "She took your truck. Said something about buying feed for her chickens, which she'd planned on doing when she thought she was going to be home yesterday. Said you could run her home once you were awake and could see straight."

His brother leaned his forearms on the counter and dropped his head to rest as well.

"Because even the morning after *you* don't. That right?" How long would he be able to chalk Walker's drinking up to age and immaturity? He was twenty-five already. As much as he feared for his own hereditary instincts, it scared him more to see it in one of his brothers. But Walker wasn't one to talk, nor to listen or give a shit about what his big brother feared. The only way to get through to him was to use his own language.

Walker's head rose lazily, but there was serious intent in his steely gaze. The coffee finished brewing, and he poured himself a cup. "There's no sugar," he said.

"I'll take it black." Jack stumbled toward the kitchen wearing nothing but his jeans from last night. He scratched the back of his head, felt his hair standing out at strange angles as he opened the cabinet that still held the mugs. "Jesus," he said, pulling out the one with a collage of the three brothers when they were kids. *Before.* He remembered his father, in a drunken outburst, backhanding the mug off the counter. "The handle had broken off," he said, more to himself than to his brother. "Exploded into a bunch of pieces. I was there. I saw it."

But even as he inspected the mug, he knew he wasn't looking at a replica. He ran his finger over the handle, felt the slight ridges where the separated ceramic had been glued back together. But to look at it—you'd never know. Unless you knew.

"He fixed some of the things he broke," Walker said. And Jack heard in his brother's voice what neither of them would even think about saying. Because damn if the three of them weren't still just as broken as they had been when they were removed from their father's care and sent to live with Jenna.

"Who's hungry?"

Their aunt's question sing-songed through the front door as she burst into the house—all smiles and sunshine, a welcome interruption to wherever the conversation was veering between him and Walker. He never knew how she did it. Even when she'd been barely twenty-five, without parents of her own, and found herself the legal ward of three teenage boys, she'd rarely faltered.

The two men turned toward her, and Jack was sure he smelled . . . bacon.

Walker, suddenly steady on his feet after one sip of coffee, strode in her direction. "Bring on the grease," he said, and she held out a bag that was soaked through with it.

"There's a farmer's market midway between my place and yours. Turns out this guy—new to the area. He's opening a little diner out that direction soon, and he just so happens to be looking for an egg supplier."

Walker tore open the bag and pulled out one of three wrapped sandwiches. He moaned as his teeth sank into the first bite. "Damn. I love a good buttermilk biscuit," he said, his mouth full of food. "What the hell is a diner owner doing at a farmer's market?" he asked. "Not that I'm complaining," he added, pointing at her with what was left of his nearly demolished sandwich.

She shrugged. "He likes to buy fresh ingredients from the locals." She playfully batted her lashes. "Like me," she continued. "And he's trying to advertise his new place. So he rents a booth and sells samples of his upcoming menu."

Jack poured his coffee, only realizing after the fact that

he wished he'd switched mugs. He slid into a chair at the kitchen table and unwrapped his own sandwich.

"I don't remember this," he said, knocking on the table-top. "If Jack Senior had to mortgage the property for that damned vineyard, what the hell was he doing buying furniture?"

Jenna grinned and bounced her hip against Walker's. "*He* made it."

Walker coughed and looked away as Jack's eyes met his.

"You *made* the table?" Jack laughed, and Jenna narrowed her eyes at him. "Wait. You're serious?" Jack had never seen his younger brother show interest in anything besides women or booze. The weight that had been pressing on his chest since he'd entered the town limits got heavier. Apparently he'd missed more than he'd realized.

Walker's eyes remained focused on his sandwich as he shrugged. "I did an apprenticeship with one of the Callahan brothers. Ain't made anything worth its salt other than that table, though."

"It's good." Jack ran his hand along the wood grain. "Real good."

"Yeah, whatever," Walker said, filling his mouth with food again, effectively ending that little tidbit of brotherly bonding. And since he wasn't here to push, Jack let it slide.

"Where's Luke?" Jack asked, realizing they were one short. Then he finally tore into his biscuit and let out his own moan. "Christ, this is good."

Jenna rolled her eyes. "Luke's out riding bareback like a maniac, I assume for some rodeo coming up. And you're welcome, by the way."

Both men grunted out a *thanks* while they continued to eat. Jenna poured herself some coffee and then opened the fridge.

"Shit. Y'all don't even have milk. Tell me you know your way through a supermarket, Jackson, because I'm not sure this refrigerator ever gets fully stocked if I'm not stopping by with groceries."

She took a sip of her black coffee and grimaced. "Hell, Walker. I bet a spoon would stand up in this sludge."

Walker grunted. "Keeps the hair on my chest."

She set her mug down on the table and blew out a breath. "Yeah, well, I don't need or *want* any hair on mine, so I'll pass. I had a cup at the market, anyway. With a new friend. I don't really need a second."

Jack's eyes darted up to meet hers. "With the egg guy?"

She shrugged. "Maybe." Her cheeks flamed.

Both men stood in unison, their chairs skidding across the wood floor.

"What's this asshole's name?" Walker asked.

"What do you know about him other than he's opening some diner? Did you get the name of it? He's not coming to your place to pick up the eggs, is he?"

She burst out laughing. "Is that a euphemism? *Picking up eggs?*"

Jack crossed his arms and Walker popped the rest of his breakfast in his mouth, staring her down as he chewed.

"You," she said, pointing at Walker. "I appreciate the attempt at big-brotherly protection, but I got more than a decade on you. So, simmer down, cowboy."

Walker scowled.

Jack cleared his throat.

"And *you*," she said, turning her gaze to her oldest nephew. "Put on a damn shirt if you want me to take you seriously."

He glanced down at his bare torso and shrugged. "I can still big brother you without a shirt."

She scoffed. "I was already reading Judy Blume by the time you were born."

Walker's brows rose. "The sex one? Go, Jenna."

Now she groaned. "God. No, Walker. I was *eight*. And how do you even know about *Forever*?"

He shrugged. "There was this girl in high school I wanted to make out with. She wanted to read me Judy Blume. We compromised."

Jenna shook her head. "You're impossible. And I was talking about *Superfudge*."

"Is *that* a euphemism?" he added.

She backhanded him on the shoulder. "I don't even know what that would mean!" she cried.

Jack tried to bite back his laughter, but it was useless. Plus, this felt *good*, he and Walker giving Jenna shit about dating like they used to do when they were in high school. Their situation had never been a normal one, but they'd found their rhythm back then, and it felt like maybe they were finding it again now.

Jenna swiped the third sandwich from the table and then held up her hands in defeat. "I'm going to go check on Luke. Bring him his breakfast before you two animals devour it."

She spun on her heel and headed back toward the door.

"What's his name?" Jack called after her.

"Or do we call him *Egg Man*?" Walker added.

Using her free hand, she answered them with one finger.

"*Egg Man* it is!" Walker shouted before the screen door slammed behind her.

Jack lifted his coffee mug from the table and held it out toward his brother. "Well done," he said.

Walker gave him a sly grin and held up his own mug. "You're still an asshole."

Jack leaned back against the counter. "And you're still a dick." He sipped his coffee.

"They let you say shit like that in your fancy lawyer office?"

He laughed. "Is that what you think San Diego is? Look around you, brother. You grew up in the middle of *wine* country. You're one-third owner of a vineyard. You're so goddamn fancy, I'm finally feeling underdressed without a shirt."

"Fuck you," Walker said, eyes peering over the top of his mug.

"Fuck you right back." And with that he strode back to the couch to retrieve his shirt. He threw it over his head and then padded toward the front door where he hoped his boots were, found them, and pulled them on. "I'm gonna grab my shit from the truck, shower, and take Jenna home. You can spend the rest of your morning wrapping your head around 'fancy' because we're gonna have to keep that vineyard."

Regardless of how much he'd had to drink the night before, he hadn't forgotten the simple math of the whole situation. The mortgage Jack Senior took out on the ranch was more than he guessed their piece of wine country was worth—at least not while it wasn't thriving. If they could get it up and running, then maybe they could turn a profit—or at the very least break even.

He'd stay long enough to see that his brothers were headed in the right direction. And maybe he'd check in on Egg Man as well. Not that Jenna needed looking after, but still. He felt like he should take care of her—of all of them—while he was here. It wouldn't make up for the years he'd been gone, but it would count for something. Wouldn't it? Luke and this rodeo bullshit. Walker and the furniture making—and drinking. Visits to Jenna's throughout the years had been tense, but he guessed now they'd all been on their best behaviors, not wanting to rock the boat. But there was no pretense now. He'd come back to more than he'd expected and had lost more than he'd anticipated being gone so long. He'd bridge the gap between him and his brothers. Jenna as well. He had to.

Jack hefted his bag out of the truck's cab and rolled his head along his shoulders. He wouldn't survive another night on that couch, but he wasn't sure how well he'd sleep in his old room, either. No. He *was* sure. Because he was a shitty sleeper no matter where he was. Unless, apparently, multiple shots of tequila were involved, and he knew better than to make that a habit. Despite the name they shared, he wasn't his father...yet.

That's what he'd been telling himself for ten years. Soon, he might even believe it.

"You were never planning on going home yesterday, were you?" Jack glanced toward Jenna in the passenger seat.

She shrugged. "I knew y'all would need to reconnect, but I also knew you wouldn't do it without a little push. So...I pushed."

He shook his head as he pulled onto her narrow street. "You think you know me that well, huh?" But she was right. That was his way—jumping right into the fray when it came to his brothers. But then he'd taught himself to pull back as well, to maintain just enough distance so it wouldn't hurt too much to leave.

"You've been pretty quiet this whole ride," she added. "Figured you needed some time to think. But we're almost home, and I got some things to say. So I'm gonna say them, okay?"

He kept his eyes on the road now and simply nodded.

He'd been grateful for the silence. The least he could do was let her say her piece.

"I've never once in all these years told you what to do. Hell, I barely knew you anymore when you came to stay with me, and then I only had you under my roof for the better part of a year before you took off for college."

"Mmm-hmm," he said, jaw tight. He wasn't sure what was coming, but her tone told him it wasn't anything he wanted to hear.

"And I'm proud of you. Real proud. Your brothers are, too."

He let out a breath. "I think you're mistaking pride for resentment."

She crossed her arms and angled herself to face him. He still maintained eye contact with the road ahead of him, but he could feel her gaze now, boring into him.

"Now what on earth ever gave you the idea those boys..." She shook her head. "I guess they're grown men now, aren't they? Jack, how can you think they did *anything* but look up to you, especially after what you did for them? What you've *done* for them."

"Don't," he said, his voice firm. "Jenna—don't. I'm not a martyr. I was a dumbass kid who thought...Shit. I don't know what the hell I thought." But he always knew that as long as he was on the receiving end of his father's fist—or sometimes boot—his brothers weren't. All it had taken was one time. A thirteen-year-old Walker trying to pull what he'd thought was an empty bottle from what he'd also thought was a sleeping Jack Senior's hand. But passed out drunk was worse than asleep, because when he woke with a start—dazed and disoriented—Jack Senior backhanded his youngest son across the cheek so hard it knocked him to the ground.

Afterward, Walker locked himself in his room for two days. Even missed school. Jack Senior had miraculously stayed clean for a full week after that, promising it was the last time anything of the sort would happen. Of course it wasn't. Jack and his brothers had gotten used to those kinds of promises—and them not sticking.

Walker was never the same after that. None of them were. But of the three of them, he had been the one who was still a kid—who'd still had that spark of hope. And just like that it was extinguished.

Jack pulled into Jenna's drive and was grateful for the timing, hoping it would end this conversation, or at least send it in another direction. The truck rolled to a stop, but she made no move to open her door. Instead she kept her gaze fixed on him.

"What are you still runnin' from, Jack? You can be a lawyer anywhere. If you just love San Diego to pieces and can't bear leaving, tell me. I'll believe you. Otherwise, when's it gonna be time to come home?"

He felt the muscle in his jaw tick, ran his fingers through his overgrown hair. He'd always thought the time would be now, when Jack Senior was gone and he could finally start over. But he'd built a life in San Diego—one safe from the memories that he could only keep at bay with physical distance. And now he had a chance to get even farther—as far from here as he could go without leaving the country.

"Stay 'til the vineyard's up and running," she added. "See this thing through, and *then* go back to San Diego."

Although they'd stopped, he gripped the steering wheel with both hands. "It's not that simple. You know it isn't. It could take months. Years, even, depending on what rudimentary knowledge of farming we have from . . . what? Living with our aunt for a few months?"

"Years," she corrected him, blowing out a breath that sounded like exasperation. "Luke and Walker were with me for years. And *yes*. I know it's not that simple, but if you get someone out there who knows grapes, you'll figure it out. You always do."

He could sense there was more coming, but she trailed off and turned toward the car door.

Now? She was getting out now that she'd baited him with that tone? Well, he wasn't biting.

She sat there, hand on the lever and facing the window, but she still didn't move.

"Fine," he growled. "I'll bite. What about getting someone out there who knows grapes?"

She shrugged and glanced at him over her shoulder. "You don't think I missed you sneaking out after curfew back then. Did you?" She laughed. "Look, I know things were a mess when you left. But this isn't one of your whirlwind visits where you're in and out in forty-eight hours. Do we still have to pretend the Ellis girl doesn't exist?"

There it was, the real reason for his silence. Yesterday he'd driven from San Diego to the ranch in a daze. Call it lack of sleep or lack of connection after being gone for so long, but he'd been able to keep his emotional distance on that drive. Yet one night with his brothers and Jenna had flipped a switch, and now he was here. Walking distance from the Ellis place and their vineyard...and what he'd done to prove that he wasn't good for her.

"You knew about her," he said. Not a question but a realization. Jenna had tiptoed around him in those early months after he'd left the ranch in an ambulance, the last time he'd been there before yesterday. He'd come home from the hospital—to Jenna's home, in an unfamiliar town—with a broken tibia, two fractured ribs, and no desire to *talk about his feelings* despite the few visits they'd forced on him with the hospital psychologist. Somewhere, deep down, he'd known it was for his own good, but all he'd wanted to do back then was forget.

And then there was Ava Ellis, the girl who'd chipped away at his foundation until she finally broke through. Shit. He could see her now talking to the assistant in the school office, those long, cinnamon waves framing her snow-white, freckled skin.

"I'm going to trig, too," she'd said, lingering as he waited for his schedule. Nothing like starting a new high school six months before graduation. "I could walk you there."

He remembered glancing down at the plaster that had peeked out from his jeans.

"I can walk fine," he'd said like an asshole. But to be fair, he'd felt entitled to a little bit of asshole at the time. He'd paid his dues.

"Right," she'd said, brows raised. "I can see that. Just thought you might want to know the way." Then she'd stalked out the office door, her head held high—and had waited for him a few paces down the hall.

That was all he'd needed—her not taking his bullshit—for him to realize maybe he didn't want to dish it out. At least not to her.

"Of course I *knew*," Jenna said, bringing him back to the present. Finally she opened her door and hopped out of the truck.

He followed her, grabbing her bag from the pickup's bed and hoisting out the sack of chicken feed as well. He set the second on the ground.

"Why didn't you say anything?" he asked. "About me sneaking out? Ignoring any semblance of a curfew you tried to impose? About any of the shit I pulled? I couldn't have made things easy for you."

Jenna turned to him and reached for her bag, and he handed it over.

"Your mama and me, we lost our daddy when I barely knew my ABCs. I lost her when I was just learning how to be a grown-up and then our own mama a few years later. I might have been twenty-five when you boys came to me, but I was an orphan. I *needed* all of you as much as you needed me. And if sneaking out 'til all hours of the night with the Ellis girl made you happy, then it made *me* happy, too." She reached a hand for his cheek, and Jack realized how long it had been since he'd felt this surge of affection for anyone. "I didn't have a clue how to be a parent, but I hope I did right by you boys." A tear escaped down her cheek, and she laughed. "I need to stop saying 'boys.' You're almost thirty, for crying out loud."

He bent his head and kissed the top of hers. "Not for another eighteen months," he reminded her. "And you did more than right by us, Jenna. You kept us a family. I would have—the state could have—" He broke off. "I don't know if I ever really thanked you."

She shook her head. "You did what you had to do to keep you and your brothers together."

"So did you," he added. "*Thank you* for that."

She shrugged and swiped at her damp eyes. "Then I guess we're even. Or something."

"I guess we are."

"You coming inside?" she asked.

Like a magnet, his head turned in the direction of the Ellis Vineyard, only a mile walk from where he stood. He squinted in the sunlight. After all that had happened his last week in town, he'd never forgotten that red hair—or the freckles on her shoulders and across her nose. He'd also never forgotten that his only possible reason for coming back had told him they were nothing more than a fling when he'd been foolish enough to think it was love.

"She's not there anymore," Jenna added.

He felt a sudden jolt of something that he couldn't name and turned back toward his aunt. He kept his voice even. "Did they sell the property?"

"No. But she and her mama left the area soon after Thanksgiving your first year at school. I've seen her since then—Mrs. Ellis. But not *her*."

He scrubbed a hand over his stubbled jaw. Not wanting to risk running into her, he hadn't come home for any holidays that first year. The joke was on him, he guessed. She'd left, too.

"Ava," he said. "I'm not gonna lose my shit over a name."

Those three letters tasted bittersweet on his lips. He'd gotten past that last terrible night, but he wasn't sure he'd ever gotten over it. Or her. Wasn't that the saying? *You never get over your first love?* He'd always thought she would stay close to home. She'd been accepted to Cal Poly for art. He remembered that. He remembered too much.

Where the hell had she gone?

High school felt like a lifetime ago. He wasn't that kid anymore, the one who let a beautiful girl make him believe in a future that held something better. Still, there was that jolt of something again, of knowing she wasn't there. It was like missing something he'd never had, if that was even possible.

"You never said anything before," he said. "I *have* been back."

"I can count on one hand how many times."

He narrowed his eyes at her.

"And," she added, "you never asked."

He scratched at the back of his neck and let out a breath. "I wasn't asking now. So why say something after all these years?"

Jenna crossed her arms. "Because you never looked wistful like that before, staring down the road and all. This is what I mean," she said, waving a hand in front of his face. "Maybe you still need some closure. Maybe if you found her and talked about that night..."

"Stop," he said, cutting her off. She flinched. He hadn't meant for the word to sound so harsh, but enough was enough. "That relationship wrecked me, okay? Is that what you want to hear? I was a goddamn mess to start, and then I went and put a kid in the hospital. I don't blame her for ending things, but it doesn't mean I took it well. Especially after—"

"After all the terrible stuff you had to deal with for years," she interrupted. "You made a mistake, Jack. A big one. But that one night doesn't define you."

It did for the one person who'd seen past the rumors only for him to prove them true.

This was only a fling, Jack. It was always going to end.

Jesus, that was ten years ago. Enough already.

"I gotta head back. We have a shitload of work to do in the house before I figure out this vineyard thing. Will we see you later this week?"

She sighed but smiled at him. "As soon as my car's all fixed up. Had a little fender bender last week. That's why Luke picked me up."

"What the hell? You never said—" He started checking her over for signs of injury, but she waved him off.

He used to call to check in once a week. Then the calls

moved to once a month. And soon, distance made this part of his life seem a million miles away instead of only a few hundred. Now the guilt hit him in small, unexpected waves every time he realized something he'd missed.

"I'm *fine*," she insisted.

She was. He believed her. But who was around on a regular basis to make sure?

"The egg man—he a good guy?" he asked.

She blushed a little and smiled. "Yeah. Yeah, I think he is. But maybe I need to ask him out *before* he buys my eggs. Avoid any conflict of interest."

Jack laughed. "Is *that* a euphemism?"

She rolled her eyes and reached for the bag of feed before he could hand it to her. Then she started backing up the drive. "Welcome home, Jack." She turned and headed toward the house.

"Jenna?" he said.

She stopped, but kept her back to him as if she could tell she didn't want to hear what was coming next.

"They're making me a partner," he said. "My firm...in their New York office."

She spun on her heel, and he braced himself for an earful. But Jenna's gaze was soft, gentle even.

"Congratulations, Jack."

And then she made her way to the front door.

He watched to make sure she got in okay. It didn't matter that she was older, that she'd lived on her own before he and his brothers came or had continued to do so after they'd all left. He was going to start making up for the years he'd been away. For however long he had, he'd be the brother— or nephew—he should have been...even if he was picking up and leaving again.

CHAPTER FOUR

Mowing the lawn hadn't taken enough time. Ava was back inside now, not daring to enter the painting room again, and she just couldn't take it. Even when she wasn't torturing herself trying to re-create that stupid tree, the house was *too* quiet, and damn it, she was used to noise. She should have at least kept the dog home instead of sending him along for the sleepover at her parents' house. That would have been a decent distraction. But she'd thought complete and utter solitude would somehow spark her long-dormant creative juices.

She'd thought wrong.

So it was settled. She wouldn't wait for the noise to come to her. *She* would head to *it*.

She pulled out her phone and rattled off a text to her parents.

Know you guys are out till after lunch. Heading over to check stock in the tasting room.
    See you this afternoon.

It was Sunday, and her parents had one of their weekend employees working the tasting room. She could stop by, check on the gift shop, busy herself with something other than her empty, quiet home.

She hopped into her cherry red Jeep Renegade and practically peeled out of the driveway—a woman on a mission. It was only a thirty-minute ride to the Ellis Vineyard and she'd made it there in twenty-seven, only to swerve off the narrow road as she approached the entrance. A white pickup truck idled on the wrong side of the road, blocking her turn.

"Shit!" she yelled, throwing the car into park once she came to a stop in the grass. She was grateful she was in the car alone, knowing she'd never hear the end of letting profanity slip in certain company—again.

She hopped out of the car and stalked toward the driver's side of the truck, ready to give whoever was in there a piece of her mind. But he was out and heading toward her before she had time to think of what to say. And then she lost her words altogether as the dust cleared and she saw Jack Everett striding in her direction.

Her stomach dropped, and she wondered if she was falling. She stumbled back a couple of steps until she was able to brace herself against the hood of the Jeep, but she *was* still standing.

"Ava?" he said, taking a step forward, those stormy blue eyes laced with concern. "Shit. Are you okay? I didn't think—"

She held up a hand, halting him from moving any closer.

"I'm fine," she said, though she was anything but. Physically speaking, she didn't have a scratch. But her heart—she thought she could actually hear it beating, it was thundering so loud. "I just need a minute," she added. But for what? There was no way one minute was sufficient to accomplish anything, let alone ten years of *everything* flooding back at once.

Her chest ached being this close. She remembered walking him to class on his first day at Los Olivos High, how he was so broody and intent on keeping his distance—how gorgeous he was anyway and that she'd wanted to do anything to make him smile. Once he had, she was a goner.

Now he stood there in that untucked flannel shirt and faded jeans with his arms crossed, silent and stoic and as devastatingly gorgeous as she remembered. His blond hair was just enough on the long side that he was probably due for a trim, but God it looked good on him, especially with that golden scruff along his jaw. He wore the past decade well, and she'd missed all of it.

"Ava," he said again, and this time he closed the distance between them, stopping when his boot came toe to toe with her sandal. "Are you *okay*?"

Okay? How was there anything okay about seeing Jack again after the way things had ended? He'd left thinking she was afraid of him—and she'd *let* him—when nothing could have been further from the truth. But the alternative would have been forcing him to stay in a place that was poison to him.

The tenderness in his words tore at her, but that voice belonged to a man now. A man she didn't know. Gone was the boy who'd stolen her heart—and broke it *twice* without ever knowing. She wondered what he saw when he looked at her, if she stirred as much in him after all these years as he did in her.

Time was supposed to heal. Wasn't it? Make the past easier to bear. But when she looked at Jack, all she could think was how much she'd give to turn back the clock and try things differently. Then, maybe, she'd deserve the warmth she heard in that voice—the hint of affection.

She cleared her throat and stood straight. "I'm *fine*," she lied. "Did you just get back from England or something?"

His brows pulled together.

"Driving on the other side of the road?" she added, the dizzying effect he had on her diminishing as she turned her thoughts to the here and now.

The corner of his mouth teased at a grin, and with that gesture the dizziness returned. But she could not, *would* not, fall under his spell. Too much had happened since they'd last seen each other to let herself get carried away by feelings she'd long since buried. Besides, she'd already put her foot down. This was the year she got her life back on track—the year she finally let herself pursue the dreams she'd put aside for a decade. A chance encounter with Jack Everett—who hadn't as much as sent her an email in all that time—wasn't going to change things.

Okay, it might change *one* thing. The truth always did that.

"No," he said, drawing out the word. "I was driving Jenna home, and she said you'd moved away." He shook his head. "I don't even remember deciding to drive by." He ran a hand through that overgrown hair and squinted toward the sun. She watched as fine lines crinkled at the corners of his eyes, lines that hadn't been there the last time she saw him. "I just got back in town," he said. "My father died."

He said it so matter-of-factly it took a few seconds to register, and when it did, instinct took over, and she stepped forward, wrapping her arms around him.

"Oh, Jack. I'm—I'm sorry."

She didn't know if those were the right words or if hugging him was anywhere near appropriate, but that's what you said and did when someone died. And this was Jack Everett. *Jack Everett.* In her arms. As the warmth of his skin seeped into hers, a part of her she'd tucked away for ten long years began rising to the surface.

He said nothing at first, simply stood there as she hugged him, breathing in the scent of fresh soap, the outdoors, and something so inherently *Jack* she swore she'd know it was him with her eyes closed.

Then his arms enveloped her. She could feel his hesitation, though, the way he didn't squeeze too tight, didn't breathe too deep.

"I was just going to check up on some things in the tasting room," she said, reluctantly pulling away.

She still had a few hours before everyone returned. It would be time enough to ease into this reunion—to tell him what she'd planned on telling him when he came home after finishing his degree. Except as far as she knew, he never did return. At least, he'd never contacted her if he had. Not that she blamed him.

"Come inside for a drink?" She laughed nervously. "If wine isn't your thing, we have a fridge in the office. I'm sure there's soda or bottled water. Or something."

She wasn't sure if she'd ever expected to see Jack Everett again, not after he hadn't come home—and she'd sought him out in Los Angeles only to find that he'd definitively moved on before she'd ever had a chance to see him. But now that he was here, nearly forcing her off the road, she felt the desperate need to get him to stay. Maybe his father's death wasn't the right time to shake up his world even more, but she'd always promised herself that if he came back—if *he* chose for their paths to cross again—she'd tell him all the things she couldn't say when they were teens and she knew that no matter how he felt about her, he'd needed to get as far away from here as he could.

He shoved his hands in his pockets. "I'll follow you in" was all he said before heading back to his truck.

Had there been a ring on his left hand? She hadn't thought to look until it was too late. Or was she avoiding what she didn't want to confirm? She guessed they'd get to that soon.

Oh God. Jack Everett was really here, and he hadn't bolted at the first sight of her.

She rounded the bumper until she was at the driver's side again, and then somehow she made it back behind the wheel, navigating through the property and to the winery while she tried to process how the hell to tell him—*everything.*

The drive down the winding path behind Ava's Jeep was hardly enough for Jack to get his shit together. She wasn't supposed to be here, and he sure as hell wasn't supposed to force her off the road.

She wrecked me.

It had been minutes since he'd uttered the phrase to Jenna, and now here he was going to have a drink with Ava Ellis. He was out of his fucking mind. But then again, the him she'd destroyed had been an eighteen-year-old mess who had one foot out the door the whole time they were together. Except he'd always planned on coming back after college...for her.

This was only a fling.

It was always going to end.

All it had taken was a few words for his plans to change.

He heard the door of her Jeep slam and realized he was still sitting in his truck despite the fact he'd already parked. He pulled the key from the ignition and stepped out of the vehicle to see her leaning against her bumper, arms crossed as she watched him exit. She offered him a nervous smile but before he could consider reciprocating, they were interrupted.

Tires crackled over gravel, and both their gazes shifted to a sedan rolling toward them.

"Looks like you got new customers," he said.

Her eyes flashed toward his, and despite the sun's glare, he could see a desperation he hadn't been expecting—not that anything about this meeting had been expected. But just as quickly, she schooled her features and held out her arms as a young boy barreled out of the car and headed straight for her.

"Mom!"

The boy threw himself at her so quickly, clinging to her, that Jack didn't even get a chance to see his face, just the auburn waves—exactly like his mother's—where Ava now buried her face, peppering his head with soft kisses as she did.

"Mom?" he heard himself ask as something inside him clicked into place and then sank.

"Owen!" she cried, falling against the back of her car, unable to contain her laughter. "You're getting too big for me to hold you like this," she added as he slid down her torso so he was standing on his own two feet.

"Grandpa got your text, and he asked if I wanted to go to the park and practice pitching or if I wanted to surprise you instead."

She ruffled his hair and as he took a step back, Jack could make out the color of the boy's eyes. Not green like his mother's, but blue.

A chocolate Lab bounded out of the car after the boy, stopping only to give him and Ava sloppy kisses as the two of them roared with laughter.

Not green like his mother's.

Did he have his father's eyes?
Owen.

"My mother's maiden name was Owens," he said, his voice sounding rough and far away.

She bit her lip. "I know."

"Margaret, take Owen inside."

An older man and woman approached, and Jack recognized Margaret and Bradford Ellis, Ava's parents. Mr. Ellis narrowed his eyes at Jack.

"Come on, honey," her mother said, motioning to Owen. "You and Scully come in with me while Grandpa talks to Mom for a second."

The boy—Owen—backed up and glanced at Jack.

"Who are you?" he asked, with the unreserved curiosity only acceptable from a child.

Ava's father patted his grandson on the shoulder. "No one, son. Follow your grandma. She'll get you and Scully something to eat."

"But I thought the rule was no dogs in the wine shop."

Mr. Ellis let out an uneasy laugh. "We're bending the rules, only for today."

Owen pumped his fist in the air. "Yes! Come on, boy!" He kissed Ava quick on the cheek and scampered off after his grandma, Labrador in tow. As soon as they were safe behind doors, Bradford Ellis dropped his painted-on grin and turned, teeth gritted, toward Jack.

"Dad, don't—" Ava started, but Jack knew the look of a man with an agenda. Just like he'd done time and time again with his own father, he stood his ground and braced himself for whatever came next.

"I know who you are," he said. Her father was a tall man, still well built, but Jack had at least an inch or two on him. "I knew it the second I saw that piece-of-shit truck."

Jack's jaw clenched as he thought about the accounts he'd set up in Luke's and Walker's names, about how much more this new position in New York would help get them back on their feet after Jack Senior mortgaged the property. Every goddamn cent he made—other than what he needed to live—was put away for his family. But he wasn't going to dignify Bradford Ellis with an excuse for the vehicle he drove. Instead he stood there, impassive, as the man lit into him. As the unmistakable reality of who the boy was sank in, and as it registered that Ava's father had called Jack *no one.*

"Nice to see you, Mr. Ellis," he said, fighting to keep his voice even.

"You put the Wilkes boy in the hospital," the other man said in a low, warning tone.

"For assaulting your daughter," Jack retaliated, though he knew it was a shit excuse. He'd pulled Derek off of Ava without issue. He could have left it at that. But when he saw those bruises...

"Ava didn't press charges," Mr. Ellis snapped.

"Dad!" Ava cried. A look passed between father and daughter that Jack didn't understand. "Stop. Please."

"Ava," the older man said, addressing his daughter but still facing Jack. "You told us it wasn't him. You said he wasn't the father, and we took you at your word."

"It's complicated," she said, her voice starting to shake. "I told you what you wanted to hear—what would make it easier for everyone."

Jack couldn't move. He was frozen where he stood. So he just listened to this warped version of his past play out.

"*We* raised that boy with you. We helped feed him and clothe him. You put off school and took a job at the vineyard, *our* family's business, and have never wanted for anything. We're Owen's family, Ava. Not him. If he thinks he can show up after ten years—after what he did—and be a part of your life—a part of Owen's life—without our say?"

"Dad, I said *stop.*" She cut him off.

Jack turned at the sound of Ava's voice. Mr. Ellis did as well.

She faced Jack with pleading eyes. Jack glanced back toward the winery, to where *his son* had disappeared behind closed doors.

His *son.*

"Christ, Ava."

She covered her mouth, and her green eyes glistened.

He pressed the heels of his hands into his own eyes. Then he stared at her for several long beats. He thought about the baseball scholarship he'd almost lost because of his broken leg senior year. Then, without warning, he thought of loss in a whole new way. But there wasn't time to process.

"He plays ball," he said. "He has *my* goddamn eyes, my mother's *goddamn* name, and he plays ball?"

"I'm so sorry. I'm *so* sorry," she repeated, the tears pooling now.

He slammed his palm against the side of the truck bed, and Ava yelped.

"Hey!" her father yelled, taking a step toward Jack and then lowering his voice. "That's my daughter. And *my* grandson in there," he said, pointing toward the winery. "I will do anything I need to do to protect them, even if it means calling the cops on you right now. No one forgot what you did, Everett. Or who your daddy is. I don't care what happened between you and my daughter in the past. Because there is no future for you here. You're not good for either of them."

Jack felt the sting in his palm and started backing toward the driver's side of the truck.

"Was," he said, and he watched the other man's brows furrow. "You know who my daddy *was*," he amended. "He died earlier this week."

Ava let out a quiet sob that mingled with his name.

"I shouldn't have come," he said, his voice tight with strain, his hands balling into fists. He fought to maintain control, to keep from scaring her again. But his anger was justified. He knew that much.

He shook his head and spoke softly. "Fucking hell, Ava."

Bradford Ellis took another step in Jack's direction as he pulled open his truck's door.

"Please, Dad. Stop. Please." Ava pressed her hands to her father's chest and urged him back again. But he kept speaking over her shoulder.

"You're trespassing, Everett. I suggest you head on out, now."

Jack didn't wait to see if she'd turn around again. He was in the truck, engine roaring to life, before he lost it completely.

He had a *son*.

In the span of ten years—and ten minutes—Ava Ellis had wrecked him not once, but twice.

And here he was, doing what he did best—leaving.

CHAPTER FIVE

Ava had been in a fog ever since Jack Everett had sped off the Ellis property yesterday. The proof was in the coffee. She couldn't even stomach a cup, and she didn't normally acknowledge the morning until she'd had at least one, if not two. Her mug rested full and steaming in front of her, but all she could do was stare at it. Owen sat across from her at their round, wooden breakfast table, shoveling Cheerios into his mouth like they were his last meal.

"Hey there, slugger. Slow down. The bus isn't coming for—" She glanced at the clock above the stove. "Shit!" she yelled, sliding her chair back from the table with such momentum that she knocked the full mug over.

Owen jumped up, bowl of cereal and spoon in his hands as he protected his precious cargo. *"Mom,"* he scolded in that sweet boy voice of his, but he was giggling. "You swore *and* almost gave me *coffee-Os.*"

Both their heads turned toward the front of the house as the slow hiss of a school bus stopping sounded outside.

"Shit," Owen said under his breath and swallowed his last bite.

"Language!" Ava yelled. "Quick. Grab your backpack. And your baseball bag. Are your cleats in the bag? I'll grab your lunch from the fridge. And—shoes! Put your shoes on. Did you brush your teeth? Doesn't matter. You'll do it before bed tonight. Twice."

The two of them scrambled through the kitchen and into the living room, Ava snagging her son's lunch on the way while he frantically tied his shoes and stuffed his cleats in his baseball bag. She stuck her head out the door and waved at the bus driver, who tapped at his wrist as if she didn't know they were running late.

"Lunch!" she called, and Owen looked up just in time to catch the paper sack and drop it into his backpack. "Grandma's gonna pick you up and take you to practice, and I'll be there by the time it's over." He had a bag on each shoulder and was halfway through the screen door.

"Love you!" She strode toward him and planted a kiss on his tousled mop of hair.

"Love you!" he echoed as he bounded off the porch, across the yard, and up the steps onto the bus.

"Thank you!" she cried, waving to the driver. "Sorry!"

Then she stepped back inside and fell against the door, closing it with her butt and letting out a labored breath. That's when she heard the off-tempo, staccato drips against the kitchen's tile floor—along with what sounded like a tongue lapping the spilled liquid.

Shit.

"Scully!" she yelled, sprinting the few feet into the kitchen, stopping short at the scene before her. Her lovely Kona blend blanketed the kitchen table, puddles forming under the edges where the coffee had run off and onto the floor. Their Lab stood, paws in puddles, slurping up the spilled coffee. "Scully, *get!*" His head shot up, his wide eyes meeting hers. She pointed toward the doggie door that led out to their fenced backyard. *"Out!"* The dog obeyed,

traipsing caramel-colored paw prints across the tile as he
went.

She surveyed the damage, which was still significant,
and decided that catching him after only a few sips—along
with the milk and sugar she used to dilute the liquid—had
probably kept him clear of any caffeine-related danger, but
she'd call the vet to make sure. First, though, she had to
clear her head, which meant processing what had put her in
this fog to begin with.

She'd satisfied Owen yesterday afternoon, explaining
away her reddened eyes as having been surprised and excited to see an old friend she'd missed for a long time.

Owen understood the concept of a happy cry and didn't
think much of her lie of omission, but Ava knew that's what
had kept her up all night and this morning settled into an
aching knot in her gut.

She had lied to Jack, and now her son had *seen* his father,
and she had lied to him, too.

Then again, she'd been lying for ten years. Hadn't she?
Owen hadn't really grasped the concept of *father* until he
was in preschool. And when he'd asked if he had one, she'd
simply told him *yes*, that she loved his dad very much, but
he'd had to move away before Owen was born.

But damn it, there was a right way and a wrong way to
do this, and getting surprised by Jack like that—and then by
Owen, too—wasn't the *right* way.

She grabbed the paper towels from the counter and set
to work cleaning up her mess. Well, the one that could be
easily absorbed with a roll of Bounty Select-A-Size. That
other, bigger mess—the one she planned on tending to as
soon as she de-coffeed her kitchen—was another story.

Fifteen minutes later, Scully's paws were clean and he
was back inside. The vet had assured her he hadn't con-

sumed enough caffeine for her to worry. Now she sat in her Jeep, smelling like she'd just come off a ten-hour shift at Starbucks. Smelling like coffee was the least of her concerns, though. She pulled her phone from her purse and set an alarm for 3:00 p.m. so she didn't lose track of time this afternoon like she had this morning. It would be one thing for Owen to miss the bus—she could have driven him the fifteen-minute ride to school, the only consequence his disappointment at missing out on the extra time with his friends. But forgetting him at practice? It wasn't as if anything like that had ever happened before, but then the events of yesterday afternoon had never happened before, either.

She did a final check in the rearview mirror, decided she looked about as frazzled as she felt, and thought *To hell with it* as she backed away from her house, headed on the hour drive to Oak Bluff.

Ava's tires crackled over the gravel driveway in front of the Crossroads Cattle Ranch. The knot in her stomach tightened not only at the thought of seeing Jack again but at what it must be like for him to be here after all this time. He hadn't talked much about his parents when they'd met. He didn't need to. The gossip preceded his arrival. And once they'd become close, the most he'd done was confirm that his mother had died years before and that his father's drinking and abuse was the result.

She thought about her own father's behavior yesterday afternoon. She'd hated him for it in the moment, but realized she had what Jack never did—parents who'd do anything to protect her.

Tears pricked at her eyes as she rolled to a stop behind the white pickup that had caused her to swerve off the road less than twenty-four hours before, but she swallowed them back. She had no right. *He* was the one who'd had the rug pulled out from under him, not her.

She reached for her key, ready to pull it from the ignition, and found that it and the rest of the keys on the ring already lay in her lap. Huh. So she'd turned the car off. Must be that brain fog again.

She yelped when someone rapped their knuckles against the driver's side window. She turned, heart in her throat, to find Luke Everett grinning at her. He might have aged a decade, but she'd never forget that devil of a smile.

He stepped back to let her open her door and she climbed out, albeit on wobbly knees. There was no turning back now, not that she would. She owed Jack an explanation at the very least. At the most—well, she owed him ten years she couldn't give back.

"Red," Luke said, invoking the nickname Jack had given her when they were teens. He took his hat off and squinted at her. "Well, you sure as shit look the same as you did in high school. Lemme guess. You heard about dear old Dad and came to pay your respects?"

Luke *had* changed. He must have hit a growth spurt sometime after Jack left, because the boy she remembered had been a head shorter than his big brother and lanky as the day was long. The man who stood before her was exactly that: a *man*. Tall and broad with corded muscles lining his exposed forearms. And a nasty gash across his cheek.

Ava made an attempt to smooth out the wrinkles in her peasant skirt, then remembered the wrinkles were meant to be there and forced her fidgeting hands to stay still.

"Are you—okay?" she asked, pointing at her own cheek.

He winked. "You should see the bull," he said, then laughed. "Not a scratch on him."

She bit her lip. "Jack told me about your dad," she said but then paused. She knew *sorry* wasn't exactly the right word but also knew that she didn't wish death on anyone, no matter how awful a person was.

"I know," Luke said, as if he was reading her thoughts. "What do you say about a man who knocked his kids around and drank himself to death? I don't think they make a greeting card for that."

He offered her a warm smile, which put her more at ease. She still wanted to throw up from nerves—but to a lesser degree.

"Wait a second," Luke added. "Jack *told* you? I didn't know you two were still in touch."

"No." She swallowed, her level of nervousness climbing the chart again. "I mean, yes. We spoke yesterday. Did he—did he not say anything about running into me?"

He ran a hand through his blond hair and dropped his hat back on his head.

"Well, shit," he said. "That explains him going on a bender with Walker for a second night in a row. He came home yesterday afternoon, did some work in Dad's office, and then helped Walker finish off a bottle of whiskey. I thought he'd still be sleeping it off, but he took off for the vineyard thirty minutes ago." He gave her a nod. "You did some number on him back in the day, Red. Guess you still have that magic touch."

She blinked a few times as realization set in. He hadn't told his brothers about Owen.

"Vineyard?" she asked. "I thought this was a ranch."

"It is. But apparently Jack Senior bought a vineyard without letting any of us know. Just off the property. So big brother thinks it's on him to figure out what to do with it." He shrugged. "If you ask me—which he hasn't yet—he ought to sell it right back to the first buyer he can find so we can try to get the deed on the house back, though I doubt we'd break even. I've got some money saved up, though. Maybe we can dig this place out of debt. Then Walker and I can get back to ranchin', and Jack can get back to lawyerin' and pretending this place doesn't exist."

She heard a bitterness in his tone that didn't quite mesh with Luke's playful disposition. But he painted that smile back on quick enough that she almost second-guessed herself. *Almost.*

"You said he's at the vineyard now?" she asked, already feeling like she was overstepping her welcome yet doubting she'd be welcome at her next destination at all.

Luke nodded. "If you back out of the drive and head west, take the second right onto the main street, Oak Bluff Way. It's a mile from there, right through town." He looked her up and down, taking in her top, skirt, and sandals. "It's a nice walk through the ranch property, too—if you're dressed for it." He winked at her again.

That must have been what Jack had done, seeing as his truck was still here.

"Thanks," she said. Her heart twisted as she realized how much Owen would like his uncle if he ever got to meet him. "I'm good with driving." She held out her hand, not sure what the proper parting gesture was between two people who shared a short past—and maybe, she hoped, some semblance of a future. Between Jack and his son. She and Jack were the past, right? They were different people now. Plus, she had a college application to complete, a long-awaited education to begin the following semester, and *he* had a life in San Diego. They'd both been moving in different directions since the day they'd said good-bye, and it seemed they were still on two different paths that weren't meant to intersect.

Look at what he'd done—college, law school, joining a successful practice. She'd followed his career from afar. Even if she'd chickened out trying to contact him, she knew he'd done well, and part of her found satisfaction in that. Pushing him to leave *had* been the right decision at least in that respect.

Luke took a step toward her and dipped his head to kiss her on the cheek, snapping her out of her reverie. "You look good, Red."

A sudden warmth spread through her. At least one member of the Everett family was happy to see her.

"You too," she said. "Say hello to Walker for me."

He laughed. "Now he *is* sleeping it off. But will do when he rejoins the land of the living."

She smiled and stepped back toward her car, opening the door. "Thanks," she said.

Ever the gentleman, Luke gave her a quick tip of his cowboy hat. "My pleasure. And if he's pissed at someone interrupting his alone time, be sure and tell him I sent ya."

She laughed at that and settled herself back into the car. But as she slammed the door and pulled slowly back onto the street, the ease of being in Luke's presence gave way to the sinking feeling she'd had since she'd watched Jack lay eyes on his son for the first time. She'd explain as best she could, and that would be that. That was why she'd made the drive today, to get everything out in the open. Owen was what mattered now, and if Jack decided he wanted to be a part of his son's life, they'd figure out what that meant for them. They could make their version of a family work for Owen's sake.

Even if Jack never forgave her.

CHAPTER SIX

The breeze cooled Jack's skin, and he was grateful for it. It was seventy degrees at best, but the cloudless sky made the sun feel much stronger. It didn't help that he'd left his hat in the truck—or that he still felt like he'd been hit by a freight train. Whether that was because of the booze or his encounter with Ava the day before was still in question, though he guessed it was probably both.

He walked the rows of grapevines slowly, his steps measured and his head pounding. The whiskey had helped his inability to process what had happened at the Ellis Vineyard, but it wasn't doing shit for his capacity to remain upright. Maybe he should have waited the ten minutes it would have taken him to make a pot of coffee, but after two nights in that house, the walls were closing in on him. He needed out.

He ran his hand along the leaves. Here and there he found a clump of grapes, most of them wilted.

"How the hell are we gonna breathe new life into *this*?" he asked out loud.

"With a hell of a lot of blood, sweat, and possibly tears?"

He stopped mid-step and tilted his head toward the sun, allowing himself one long breath before he spun to face her.

Her red waves rested on her shoulders, radiant in the sun, and his breath caught in his throat despite his anger. Because he *was* angry—and so many other things he couldn't yet name. Whatever he was feeling, though, Ava Ellis was responsible, and he sure as shit didn't like anyone having that kind of power over him.

"What the hell are you doing here, Ava?" It wasn't as if he didn't know the answer or that their meeting again was inevitable, but he hadn't counted on *inevitable* being *this second*, and he wasn't sure he was ready for whatever came next. And despite the lightness he felt at her nearness, he wouldn't let the sliver of happiness he'd felt at seeing her yesterday override the betrayal he felt now.

She took a step toward him, and he did nothing to encourage her. He did his best to remain impassive even as his head throbbed in time with his pulse.

"I just want a chance to explain," she said, her voice soft and tentative. "I don't expect you to forgive me, but I do need you to understand *why*."

He crossed his arms over his chest. "Really?" he asked. "Because I spent the whole ride back here yesterday trying to answer that same question. And when I couldn't, I drank myself into a fucking stupor." He pinched the bridge of his nose and squeezed his eyes shut for a second, trying to keep the pounding at bay. But it was useless. "I took off from this place so I could leave that shit behind. So I wouldn't become *him*. I'm back two damned days, and I'm already acting more like Jack Senior than I did when I lived here."

Bitterness and blame dripped from each word, and he knew she wasn't responsible for all of it. He had free will, made his own decisions. But that didn't change the fact that he couldn't figure out how to process what had happened since his return without simply numbing himself to it.

A tear slipped down her cheek, and she was close enough that if he wanted to, he could swipe it away. But he wasn't relinquishing any more control.

"That," she said, the one syllable word breaking as she spoke. "That's *why*. You needed to *go*."

He shook his head. "Without knowing?"

"Yes." Another tear fell. "Would you have gone otherwise?"

He ran a hand through his hair, tugging at the too-long strands. "Christ, Ava. That wasn't your decision to make. I should have had a goddamn choice, but you didn't give me one." The volume of his voice rose, and he could feel the beat of his own pulse in his neck.

She wiped away her tears, but they were falling faster now, and another one simply took the former's place. "I was *eighteen*," she said, her voice rising to a level to meet his. "And scared. I was so scared, Jack. I was going to tell you at the party. And then—well, I couldn't. I called you to meet me the next night so I could. But once you got there and told me about Walker...that, after what happened with Derek, I couldn't do it."

He'd started to pace, but the mention of his brother's name stopped him cold. "Walker? How the hell does he have anything to do with this?"

She wiped her eyes again and then wrapped her arms around her shoulders. As she did, he felt the slight shift in temperature, as if the ocean breeze had made its way ten miles inland.

"Do you...remember what happened?" she asked, and he could tell she was proceeding with caution. "Do you remember what you said to me?"

He was the one stepping closer now because this cryptic bullshit was going nowhere, and he wanted to make sure she heard him crystal clear.

"I remember plenty," he said, jaw tight. He swallowed back the ache he felt as he neared her. "I remember you walking away. I remember calling you every fucking day before I left and you not answering." He shook his head and opened his mouth to say something else but stopped when his eyes met hers, their brilliant green now clouded and reddened by tears.

"Jack," she said, and his name was a plea.

She didn't want to say whatever came next. He could sense that with every fiber of his being. But she had to. Whatever it was, he knew she had to.

"What?" he asked, his voice strained.

She moved in, close enough that he could smell her morning coffee and the sweet citrus scent of her skin.

"Walker's fifteenth birthday was the next day," she said, the words followed by a soft, hiccupping breath.

The weight that had been threatening to crush his chest dropped to his stomach, and he had to keep himself from staggering. Ava must have noticed, because she made a move to reach for him but pulled her hand back almost as quickly.

He clasped his hands behind his head and tilted his head toward the sky. That's when he felt the first drop of rain— and with it, the undeniable anguish of the memory.

He dipped his head so they were eye to eye, shoved his hands under his arms to keep himself from hitting something because there was nothing to hit other than the fucking vines.

"Jack Senior sent him that pint bottle of whiskey," he said, his voice rough and almost unrecognizable as his own.

"And he drank the whole goddamn thing before he'd even made it back from the mailbox."

She nodded but didn't speak. So he went on even though he didn't want to—knowing that he *had* to. To understand everything that happened in the aftermath of the party, he had to relive it because he'd apparently blocked it all out— tucked all of those memories somewhere safe where they couldn't knock him on his ass again. Yet here he was. "There wasn't even a card," he added. "Just a note telling his *fifteen*-year-old son that if he ever needed to forget, the bottle would do the trick."

"I know," she said, not stopping herself as she reached for him now, resting her palm against his chest. Heat spread through him, and he didn't—*couldn't*—push her away. "I remember."

He shook his head. "Did I tell you what it was he wanted to forget, though? How two years wasn't enough for my brother to get past his father backhanding him across the face so hard it fractured a goddamn bone in his cheek? And just like I did, he protected Jack Senior. Told the ER doc it was one of the horses."

Walker's birthday *gift* and his first experience with liquor had all happened the day after the party.

"Deputy Wilkes sent me home after taking my statement. I still don't get why he didn't press charges after what I'd done to his son. And then Walker..."

Everything was falling into place. Every part of that weekend played out like the worst of his nightmares come true. And that's exactly what it had been.

Her hand fisted his shirt and the other flew to his cheek. The rain fell freely now, and he watched as the water obscured her tears. He was powerless against her touch, powerless against the memory. Because he knew what came next—the part he hadn't given a second thought. But he knew it meant everything now.

"I told you right then and there that I didn't want kids."

She nodded slowly, hand still on his cheek.

"After what I'd done to Derek and the way Jack Senior kept his hooks in us even when we weren't under his roof, I said I'd never take the chance I'd turn into him. That I'd never become a father if I could help it. I said that to you while you were pregnant with our child."

She covered her mouth with her hand, nodding once more.

"We're one hundred percent them," he said, the truth of it setting in. "My parents. They got pregnant with me when they were teens, and look how the hell it all turned out."

"You had to go," she said. "I brought you there to tell you about Owen, but I knew—after the party and Walker I knew I couldn't. I couldn't force you to stay in a place that brought you so much pain. Because even though you were off the ranch, it wasn't over. So I had to say whatever I could to make sure you'd go." She paused, letting the rain pelt her skin, and he watched it run in rivulets down her cheeks. "You always said you'd come back—and a part of me believed that even after what I'd said, you would, that I'd get the chance to tell you when you were ready." She shook her head, pressing her lips together to stifle what he guessed was a full-on sob. "But you never did. Not until now."

He backed away. "I felt like a goddamn monster, Ava. And you telling me to go ... I swore that's what you thought of me, too."

She sucked in a sharp breath. "I'm sorry. I didn't know what else to do. We were so young, and suddenly I had to deal with what Derek tried to do, what you did to him, and the fact that I was pregnant. It was too much."

"What about when Owen was a year old? Two? Jesus, Ava, I get why you didn't tell me that night, but ten years? Ten *fucking* years?"

"You were engaged!" she cried.

His eyes widened. "What the hell are you talking about?" He wasn't denying it, but how in God's name did she know?

"I *went* to UCLA," she said, bitterness dripping off her words. "When you didn't come back for me, I went after *you*." She laughed, but her smile didn't reach her eyes. "I found out you were a clerk at a local law firm, and I went to see you. To tell you everything." She blew out a long breath. "I sat there in that office while the receptionist went on and on about how much the partners loved you, that you were exactly like your fiancée—putting work and school above everything else." Her hands fisted at her sides. "I left, Jack. I left as soon as she went down the hall to find you." Now she crossed her arms over her soaked torso, and that warmth he'd seen in her eyes turned to something he recognized all too well—resentment.

"Ava—"

But this time she was the one to shake her head. "You— you were getting married after I'd spent years changing diapers at four in the morning...joining the preschool PTO because yes, there was one...buying two extra car seats because the only way to be included in the carpool clique was to have all of the necessary equipment!"

She was yelling now, and he wasn't sure if it was from the rain or because she was pissed.

He closed the distance between them. "*You're* angry?" he asked, incredulous.

She groaned through gritted teeth. "Yeah! *I'm* angry!"

He was the one laughing now, the sound just as bitter as

hers. "So, what? Am I supposed to apologize for not keeping you up to date on *my* life? Or for not being there for a kid I never knew about?"

Her chest was heaving. "Yes!" she cried. "Yes! I know it doesn't make sense and I'm being completely irrational, but there you go. I want you to apologize for finding happiness without me even though that's what I wanted for you. Because I never found it without you!"

He held his left hand in the air, brandishing it at her. "There's no ring, Ava! No goddamn ring. And no happiness. Just the same messed-up guy you sent packing ten years ago."

Even with the rain, he could hear her breath catch in her throat.

"You're...divorced?"

He pressed the heels of his hands into his rain-drenched eyes. Then he looked at her. "No," he said, his voice calmer now. "I didn't marry her."

She stood there, mouth hanging open, but she said nothing.

"You had your reasons for pushing me away...and I had mine for not being able to truly move on."

"Closure," she said quietly, but he could still hear her over the rain.

Maybe that's what she was hoping for, too. Because none of it had felt right back then. He'd fucked up. Bigtime. But he'd also known that what had happened between them was more than a fling. He'd *known* she was lying to him, which was why he called her every day before he left for baseball training—and at least once a week the first month he'd been gone. But she'd always sent him right to voice mail. He might have loved her, but he wasn't an idiot, and his pride could only take so much. He'd finally let himself believe she'd stopped loving him, and that was when he'd stopped calling.

What else could he have done when she'd locked him out of her life so completely?

"I want to hear you say it," he said finally.

"What?" she asked.

"I want to hear you say that you loved me when you made it clear that you didn't." He tried to tell himself that her coming to find him didn't matter, that what she said now wouldn't change how he felt. It couldn't. But maybe it would heal the wound that had refused to close up for ten long years.

They were near soaked at this point, but neither seemed to care. The only thing that mattered was what she said next.

She didn't hesitate to answer.

"I loved you, Jack. I loved you *every* day we were together, and I'm pretty sure I'd fall for the man you've become if I had the chance to." He reached for her but stopped himself. "I love our *son*," she continued, "and I'm so sorry I deprived you of the chance at that kind of love, that Owen never knew—"

Before he knew what he was doing, his mouth was on hers, his hands cupping her cheeks, skin slick with rain and tears. She kissed him back, and despite the chill in the air he felt heat beneath his palms. Ten years of loss and ache and longing for something he hadn't known still existed poured from his lips. Her tongue plunged into his mouth, and he knew whatever it was he was giving to her he received in turn.

This was Ava—*Ava Ellis*. He'd kissed these lips hundreds of times, yet everything about them was foreign to him now. The girl he knew didn't exist anymore. The person he held in his arms was all woman. He slid his hands down her sides, following her curves until they rested on her hips. He might not know her like he had a decade ago, but his heart sped up just the same at the mere memory of how she used to make him feel.

Hopeful.

Whole.

Loved.

She stumbled backward, but he caught her with a hand on the small of her back. His fingertips pressed firm against her soaked shirt, and he felt the heat of her skin against his. He kissed her harder, searching for the connection he knew was buried deep. Ava's hands splayed against his chest, his heart thundering against her palm. He felt it—their past and present colliding in the clattering of teeth as her pelvis rocked against his. He was hard in an instant, yet in that same moment knew it didn't matter. That this was wrong. All of it. No matter how right his mouth felt on hers.

He pressed his hands to her shoulders and pushed her from him, freeing himself from the momentary spell as the pieces of their chance meeting yesterday fell back into place.

The tips of her fingers brushed her kiss-swollen bottom lip, and he ignored the urge to say *To hell with it* and suck it between his teeth.

"I'm not welcome in your life!" he called over what was quickly becoming a downpour. "Or did you miss that exchange between me and your father?"

He knew there was more to his hesitation than that, that if this went any further he'd have to deal with the real issue. Without warning, he'd become what he'd sworn he never wanted to be—a father.

He started to back away.

"I told them you weren't the father," she said. "And they chose to believe it because it was easier for them—and easier for me." She shook her head. "I was so scared if they knew—if my father knew—he'd find a way to make Deputy Wilkes change his mind—or worse."

"Worse?" His head was swimming.

The police had questioned everyone at the party, but there'd been no arrests, not even for the alcohol. It was like the whole thing got swept under the rug, and he'd never understood why.

He'd deserved a night or two in jail, if not more. Instead they'd hauled him into the station, taken his statement, and for reasons he couldn't fathom, sent him home.

He'd always known that once news of his home life in Oak Bluff traveled to Los Olivos, people would look at him and his brothers differently. And it had happened almost the minute they'd arrived. Kids from the other side of the tracks, so to speak. Sons of an abusive drunk with one brother, after one messed-up night, already showing signs of following in his father's footsteps. Why the hell wouldn't her parents suspect the same from him? Wasn't that why he and Ava had kept their relationship a secret? Wasn't it exactly what he'd feared himself?

"They took my statement, too," she said. "I told them about what Derek did and agreed not to press charges against *him* as long as he sought treatment—and as long as no charges were pressed against you. If after all of that my father found out you were Owen's dad? He was tight with the deputy. I wouldn't have put it past him to try and threaten jail time to make you sign away your legal rights to your own son."

The cops had let him off with a warning and one

stipulation—that he send paperwork proving he was seeing a counselor to deal with whatever had led to him pummeling Derek that night.

"So you're the reason I didn't go to jail. And why I spent my entire freshman year seeing a campus psychologist." Maybe he'd been forced to seek help, but it was help he'd needed. He'd just been too young and too damned stubborn to admit it.

He slicked his rain-soaked hair off his face. It was too much—all of it. Too damned much.

"Maybe I overstepped, but it was the only thing I could think to do for you that you might not do for yourself. I still believe my father was wrong about you then, and I'm willing to bet he's wrong about you now. You had *one* bad night after years of hell that I can't even imagine. But I never for one second thought you were a monster." Her teeth chattered as she spoke. "I don't expect anything from you that you don't want to give, Jack. But you're welcome in Owen's life. If that's what you want."

That was the thing. All he'd ever wanted was to leave. She'd gotten that part right. If he took her up on her offer, he ran the risk of wanting to stay, and he wasn't sure what the hell to do with that.

"Let me drive you home," she added. "And then I'll leave you to think about—about everything."

She was soaked, visibly shaking, and her eyes were bloodshot from the salt of her tears. She was in no shape to drive. And him? Well, he'd been better. But he'd been steady behind the wheel on no sleep. He could be steady for the mile drive back home.

Steady. It was what Jack Everett did, and despite everything, he'd do it for Ava now.

"Give me the keys," he said, and she didn't even question him as she reached into some hidden pocket in her skirt and handed them over.

He nodded, and they both strode in the direction of the closest road, where she had parked on the shoulder. He unlocked the Jeep with the key fob and pulled her door open, instinctively grabbing her arm when her foot slid in the grass. Once inside himself, he started the car, turned on the heat full blast, and drove.

Neither of them spoke a word, but it didn't matter. The past ten years filled the space between them. And even though they'd escaped the downpour, Jack couldn't help but feel like he was drowning.

CHAPTER SEVEN

Ava stood on a rug in the front foyer of Jack Everett's childhood home, her skirt turning it from a place to brush off your shoes to a squishy, spongy swamp.

"Wait here," Jack said, stepping around her and disappearing toward the kitchen.

She attempted to shrug, but it felt like a shiver, so she waited. What else was she going to do?

"Who the hell are you?"

Her eyes widened as she followed the sound of the voice to the top of the stairs in front of her.

The man staring down at her wore nothing but a pair of low-slung jeans. He scratched at his abdomen and then at the back of his head, his dirty-blond hair sleep tousled. His almost-beard made her do a double take, since she was sure the last time she'd seen him he hadn't even been able to grow facial hair.

"Walker?" she asked, knowing it had to be him, since she'd already seen Jack and Luke. She was no math expert, but the odds were pretty much in her favor that either it *was* the youngest of the three brothers, or the Everett boys multiplied in the rain.

He narrowed his eyes and made his way down the stairs

until he was standing in front of her, arms crossed. He looked her up and down as she stood there in her ever-growing puddle, and his eyes finally glinted with recognition.

"Ava-fucking-Ellis," he said. "And here I thought Jack Senior's passing would go unnoticed by the rest of the world. Guess it brought someone out of the woodwork. Just wasn't thinking it would be you."

She swallowed hard, then rubbed her hands on her arms, trying to fight against the shiver of cold and realization.

Neither Walker nor Luke had any clue what she'd kept from their brother.

Jack reappeared with a towel and what looked like clothing stacked on top of it. He offered the pile to her, though he was still drenched himself.

"There's a bathroom off the living room, across from the kitchen. I'll throw your clothes in the dryer after you change. Can't let you drive home like that."

While it was a sweet gesture, his voice was flat, and she knew it was just Jack being Jack—performing his obligatory duty for someone else in need. It was what made her fall for him in the first place—the way he took care of his brothers, even in the early weeks when they'd first met and he'd been in a cast. Her insides felt like they were caving in as the memories also brought her back to their first kiss—and Jack wincing when she'd pressed her palm against his torso. She'd never forget the bruises over his ribs, a terrifying kaleidoscope of purple, blue, black, and yellow. But that had been the type of pain that would heal. What lay beneath was something she'd never truly be able to understand.

"Thanks," she said, grateful for anything other than the cold clothes stuck to her body. She grabbed the offering and headed toward her destination. As she did, she heard Walker mumble something about a bigger bathroom upstairs—and Jack responding with an emphatic *No.*

She didn't know the full details of Jack's last night in this house as a kid, but his father knocking him down those same stairs where she'd been reacquainted with the youngest Everett brother was all the information she needed to understand. Once inside the bathroom, with the door shut and locked behind her, she let out a long, shaky breath.

Of course he never came back—not for her. Not for anyone. And she didn't blame him, either.

She steadied herself, swallowing back the memories, and peeled off her wet clothes. The towel provided welcome warmth, but when she pulled the gray T-shirt over her head, she startled at Jack's scent, at the nearness of him, and her thoughts zoomed in on that rain-soaked kiss.

There'd barely been enough time for her body to react when it happened. She'd been wrapped too tight in the emotion of it all, but now something long ignored, long dormant, suddenly woke. Her nipples peaked against the thin cotton of his shirt, and she knew it had little to do with body temperature.

She'd kissed Jack Everett the boy years ago. Fallen for him. Made love to him. And though there'd been other men since, she'd never ached for their touch like she did for his now. Funny how the heart and body could reconnect, even after all this time.

I loved you every *day we were together, and I'm pretty sure I'd fall for the man you've become if I had the chance to.*

Chance or no chance, it didn't matter. She knew it the day she'd shown him to his first class at Los Olivos High, the second he stepped out of that truck yesterday—and again when she found him at the vineyard this morning.

But there was more at stake this time around. Her future, for one. She'd put her life on hold to raise Owen, and there were no regrets there. But she was getting back on track now. All that stood between her and art school was one stupid painting that she *would* produce. But her son—*their* son—was still the most important person in her life.

Owen came first. Before she even thought about protecting her own heart, she had to protect his.

She emerged in the too-long T-shirt and shorts she'd had to creatively fold and roll at the waist to keep them from falling down. Jack stood at the kitchen counter in a fresh T-shirt and jeans himself, his feet bare, a steaming mug of coffee in his hand. He tilted his head toward a second mug on the kitchen table.

"I hope black is okay. We're out of everything." He forced a small smile, and she tried not to read too much into it. She'd dropped a bomb on him, and not in the way she'd hoped to do it. He'd need time to adjust, and she'd give him the space.

"Black is fine," she lied. "My clothes—I should run them to my car." Her eyes dropped to the towel-wrapped bundle in her arms, and he quickly set his coffee down and moved toward her.

"No," he said, taking the clothes from her. "I said I'd take care of that."

"Thank you." She ran a hand through her wet hair, trying to finger comb the tangles and keep herself from fidgeting in the presence of this strange yet familiar man who'd just kissed her until her lips were swollen.

He walked through the kitchen to what must be the laundry room, calling over his shoulder. "Everything here dryer safe?"

She laughed absently as she followed him, pausing in the open doorway. "I'm a single mom. I don't have time for clothes that *aren't* dryer safe."

A thick silence filled the air after that, punctuated moments later by the forceful slam of the dryer door. His back was still to her, and she swore under her breath.

"I'm sorry," she said softly. "That came out wrong. I mean, it's a mom joke, single or not. Shit. I don't know how to be me around you, Jack. I don't know how to do this." Not that she knew what *this* was. Was the coffee a peace offering or another obligatory gesture while she waited for her clothes to dry? Could he not even stand to be in the same room with her, or did a tiny part of him want her here?

He started the dryer and turned to face her, arms crossed and expression, as always, unreadable. Damn him for being able to hide like that when she wore her emotions like an obnoxious holiday sweater—screaming at you whether you wanted to see them or not.

"Yeah, well," he said, "I don't know how to be angry with you while a part of me still wants you, so I guess that makes two of us."

She exhaled. She'd spent all these years mired in guilt for not telling him, then resentment for thinking he'd found the life she'd always hoped he would—without her and Owen. Now she was wearing his clothes, and he *wasn't* wearing a ring, and what the hell did all of it mean?

She had no freaking clue. Still, she took a leap of faith with one tiny step over the threshold so they were now in the same room.

"So—you don't *hate* me?" she asked in complete earnest. Because right now that's all she needed to hear, that there was something salvageable between them, no matter how small.

He dropped his arms and pressed his hands against the dryer behind him, his gaze boring into hers.

"Shit, Ava. No. I don't hate you. I may not like how things went down, but that doesn't mean I don't get it—that I don't claim some of the responsibility. I've spent so god-damn long reminding myself what you did to me. I'm only now realizing what I did to you, and I need some time to wrap my head around that. Around all of this."

"I can live with that." She shivered.

"You're still cold," he said. A pile of folded towels sat atop the dryer in a basket, and he pulled one from the bottom and draped it over her shoulders. As soon as she felt the heat she understood why.

"You gave me the warmest one," she said, suppressing a smile. She wasn't going to let this silly bit of chivalry get to her.

Except it was already getting to her.

He tugged the cozy terry cloth around her, and she stumbled forward into his chest. She moved to step back, to pull at the tether that still seemed to bind them, but he kept each end of the towel firm in his grip—which kept *her* firm against *him*.

She swallowed and then took a chance, pressing her palms against his chest.

She felt his heartbeat, so strong and sure, and she wanted that sureness to be about her—about them. But they were strangers now. They had to proceed with caution.

For several seconds they just stood there, their mouths close enough so that warm breath mingled between them, but their lips didn't dare meet. Her heart rose in her throat as her pulse thrummed in her ears.

There was something in that moment before a kiss, in the anticipation of it. An exquisite ache. A rare hope. The promise of amazing—or of unimaginable heartbreak. Ava felt all of those things in Jack Everett's arms, and for this one moment she threw logic out the window and welcomed every single possibility if it meant his lips on hers again.

"I'm so goddamn angry." His voice rumbled in his chest, and she could feel the vibration of it against her palms.

"I know," she said, and she also knew that anger went deeper than what had happened between him and her.

"I spent so many years hung up on a warped version of the past. Now here you are—showing me what I've missed—and I don't know what to do with all of it. I just need a few minutes where I don't have to think about what comes next."

His breath was ragged. She could feel that same need—feel it building up until she thought she'd burst.

"No thinking," she agreed. She could do with forgetting, just for a few minutes, what it was that had gotten them to this moment.

And just like that, the towel dropped to the floor. His hands cupped her cheeks, and hers slid around his neck. As their lips met, still hungry yet more cautious than before, everything else fell away. Gone were the past ten years—her heartache, her regret, and her longing for something she wasn't sure she'd ever find.

All that mattered was this moment—Jack's hands on her skin, the electricity building between them as his tongue slipped past her parted lips and she tasted a sliver of redemption. Restoration. Release.

His hands slid down her neck and then her sides, and a new kind of shiver ran through her as they rested on her hips, his fingertips kneading her over her shirt.

She unclasped her own hands from his neck and grabbed his wrist, moving his palm beneath the fabric of his T-shirt that she wore and onto her bare skin.

"Jesus, Red," he growled.

And there it was, the nickname he'd given her finally rolling off his own lips.

"I thought only Luke remembered what you used to call me," she said.

He shook his head and leaned back. "Didn't seem right before."

Does it seem right now? She wasn't going to ask.

"Stop thinking," she whispered. "We agreed. No thinking. Just for right now."

She guided his hand higher until the tips of his fingers brushed her taut nipple, and he hissed. She hoped this meant he'd listened to her request because her ability to speak, let alone think, no longer existed. She answered his touch by kissing him harder, deeper, begging him for more.

His thumb and forefinger pinched her tightened peak, and she drew in a sharp breath. Their bodies vibrated against the thrum of the dryer, and every one of her nerve endings was on heightened alert. She'd never been so sensitive to another man's touch, and it was this realization—this momentary weakness of logical freaking *thought*, that had her gasping and pulling away this time.

His blue eyes were a tempest of emotion, confirmation that this had gone too far.

"I'm sorry," he said. "I thought—"

"I told you not to think. I *wanted* you not to think." She shook her head. "But as much as I want to, I can't turn off my own voice of reason. The thing is, there's a little boy caught in the middle of this, and he has no clue about any of it. It's not fair to him, Jack." She had to force herself not to wince at his stricken expression—and not to fall apart when she saw his walls go back up, hiding any part of him he'd let slip through. "And it's not fair to us," she added.

He nodded.

"I'd like you to meet him," she said. "If you want to. I won't tell him who you are. Not until you're ready for him to know." She swallowed hard at the next thought. "And if you decide you don't want him to know—then we'll cross that bridge when the time comes. But I won't get his hopes up when there's the chance of them being shattered."

Jack's brows pulled together. "How would you—"

He didn't finish the question, but she'd guessed what he was asking. She'd spent the whole night before working it out, how she could let her son meet his father without any pressure of what came next.

"I told him you were a friend I hadn't seen in a long time. Once I tell him you played baseball all through high school and college, you'll automatically be his friend, too."

His lip gave a slight twitch, and although he didn't smile, she knew a part of him wanted to.

"He's a pitcher?" Jack asked.

Ava smiled. "He's really good. A natural. My dad gives him some pointers every now and then, but that part of Owen is all you." She glanced down at her attire and then lifted her shoulders. "I should go. I'm gonna write down my number. You can call me if you want to trade our clothes back—and if you want to see Owen again."

He stood there, jaw tight, his expression stoic.

She stepped toward him, leaning close to place a soft kiss on his cheek.

His shoulders relaxed.

"Thank you for hearing me out," she told him. "And for maybe, in some small way, understanding."

He nodded. "You're welcome. And Red?"

"Yeah?"

"I'm sorry you did all this alone."

She swallowed hard and started to back away toward the kitchen but paused as another idea struck that was either brilliant or foolish or both.

"The vineyard's beautiful," she said. "If you decide to keep it, I could help you get it up and running." She gave him a nervous smile. "Strictly business, of course. Though I wouldn't charge you much."

He pressed his lips together, not quite a grin but not a frown either.

"I'll consider your offer," he said, and she decided not to ask which one.

That night she lay in bed, exhausted but unable to fall asleep. At a quarter past eleven, her cell phone vibrated on her nightstand. She assumed it was a text, but when the vibrating continued, she remembered that she'd turned her ringer off after Owen had fallen asleep. She grabbed the phone quickly and accepted the call even though she didn't recognize the number.

"Hello?" she said in a half whisper, tiptoeing to her door and closing it so she didn't wake her son.

"You were sleeping. Shit. I shouldn't have called so late. Sorry if I—"

"Jack?"

"Yeah."

"I wasn't asleep."

"Oh."

"And—I'm glad you called."

He was silent for a few beats, so she waited, giving him his space.

"Red?"

"Yeah?"

"He's my son."

"Yeah," she said again, her voice breaking softly as she crawled back into bed. He'd said it with such conviction she wasn't sure what to make of it. But that didn't matter. He knew about Owen and acknowledged him, and that was already more than she could have hoped for after all this time.

"Of course I want to meet him. I never for a second should have made you think I didn't."

"It's okay." She swiped at a tear, then rolled her eyes at herself. Hadn't she cried enough for one day? But this was a happy tear. A hopeful one. She kind of liked it for a change.

"No," he said. "It's not okay. I was an asshole for letting you leave today without saying anything, but it's been a hell of a two days."

She laughed at this, and God it felt good to smile. The weight hadn't lifted from her chest, but it was suddenly a lot lighter. "I think you've earned a free pass or a get-out-of-jail-free card. Or something."

A deep, soft laugh sounded in her ear, and it only made her smile broaden.

"Jack Everett, did you just laugh?"

She heard the sound again.

"I think maybe I did," he said.

She opened her mouth to say more but then bit her tongue. She liked being the reason he laughed, but knowing it was enough. She wasn't going to break the spell by gloating.

"What about tomorrow after school?" he asked.

She grinned. "He gets out early. Noon, I think. Teacher in-service day or something like that. Are you free for a late lunch?"

"How about this great little barbeque place in town, BBQ on the Bluff? I hear they buy local, and from what Luke and Walker tell me, Crossroads Ranch has some of the best beef in the area."

She laughed again. "Did you make a joke?"

"I think maybe I did."

"We'd love to meet you for lunch," she told him. "And as far as Owen knows, you're my good friend Jack who I haven't seen in years."

He cleared his throat. "So, one o'clock?"

She let out a long breath and nodded, then remembered he couldn't see her. "Yeah. One o'clock. We'll see you then."

"Red?"

"Yeah?"

"I'm glad I called, too."

And then he was gone.

After the adrenaline wore off, her head sank against her pillow. She barely had time to double-check that her alarm was set before she drifted off into her first restful night of sleep in years.

She dreamed of kissing a boy under an olive tree—and what it would have been like if he'd stayed.

CHAPTER EIGHT

Jack's brothers both sat at the kitchen table, a spread of sandwich fixings laid out before them. The last of what was left in the fridge, he guessed. Both had risen early to do some work in the barn while Jack tended to paperwork regarding the mortgage and the inevitable sale of the vineyard. Walker must have had a tame evening because he was awake and alert as early as Luke had been. This had set Jack somewhat at ease for the morning. Maybe he wouldn't have to worry so much about his youngest brother once he went back to San Diego. And since he had the two of them together—sober—he figured this was as good a time as any to tell them.

"I'm meeting Ava for lunch."

The two of them barely looked up, let alone acknowledged, he'd said anything at all. He got it. After a morning of manual labor, nothing stood between a man and his next meal.

"She's bringing her nine-year-old-son," he added. Luke offered a nod, and Walker grunted something that probably meant *I don't give a fuck*. So Jack decided to go in for the kill. "His name is Owen. And he's mine. Which means you two assholes are uncles. Congratulations."

Walker coughed on a piece of roast beef he'd just shoved

in his mouth. Luke stopped mid mustard spread. Jack crossed his arms and raised his brows. Silence rang out for a beat. Then another. And one more after that.

Finally Walker swallowed. "You got a fucking kid?" he said.

"It appears that I do."

"Did you know?" Luke asked.

Jack ran a hand through his shower-damp hair, hoping the gesture would mask his erratic heartbeat. His first reaction to the news had been fight or flight, and he'd chosen flight. Now—now he was going to meet this portion of his past head-on. He still didn't think he had what it took to be a father, let alone a good one, but he owed it to the boy—to *Owen*—to see.

"No," he told them. "And before you start talking shit about Ava for keeping this from me, know that the whole situation is complicated as hell."

Walker finished piecing together his sandwich and took a savage bite. "You know how you keep things *un*complicated, big brother?" he asked without giving two shits that half his snarling mouth was full of food. "Cover your dick, or keep it in your prepubescent pants."

Luke snorted.

Jack ground his teeth. Some things were funny as hell, but his past with Ava—how Owen came to be—sure as shit wasn't. "Everything's a joke to you, asshole," he said. "Christ, we were eighteen. We used protection. It didn't work. I didn't know until two days ago. End of story."

"Didn't know what?"

Jack pivoted to see Jenna standing in the doorway, tote bags in each hand with what looked like groceries.

She wasn't kidding. His brothers would probably starve without her help.

He strode to where she stood and relieved her of half the bags, welcoming the diversion even though he knew it would be short-lived.

"That we're uncles," Luke said, standing to peek at what she'd brought them. "Eggs," he added. "I like eggs."

Jenna deposited her bags on the counter and spun to face Jack, who was ready and waiting for her reaction.

"Why are they uncles?" she asked, and his brows pulled together. Jenna backhanded him on the shoulder. "Why are they uncles, Jack?"

He could hear the hysteria building, which was not a good sign considering Jenna didn't get hysterical. She didn't get *anything*, really. They'd gone from walking on eggshells around Jack Senior to someone who rarely let them see her angry at all.

He put a hand over hers, hoping the gesture and his attempt at a soothing tone would reassure her. "Ava," he said. "Ava Ellis. We were—well, we—that spring—"

"Oh for fuck's sake," Walker interrupted. "He knocked up the Ellis girl and then skipped town for a decade."

Jenna gasped, and Jack whirled on his brother, who was standing now as well. He grabbed Walker's collar, fisting it between his fingers.

"I didn't know, damn it!" Jack said through gritted teeth. "Christ, I didn't know. So cut me some slack or shut the hell up."

Walker's cheeks flamed with a building rage Jack hadn't seen before. He let go of his youngest brother and took a step back.

"There's a lot of shit you don't know, *Junior*."

Jack winced at the nickname. His father had first called him that when he was child not much younger than Owen. Later that name became a warning.

*Watch it, Junior. You better shut the hell up, Junior.
Pour my bottle down the drain one more time...Junior.*

Walker threw open the fridge and found himself a beer.
"Lost my appetite," he said, brushing past them all and out
through the back door.

Jack pressed his palms against the counter where Walker
had stood. He knew being back in this house would have
its challenges, but he hadn't anticipated his brothers being
one of them. They'd been allies once. He'd been their pro-
tector, and he didn't expect recognition or thank yous or
anything like that. Yet he'd somehow taken for granted
that they'd remember what he *had* done—assumed that being there back then, when he knew they truly needed him,
would make up for being gone.

But intermittent visits, emails, and texts hadn't been
enough. He didn't know his brothers anymore.

He felt a hand on his shoulder and knew the gentle gesture
came from his aunt. When he turned, he saw Luke striding
out the front door, sandwich in hand, and he wondered what
his brother's ever-present grin hid beneath the surface.

"I didn't think it'd be this hard," he said, and she gave
his shoulder a soft squeeze.

"If it was easy, everyone would do it."

"If *what* was easy?"

Jenna shrugged. "Coming home, facing your past, mend-
ing fences. Meeting your *child* for the first time?"

He let out a long, shaky breath. "I have a son," he said,
the word still so foreign on his tongue. "She named him
Owen."

Jenna's hand flew to her mouth, stifling a gasp—or
maybe a sob. Because the word—his son's name—was like
an automated switch, and a tear that seemed to come from
nowhere sped down her cheek.

Jenna *Owens*. It was her name, too.

He was ready to apologize for—he wasn't sure what. But he knew that whenever he opened his mouth lately, someone seemed to get upset. Before he could say anything, though, she dropped her hand to reveal a beaming smile.

"I'm a great-aunt!" she said, laughing. "Well, shit. You just aged me a half century."

Her joy was contagious, and Jack found himself smiling, too.

"We're not telling him who I am. Not yet, anyway," he said.

It took less than ten words for Jenna's expression to fall. "Of course," she said, feigning nonchalance. "Of course. You and Ava have a lot to figure out. I didn't think—" But she stopped herself, and Jack could tell she was fending off a different kind of tears.

He hugged his aunt. "I don't know how you do it," he said.

"Do what?" she asked, wiping the back of her hand under each eye. "Turn into a basket case almost every time you see me?"

He shook his head. "Your first instinct with me and Luke and Walker—when you hadn't seen us in years—was to take us in. You have this heart that's bigger than anything I've seen. You haven't even met Owen yet, and you love him already."

"Family is everything," she said. "And you feel something too, Jack. I won't let you pretend you don't."

He shoved his hands in the front pockets of his jeans. "Maybe. But I don't know how to love like that—like you do."

Jenna pressed her palm to her chest. "Oh, honey. You

were too young to remember, but I do—how your mama and daddy looked at you like you had the power to make the sun come up in the morning. I was so jealous of all the attention my big sister gave to you." She smiled wistfully. "They loved *you* like that. And I know somewhere in that protected heart of yours, you have the capacity, too. You just need to unlock it."

Jack's jaw tightened. It wasn't that he didn't appreciate what his aunt was trying to do. But the only father he remembered was some sort of funhouse mirror reflection of the man she tried to recall for him now. Where she remembered smiles, Jack saw a sneer. Terms of endearment were twisted into angry words filled with disdain and blame.

If she didn't have to work so hard taking care of you boys, she never would have gotten sick.

"That's not the man I knew," he said with such force it made her flinch. "Shit, Jenna, I didn't mean—"

"It's okay," she interrupted. "I mean, no. It's not okay to talk to me like that, but I'm going to let it slide. You've come against more than I reckon you bargained for coming back home, and I'm sure it's a lot to take in." She reached up and brushed off his shoulders and then slapped her hands against his cheeks. "You look good, nephew."

He looked down at his checked shirt and worn jeans. It was fine attire for a barbeque, but for meeting his son?

"I don't know what the hell I'm doing here. I really don't." He scrubbed a hand across his jaw. "I'm out of my goddamn element. I don't know how to talk to kids. And he could hate me the second he meets me. Not sure if you noticed, but I'm not exactly the easiest guy to be around these days." He cleared his throat. "And I shouldn't have snapped at you. I'm sorry. You're right about that much."

"I know I am, darling," she said with a grin.

"But," he added, "it doesn't help to hear what kind of man my father used to be. Because that's not the man he was in the end."

He kissed her on the cheek and backed toward the front door.

She pointed a finger at him. "It also says nothing about the man *you* are, Jack Everett."

He swallowed hard but kept moving, wishing he could believe her. But Jenna had just reminded him that his father was someone else entirely before his mother got sick. Maybe once he'd seen his son as someone who could light up the world. But then he plunged himself into complete darkness at the bottom of a bottle, blaming his own children even though they had lost their mother, too.

He was at the door now, but neither of them had broken eye contact. He thought about making his aunt flinch, about slamming his hand against his truck when he was at the Ellis Vineyard, of all the times he'd had to remind himself to rein in the anger before he simply exploded like he had with Derek Wilkes.

You're not good for either of them.

Ava's father's words ran on a continuous loop in his head.

"Actually, Jenna, it says everything."

CHAPTER NINE

Owen squirmed in the wooden booth next to her. "Mo-*om*. I'm so hungry I think I'm going to die."

Ava laughed, hoping her son couldn't see through the reaction to the nerves that lay beneath. Normally she'd give him a snack in the car—a bag of goldfish crackers or one of those squeezie applesauce pouches—but she hadn't wanted him to be full once they got to the restaurant. He needed the food to keep him from getting bored. And to keep him from being idle enough to scrutinize anything about Jack he might not want scrutinized.

"In a few minutes, bud. Promise."

But it was five minutes to one, and Jack wasn't here. *Yet.* Because of course he was coming. She hadn't spent the whole hour mentally reassuring herself only for him not to show.

Oh shit. What if he didn't show?

She'd chosen to sit with their backs to the door. Otherwise her eagerness to see Jack enter would get the best of her. But this only made things worse. More than once she'd attempted to casually look over her shoulder only to meet the curious eyes of several BBQ on the Bluff patrons.

"Are you two ready to order, or are you waiting on someone else?"

Ava startled as a young woman with a blond pixie bounced a pen against a pad of paper. "It's cool if you're still waiting. I've got a couple of nephews, though, probably around your little guy's age, and all they ever do is *eat*. Figured he might be hungry."

Ava smiled and turned to Owen, who gave her a pleading look.

"We *are* waiting for someone, but I guess it couldn't hurt to—"

"Lily Green, since when do they let the cook out of the kitchen?"

At the sound of Jack's voice, a warmth spread through Ava's veins like chocolate fondue, hot and sweet and delicious. She shook her head. This was *not* the place to let his smooth baritone start—*doing* things to her.

"Since I'm short two servers this afternoon," the other woman said with a grin. "And how about you tell me why I've already seen you twice in the span of four days? Luke told Tucker you'd be hightailing it out of Oak Bluff first chance you got." She turned her attention to Ava. "My husband and Jack's little brother, Luke, are good friends. Best friends, actually. But me and Luke? We butt heads like you wouldn't believe. Wonder if big brother here is as difficult as the other." She winked at Jack.

He smiled and slid into the booth across from Ava and Owen.

"Am I late?" he asked, and Ava shook her head. He glanced back at the woman with the notepad—*Lily*. And Ava couldn't help the surge of relief she'd felt when the woman said *husband*.

"Start us off with that cornbread you sent over the other night, will ya?" Jack added. "I've been craving it ever since."

Lily shoved her pen behind her ear and dropped the pad into her apron pocket. "You got it. I'll get the rest of your order when I deliver the goods."

Only after Lily was gone did Jack give Ava his full attention, and she had to remind herself to breathe when he looked right past her and let his eyes fall on Owen.

"Hey, bud," he said. "You like cornbread?"

Owen narrowed his eyes at Jack—at his father—and Ava watched as the boy studied the man. Finally, her son nodded.

"Yeah, I like it," he said, then looked back and forth between his parents. "My mom calls me that, by the way. *Bud.*"

She held her breath, and Jack cleared his throat. He was nervous, and Owen was already giving him the third degree. But then Jack crossed his arms and smiled. She wasn't sure what she was expecting, but he seemed ready to take whatever Owen had to dish out.

"What should *I* call you, then?" Jack asked him, and Owen crossed his arms as well.

"You're a friend of my mom's?"

"I am," Jack said.

"A *good* friend? Because if you were a good friend I think I would have heard of you before."

Jack let out a nervous laugh while Ava seemed to ignore her earlier directive reminding herself to breathe.

"Truth is," Jack started, "your mom and I used to be real good friends. Then I left town, and we lost touch for a while." He turned his attention to her, his blue-eyed gaze steady and intent. And Ava's heart stuttered like it had the first time she saw him in high school. "But I think I'd like for us to be friends again."

Owen tilted his head toward her so that both of their gazes were fixed on hers.

"Do you wanna be friends with him again?" Owen asked.

Ava cleared her throat. "Yeah, bud. I think I do."

Because friendship she could admit to wanting. Friendship was a start. What she wouldn't do was hope—this early on—that it would lead to more.

Owen nodded and faced Jack again. "One more question."

"I'm all ears," Jack said, his lips hinting at a grin.

"Marvel or DC?"

Jack's brows raised, and Ava bit her lip.

"And here I thought I was going to get a *hard* question," Jack said. "Because the only right answer is Marvel, and the top Avenger, of course, is the first Avenger, Captain Steve Rogers."

Owen pumped his fist in the air and shouted, "Yes! Okay, Mom. This guy's cool. I think you two should be friends again."

Ava's breathing finally steadied, but she had a rising tide of emotion. Because Jack and Owen had connected. Her son had just given his own father the seal of approval. And she—well, she'd never expected this day to happen, let alone have it be a success.

"Cornbread for all my friends!" Lily said, placing a basket on the table.

The spell was broken, but a new one took hold as Owen devoured a piece before Lily even had time to leave the table. They all watched as he sank into the booth as he swallowed—satiated for the moment.

"Did he even chew that?" Lily asked.

Owen grinned and rubbed a hand over his belly. "Whatever I did, I'm gonna do it again." He reached for piece number two, but Ava's hand landed on his wrist before he could swipe another golden square.

"Drink something, bud. You're gonna choke or make yourself sick if you don't slow down."

Jack scratched the back of his neck and squinted at Lily. "I remember my brothers saying this place had the best strawberry lemonade. You still got that?"

She shook her head, and Ava watched as Owen deflated.

"I change the menu monthly. But I've got a frozen strawberry limeade that'll knock your socks off. What do you say?"

Owen perked up again. Ava smiled and lifted her shoulders. Jack slapped a palm down on the table.

"I guess that settles it," he said. "Three strawberry limeades, and judging by this guy's appetite, I think we're ready to order."

Forty-five minutes later, Owen was working off his short ribs at the vintage Pac Man machine with a stack of quarters—courtesy of Jack. Ava was still picking at her brisket sandwich as she watched Jack take a long, slow swig of his limeade.

"You're good with him," she said softly, and the anticipation of his response made everything inside her constrict.

He set his glass down on the red and white checkerboard tablecloth, running his thumb down the cool condensation. "I'm flying by the seat of my pants, here. I'm just lucky you raised an amazing kid," he said, eyes trained on the hand still holding the glass, his voice rough. "Made today a whole lot easier."

She took a chance, bold as it was, and laid her palm over his free hand. "*We* made an amazing kid," she whispered. "That's not all me, there."

His eyes met hers, clouded with too much emotion for her to read. She guessed there was still anger—at her in particular. She owned that and would continue to do so. But pain lay beyond those blue irises, too. A pain she'd always wanted to take away, even when they were teens. But she learned too late that she hadn't possessed that kind of power. And maybe she never would.

But Owen was pure magic. She'd felt that every day for almost nine-and-a-half years. And if Jack could lasso even a thread of it, maybe he'd understand the type of joy only a child could bestow.

"You mean baseball and Marvel? That just means he's smart." Jack laughed. "I gotta be honest," he added, and Ava noticed he hadn't pulled his hand from hers yet. "I didn't think it would be a good idea to let this go beyond lunch."

She sucked in a sharp breath, soft enough, though, that maybe it went unheard. But he did hear, because his hand left the glass and covered hers, her palm sandwiched between his.

Now her breathing grew shallow for an entirely different reason. She knew this discussion was about Owen, but Jack touching her was something else. Because his thumb moved in slow, soft strokes against her skin, and her stomach flipped with each small movement, making her forget for a moment what they were even talking about.

Owen. This is about Owen. It wasn't the time for her to lose focus or get lost in thoughts of what might have been...or what could be. Owen and Cal Poly. That was all she could handle right now.

But this man who'd been so afraid of who he'd become already knocked it out of the park with their son, and she wasn't sure what should come next.

"And now?" she asked, reeling herself back in.

"Now I kinda don't want to let him out of my sight. Not yet. I mean—if it's okay with you, I'd love for you both to come by the ranch after we settle up here. I could show him around, maybe even introduce him to the two assholes who live there."

She bit her lip, hesitating. She'd already gotten more than she'd bargained for out of this day. She wanted to be near him—God, yes she did. But she didn't want to fall for someone who might not stick around. She wouldn't survive it again.

"I'm not sure that's—" she started, but he interrupted.

"As friends, of course," he said. "I'll call ahead and let everyone know the situation."

"Of course," she agreed. "And maybe," she added, knowing she needed to get the words out before she lost her nerve, "we should keep it as just friends, too. For now. While we're figuring this out." Her world was already spinning out of orbit. Anything more than friends would knock her off her axis wholly and completely. Then where would she be?

Just uttering the phrase made her chest feel hollow. There had been so much pent-up emotion in their first frenzied kiss—and in their stolen moment in the laundry room yesterday. So much that they couldn't put into words was spoken in the touching of their lips. But Owen was the first priority. Plus, she'd gotten her hopes up about inviting Jack back into her life before, and it had crushed her to see he'd moved on. Simply because he hadn't gone through with the marriage didn't mean whatever was brewing between them meant anything.

It was probably nothing more than heat. Pent-up chemistry that would dissipate with time.

Jack stirred his straw in his glass. "Of course," he said again, this time with less conviction.

"I'll do anything I can to keep from hurting him, Jack. *Anything*. You need to know how much I want you in his life, but if he finds out who you are and you leave again? That will crush him."

Because the crux of it was that she hadn't meant to hold a torch for him all these years. But the reminder of how much she'd loved him was in her son's eyes—in his very essence. Jack Everett had always been with her. After her failed attempt at reconnecting with him in L.A., she'd given up hope of ever seeing him again. If he'd ever come back to his aunt's place, he hadn't come looking for her. Now here he was, the man she always knew he'd become—and he had more power to hurt her than he ever did.

"You're right," he finally said, then slid out of the booth. He laid a couple of twenties on the check Lily had left. Ava opened her mouth to protest, but Jack simply shook his head. "Your money's no good here. Besides, you heard how she's married to Luke's buddy, Tucker. They've been struggling a bit, so I want to leave a little extra—not that it will help."

Ava slid out of the booth as well, marveling at Jack's generosity. She wasn't surprised at the man he'd become, not one little bit. But he wasn't the only one who'd missed out on these past ten years. He was a natural with Owen. He could have been back then, too, if she'd have been brave enough to have given him the choice.

"I want to help you and Owen, too. I mean—" He scratched the back of his head. "I have money. And a promotion in the works. No matter what, you and Owen won't want for anything, financially speaking." He laughed. "As long as this damn vineyard doesn't sink the ranch further into the hole."

"I take care of Owen just fine," she said, the words coming out sharper than she'd intended.

"Of course. I didn't mean..." He trailed off.

"Look. I appreciate what you're offering." But this time she was the one without words. Because how did she tell him that she wasn't looking for financial stability to come from anyone else? She'd fallen back on her parents in terms of money and an easy income since she'd graduated high school. She didn't bring Owen here to meet his father just so Jack could offer them more money in the bank.

That was why she was finally applying to school again—why she'd take every cent of financial aid she could get and repay it with an impressive graphic design job—or maybe she could restore pieces at the San Luis Obispo Museum of Art. Whatever it was, *she* was going to do it. Owen didn't need money. He needed a father. And *she* needed... Was it fair to insert herself into this scenario when she should put her son first? Because no matter how hard she tried, she couldn't stop thinking of the *what ifs*.

What if she fell for him again?

What if he stayed?

What if he left?

Finally she crossed her arms and smiled. What they *both* needed was a subject change. "Is this where you take me up on my offer to help you get it up and running?"

He sighed. "Jack Senior's lawyer doesn't think we'll get

back what he bought it for without it thriving. Keeping it until then might be the only option."

"Just tell me you need my help, and it's yours," she said. "It's not harvest season, so things are slow at the Ellis Vineyard. I manage the shop and tasting room, mostly, but it's not hard to get coverage for that if I need to. Plus, I've never taken a vacation, and I know the owners. I'll just have to ply them with extra time with their grandson."

He raised a brow. "You gonna tell them what you're doing? Who you're spending your time with?"

"I don't answer to them," she spouted, a little too defensively. Because despite being a grown woman, in a way she did. If it wasn't for her parents, raising Owen these past nine years would have been a hell of a lot more difficult. "But I also have nothing to hide. So yes, I'll tell them." Until she knew *how* Jack was going to fit into Owen's life, she wasn't sure what to tell them.

"Fair enough," he said, not pressing her to say more. So she didn't. "Then I guess all that's left is a question." He cleared his throat and cocked his head to the side. "Ava Ellis, will you help me restore a vineyard?"

She grinned. "Well, Jack Everett, I thought you'd never ask."

And just like that, the deal was done. He promised her he'd be in town for at least a month, and in turn she promised him she'd make sure Luke and Walker were well on their way to producing the maiden vintage by the time he left, if that's what he decided.

For now she'd convince herself that the compromise would be enough. After all, none of this was part of Jack's plan. She understood that.

He hadn't planned to drive by the vineyard the other day. But he did. He hadn't planned on fatherhood, yet he'd just spent the better part of an hour dissecting the friendship between Captain America and the Winter Soldier with his son.

He hadn't planned on the vineyard, but he was staying to get it off the ground. And maybe—just maybe—Oak Bluff wasn't where he saw his future.

But maybe now that things had changed . . . it was.

CHAPTER TEN

"Do not let Luke or Walker mess this up," Jack barked into his cell phone, and a long pause stretched out between him and his aunt. "Jenna? Did you hear me?"

What *he* heard was a soft sniffle. Christ. Maybe it wasn't his brothers he needed to worry about.

"Jenna?" he said again, drawing out her name, and she cleared her throat.

"We—we get to meet him? We get to meet Owen?"

He sighed. He should have realized this would be almost as big of a deal for them as it was for him.

"Yes," he said. "But we're going to be there in a couple of minutes, and I need your word that the three of you can handle this, that you can handle not letting him know who you are yet."

Jack glanced in his rearview mirror to see that Ava's red Jeep was still behind him. "Of course," Jenna said. "We can handle this. We won't tell Owen anything before you do."

"We can handle it, asshole!" he heard Luke yell into Jenna's phone. "She's the one getting all weepy and shit. No worries, brother. We're not going to blow your cover."

Jack let out a long breath as they were pulling up the ranch's driveway. He guessed he'd have to trust them.

Maybe it was a foolish, impulsive decision to invite Ava and Owen back, but something warred within him not to let them go home. Not yet. It had just been lunch, but it was also something entirely more. And Jack had no idea what to do with more. So instead of handling it himself, he'd pawn that responsibility off on the most dysfunctional of families—his own.

He hopped out of his truck and turned to where Ava pulled in behind him. He crossed his arms and tilted his head toward the sun, squinting.

Here went nothing.

He dropped his gaze toward his guests and was startled to see Owen mirroring his stance—arms across his chest and head raised to the sky. Something in his own chest sank. Or maybe it lifted. He couldn't tell. All he knew was that the sight of this boy—and this place—knocked him off-kilter.

"What is it?" Ava asked, striding toward him.

Jack shook his head. "Nothing. Let's—uh—go inside."

Ava shrugged, and Owen's head dropped so their eyes met.

"This is your house?" the boy asked. His eyes volleyed from the ranch, to the barn and stable, to the cows grazing in the pasture beyond the residence. "Is it a farm?"

Jack chuckled softly, grateful to Owen for breaking the ice, even if he didn't realize he was.

"This *is* my house," he said. "But I don't live here anymore. My brothers do. And it's not a farm. It's a ranch."

The three of them headed for the porch's front steps, for the door he knew would open to let Owen and Ava in—to let them past the threshold that was his life.

"What's the difference?" Owen asked, and Jack ruffled

his hair, the strands thick and wavy beneath his fingers. Like his own, yet softer—and red like his mom's.

His fingers twitched. Then he pulled his hand away.

"Well," Jack said. "For starters, we don't grow anything but cattle. And farmers tend to know a lot more about the land—about growing things from the earth."

Owen nodded as they climbed the steps. "Like Mom and our family does with grapes?"

Out of the corner of his eye, Jack saw Ava smiling at them. "Yep. Growing grapes is like farming. And it so happens I have some grapes of my own to tend to, and your mom offered to help me learn how."

He pulled the screen door open and gestured for Owen and Ava to walk inside.

"She's a good teacher," Owen said, stepping into Jack's childhood home. "She taught me how to ride a bike and tie my shoes. She even taught me how to memorize the fifty states in alphabetical order—but not a whole lot of my friends think that's cool, so it's kind of our secret." He looked at his mom and then back at Jack. "I guess you're in on the secret now, too."

The boy, unassuming and unafraid, strode past Jack and his mom, his curiosity seeming to take over as he started down the hall and toward the kitchen.

"He knows how to ride a bike and tie his shoes," he said, an unexpected twinge of envy socking him in the gut.

"Yes," Ava said softly, keen understanding in her tone. "But there's still so much for him to learn." She paused for a moment, worrying her top lip between her teeth. "You just taught him the difference between a farm and a ranch. I'm guessing there's a lot more you could teach him...if you wanted to."

But there wasn't time for him to respond because as

the door clicked into place behind them, he caught sight of Jenna emerging from the kitchen, her hand outstretched to shake Owen's.

What *did* he want? Jack wanted to do right by this kid who had no idea his world could be turned upside down at the drop of a hat. He wanted to do right by his brothers, his aunt, and the woman who'd sacrificed her own future to give him the one she thought he wanted.

The one *he* thought he wanted.

New York. He was moving to New York. *That* was his future—one where he could keep the ranch and vineyard financially afloat. One where he could make sure Ava and Owen never wanted for anything.

But even he knew that wasn't what it meant to be a father. *Or* a brother. New York was the logical next step in his career. But was it still the logical next step in his life?

Owen turned to them as they caught up. "Mom. This is Jenna, Jack's aunt, and she said that I can go to the stables with Jack's brother and that I can ride a horse and go see all the cows, and I know you're going to say that I've never ridden and I could get hurt, but *please* say yes. I'll be careful. *Please?*"

Jenna smiled sheepishly. "I'm sorry. I maybe should have asked you first, but I get a little excited around sweet kids like this one, and he just walked in here, introduced himself, and I couldn't help myself."

Jack understood Jenna's nervous energy, but he kept quiet, knowing this was Ava's call. He didn't have a say in what Owen did or didn't do.

Luke sauntered in from the laundry room off the back of the kitchen and tipped his cattleman hat to his guests. "Did Jenna say I'm taking Shortstop here for a ride?" he asked with a knowing grin.

"Shortstop?" Owen asked, crossing his arms again as he'd done outside. "I'm taller than most of the other kids in my grade. *And* I'm a pitcher."

Luke crouched before his nephew, resting his elbows on the knees of his dirty jeans.

"A ball player, eh? Like your friend Jack." Luke raised a brow at his brother before turning his attention back to Owen. "You may be taller than the other kids," he said, sizing his nephew up. "But you sure as shit ain't taller than me." He winked. *"Shortstop."*

Jenna playfully slapped her younger nephew on the back of the head as he stood. "Language, Luke."

Owen shrugged. "It's okay. Mom says it all the time."

Ava gasped. "I do *not*!"

Jack's eyes widened with amusement as he waited for the story to unfold.

Owen nodded. "Sometimes when you leave the window open in your painting room, I hear you when Scully and I are playing out back." He pressed his lips together and looked at the rest of them. "Painting pisses her off."

Ava's mouth hung open, and Jack tried to ignore the implication of what Owen had just revealed. The Ava he remembered had loved painting above everything else. Painting didn't make her upset. It was what she did when she was already pissed off in order to calm down.

"Owen," he said. "This is my brother Luke. There's two things you need to know about him. One, he knows horses, and there's no one better to teach you how to ride one. And two—once my brother gives you a nickname, he's not likely to call you anything else, so get used to Shortstop. Wear the name with pride."

Owen let out a breath. "Can I ride, Mom? *Please?*"

Luke took his hat off and held it against his chest. "I'll

take him out on Cleo. She's our gentlest, doesn't mind being led. I'll never let her go beyond a walk."

Ava's shoulders slumped. "You promise he's safe?" she asked, squinting at the still healing wound on Luke's cheek.

The man winked again. "Don't worry. I'll save the bull riding for lesson two." Luke clasped a hand on Owen's shoulder. "What do you say, *Shortstop?*"

Owen groaned, but he was smiling as Luke led him back the way he came. Ava pressed her lips together—a wince she seemed to be forcing into a smile.

"Don't worry," Jenna said. "Luke may be a daredevil when it comes to his own safety, but Owen's in good, capable hands with him. No one knows those horses like he does."

The back door opened, and Walker ambled in from the deck.

"Nice of you to make an appearance," Jack said.

The youngest Everett brother raised the bottle of beer that was in his right hand. "Figured you wanted the family to make a good impression on the kid," he said with a mild sneer. "And I wasn't really in the mood to impress."

Jack opened his mouth to say something but Jenna put a hand on his arm.

"Don't," she said softly. "Not today."

There was enough genuine concern in her tone that Jack let it slide.

He hadn't realized Walker's drinking had become this—regular. And how often did Luke get injured with the rodeo shit? Was Jenna happy? And Christ, he had a son who already knew how to ride a bike, tie his shoes, and say the fifty states in alphabetical-fucking-order.

"Jack?" Jenna said, and it sounded like it wasn't the first time she'd said his name. "Are you okay?"

He shook his head softly, bringing himself back into the moment, and realized Jenna, Ava, and Walker were all staring at him.

"I'm fine," he said, his words short and clipped. "Ava says we can get the vineyard up and running, that she can help. Once we see if we can turn a crop, we can decide whether or not to put it back on the market. So I thought we could all sit down and talk, figure out a game plan."

Jenna clapped her hands together. "Is there going to be a tasting room? A gift shop? Y'all are pretty handy, right?" She looked Jack and Walker up and down. "You could, like, build something, right?"

Walker brushed past them, set his empty bottle on the counter, and tore open the stainless steel refrigerator to retrieve another. He peeked around the corner of the door.

"I'm assuming we're going to be at this awhile. Who else wants one?"

Ava and Jenna both declined, using the fact that they'd both be behind the wheel soon as their excuse. As much as he'd love to dull them, Jack wanted to keep his senses razor sharp. Everything hinged on this damn vineyard—on getting it running so he could get his life back. Whatever that meant.

Walker shrugged. "At least no one can accuse me of not sharing." He dropped into one of the high-backed wooden chairs at the long kitchen table that Jack still couldn't believe his brother had made. Jenna and Ava took their seats as well.

"I'm going to grab the paperwork," Jack said, and made a detour to his office before returning. He sat down, opened a leather-bound binder, and ran a hand through his hair as he started skimming pages.

He shook his head. "What the hell is a *Burgundian varietal*?" he asked.

Ava's eyes brightened. "May I?" she asked, motioning for the binder.

"Please," Jack said, sliding it in her direction. "Translate."

She laughed. "We grow the same grapes," she said. "This will be easier than I thought. I mean, I know the varietals and what we can make—pinot noir, maybe. Chardonnay. But I saw the plants, and they've not been tended to properly in quite some time. The trick will be producing a viable harvest first."

"Well," Walker said, popping the top off his bottle. "You gonna be able to teach us how to do magic?"

Jack shook his head, but she held his brother's gaze.

"Yes," she said. "If you're all up to the task, then so am I." She looked at Jenna. "And your aunt is right. You should think about a tasting room, something to get customers in the door so they learn the difference between Crossroads Ranch and Crossroads Vineyard."

Jenna beamed. "Crossroads *Vineyard*. I don't know about y'all, but I love the sound of it."

Walker leaned forward, resting his elbows on the dark wood of the table. "There is a structure on the outskirts of the property. It's not complete, but I've been out to inspect it. I think that's where all the tanks and barrels and shit are supposed to go."

"Liking the sound of it isn't enough. I'm sorry, Jenna." Jack rubbed his eyes with the heels of his hands. "Shit. It'd be easier to sell it at a loss. This is going to be more than an investment of time. You know that, right?" He hadn't directed the comment at anyone in particular, but he was sure they knew he meant Walker.

"There is the life insurance payout," his brother said, and Jack nodded.

"That might scratch the surface," he added.

"And Jack Senior may have been pissing away his own savings, but I've been putting money away—my own account, not that one you set up for me. Plan was to build my own place eventually, but maybe I don't need to. Not right now."

Jack's eyes widened, and the two women looked on, watching whatever was about to unfold—unfold.

"I can't ask you—" Jack began, but Walker cut him off.

"You aren't the only asshole who gets to make decisions around here, *big brother*. If this is what's best for the financial state of the ranch, then this is where I'm putting my money. Luke can decide what the hell he wants to do, and if you want to add some of your precious lawyering cash to the heap, that's *your* decision. But I've made mine."

Jack gave his brother a slow nod. Issues aside, somewhere underneath Walker had a good head on his shoulders. And no matter their differences, his brother was still putting family first.

"I'm in," Jack said. "Adding my cash to the heap."

The corner of Walker's mouth twitched into something that almost resembled a smile.

"Who's in?"

Luke and Owen traipsed in from the mudroom.

"Are you done with your ride already?" Ava asked, and Owen shook his head.

"Luke showed me how to brush Cleo and put her saddle on and—I got thirsty."

Luke clapped his hands together. "Came back for some lemonade, but it looks to me like I'm walking in on something pretty big."

Jenna beamed. "Jack and Walker are investing in the vineyard. Ava's going to help get us on our way to harvest, and..." She paused for a few seconds. "And I'm just so damned happy to see you three together again."

Luke raised a brow but said nothing as he headed for the fridge and emerged seconds later with a pitcher of lemonade. He poured Owen a glass, then filled four more, setting one in front of Jenna, then Ava, and then Jack. He finished off the pitcher on a final glass—his own—then raised it.

"I'm in," he said.

Walker held up his bottle. "To fucking grapes."

"Language!" Jenna yelled, but she was laughing.

Jack laughed, too, and then the rest of them said in unison—Owen too, "To fucking grapes!"

Every single one of them bore some semblance of a grin, even Walker. It was one hell of a sight, one Jack wanted to enjoy awhile longer.

He'd tell them about New York tomorrow.

CHAPTER ELEVEN

Owen drummed his hands on the passenger seat headrest in time with the music playing on the radio. Ava didn't recognize the song, but then again, her mind kept wandering somewhere else.

Her world had been so small for so long—only her, Owen, and her parents. But in a matter of days, Owen's family had grown exponentially to include a father, two uncles, and a great-aunt, all who'd welcomed him into the fold like he'd always been one of them. She swallowed back the guilt at what all of them had missed out on these past ten years. After she'd given up hope about Jack coming home after college, she'd resigned herself to this solitary life, convinced that her son was enough. In many ways he was. But she knew now, after seeing Owen with the family he'd never known existed, that it wasn't enough for *him*.

"Did Jack really play college baseball?" he asked, forcing her back into the moment.

Ava grinned.

"Yeah," she said. "He did."

"Did you know him then? When he played?"

She shook her head. "When I met Jack, he was injured

and couldn't play. A broken leg. Once he went off to college? Well—we lost touch."

Owen bounced in his seat. "I bet it was from an epic slide into home. Or maybe he had to wrangle some cattle with Luke and Walker and he got trampled or something." She caught sight of him in the rearview mirror, his eyes bright with excitement. "I can't believe there are real cowboys right here in our county—and that you *know* them."

She forced her smile not to falter and kept her eyes trained on the road. How she wished that was Jack's story—an *epic slide into home.* She couldn't imagine what it was like for him to be in that house with those memories, a place that held far more pain than anything she'd ever endured. She'd expected today's meeting with Jack to end with lunch, and instead he'd invited her and Owen to cross a threshold of sorts. She knew Jack was strong, but to let them in like he did today? She wondered if he had any clue how strong he really was.

"You liked the Everetts, huh?" she asked.

Owen laughed. "If you promise not to tell him, I even sort of like Luke calling me *Shortstop.* It's like having a big brother or something."

Ava couldn't control the tear that escaped the corner of her eye, but she wiped it away without a sniffle, hoping Owen didn't notice. He was quiet for several long seconds, and because she didn't know what else to say, so was she.

"Do you think *he* does cool stuff like the Everetts?" Owen finally asked, and she knew what was coming. It had been a long time since anything had triggered questions like this.

"Your dad?" This time she did sniffle, because today had been amazing and wonderful and everything she'd wanted. Yet it had also been a lie. But the ball wasn't in her court anymore. It was in Jack's. She owed it to him to let things unfold on his timeline, to be sure about what role he wanted to play in his son's life before they told him.

"Yes," she answered him. "I think he does a lot of amazing things. You know he wouldn't have left if he didn't have to, right? I know it's hard to understand, bud, but he was—*is*—a good man. I'm sure of it. But sometimes, even when people care about each other, their lives go in different directions. And that's what happened with us."

The tears were impossible to hide now, so she let them flow, rummaging in her purse for a tissue as they did.

"I'm sorry, Mom," Owen said softly. "I didn't mean to make you sad."

"Never apologize for asking where you come from, sweetheart. It's okay to be curious," she said. *And it's your right to know.* She was caught between two of the most important men in her life. She knew now, though, that whatever Jack decided about Owen—being in his life or not—they *both* owed their son the whole truth, which meant the pivotal role Ava played in all of this.

"Did he know about me?" Owen asked. "I know he left before I was born, but did he know I was...you know...on the way when he did?"

The last time he'd asked about his dad was a couple of years ago, and he'd always readily accepted that he'd had to leave before he got a chance to meet his son. She'd let him come up with theories of him being a secret agent or a superhero, telling herself it was okay to indulge his imagination because it comforted him. But the one question he hadn't yet asked was the one he was asking now, and Ava didn't want to lie anymore.

"He didn't," she admitted. "Not when he left. I was too scared to tell him because I knew he needed to go. It might not make sense to you now, but if I had told him, his life would have turned out much differently. Staying here would have been very painful for him." She finally ditched the sunglasses so she could use the tissue to dry her tears. "That doesn't mean that having you in his life wouldn't have been a good thing, Owen. That's not what I'm saying. But if he had stayed? I'm afraid some bad things would have happened to him, and I loved him too much for that."

It was all the truth, as much as she could tell him without letting Jack tell his own part of the story.

They were finally on their street, approaching the safety of home. She reached her free hand toward the back seat and squeezed Owen's knee. He rested his hand on top of hers.

"So you were kind of a superhero, too, then. Right?"

"What do you mean?" she asked.

"You saved him," Owen said, matter-of-factly.

Maybe she had saved him from something bad, but she'd also robbed him of so much good, and now she couldn't decide which fate would have been worse.

"Did he love you as much as you loved him?" Owen asked, and she gave his knee another squeeze.

"Yeah, he did." And Ava had broken his heart, as Owen would believe, to *save* him.

"Do you think he'll ever come back? That he'd ever want to meet me?"

"I really do," Ava said.

She pulled into the driveway and put the car in park. Then she spun to look at her son—this beautiful, understanding boy who she knew someday would be an amazing man, just like his father.

"You're a lot like him, you know?" she said, and her boy beamed.

"That's a good thing, right?"

"It's all I could hope for," she admitted. "I'm so proud of you, Owen. And he would be, too."

He undid his seat belt and leaned forward, giving her a kiss on her tear-soaked cheek.

"I'm gonna go toss the ball with Scully out back," he said. "He's probably been so bored all day."

She nodded. "Have fun, *Shortstop.*"

He laughed and bounded out of the car.

The lights were on already inside, which wasn't a shock, especially since her father's car was also in the driveway. She'd barely made it through the door before her parents appeared in the small foyer, her mom greeting her with a glass of red.

Ava smiled at the woman who was a mirror image of her own self, twenty-five years in the future. Maggie Ellis wore her long, red hair in a braid over her right shoulder, the silver strands woven throughout looking more like highlights than a sign of age.

"Thank you," Ava said, kicking off her shoes as she reached for the glass.

"It's from the new barrel of pinot noir," her mother said.

Her father opened his mouth to add to the conversation, but Ava knew once he did, the pleasantries would be over. So she held up a finger as she took a long, slow sip, then craned her head to peek through the kitchen and through the back door to make sure Owen was outside with the dog.

She sighed. "Dad—before you say anything, I've already agreed to help the Everetts get the vineyard back on its feet, so I'll be spending some time in Oak Bluff over the next few weeks."

He crossed his arms. "He lay claim to his boy yet?" Her

father spoke soft enough so that only she and her mother could hear.

"Bradford!" her mother whisper-shouted, backhanding him on the shoulder, but his sturdy frame didn't budge. The man was as strong as he was stubborn. For most of Ava's life the former had made her feel like the safest girl in the world. But she knew now she was dealing with the latter, and first impressions were hard to erase, especially when the man had made up his mind about Jack Everett a decade ago.

Ava sipped her wine again before answering, letting the liquid heat her veins and soften her reaction. "Jack and I will tell Owen when we're both ready," she simply said.

When we know whether he's going to be a regular for our son or if he's going back to San Diego where he has his own life—the one I wanted for him.

That much she kept to herself.

"And until then?" he asked.

Ava shrugged. "Until then I help him and his brothers figure out how they're going to run a ranch *and* a vineyard. Until then I let Jack and Owen get to know each other as friends so that when we do tell him the truth, there is a foundation set between them already."

"And if I forbid this?" her father asked.

"Oh, Bradford," her mom said, calmer this time as she rested a palm on her husband's forearm. "She's not a child anymore. We have to trust her and let her do this her way."

Ava polished off the rest of her wine. She was usually one to savor a new vintage, but she was too on edge to take things slowly.

She strode past her parents, kissing them both on the cheeks. "Thanks for coming over. And making dinner. I'll call Owen in to eat."

And because her son was the one person her father couldn't argue with, they sat and ate as the boy recounted his day at the ranch—of lemonade and riding a horse and his overall fascination that real cowboys lived right in the middle of wine country.

That night, after Owen had fallen asleep, Ava sat in her painting room with another glass of the pinot noir and a paintbrush in her hand. She was finally able to slow down—to enjoy not only the new vintage but her ability to do what she hadn't done in years.

Not the tree. She still couldn't make any headway with that. But she'd painted something, and something was definitely a start.

In the morning she made sure to hide the drying canvas where Owen wouldn't see the portrait of a boy with auburn waves playing catch with his dad.

This could be her ticket into art school, but it felt premature to think that way. Because if this all blew up in her face, so would the image she'd seen in her mind's eye that finally allowed her creativity to flow.

She was no hero, and neither was Jack. They were human. And they'd made mistakes. Maybe she'd protected Jack from more pain, but she'd also stolen from him the immeasurable joy she hadn't known was possible until she'd first held her son in her arms.

No. She was no savior. But now that Jack was back, maybe—just maybe—their son would save them both.

CHAPTER TWELVE

Jack pulled the navy thermal shirt over his shoulders and shook out his damp hair. The floor creaked as he padded through the living room where Walker was still passed out on the couch from the night before. Luke, he assumed, was asleep upstairs. It wasn't even dawn. As ranchers they'd always woken early, but they could usually stay in bed until at least sunrise.

Yet several years of living in the city hadn't done a thing to give Jack a restful night's sleep.

Besides, there was work to be done, and the sooner he did it, the sooner—what? Wasn't that the million-dollar question? Once he and his brothers got the vineyard in shape for a potential harvest, what the hell came next?

He didn't have much time to think about it because the second he pulled on his work boots and stepped outside, he was greeted by blinding headlights rolling up the drive. By the time his eyes adjusted, he was able to make out Ava's red Jeep.

He stood, arms crossed, waiting for her to emerge. And when she did, he was grateful both for the sliver of predawn light and the cover of darkness. Because damn she was a sight for weary eyes, and he wasn't prepared for how much he'd wanted to see her until she was right there in front of him.

He could tell himself again and again that they were going to take things slow, but the surprise of her presence blew logic out the window. All he wanted now was to be near her. To run his hands through her hair. To trace a pattern from one freckle to the next.

He licked his lips, suddenly parched.

"What are you doing up so early?" he asked as she strode toward him with two to-go cups of coffee in her hands. "You're not supposed to be here for at least two more hours."

Her long-sleeved T-shirt hugged her curves atop snug-fitting jeans. As she came closer, he could see how the green scarf around her neck brought out her eyes— eyes that narrowed at him before responding to his question.

"You were never much of a sleeper," she said, offering him one of the cups. He took it. "I was a little restless myself. Figured I'd take a chance you were up, too."

"What about Owen?" The name still felt strange on his tongue.

"He slept at my parents' house. They'll get him to the bus today," she told him, pressing her palms to the cup. Her sleeves had those holes for her thumbs, so she wore them like fingerless gloves.

He watched a shiver run through her body.

"You're cold," he said, stating the obvious. But what else could he do? He hadn't brought a jacket. It wasn't like he could pull her to him and let body heat do the trick, no matter how much he wanted to. They'd *both* agreed to step back, that there was more at stake here than their physical attraction. So despite wanting to warm her body with his own, he stood there, one hand in the pocket of his jeans, the other occupied with the coffee.

She shrugged and took a careful sip from her cup. "That's what this is for," she said, smiling. "I'll warm up once we get working."

"If Owen slept by your folks, that means they know where you are today?"

She nodded. "They know." But she didn't offer much else.

He cleared his throat. "Speaking of working... What *are* we actually doing today?"

She glanced back at her Jeep, which was now blocking his truck. Then her eyes rested on his again.

"Hop in, and I'll show you."

He shook his head. "Give me the keys."

She hummed out a laugh but pulled her keys from her pocket and pressed them against his chest. "Does the big, bad cowboy need to be in control at all times?"

Despite the chill in the air, her fingers were warm on his chest. He took the keys. "Behind the wheel? Always."

She gave him a pointed look. "Says the man whose terrible curbside manner forced me off the road as soon as he got back to town."

He ground his teeth together, steadied his breathing, and decided not to dignify her very accurate recollection with any sort of response. The truth was, he *had* lost control that day. Just seeing her house and letting the memory of their past seep into his conscious thought had thrown him off-kilter. Then everything that came after? Yeah, it was safe to say that after the events of that day, he'd been using any means necessary to stay in as much control as he could.

"Let's go," he said, then headed for the driver's side of her car. He climbed in behind the wheel and let out a long breath before depositing his coffee into the cup holder. Glancing toward the back of the vehicle, he found a copy of *Sports Illustrated* open to an article about the new pitcher who'd just been drafted by the Dodgers.

Ava's door opened and she slid in beside him.

"He's reading *Sports Illustrated*?" Jack asked, reaching for the magazine. He turned on the interior light and started skimming the article. "This new kid is really good," he continued.

"Kid?" Ava asked with a soft laugh. "Last time I checked, twenty-eight wasn't that old. And yeah, Owen's a great reader. I've tried to get him into *Harry Potter*, you know? Something we can read together. But I cannot pry the sports magazine from his little hands." She sighed wistfully. "His hands aren't so little anymore."

Jack's jaw tightened, and he shut off the light and tossed the magazine back on the seat. He didn't say anything else as he started the Jeep and reversed down the driveway.

They rolled quietly along Oak Bluff Way, where every shop and local eatery was dark except for Baker's Bluff, the town's bakery, and judging by the logo stamped on their coffee cups, a place Ava had already been before showing up in his driveway.

"You're quiet this morning," she finally said.

"It's early," he grumbled.

"You don't sleep," she reminded him.

Just because that was true, though, didn't mean he was a morning person.

"You haven't touched your coffee," she pointed out, and he opened his mouth to say something but then thought better of it. Or maybe it was simply that he wasn't sure what the hell to say.

"Are you—*always* this much of an asshole before dawn?" she asked.

When he didn't take her bait, she settled into her seat and sipped her coffee. It wasn't until he parked along the street lining the vineyard and let his head fall back against his own seat that he was able to put words to *why* he was being an asshole. Because she was right. He was.

"You're good at it," he said softly, eyes trained on the car's closed sunroof.

"At being a morning person?" She barked out a laugh. "I'm only conscious because I *couldn't* sleep last night. If you tried to wake me this early on a normal morning, I'd have turned into a dementor and sucked out your soul."

He looked at her, brows drawn together.

She groaned. "Harry Potter."

"You *really* want him to read those books," he said.

"I really do."

She smiled, and he felt an unexpected warmth rush through him.

"And I wasn't talking about being a morning person," he said. "Even though I admit I'm not." He glanced around the car, nodding toward the back seat. "I mean *this.*"

Her mouth opened to say something, and her brows rose. He could tell she was still confused. Christ, that made two of them.

"You're *good*—at being his mom," he told her. He was certain of *this*. Where the confusion came in was *how* she'd done it.

Her green-eyed gaze softened on his. She lifted her hand as if she was going to reach for him but dropped it just as quickly.

"I've had almost a decade to work on it," she said, then laughed. "It's not like I held this tiny bundle in my arms at eighteen and had any sort of clue what the hell to do."

His chest ached at the thought of her going through the birth without a partner.

She kept talking, the smile on her face enough to tell him she didn't know her recollections had any effect on him. "And you've only seen a tiny snapshot of my parenting skills. You missed me bathing the kitchen floor in my morning coffee the other day when I was scrambling for Owen not to miss the bus. Or that time I forgot I was on snack duty for his baseball game last year and had to divide up three Larabars and a box of Wheat Thins among ten sweaty, hungry boys."

A smile tugged at the corner of his mouth, and she shrugged. "I don't get a lot of sit-down meals," she said. "My car stash has saved my life more than once."

He raised his brows and let his eyes trail from hers toward the other recesses of the vehicle.

She backhanded him on the shoulder. "My snacks are safely stowed in the trunk. And yes, I've got us covered for breakfast."

The realization of what she was saying damn near floored him. With all that she'd had to do on her own these past ten years—with all she did on a daily basis—she'd still thought of him this morning in a way no one else had in a long time. Possibly ever.

He pulled the keys from the ignition and laid them in her open palm.

"Thanks," he said. "For letting me take the wheel... and for the coffee."

"It was nothing," she said, her voice soft and sweet. It wasn't the voice he remembered exactly, but it was Ava.

And though he couldn't put words to it, he knew she was wrong. Whatever was happening between them, it was *something*.

Ava bit the tag off a pair of men's work gloves and handed them to Jack. After he pulled them on, she reached back into her bag of tricks to pull out a rubber-handled tool, which she effectively slapped into his palm.

"Pruning shears," she said.

"Yeah. I guessed."

The sun was finally peeking between the few scattered clouds, illuminating her face so he could connect the dots with each and every one of her freckles if he wanted. And yeah. He wanted. Despite their agreement, he reacted to her in ways that, in his own imagination, weren't stepping back at all.

"Today's lesson is on spur pruning," she said. Then she pulled off her scarf, revealing her long, slender neck. His eyes dropped to the V-neck of her top, and as they trailed back up to her face, he watched as a soft flush followed the same path all the way up to her cheeks.

Looked like he wasn't the only one with an active imagination.

She busied herself tugging on her own work gloves and grabbing a second pair of shears.

"Not cold anymore?" he teased, though he fought to keep his expression unreadable.

She cleared her throat. "Coffee did its job. Plus, the sun's up."

He nodded. "All right, *Teach*. Show me what you want me to do."

Ava took a deep breath and exhaled slowly. She lifted her hand to the opened trunk, and Jack stepped out of the way so she could lower it. They walked in silence from the road to the nearest row of vines.

"This," she said, grabbing what to Jack looked like a random branch growing upward, "is a spur. And this"—she stroked her hand across the plant's longer, thicker, horizontal stalk—"is the cordon. We'll need to take a look at both eventually, but today we're only focusing on the spurs. Because the vines have been left unattended, most likely since your father purchased the property, you've got too many buds per spur fighting for nourishment."

"Too many mouths to feed," Jack said with a slow nod, the words escaping his lips with a bitter tone he hadn't intended.

She pressed her lips together and forced a smile. "Yeah. Exactly. So, we need to cut them back. Anything more than three of these stalks growing from a spur"—she gripped the thick, wooden base from which each of the thinner branches grew—"needs to go."

"Sounds easy enough."

"It is. All you have to do is clip it right here at the base." She demonstrated and then smiled. "And that's it."

His eyes widened as he stared down the rows upon rows of plants.

She laughed. "We'll do as much as we can today, and that will help us determine how long it will take to finish the job. Once you show Luke and Walker, you guys will get it done in no time. You'll all be vintners before you know it." She dropped her gaze back to the spur she was pruning and clipped another branch. "I mean *they* will. I know you have a job to go back to."

He didn't respond because what would he say? He *did* have a job to go back to. In New York. He was supposed to come home to tie up loose ends and give himself the closure he needed here in Oak Bluff. Instead he'd found unexpected doors opened, doors he was both terrified to walk through as well as slam the hell shut.

So instead of saying anything else, he watched in silence as she deftly went to work. And then he moved from her side to the next row of plants and started on his own.

He was used to his ghosts. They'd been his company for the better part of ten years. What he wasn't prepared for was the pull from the land of the living.

His brothers.

This woman.

His *son*.

He hadn't planned on wanting anything in a place that hadn't felt like home for the majority of his life. A place that had taught him all the things he never wanted to be.

But most surprising was the ache in his gut at what saying good-bye to it would mean this time around.

CHAPTER THIRTEEN

It was nearly eleven when Ava decided to check on Jack, who was now a couple of rows down from her. The sun had melted away the clouds, and she had already stripped down to the tank beneath her long-sleeved shirt. She'd expected to find Jack had done the same—ditched the navy thermal that brought out his stormy blue eyes for a tight-fitting undershirt.

She mentally prepared herself for the sight of him, for how the cotton would cling to the taut muscles of a man she'd only known as a boy. What her brain had not counted on, however, was for him to be wearing *no* shirt at all.

She dropped her shears, and her mouth followed suit.

Look away, she willed herself, but free will didn't seem to exist at the moment.

A soft sheen of sweat glistened on his shoulder blades. His jeans hung low on his hips, and she followed his tanned skin, the muscles that moved and worked in precision, to the band of his boxer briefs that peeked out from the worn denim.

And then...she yelped. "Shit!"

She slapped at the back of her neck as Jack spun to face her, grinning.

"Shit. Shit. *Shit!*" she yelled, and his smile quickly faded as he strode toward her.

"What's wrong?" he asked, his brows creasing in concern.

Her hand was cupped to her neck, but it wasn't the pain of the sting that made her breath catch in her throat. It was Jack Everett, sweaty and shirtless and skin dusted with dirt—everything about him so far from the boy he was and instead so inherently *man.*

"A bee," she said, her voice shaky.

"Shit," he hissed, echoing her earlier sentiment. "Let me see."

He shoved the shears in his back pocket, which tugged his jeans a little lower, and she followed the line of golden hair that trailed from his belly button to whatever lay beneath the denim and cotton.

It wasn't like she was unaware of what was there or even that she hadn't seen it. But this brooding specimen before her was, himself, unknown to her. And as he pulled her hair back to investigate the wound, the strange man who was Jack Everett sent chills across her heated skin.

"The stinger's stuck. You got a tweezers in that bag of tricks back in the truck?"

She shook her head, wincing as his hand brushed against the sting.

"Sorry," he said, his voice rough as he stepped back to face her. "I'm ready for something other than a banana and a health food bar anyway," he said with a soft smile. "Let's head back, get rid of that stinger, and regroup. You're not allergic, are you?"

She shook her head again. For someone who worked most of her adult life outside, she'd been stung plenty and had needed to remove a stinger once before. Okay, so her mom had done it because it had hurt like hell. But she could handle the pain now. Hell, she'd given birth—had endured an IV, an epidural, and an eventual C-section. She could certainly manage a bee sting without her mother's help.

Jack drove again, and she willingly let him. She sat in the passenger seat and piled her hair into a messy bun, securing it with the hair-tie she wore around her wrist. The breeze from the open window both soothed her burning skin and irritated the lodged stinger, so she gritted her teeth for the short drive and appreciated, for once, that Jack was not the chatty type.

The house was empty when they returned, and Jack led her straight to the bathroom next to the guest room where he slept. He found the tweezers in the medicine cabinet and set it on the counter before washing his hands.

He was *still* shirtless.

"I got it," she said nervously. "Thanks. I'll be out in a minute."

He raised a brow. "You don't want my help removing a stinger from the back of your neck."

His words weren't a question, merely a statement outlining her stubbornness.

She went to work washing her own hands. After drying them on the towel hanging next to the medicine cabinet, she shook her head, the movement sending a shock wave of pain from the site of the sting straight through her entire body.

She hissed in a breath through clenched teeth. "I've got tweezers and a mirror," she said. "I'm all good."

Jack held his hands up in surrender and backed out through the doorway.

"Call me if you need me."

She pressed her lips into a tight smile—and closed the door.

Ava wasn't *in*flexible, but the position she was in now, butt against the counter and head craned to try to see the bee sting in the mirror, was ridiculous. When she brought the tweezers toward its target, she misjudged the distance between her hand and her neck, effectively stabbing the swollen, inflamed skin.

She swore, then groaned at her inability to take care of what should be a simple task.

A soft knock sounded on the door.

She spun to face herself in the mirror, rolling her eyes at her dirt-smudged face, at the spots of color on her cheeks that spoke not only of the jolt of pain at her miscalculation of depth but also at embarrassment.

"Can I come in now?" Jack asked when she didn't respond to his knock.

Needing his help for this didn't mean she *needed* him. She could have gone home, called one of the other baseball moms who weren't *exactly* friends. Because who had time for friends when she was running to practices, games, the school book fair, and the bake sale? She still had her girlfriends from high school, but they were only now starting to get married and have kids. While she was at double-header baseball games, they were dealing with colic and diapers and ohmygod—Ava had no one to call in a pinch for a stupid bee sting.

She huffed out a breath. "Fine," she said. Then only to herself added, *And please be wearing a shirt.*

The door clicked open, and he was, of course, still half naked. He set a glass of ice on the counter.

"Hand 'em over," he said, palm up, as he turned his attention to the tweezers.

She did. But before he brought metal to flesh, he set the instrument next to the glass and instead reached for an ice cube, bringing it to her neck where he rubbed small circles over the sting.

Her shoulders relaxed, and she let out a soft moan. "God that feels good," she admitted. She looked up to meet his reflection in the mirror. One strong hand rested on her left shoulder while the other, the one with the ice, kept up at soothing her skin.

"Helps if you take down the swelling a bit. Makes the stinger easier to grab."

"Mmm-hmm," she hummed, eyes closing as relief—and desire—spread through her. She didn't bother asking her body to shut off its response. There was no use. She'd all but forgotten about the bee sting.

"All done," Jack said.

"Huh?" she asked absently, eyes opening wide to see him shaking the tweezers into the sink, the tiny shard that was the stinger falling into the porcelain bowl next to a partially melted ice cube.

Cold water dripped down her shoulder as her gaze met his, and he gave her a self-satisfied grin. "The ice also works as an anesthetic for patients who might be a little more skittish."

She narrowed her eyes. "I am *not* skittish. And how did you become so adept at tending to bee stings, anyway?"

The hand that was on her shoulder slid down her side, coming to rest on her hip.

She swallowed.

"Walker wasn't always so standoffish," he said in a low tone. "There was a time, when he was much younger, that he let me help when he got hurt. When he actually admitted to needing my help."

She sighed and reached for his free hand, the one pressed to the counter next to hers, and gave it a soft squeeze. "*You're* good at it, Jack."

It was his turn to close his eyes, to avoid her fixed stare. But that didn't keep her from continuing.

"You raised them. As much as you thought you weren't cut out to be a father, that's exactly what you were to your brothers. They needed a father figure when yours wasn't up to the task, and you stepped in without a second thought."

His forehead fell against the top of her head, and he released a breath.

"What about what *you* need?" she asked him, and his fingertips pressed into her hip. "Who helps *you*?"

"Ava, don't—" he started, but her hand was already pulling his from the counter and to her other hip. He lifted his head, his eyes locking on hers.

She saw the heat that mirrored her own.

"I know we agreed to take things slow, to step back. But maybe we need to get this out of our systems first," she said.

She needed to get *him* out of her system once and for all.

"I'm leaving," he said softly, and her throat tightened.

"I know. Your life is in San Diego. A see-you-for-the-weekend dad is still more than anything Owen could have possibly dreamed of. And I don't have any expectations beyond right now—"

"Not San Diego," he interrupted.

Somehow, studying his gaze through the mirror's reflection gave her the illusion of safety, that whatever came next, she'd withstand it.

"What do you mean?" she asked.

She felt his chest rise and fall against her back as he tilted his head up and then back down again so his eyes met hers.

"I'm not taking a leave of absence because of the funeral and the vineyard. I'm moving. I've already packed up my apartment and shipped most of my things to New York."

"New York?" she blurted, turning to face him, and the safety of the mirror was gone. Nothing was between them other than a few centimeters of space, the air thick with the remnants of their past and a future that seemed impossible—especially where Owen was concerned.

He nodded once. "It's a promotion. I already accepted. With the ranch mortgaged, it's a chance for me to help Luke and Walker more than they've ever needed me to before, especially if the vineyard tanks. And I know you said you and Owen are fine financially—"

"We are," she blurted, though she knew in his way he was just trying to do the right thing. That part of him hadn't changed. "I'm starting my degree in the fall. Part-time, obviously. Between that, and Owen, and still working at the vineyard, my life is going to be pretty crazy, so it's not like I'm expecting whatever this is between us to be anything more than..."

Than what? Because right now it was a distraction, and she wasn't about to let Jack Everett, those eyes, and his ability to swoop in and save the day knock her off course again.

He was ready to offer Owen a secure financial future. But not a personal one.

What did she really expect—that he'd uproot his life for them once the truth was sprung on him?

Fine. Yes. Maybe a little bit. But that was about as rational as what she was doing right now—raising both of his hands to cup her breasts.

"Christ, *Red*."

She wasn't wearing a bra.

He let out a soft growl. "Jesus, Ava," he ground out, his thumbs stroking her taut nipples. "What the hell are you doing?"

She arched into his palms. "Getting *you* out of my system so I can freaking think straight. This is it," she assured not him, really, but herself. "This one time. Then we can both move on."

She spun in his arms again so she could only see him in the mirror, then clasped her hands around his neck. He dipped his head so his lips brushed against her ear.

"Are you sure this is what you want?" He peppered her jawline with achingly soft kisses. "Because I'll stop if it's not."

His voice was rough. And sexy. And stopping—for her—was not a possibility.

"It's what I need," she whispered. "What do *you* need, Jack? Tell me, and I'll give it to you."

He pinched one of her tight peaks and grazed his teeth along her neck.

Her breathing hitched.

"This," he whispered. "I need *this*."

They didn't need each *other*. Only *this*, their bodies' combined demand for release. Everything else would be clearer once whatever was brewing between them was allowed to boil over—and then simmer.

She grabbed his hands and guided them to the hem of her tank, hesitated for a second, then lifted her arms so he could pull it over her head.

Her jeans rested low on her hips, and he traced the line of the faint scar across her pelvis.

"Owen went into distress during labor," she said. "The cord was wrapped around his neck. I had to have a C-section."

His hand stopped moving, and she dropped her head and groaned. "I suppose childbirth talk kind of kills the mood, huh? Not the sexiest of subjects."

He hooked a finger under her chin, gently lifting it so his eyes could once again lock on hers. Then he shook his head. "You're the sexiest woman I have ever seen," he said. "And the strongest. There is nothing you could do to make me not want you like this. Don't you get that?"

What she got was that she wanted *him* like she wanted air. She wanted his hands on her, *in* her. His lips hot against hers and the taste of him lingering on her tongue long after they parted. She tried to give voice to all of this, but all that came out was a soft "Okay."

He spun them both so their hips were against the sink, their bodies perpendicular to the mirror so he could still watch as he bent to take one of her rosy nipples into his mouth.

She dug her fingers into his hair and cried out as his teeth nipped.

All the while she watched him watching them, and every synapse of every nerve fired off at the thrill of it.

She unbuttoned his jeans and gripped his hard length through his briefs. He repaid her with another satisfying growl.

"We should shower after all that hard work," she said, breathless from his touch—from touching *him*.

She snuck her thumb inside his waistband and swirled it over his wet tip.

"Ava," he groaned, then backed away from her to pull the shower curtain from the tub so he could turn on the water.

Wordlessly they finished undressing each other. She stared at the man before her for several long seconds—the light dusting of hair on his chest, the ridged muscles of his abdomen, the sheer solidness of his form. He was beautiful in a way that made it hard to breathe.

He pulled her over the lip of the tub into the warm spray, leaving the curtain open as he pressed himself to the tiled wall and pulled her back against him, their naked forms framed once again in the mirror.

She didn't protest.

"God, you're gorgeous," he said in her ear before he lightly bit her lobe.

She watched his hands cup her breasts, and then one traveled south, below her belly button, her scar, and finally between her legs.

Her breath caught as he parted her, teasing her entrance before one finger slipped inside.

"Jack," she cried softly, and his cock ground against the flesh of her back.

No sir. This was not the boy she'd fallen in love with. This man knew a woman's body—knew hers in a way he couldn't have when they were two inexperienced teens figuring this out together.

"You're like warm fucking silk," he said, exiting her slowly until his slick finger reached her swollen center.

She whimpered, grabbing his wrist. "More," she squeaked. *"Please."*

He smiled wickedly at her in the mirror. Two fingers entered her this time, and she threw her head back against his chest, eyes squeezing shut so she could try to keep it the hell together.

She writhed against his erection, and he swore.

"Inside me," she said, almost unable to form the words. "Please," she begged.

"Open your eyes, Ava." He pumped his fingers inside her warmth, and her legs went completely boneless. Somehow, though, she didn't fall.

Jack wouldn't let her.

She opened her eyes, meeting his in the slowly fogging reflection of their need.

"I'm not gonna lie," he told her. "I want to make love to you. But not like this."

He exited her again, his fingers now tracing maddening circles around her clit.

"Not...like...what?" she asked, gasping between each word.

The steam won out, and she could no longer see him— see what he was doing to drive her out of her mind.

He spun her and backed her toward the tiled wall of the tub, pressing her against it and then kissing her until she nearly forgot her own name.

"Not when you're driving me so crazy I'm not sure how long I'll last inside you." He kissed her again. "Not when I won't be able to lay you out properly and give every inch of your skin, every freckle, the attention it deserves." Another kiss. "And not when I can't promise you anything beyond these next few weeks."

There it was again, that tightening in her throat that made her unable to respond with any words at all.

"I can still stop," he said, apparently reading something in her expression. "The last thing I want is for you to regret this."

She shook her head. "Don't stop," she managed to say. "Please don't stop." Because whatever came after this, she didn't care. Not now. Not when she could have him for to-day. For this one moment, even if it was their last.

And before he could ask her again if she was sure, she kissed him and grabbed his cock, stroking him from root to tip.

"Ava," he groaned against her lips.

And then he was kissing her cheek, her jaw, down her neck and breasts until he lowered himself to his knees where he sprinkled kisses on the inside of each of her thighs.

She sucked in a sharp breath anticipating what would come next, but nothing could prepare her for his hot breath against her folds, for the sensation of his tongue sliding along her opening and then circling her aching arousal in achingly precise strokes.

She was nothing more than a blob of freaking Jell-O, her knees buckling as he slipped two fingers back inside while his tongue worked her expertly into complete and ut-ter madness, all while he somehow kept her from melting into a puddle onto the bathtub floor.

The orgasm came over her like a fifteen-foot wave, pulling her under until she was gasping his name—and for air.

He held her close as she shuddered against him, as she slid down the wall and into the tub in front of him, standing no longer an option.

Who the hell was she kidding? *Get him out of her sys-tem?* She'd just let him right *in* to her goddamn system.

He was leaving. She was taking control of her life and career.

This. Was not. The plan.

He brushed her wet hair from her face and pressed a soft kiss to her lips. *"That's* what I needed."

She forced herself back into the moment. "But what about...?" She stared at his rock-hard length.

"I'm fine," he started to say, but she closed her hand around his base and squeezed. "Fuck. Red." She stroked him slowly. "Jesus."

"Stand up," she said. "Your turn."

CHAPTER FOURTEEN

He would have been satisfied with simply bringing her to climax. He could have set her up in the kitchen with something to eat for lunch and then come back for a cold shower of his own, where he'd take care of his own release.

Because shit—he needed it. He just wasn't prepared for needing *her*.

Seeming to have regained her sea legs, Ava stood and held her hand out for his. He was still kneeling, still savoring the taste of her and wondering how he'd gone his entire adult life without it.

"Ava—" he said when they were both standing, but she shook her head and splayed a hand across his chest.

"It's only this once, remember?" she insisted, but even with the water beating down on them, he detected a hint of uncertainty. Or maybe it was him. "And despite what you might think of me," she teased, "I'm not a selfish woman."

"I never said—" he started, but she kissed him, silencing him because he couldn't say no to her lips on his. "Red," he groaned as her teeth tugged on his bottom lip, but she wouldn't respond, and he knew if he didn't get the words out now, he never would. *"Ava."* She stopped and tilted her head up, her emerald eyes meeting his. "I don't want to hurt you," he said. "I already did that once, and that's not my intention here."

She nodded. "But you didn't know," she said. "And I hurt you, too."

His forehead fell to hers. She'd destroyed him—the messed-up kid he was then. But she'd been a messed-up kid, too, one who thought he wouldn't want their son, and back then...who could say he wouldn't have reacted exactly as she'd expected?

"If we know what we're getting into, then no one gets hurt," she said, then kissed the line of his jaw. "Right now, though, you need to let someone take care of *you*."

And before he could argue, her kisses traveled south, down his collarbone, his abdomen, each of his hips, until her tongue, warm and willing, swirled around his tip.

She teased him for what felt like hours—licking, tasting, stroking. Time seemed to stand still when she was near, or maybe it was that he wanted the minutes to stretch out before them. If this was his one-time-only with her, he wanted *only* to be infinite.

But without warning, the teasing was over. He gritted his teeth and dug his fingers into her hair as she swallowed him down to the base of his cock. She gripped him tight, her hand following the trail of her lips as she came back up for air. Again and again she took him into her mouth, her hand working him until he thought he might lose his mind.

The water still beat down on them, steam clouding the air, and it was as if they weren't really there. As if this wasn't exactly real. It was this realization that let him relax his shoulders, that gave her permission to take him to the edge, where he spilled over with silent release. He couldn't fully let go, but he could trust her enough to let her take the wheel—to let the smallest piece of his decade-old walls crumble here—in this fantasy world they'd created, and then piece himself back together as soon as the steam cleared.

She stood and buried her head beneath his chin, his chest heaving against her.

"You gave up control for me," she said softly. "I don't suppose that was easy to do."

She stepped back to look at him, and as much as he knew he was a dick for doing it, he shuttered his expression.

He couldn't let her see that even after climax, he still needed. He needed her close, needed her hands on him to steady the erratic beat of his heart. Needed her kiss to reassure him that this was something more than her getting him out of her system.

If she knew how far that was from how he saw things, she'd know how much control he'd truly lost, and nothing terrified him more than letting her see that.

He had no right to need these things from her, not when he was moving to the other damned side of the country.

Her smile quickly fell, and she shook her head. "You keep so much of yourself locked away," she said, then kissed the spot on his neck where he could feel his pulse thrumming against her lips. "If you're ever ready to let some of it go, I'm here for you."

She pressed her lips to his and then stepped out of the tub, wrapped herself in a towel, and exited the bathroom with her clothes in hand.

He let his head thud against the tile while the water, cooling off now, pelted him in his chest.

She was right, of course. Not that he'd say it aloud. Not that he *could*. He didn't just keep his past at bay for himself.

He did it for everyone around him. That's why San Diego was easy, why New York would be even easier.

But here? Even ten years after the fact, Ava *knew* him. He'd let his guard down for a matter of minutes, and she'd seen right through to his goddamn core.

She deserved better than that. Better than him.

When he emerged fully clothed into the kitchen, the place was a flurry of activity. Ava was carrying a tray of burgers out the back door to where he saw Luke firing up the grill. Walker stood next to the sink, slicing tomatoes on a cutting board.

Jack cleared his throat, and Walker looked up.

"What?" he said, already on the defensive.

Jack shrugged. "Nothing. I guess I didn't know you were so—domesticated."

He was used to seeing his youngest brother eating whatever he could find right from the fridge, not bothering to take the time to do anything more than open his mouth and insert food. As a teen he'd always been on the move, agitated. Jack understood. The anticipation of their father's mood was almost worse than what happened when he was in a bad one. Almost.

"I guess it's just nice to see you—relaxed," Jack added.

Walker picked up a half-empty bottle of beer and raised his brows. "Meet my brand of medication," he said before taking a sip and setting it back down. Jack normally would have worried about his brother drinking and wielding a knife, but he could tell Walker was sober. He did, however, second-guess himself as his brother pointed his knife at him. "I can take care of myself in the kitchen," he said. "But you tell anyone I know how to julienne and shit, and I'll lay you out cold."

Jack couldn't hold back the laugh. "Do you—julienne and shit?"

Walker returned to cutting, his back to him once again. "You're a dick," he said under his breath.

"And apparently you're not only Mr. HGTV but Gordon Ramsay as well," Jack said. "Who'd have fucking guessed?"

"I need cheese!" Ava said as she came back through the kitchen. She headed straight for the fridge, grabbing a block of cheddar Jack hadn't even known they had and then opening and closing drawers until she found a knife fit for slicing it. "You still take yours medium rare?" she asked, elbowing Jack in the side but not waiting for his answer before she was out the door again.

Walker turned to face him, crossing his arms as he shook his head.

"What?" Now it was Jack's turn to play defense.

"I know I don't know my elbow from my asshole sometimes, but I'm pretty damned sure you're gonna ruin that pretty woman when you leave."

Jack crossed his own arms, a mirror to his suddenly perceptive brother. "What the hell do you mean?"

Walker strode to the fridge and retrieved another beer, twisting off the top as he spoke. "I mean I'm not blind. And if you'd open up your damn eyes, you'd see it, too." He swigged from the bottle, then wiped the back of his hand across his lips. "That girl carries a ten-year-old torch. And let's not forget the offspring. Seems like a good kid. You gonna be the father that fucks that all up?"

Jack's hands balled into fists. He started forward, ready to unleash his frustration on his brother, but knew it would only leave him hollow. Instead he turned toward the front door and walked out.

Luke found him out by the stable, beating a bale of hay on the far outside wall with the bucket of balls he'd found still tucked away in the garage.

"You still got a mean curveball," he said over Jack's shoulder.

He threw a few sliders. Then a changeup. And then several fastballs until the bucket was empty and his elbow ached. He shook his arm out and then collected the balls, gearing up for round two.

"I've stayed too long already," Jack said, tossing the ball into his glove. He could still get his hand inside it, but the fit was too small. It was the glove his father had gotten him when he'd started the new season junior year.

Jack Senior had had a rare, lucid afternoon. He'd found Jack in this very spot, fighting with his then too-small glove.

"Jackson!" he'd called as he approached, and Jack had held his breath, bracing himself for the blow. But when it didn't come, his father had simply nodded toward the glove and said, "C'mon. You won't make it through the season with that."

And they'd driven to the next town over where they had a sporting goods store—Jack behind the wheel, of course, since Jack Senior was with it enough to hand the keys over.

That was the closest his father had come to showing him affection in the years following his mother's death, so he filed it away under memories he let surface. It wasn't an apology or an end to the drinking. But it was something.

"Or maybe you haven't stayed long enough to let this place sink back into your bones."

Jack missed the hay bales and drove the ball right into the side of the stable, the wood splitting on impact.

"Shit." He shook his hand out of the glove and went to

survey the damage. As soon as he touched the point of impact, the old wood cracked clear through so he could see one of the horse's stalls.

"Looks like you'll have to hang around a bit longer to patch that up. And while you're at it, we could call one of the Callahan brothers. I was thinking we could talk to them about adding on the tasting room to the structure where we'll do all the fermenting and shit. I bet they'd fix up that wall pro bono if we gave them the contract for the tasting room."

Jack ran a hand through his hair. "I can handle a hammer and some plywood."

"Good as you can handle your pitching arm?" He grinned.

Luke was always grinning. Did nothing faze the guy?

"Look," Luke added. "You're gonna do whatever it is you need to do, and if that means getting us up and running and then heading to New York, then that's your call. But you fit here once, Jack. You could fit here again."

Jack's eyes widened. "Jenna told you?"

He crossed his arms and shook his head. "She didn't need to. I know you think you're the one who keeps tabs on us, but I can read. I check on the *San Diego Sun* every now and then. Caught the article on how your firm was making you its youngest partner—in their New York office."

"Shit," Jack hissed.

Luke laughed. "It's a good gig. Walker'n I have just been waiting for you to grow a pair and tell us."

"I was waiting for the right time," he said, not taking his brother's bait.

"Hope you're taking it because it's something you love to do, though," Luke added. "Not because you think we need the money."

"You *do* need the money," he said. "You got a mortgage to pay."

Luke shrugged. "Ranch isn't in the red yet. And do me a favor. Ease up on asking Jenna to keep your damn secrets. It's enough to ask her to pretend she's not that boy's aunt. Don't make her keep more from her family. That's not her way." He opened his mouth to say something else but didn't.

"It's my way," Jack said, finishing his brother's thought. "That's what you were going to say."

"Looks like I didn't have to." Luke turned and began to stride off.

"How can you stand it?" Jack asked.

His brother stopped and spun back to face him, overgrown blond hair in eyes that now squinted from the sun. "There was no alternative for me. No baseball scholarship—not that I wanted one, by the way." He laughed, but for once it wasn't an entirely happy sound. "I was born to work the ranch. Never wanted anything else." He turned his attention toward the pasture. "I'm happier out there on my horse or in the rodeo arena than I am anywhere else. Jenna was good to us, but when Dad couldn't take care of the place anymore, I *wanted* to come back."

"Why?"

"Not for him," Luke said. "No fucking way. But for *her*. For what they built for us."

Jack squeezed his eyes shut and let the sun beat down on his cheeks, trying to remember what he used to love about Crossroads Ranch. Because he had loved it once. He knew that much.

When he came up blank, he dropped his gaze back to where his brother stood, but Luke was already gone.

That seemed to be the theme today.

Ava left him in the shower.

He left the house.

Luke left him here to take his frustrations out on the stable.

Leaving had been the right answer once—when he was a messed-up kid in a messed-up life he couldn't fix.

He'd sworn things would change once Jackson Everett Senior was dead and gone, but his ghost was everywhere, reminding Jack that his life was still a mess—and that he still had no damned clue how to fix it.

But he would. He'd fix the barn, fix the damn vineyard, and fix things between him and Ava. No more lapses in judgment. He wouldn't let them hurt each other again.

He shook his arm out one more time and headed back to the house. Jenna's car was parked behind Ava's now, which meant it was a goddamn party inside. He clenched his jaw and prepared himself for his aunt's third degree. But when he entered the kitchen, they were all talking. And laughing. And passing food around the table like they'd done this a hundred times before.

Jenna patted the seat next to her, and the tension in Jack's muscles relaxed slightly. He sat, kissed his aunt on the cheek, then narrowed his eyes at a scabbed-over cut on her upper lip.

She waved him off. "Nothing more than the aftermath of me trying to give a little smooch to one of my chicks. The cute little shit nipped me."

Jack let out a breath. Jenna was okay. They were all *okay*.

Ava handed him a plate covered in plastic wrap. Beneath it was a cheeseburger piled high with all the fixings and, next to it, a grilled cob of corn.

"Hope it's still warm," she said, her smile soft and conciliatory.

We're okay, he let that smile tell him.

And for the remainder of this impromptu family meal, he let himself believe what his brother had said to him. He'd fit in here once—and maybe, for the short time he'd be here, he could find a way to fit again.

CHAPTER FIFTEEN

Ava shifted in the passenger seat, trying to admire the beauty that was San Luis Obispo wine country. The rolling green of the vineyards—endless rows of grape plants leading straight to hilltops shadowed in the setting sun. Today she sat in Jack's truck, and she should have been grateful for the freedom to appreciate the view. Instead she was restless.

Jack settled a palm on her bouncing knee and she sucked in a breath.

"What's going on?" he asked, his hand flexing at her reaction before he quickly pulled it away.

Um, we've been working together for five days now, and this is the first time you've touched me since Monday's bee sting incident. But that was their deal, right? One time only. But instead of scratching an itch she'd opened the floodgates of need. Not that she could tell him that.

"Nothing," she lied. "And you really didn't have to be my chauffeur to *and* from the ranch today. That's a lot of time in the car, and I don't mind the drive."

He shrugged, both hands back on the wheel. "You've been working your ass off this week pruning those vines. Least I could do is save you some mileage on the Jeep. Plus, it's not exactly a punishment to spend a little extra time with you."

She let out a breath and tried to force her gaze out the window instead of to her left where he sat in that fitted gray tank and jeans, his *work* uniform for the warmest weather they'd had this week. And she definitely wasn't noticing how his blond hair curled above the tops of his ears—or how a few days without shaving had lined his jaw and mouth with a sexy scruff he'd never had as a teen.

Nope. She wasn't noticing any of that. And she certainly wasn't squirming in her seat because of it.

"Something's up," he said, calling her bluff.

She crossed her arms and groaned as he slowed to turn into her long driveway.

"It's *nothing*. Thanks for the ride," she said as he rolled to a stop. Then she hopped out of the vehicle before she said anything stupid.

She was almost inside the house when she heard his car door slam, effectively stopping her in her tracks.

"Ava."

Damn him for that insistence in his tone, for that deep voice that spoke her name like no one else ever had and— she was beginning to realize—like no one could. That voice could make her core tighten and her heart ache, and it was succeeding at both right now.

She turned to find him leaning against the truck's hood, all six-foot-who-knows-how-much-more feet of him, his hands in his pockets and his biceps flexing as if to say, *You know what's up, Red. And the longer you look at me, the more powerless you are against me.*

She dropped her bag at her feet and pointed at him. He wanted answers? Fine. He'd get them.

"This," she said. "You standing twenty feet away from

me. It's been like that all week. Every day out in the vineyard you've made sure there are at least two rows between us. We've eaten lunch at BBQ on the Bluff *four* times rather than step foot together inside the ranch. And I'm pretty sure you've either been marking your territory around the vines so no rodents eat the plants, *or* you can go several hours without needing to pee because you haven't stepped foot in your own home at any time that I've been inside it since Monday afternoon when, if you don't remember, you made me orgasm until I could no longer stand." She hefted her bag from her feet and tossed it over her shoulder, trying to maintain some semblance of dignity. "Now, if you don't mind, my parents will have Owen home in about an hour, and I need to clean myself up and get dinner started. Also, Owen has spring break next week, which means he'll be home—which also means *I'll* have to be home."

He crossed his arms. "So you're not…"

"I'm not going to be able to come by Crossroads next week," she said, mustering up as much finality in her tone as she could. Because she was on borrowed time with this man. And she had an application to complete—her future depended on it. Him pulling back should have made it easier for her to do the same. Instead she was losing the ability to think straight in his presence. Or maybe she'd never had it to begin with.

Besides, she said to herself, *this is probably for the best because I need to reset my damn libido so I stop reacting to you like this.*

When he didn't respond right away, she pulled open the screen door and stepped through to safety. She was in the kitchen facing the back window, already pouring a much-needed glass of wine, when she heard his work boots scuff across the tile.

"And here I thought my dramatic exit would mean you'd drive away and forget about my verbal vomit." She spun slowly to face him, holding up her glass before taking a sip.

She watched him watch her, not sure if the heat spreading through her veins was the wine or the weight of his stare. She guessed it was a little of both.

He just stood there, strong and silent as always, yet his eyes didn't waver. He never looked away.

"It's not that easy to forget," he said, his deep voice a low rumble in the quiet house.

She laughed, the sound tinged with bitterness. "No kidding. That's why they call it 'verbal vomit.' Too much comes out." She waved her free hand in the air as she took another sip. "Makes it hard to clean up."

He scratched the back of his neck, and there went those arm muscles, flexing and contracting with the slightest movement.

"I mean *you*, Ava."

She set the glass down and wrapped her arms around her midsection.

"I never forgot about you, not since the day I forced you to push me away."

She opened her mouth to say something but he shook his head. "I won't hurt you like that again," he said, the muscles in his jaw tight. "No matter what I said ten years ago, I'm going to figure out a way to do right by you and Owen—even if that means stepping back to make sure neither of you get hurt."

He still hadn't moved from the kitchen entryway, so she took a step toward him.

"You're not *him*," she insisted.

His chest rose and fell with a few quiet breaths before he

spoke. "Neither was he for a lot of years. But things change. He got pushed over the edge and never climbed back up. This shit—there's heredity to think about."

She splayed a palm against his chest, his heart thundering against it. "Maybe you need to prove that to yourself," she said. "But not to me."

She took a chance and tilted her head to where his tanned skin met the collar of his tank, kissing him softly. He sucked in a ragged breath, but he didn't push her away. She met his gaze again.

"I know you're moving across the country—and that you'll do right by me and Owen no matter where you are. Because that's *who* you are." She swallowed past the knot in her throat. "And I'll be okay if you leave again. *When* you leave again." She forced a smile. "But I have a confession. This heat between us? Monday wasn't enough to get it out of my system. So if worrying about hurting me is the only thing holding you back, don't. I'm a big girl. I can take care of myself. But if it's something else—"

She didn't get a chance to finish because his lips were on hers—rough, insistent, and exploding with need. He pivoted her around the corner so her back was against the kitchen wall, his hands roaming up her sides to cradle her face.

The kiss was deep and unrelenting, and her fingers grappled for purchase in his thick, soft hair.

"Not out of your system either?" she managed, breathless against him.

"Fuck no," he growled, and he slid a palm up the front of her T-shirt to cup her breast.

She whimpered and arched against him as he pinched her tightened peak outside her bra. Heat pooled between her legs as he nipped at her lip, as he peppered kisses across her jaw and down her neck. He hiked her up onto his hips, and she wrapped her legs around him, his erection pressing against her pelvis. Her arms snaked around his neck as she held on for dear life.

She was wet. She could feel it. From just his damn kisses.

"I don't think I've ever gotten you out of my system," he admitted. "And now the woman you've become? I don't know how to stay away."

He ground against her, pushing her harder into the wall, and she cried out with need.

"Then I guess we're going to have to keep at this until we're both free and clear of—of whatever this is." Right now she didn't care. She wanted more. Whatever he was willing to give.

"Ava?" she heard faintly in the recesses of her mind. Or maybe she imagined it. "Ava?" The voice was louder this time. "The front door was open..."

"My parents and Owen!" she whisper-shouted and Jack all but dropped her to her feet.

She smoothed out her shirt but knew her face was flushed, her lips swollen.

Oh well. Here went nothing.

"Mom!" she said, rounding the corner into the living room. "You guys are early."

She could see her dad and Owen grabbing his school and baseball bags from the car. Scully, who must have been in the backyard, came barreling through the dog door and bounded toward the front entryway, as if he could sense his most favorite human in the world was about to step foot in the house.

Jack's presence was palpable behind her. She didn't have to turn to know he was there. Her parents would

have seen Jack's truck in the driveway, but the look on
her mother's face—jaw agape and eyes wide—told her they
weren't hiding anything.

"We left practice early because Owen said he had a
tummy ache."

Ava snapped straight into mommy mode and strode toward the door. "Why didn't you call?" she asked.

Her mom grabbed her wrist before she made it to the
door. "Because this happened ten minutes ago. I knew you
were either an hour away or already heading back, so I figured we'd wait for you. I wasn't expecting..." She trailed
off.

Ava glanced back over her shoulder at Jack, who gave
her mother a polite nod. "Evening, Mrs. Ellis."

Her dad was the first through the door, baseball bag
over one shoulder and Owen's backpack over the other. He
kissed Ava on the cheek, but his jaw tightened when he laid
eyes on Jack.

"Be nice," she insisted in a whispered plea.

And then she was stooping to hug her son while fending
off a very excited Labrador. She pressed her cheek to his,
letting out a relieved sigh when he felt cool to the touch.

"I don't think you have a fever, bud. Can you tell me
where it hurts?"

Owen shrugged. "It kind of comes and goes. I think
I maybe didn't eat enough for lunch today." He wrapped
his arms around her neck and squeezed tight. Not that he
wasn't an affectionate boy, but something felt different.

She kissed him and finally backed away so the dog could
get his fill, and in seconds Owen was on his back, laughing
as Scully lavished him with slobbery, wet kisses.

Ava's dad dropped the bags in the small entryway and
walked straight past Jack into the kitchen. She turned to her

mom, who pulled her back to where Jack stood so Owen couldn't hear above his own giggles.

"He's missed you," she said. "You're doing a good thing—helping out with the Everett vineyard"—she smiled at Jack—"but you've missed both practices this week. Plus, you're out the door as soon as the bus comes each morning, and you barely make it back before sundown."

Ava's heart sank. It had only been five days, but her mom was right. This was the least present she'd been as a mother in all of Owen's life, and the guilt seeped into her bones.

"It's my fault," Jack said. "I took you up on your offer without realizing the sacrifice. It was never my intent to take you away from your son."

"Jack!" Owen called, springing to his feet once the dog set him free. "Mom said you read the *Sports Illustrated* article about the pitcher for the Dodgers. Do you think he'll get them back to the Series this year?"

Ava stepped back, allowing her son into their small huddle, and she watched the warm smile spread across Jack's face.

"Sure as hell doesn't hurt their chances. Does it?" he asked, giving Owen's baseball cap a friendly swat. "Might even win it this time."

"Sure as hell doesn't," Owen parroted, and at this Ava raised her brows at both boys.

"Language, you two." But she couldn't help smiling as well.

"I hear he's got a wicked curveball," Jack said.

Owen nodded. "I'm still trying to figure that one out. Maybe you could show me sometime? Mom said you were a good pitcher."

It was Jack's turn to raise a brow. *"Good?"* The corner

of his mouth quirked into a grin, and Ava wondered if he knew how gorgeous he was when he did that. "Just good?"

She laughed and backhanded him on the shoulder. "I never had the pleasure of seeing you in action. I had to take your word for it—and trust that whole scholarship situation."

Ava inwardly winced at the possible memories this would bring up, but Jack's smile never faltered.

"Sure, *Shortstop*. Sometime sounds good. But I should let you all get settled in for the night."

Owen grabbed his bag from where his grandpa had set it on the ground. "Or we could do some pitching practice while Mom makes dinner?" He glanced at his mom and grandma. "I'm feeling a little better," he said, then bit his bottom lip.

Ava's heart squeezed so tight at her son's pleading eyes—eyes so much like his father's. She wouldn't ask Jack to stay. He had to want it. He had to *want* to spend time with his son.

Jack crossed his arms and tilted his head toward the ceiling, heaving in a breath before his eyes met hers. How many times had she seen Owen do the exact same thing whenever he needed to think? It only hit her now that the gesture wasn't solely her son's. It was Jack's, too.

"I can head out when dinner's ready," he said.

Her mom patted him on the shoulder and smiled. "Or you could stay."

"If you want," Ava blurted. "No pressure. I was going to grill some chicken. Whip up a salad. Nothing fancy."

Owen watched them both expectantly. Jack tilted his head down to take in his own appearance.

"Let me just grab a clean shirt from my truck." He

shifted his gaze to Owen. "I think I have a glove somewhere in the back of the cab, too. You got a handful of balls?"

Owen grinned from ear to ear.

"All right, then. How about you go on out back and get us ready while I grab my stuff and clean up real quick."

Owen shot his fist in the air and whooped as he ran through the kitchen and out the back door, Scully following at his heels. Jack headed out front to his truck, a smile still spread across his own face as well.

Ava's heart swelled. "Doesn't look like he has much of a tummy ache anymore," she said.

"He just missed his mama." Her mother gave her shoulders a squeeze. "Bradford?" she called toward the kitchen where her dad was, no doubt, sulking. "Let's leave the kids to their dinner."

Her dad emerged, his jaw set as firm as it was when he first entered the house.

"Come *on*, Dad."

He grunted. But this was not acquiescence. She knew that look. It was the one she got when she backed into the mailbox the year she got her license—the one he gave to every boy who rang their doorbell throughout her high school career—except *golden boy* Derek Wilkes. It was the look that asked, *What do you have to say for yourself?* But it was a rhetorical question. Because Bradford Ellis had the answer. He *always* had the answer.

"This is a mistake, Ava." His voice was steady. Even. The way he spoke when he knew he'd already won the argument. So she decided not to disagree.

"Then it's my mistake to make."

He let out a bitter laugh. "You're a lovesick teenager again, running around behind our backs with a boy you know isn't good enough for you."

"Dad."

He crossed his arms. "You gonna deny sneaking around with a boy who couldn't even take you on a proper date?"

Ava's eyes burned, and she could feel the heat creeping up her neck and into her cheeks. "He was in a cast for the first two months I knew him."

Her father shook his head. "You didn't answer the question. If I had nothing to worry about with you dating Jack Everett, why'd you hide it from us? Why did he *let* you?"

A throat cleared, and everyone's attention volleyed toward the front door where Jack stood with a clean T-shirt thrown over his shoulder and a baseball glove under his arm.

"Because she knew you thought the son of an abusive alcoholic might hurt her someday. And you were right."

"Jack. Don't," she said, her voice wavering. "You didn't know about Owen." She turned to her parents. "He didn't know." Not that it mattered telling them this now.

He *had* hurt her without even knowing it, broken her heart—she'd thought—beyond repair. But she'd done the same to him.

"He never raised a hand to me, Dad. He never would. Not to Owen, either."

Her father narrowed his eyes. "You're letting your infatuation with this boy blind you again. It's my job to protect you. Maybe he never laid a hand on *you*, but you saw what he did to the Wilkes boy. You saw what he's capable of. You think you can guarantee there's *no* risk of that happening again?"

"Bradford—" her mom started, but he held his hands up in surrender.

"I've said all I need to say. Even if she's right, he can still hurt her in other ways. We helped put the pieces back together the last time he left her. We'll be here to do it again. Just remember that it's not only your heart he'll break," her father said. "That boy's already taken a liking to him. What's gonna happen to Owen if he finds out the truth and then Everett leaves you both?"

"With all due respect, Mr. Ellis," Jack said, "it's up to Ava and me how to proceed with Owen from here."

Ava's mom kissed her on the cheek and then hooked her elbow with her father's, practically dragging him toward the door.

"The hell it is," he said to Jack through gritted teeth. Then her parents were gone.

Jack stood, motionless except for the pulsing muscle above his jawline.

"I'm sorry," she said, moving toward him with measured calm, as if he was an animal she might scare off and send running. "He's scared for me—for *us*. I don't condone his treatment of you, but he doesn't know how to do the protective thing without being a total asshole."

She was hoping to coax a smile from him, but she failed.

"Jack." She stood right in front of him now, close enough that she could feel the heat of his body. She could count his breaths—see how each held a slight tremor. She cupped his cheeks in her hands, and he closed his eyes. But still he said nothing.

So she did the one thing she knew she could do to make him react. She stood on her toes and kissed him.

"Ava," he finally whispered against her, the sound of his voice both an admonishment and a plea.

"He doesn't know you," she said, her lips still moving against his. "And that's on *me*. Maybe if I'd been up front from the beginning, the whole Derek incident never would have happened. At the very least I should have told them who the father was and why I pushed you to leave—" She felt the tears prick at the backs of her eyes.

He stepped back and pressed a thumb to her cheek where the first one had sprung free. "But you were too much of a mess to do that," he said. "They had to pick up the pieces because of me."

"Because of *us*," she corrected. "What happened ten years ago, that's on me, too."

"But the Derek incident *did* happen. So did Walker's birthday and me telling my pregnant girlfriend I never wanted to be a father. And then you coming to find me in L.A.?" he added. "Shit."

"They don't know about L.A.," she said.

"You dealt with that on your own—coming to tell me about Owen and then thinking I was marrying someone else? I *am* the asshole your father thinks I am."

She shook her head. "You're just someone who's still trying to put his own pieces back together. Go," she said, nodding toward the back door. "He's waiting for you."

He sighed heavily and strode past her, pulling his dirty shirt over his head before tossing on the new one. And for those few moments when his torso was bare, Ava simply stared at the beautiful man he'd become and wondered if he even wanted those pieces back in place, or if he'd already convinced himself that broken was how he'd stay.

They'd eaten outside, unable to pull Owen from his baseball glove for too long. Then he and Jack had continued practicing their curveballs until past sundown.

Now Ava looked over her shoulder to where Jack stood in the frame of Owen's bedroom door, watching her tuck their son into bed.

"You want me to sing 'Twinkle Twinkle,' little man?"

Owen squeezed his eyes shut and groaned. "I'm not a baby, Mom."

Her heart constricted in her chest. "You're right," she said. "Maybe you're getting too old for this." She kissed him on the forehead and willed herself not to lose it in front of Owen and Jack.

So he wasn't a baby anymore. So he didn't need her to sing to him. Fine. She'd be fine.

"Goodnight, bud." She stood from the side of his bed and turned toward the door where Jack waited with brows raised.

"Wait," Owen said, reaching for his mom's hand. "Maybe—just tonight. If you really want to."

Ava blew out a breath. "I *really* want to," she said, a dopey grin spreading from ear to ear. She crawled in bed beside him and softly sang the words she'd been singing since the very first time he fell asleep on her chest in the hospital almost a decade ago.

When she was done, Owen's eyes were closed, and his breaths were long and deep. So she slid quietly from the bed and turned toward the door—and Jack.

"Love you, Mom," her son said dreamily.

"Love you, bud."

"Goodnight, Jack. Thanks for the curveball help."

"Night, Shortstop," Jack said, a hesitant smile playing at his lips.

The dog lumbered in past them and hopped onto Owen's bed, stretching across the boy's feet, his paws dangling off each side.

She grabbed Jack's hand and pulled him down the hall and then the short flight of stairs until they were in the small entryway, Ava leaning against the front door.

He ran a hand through his hair, then crossed his arms as he inhaled, head tilted up.

"Ah," she said. "The thinking pose. Ya gonna let me in on what's going on in that private place of yours?"

He dropped his head so his gaze met hers. "Stay with me next week," he blurted, and her eyes widened.

"I—I can't. I told you...it's Owen's spring break, and I've been gone too much already. I can't just—"

"Both of you," he said. "Or...all three of you. I mean, Scully too. We'll work on the vineyard, and Owen and I can perfect his slider."

Her mouth opened and closed, but no words came out. It was Jack who couldn't seem to *stop* talking now.

"I'll move my shit to the bedroom upstairs so you and Owen can have the guest room. But if it will be too weird for him—for both of you, I get it. It's actually probably the worst idea I've ever had so—"

"What does this mean?" she asked warily. "If Owen gets attached to you...I don't like agreeing with my father, but he's right. It's already happening." It was for *her*, too.

"I don't know," he said. "I don't know what the hell it means other than I hate the thought of not seeing either of you next week. But you're right. It could be confusing to Owen. And you. Shit. A couple of hours ago I was ready to do what I thought was the right thing and step back—keep you both safe from getting hurt again but—"

There he went again—trying to do the right thing. The only problem was she had no idea what *right* meant for their situation.

"But Owen might not be the only one forming an attachment," she said as realization bloomed.

It was, very possibly, the *worst* idea. But this was a

chance for Owen and his dad to really connect—for Jack to see the kind of father he could be, even if from afar.

It was her chance to figure out how to reconcile these new feelings for the first boy she'd ever loved with the fact she'd soon say good-bye to him again.

But for right now, she simply kissed him.

"Is that a yes?" he whispered.

"Yes," she whispered back, her lips still on his, and then kissed him again to shut them both up because she knew. Verbal vomit was a mess that was almost impossible to clean up, and she didn't want either of them to say anything more.

Because she didn't want either of them to change their minds.

He relaxed into her, his hands gripping her hips, and she could feel him smile against her lips.

"You made his night, you know," she said.

He didn't say anything in response other than claiming her lips with his again. He didn't need to. She'd watched them both all night, the boy and the man. She'd even go out on a limb and say that Jack had enjoyed himself as much as Owen had.

It didn't matter what Jack thought he was or was not capable of because Ava had seen it right there in her own backyard.

Jack Everett was a father, and he could be a damned good one if he'd only see himself the way she saw him.

Well, now she had a week to prove it.

Except his tongue slipped past her lips, and all her bones turned to jelly. She had to stop kissing him before her brain did, too.

"You should...probably..."

But he'd taken her pause in kissing him as an opportunity to trail his lips down her neck, his stubble scratching her skin in a way that made her knees buckle. If she didn't stop him now, before he got to her breast, she'd let him take her right on the entryway rug.

"Not here," she said before it was too late.

He backed away, brows raised in question, but he was otherwise completely composed.

"How the hell do you do that?" she asked.

"Do what?"

She blew out a breath and placed her hands on her hips, even as her taut nipples were about to slice holes through her shirt. "How do you liquefy my bones and then stand there as if you weren't about to have your way with me up against my front door?"

One corner of his mouth quirked up. "You gonna catch me if I go weak in the knees?"

She swatted him on the shoulder. "That's not the point," she pouted. "As soon as you leave I'm going to have to take a really cold shower and think about doing my taxes or something."

He leaned forward like he was going to kiss her but instead let his lips brush against her ear.

"I could do your taxes," he murmured.

She groaned and slipped out from under his arm. "I just—we can't. Not here. Not yet. Owen could come down those steps at any second, and I don't want to have to explain us before I can—you know—*explain* us."

Because how could she explain to her son what she didn't understand herself?

Jack pressed his lips together and nodded slowly. Then he kissed her on the top of the head. "Your father's right. Sneaking out after curfew didn't count," he said. "Maybe ten years too late, but I'd like to make up for it."

She reminded herself that proper date or no, their lives were headed in opposite directions, with Owen the only true anchor between them. But it was no use. She was falling for this man, and if she stopped kidding herself, maybe she'd be able to admit that she'd never quite gotten back up from the first time she fell.

"I'd like that," she admitted, but she kept the rest of her thoughts to herself. Maybe the father-son bond could span the miles between one coast and another, but her heart wouldn't withstand that distance.

"Goodnight, Red." His lips brushed softly against her cheek. His warm breath tickled her neck, and goose bumps peppered her skin.

She sighed, and there was a slight tremor in her breath. She couldn't be quite sure, though, if it was due to her heightened emotional state or the fact that she was still turned on just by the nearness of him.

It was probably a combination of both.

"We'll be out there bright and early Monday morning," she said.

He nodded again. And then he was out the door.

She stayed there, peering through the window as his truck backed out of the driveway and rolled away down the street.

"I'm in big trouble," she said aloud, then marched herself upstairs and straight to her bathroom, where she turned on her shower and waited for the water to get cold enough to make her body forget how much it wanted his.

Her heart, though, that was another story.

CHAPTER SIXTEEN

I'm your buffer," Jenna said, dunking her tea bag in her mug. "You know, in case things get awkward with Ava or Owen."

"She's got a point," Luke said, smacking Jack on the back of the head as he strode toward the fridge, where he grabbed what Jack had learned was his breakfast of choice, a Red Bull and a hard-boiled egg. "You were always the socially awkward one."

Because Luke was being Luke, opting for levity over gravity, Jack let the insult slide. His younger brother's safety net was a hell of a lot safer than the way Walker dealt with things.

"Things aren't going to get *awkward*," he insisted. Then he pointed at his aunt. "You're here because you can't stay the hell away, because even though we aren't your burden to bear anymore, you can't seem to shake the mom gene." Jenna's jaw fell open, but before she could misconstrue his words, Jack stepped toward her and kissed her on the cheek. "And we love you for that," he said softly. "But I've got this under control."

He hoped. Or maybe he didn't. Having Ava and Owen here was about getting to know his son. But wasn't this also about getting to know *her* again? She wasn't his eighteen-year-old first love. She wasn't anyone he really knew anymore. But every day he was with her—every minute he was in her presence—he wanted more.

"Talk about awkward," Luke said, and then blew out a long whistle. "What the hell is that?"

Jack turned to see his youngest brother rounding the corner from the front stairway, a towel around his neck to catch the water dripping from his hair. Walker was clean shaven and wearing what looked like an equally clean black T-shirt and jeans.

Jack glanced at the clock on his smart phone, the only item indicative of the fast-paced life he'd been living just a couple of weeks ago—the one he'd been so eager to return to. True, work on a ranch was almost round the clock, but the pace of life in Oak Bluff was its own entity, a pace *he'd* been setting since he'd returned, rather than his firm and his clients setting it for him.

This morning he'd woken early to take a ride on Cleo and tend to the cattle. It was only half past eight now that they were all gearing up for vineyard work, but he hadn't counted on Walker being a part of anything before noon.

"Are you okay?" he asked his youngest brother.

Walker responded first with a glare. "'Course I'm okay," he said. "Why the hell wouldn't I be?"

Jack shrugged. "Figured you were out well past midnight again."

"Yeah," Luke said with a laugh. "I'm usually dragging your hungover ass out of bed. What's with the whole getting up on your own lately? It's like you're responsible or something."

"Fuck you," Walker countered, stalking past them all and out onto the back porch.

Jenna laid a hand on Jack's shoulder.

"I know," he said. "I got this."

He followed his brother outside, where he stood against the wooden rail of the deck squinting toward the pasture. Jack hung back several feet to give Walker some space, his hands shoved in his pockets.

"You clean up like this for Ava and Owen?" Jack asked.

Walker's shoulders rose and fell, but he kept his back to his brother. "I didn't do a goddamn thing for anyone," Walker insisted.

Jack smiled anyway, since he knew his brother couldn't see him. If he pushed too hard, he was likely to spook him. So instead he simply said, "I didn't think so. But if you had?"

"I didn't."

"There's fresh coffee," Jack conceded, the only way he could think of to thank Walker. By including him in the day's plan. "We'll head out when they get here."

Walker nodded, still facing the fields. "I'll grab some in a few."

Jack took that as the closest he'd get to *thank you* and headed back inside only to find a chocolate Lab scrambling to get off a leash being held by a not-quite-strong-enough nine-year-old boy. Owen's feet were having trouble finding purchase on the wood floor, and the corner of Jack's mouth tilted into a crooked grin as he watched Scully drag the boy from the entryway toward the kitchen.

Jenna was holding the front door open for Ava, so Jack simply turned to Owen and said, "It's all right."

With that the boy unhooked the leash, and the dog came bounding toward him, barely halting before rising on his hind legs to rest his front paws on Jack's shoulders.

Jack stumbled back against the sliding glass door as

Scully gave him an affectionate greeting. The dog had shown nothing but mild interest in him before now, which was why he couldn't help but laugh—and laugh hard. Harder than he had in—well, he couldn't exactly remember.

"Someone's getting lucky tonight," he heard Luke say from his left. And then he caught sight of Ava practically sprinting toward them, her red hair wild and glowing as the sun streaming in from the front door backlit her as she moved.

"Sorry!" she called. "Shit. Sorry about the dog! He's a nervous traveler, and I think he's happy to see a familiar face and not the vet!"

"Mo-om," Owen sing-songed with laughter in his tone. "Language?"

"Shit!" Ava said again. "Down, Scully!"

The dog gave Jack one final lap against his jaw before heeding Ava's command. The second Scully relinquished his hold on him, Luke balled up a kitchen towel and lobbed it at his brother, nailing him in the chest.

"Thought you might want to dry off after that unexpected shower."

Jack nodded his thanks, and—not that he wasn't appreciative of such affection—took to wiping himself clean.

Ava's teeth were clamped together in a pained smile as Owen dropped to his knees to rub his dog's belly. "This is a lot, right?" she asked. "All three of us? I think I just realized what a handful we are."

She laughed nervously, and Jenna spoke up from behind Jack's visitors. "Sweetie, you're hanging with the Everett brothers for a week, working for no pay, and putting up with all of them? I think we know who the bigger handful is."

Luke's head tilted back as he downed his Red Bull. Then

he crushed the can on the counter and slapped his palm dramatically against his heart.

"Say what you want about Jack and Walker." He looked pointedly at his aunt. "But a guy with my devilish good looks and charm?"

Jenna pointed at her second youngest nephew. "*Not* thinking you're a handful makes you the biggest handful of them all, no matter how damn charming you claim to be."

Owen laughed. "I like it here. You guys are funny. And loud. Our house gets kind of quiet sometimes."

Jack watched Ava's expression falter before she painted a smile back on seconds later. It wasn't an insult, what Owen had said. But he saw that flicker of loss, the same one he'd felt the first time he'd seen his son. It didn't matter that he'd never thought he'd want what had been thrust upon him. Once it was there, he realized what he'd missed. And now Ava was seeing that, too.

"Quiet's good, sometimes," Jack said, and Owen shrugged.

"But loud's a helluva lot better." Luke rounded the counter, heading toward the sliding glass door. "What do you say, Shortstop? Wanna see if your dog'll give Walker the same greeting he gave Jack? I guarantee he'll react with some loud words we can all enjoy."

Jenna gave Luke's shoulder a playful push, and for a second Jack considered leaving his youngest brother in peace. But the brotherly thing to do was to give his siblings hell, so he let Luke open the back door and usher the dog outside to an unsuspecting Walker.

"What the fuck?" Walker yelled as Scully pounced. Jenna ran out after them. Owen and Luke were right behind her, laughing, so Jack trusted all was well and pulled the sliding door shut.

He strode toward Ava and removed the large tote bag from her shoulder, setting it on the floor against the wall. "I'm gonna apologize ahead of time for any changes in Owen's vocabulary by the end of this week," he said, coaxing a genuine smile from her. Then he pulled her around the corner and out of view from the back door, pressing her against the closed guest bedroom door.

She sucked in a sharp breath as he dipped his head but stopped short before his lips touched hers. "Red?" he said, his voice soft.

She exhaled then, her warm breath tickling his lips. "Yeah?" she squeaked.

"Are you going to spend the whole week thinking this is all too much for me to handle?" He rested his hands on her hips, the tips of his fingers pressing into the soft skin he knew rested beneath her clothes.

He watched her throat bob as she swallowed. "Maybe," she admitted and hooked one finger into the top of his jeans.

"Maybe's not gonna work for me." Her eyes widened. "I need you to feel at home. Because handful or not—I want you here. All three of you. Okay?"

"Okay," she said, then licked her lips, and Jack was two seconds from losing it, but he wasn't going to pressure her.

"Anything that happens between you and me while you're here is your call. But I need to make something clear. Me keeping my distance isn't because I don't want you." His lips brushed hers. Not exactly a kiss, but not exactly innocent, either. "Because I can't watch you walk into a room without wanting to touch you. You're like the goddamn sun, and I'm the closest planet. Powerless against your gravity. But I am trying to do what's right for Owen— what's right for you so you don't get hurt again." This week meant everything because after this he'd have it all figured out. They'd been keeping the truth from Owen until they knew what the truth was—until Jack could tell his son what role he was going to play in his future. That was what this visit was really about, wasn't it? Owen. The truth. Everything. But that didn't change how much he wanted her. It didn't change how hard he had to fight for restraint when he was this close. "So if at any second in any of the days you're here you think that I'd rather be doing *any*thing other than feeling your lips against mine, know that you could not be more wrong."

He started to back away, but she fisted her hand in his T-shirt.

"Damn it, Jack Everett. You're going to say all that and then *not* kiss me?" she said, her breathing shallow as she whisper-shouted the words.

"Your call, Red."

Her breath hitched. "Every time you call me that, I feel like I'm eighteen again. Like we're—*us*. You know?"

"Yeah. I know."

His heart hammered beneath her fist, his chest rising and falling in deep breaths that were becoming less and less controlled. And he wasn't running from it this time—the thought of losing control.

"My call?" she asked.

He nodded, and that was all it took. She yanked his T-shirt, pulling him to her, and he let the last of his resolve crumble as her mouth demanded his.

His fingers dug into her hips as she parted her lips, encouraging him to do the same. Her tongue slipped past, mingling with his, and he could taste the hint of the morning coffee she probably drank on the ride over, along with something both sweet and spicy—cinnamon. Maybe a mint.

This made him grin, the thought of her popping an Al-

toid or something like that. Because maybe she'd anticipated this as much as he had.

Her hand moved from his shirt, and seconds later, the
door to the guest bedroom fell open, the two of them stum-
bling past the threshold and collapsing onto the bed he'd
made for her the night before. The room also had a small
couch with a pull-out bed. He'd bought new sheets for that
one for Owen.

Right now, though, all Jack could think about was Ava
beneath him and how long she could stay there before any
of the other four people—and one rambunctious Lab—
would come looking for them. He rationalized that they'd
hear the back door when the chaos decided to move inside. It wasn't like either of them would let this go any
further than some very heavy petting. At least not right
now.

"I can't believe we weren't doing this all week long,"
she said, her voice breathless between each feverish kiss.
She knew they were on borrowed time, too. But it was more
than this day or the little snippets of time they'd have together this week.

Jack didn't know what the endgame was, but he hoped to
hell that having Ava and Owen here for the next five days
would give him the answers he needed—would help him
figure out what was best for all of them.

He was hard. Hell, this woman did things to him. But
there wasn't time for what he wanted to do to her. As if she
was reading his thoughts, though, Ava tilted her pelvis, and
he ground himself against her. She let out a soft cry, an even
softer plea as she whispered, *"More."*

That's when the scrabble of excited paws snapped them
both back into the moment, and Jack sprang to his feet
as Scully came bounding through the door and dropped a

baseball at his feet. The dog sat panting, tongue hanging out the side of his mouth, and tail wagging expectantly.

Ava was up and smoothing out her hair by the time Owen caught up to his dog.

"I think Scully wants to play catch with you, Ja—" But the boy stopped short when he laid eyes on the room, the one Jack hadn't officially shown Ava yet.

"Whoa," Owen said. "This is like someplace a real cowboy would live."

Relieved not to have been found dry-humping his son's mom on the guest bed, Jack laughed. He ran a hand along the knotted pine panel on the wall, one of ten that ran horizontally from doorframe to corner, stacked from floor to ceiling.

"Our father built this room for our mom," Jack said, allowing flashes of a happier time to invade his memories. "She missed her friends and family from Texas, so Jack Senior—with the help of the Callahans, some family friends who ran a contracting business—put an addition on the house that included this room. And you want to know what?"

"What?" Owen asked with an eager grin. Ava, not having heard the story before, either, said the same.

"He designed this room to look like the one our mom and Jenna loved at their grandparents' ranch back in Texas, so there'd always be a bit of home here in California."

Owen's fingers trailed Jack's across the wall and then to the queen bed, covered now with a semi-rumpled quilt.

"She made that, you know." Jenna's voice came from behind him, and Jack spun to find her standing in the doorframe. "She hated every second of it—claimed she was meant for the labor of the ranch and not for something with painstaking detail like crafting a quilt. But our nan made the one in the bedroom we always stayed in at their ranch, so Clare made sure this room had the same."

Jack ran a palm across the quilt, straightening it, and cleared his throat. "I thought this was something they bought."

Jenna shook her head. "You were probably too young to remember or too busy with baseball to notice her working on it. But that was her contribution to the room." Jenna laughed. "She probably did it to spite your daddy so he wouldn't be able to take full credit for the space. They were both so competitive. And so damn stubborn sometimes."

"Please don't, Jenna," Jack said.

Her eyes narrowed. "Please don't *what*? Remind you that they were happy? That despite the man Jackson Senior turned into, he did right by your mama and she by him? I'm not apologizing for what he did..."

Jack's hands fisted at his sides, and he tried to take a controlling breath. But control in the face of *what he did* was impossible.

"You don't get it," he snapped. "It doesn't matter what happened before she died when all I can seem to recall is what he did after. I'm happy as hell he took such great care of her when she was alive, but what about her children, Jenna? What about *his* sons?"

This was a mistake—this little trip down memory lane. Especially in front of Owen.

"Jack—"

But he wasn't waiting around to hear more.

"Enough," he said, then strode past Jenna and out of the room, calling over his shoulder, "We should get to work."

Because he wasn't about to listen to his aunt get all wistful and sentimental about his parents. Whatever Clare and Jackson Everett Senior had been before his mother died—

that was fiction. The reality was that he and his brothers lost two parents *and* a good part of their childhoods. He was wrong for even entertaining the thought that good memories could override the bad. Good memories had no place here.

Walker and Luke stood waiting in the kitchen, and Jack nodded to them and then headed toward the front door.

He needed out of this house. Fresh air would do him some good. Clear his head. Sure, he was being a dick, especially to Jenna, but she at least understood him, how he operated. He'd apologize later, and she'd give him hell for treating her like that in the first place, but she'd know he loved her and needed to let off some steam. This was their routine.

Thankfully, everyone followed him outside without so much as a *What the hell?* Not even Walker.

"We need to finish pruning by lunch," Jack said once everyone was assembled. Even the damned dog. "Then we'll eat, regroup, and check on the cover crop the previous owner planted, see if that grass needs to be tilled or torn out and replanted altogether. Bottom line is we can't have weeds. If we get this place on the path to producing a crop next year, we don't want to fall on our faces because of some damned weeds."

Ava squinted at him, the sun hitting her right in the eyes. "Sounds like you've been doing your homework. I could show you how to till—and how to recognize some sneaky weeds that disguise themselves as grass."

She smiled, but he couldn't let her get to him now that he was ready to get shit done—and get one step closer to getting the hell out. The less he had to sleep under the roof of Crossroads Ranch, the better.

"I think I got it. I passed the California Bar," he said. "A weekend of reading up on viniculture ought to do the trick."

"I see," Ava said, stalking past him toward her car. "Because certainly a weekend of reading far surpasses a lifetime of experience."

"Oh, Jack," Jenna said, shaking her head.

"Hey, Mom! Wait up!"

Owen and Scully trailed after Ava.

"What the hell did I say?" Jack asked.

"You're outta practice, brother." Luke clasped him on the shoulder. "Told ya you were the socially awkward one."

"Man, you're a prick," Walker added as he headed down the driveway and toward the stable.

Ava, Owen, and the dog were in her Jeep and backing into the street. Luke and Walker were probably taking a couple of the mares over to the vineyard. That left just Jack and Jenna.

He crossed his arms and held his aunt's gaze. He could wait her out, no matter how long she stared. They used to play this game in high school, and it always ended in Jenna groaning and throwing her hands in the air.

"What's it gonna take to get through to you, Jack?" she used to ask. "When are you gonna finally let me the hell in?"

But he wouldn't answer. Never did. Because what the hell was the point of letting *anyone* in when all he ever did was make things more complicated for everyone involved?

That's how it had felt when he and his brothers had taken over Jenna's house—or when he saw the look of horror on Ava's face after what had happened at the graduation party.

Except this wasn't then, and Jenna held her ground now. She wasn't screaming through gritted teeth. No impatient exasperation. Just cold, clean resolve.

"I got all day," she said, taking a step closer.

Jack almost flinched. Forget the fact that he was at least

a foot taller than her. The woman had a serious *Don't mess with me* vibe going on.

His jaw clenched. "I was supposed to come back for a weekend. A week tops. Now there's this vineyard, and I can't leave that to Luke and Walker to take care of on their own. Then Ava and Owen. I have a son. A *son*, Jenna. He's this incredible kid, and I'm—I'm *me*. I don't know how the hell to deal with all this."

"Ya screwed up just now," she said calmly.

He opened his mouth to respond, but she cut him off.

"I know this place gets to you, Jack. And I know you built yourself a whole new life so you wouldn't have to deal with it. But you're here now. You decided to stay for however long that might be, and you got a hell of a lot more than you bargained for, which I'm guessing you thought would include a quick graveside service, washing your hands of this place, and then hightailing it out the door again. But this shit ain't about only you anymore. Not when you're under that roof with Luke, Walker, and your son and his mother. So maybe it's time to get your shit together and *deal*."

He crossed his arms and raised a brow, waiting for a beat. "You about done?" he asked.

She pursed her lips and contemplated the question for a few seconds. "Yeah. I guess I am," she finally said.

"That your version of therapy?"

She nodded. "Maybe it is. Wouldn't hurt you to, you know, deal with your demons and all that."

He let out a bitter laugh. "I did for that whole first year of college. Stipulation of my non-arrest and all." But it seemed nothing had been enough to prepare him for coming home. "Anyway, I thought that's what I was doing coming back here—dealing with my demons. You know I'm gonna take care of them, right? He's my son. My responsibility. I don't take that lightly."

She sighed. "From across the country. Is that why you haven't told him yet? That boy deserves the truth, you know."

She was right. He knew that. But he also knew that some people weren't cut out to be fathers, and he'd always put himself in that category. A couple of good interactions with his son didn't mean he knew what the hell he was doing—didn't mean he'd be any different from the man who raised him.

"What do we actually tell him? *Hey, kid. I'm your dad. Nice to meet you, but I gotta run. It's what I do.* Or *I once beat a kid unconscious for trying to hurt your mom. Hope I don't do the same to you.*"

Jenna's features softened. She never could hold on to anger for too long. "Oh, sweetie. When are you going to let yourself off the hook for something that happened when you were a troubled kid?"

He let out a long breath, grasping at the one thing in his life that made sense—the one thing he could control. "New York is what I've worked toward ever since I left. It's my career."

She stepped forward and tapped him on the chest. "A career I haven't heard you mention once other than to tell me you're moving to the other side of the country." She laughed. "Small-town ranch boy like you? You'll hate that noisy city."

"I haven't been a small-town ranch boy for a decade," he said even as he sucked in a deep breath of Oak Bluff's crisp open air.

She patted him condescendingly on the cheek, a gesture that only Jenna could make endearing. "Aw, honey. I've lived in Los Olivos longer than I ever lived in Texas, but you will never hear me say 'I ain't been a Texan in however many years.' You can take the boy off the small-town ranch..."

He rolled his eyes and shook his head. "You want a ride to the vineyard or not?"

Her shoulders relaxed, and he knew the anger was completely gone. "Before the subject is officially changed, can I say one more thing?"

He laughed. "Could I stop you if I said no?"

She shook her head. "Make things right with Ava."

He led her to the passenger side of his truck and unlocked the door.

He'd fucked up. He knew that. He had let his demons get in the way of thinking about what he said before he said it, and he'd gone and diminished her whole goddamn life's work to a quick weekend read.

Shit. How had the morning started off so well and then gone to complete and utter hell?

Oh. Right. He'd been a first-rate asshole.

"I will" was all he said, and that seemed to be enough because Jenna climbed into the truck without another word.

In a few minutes they were at the vineyard. Walker and Luke must have ridden to the far end to do the pruning there because neither they nor their horses were anywhere to be found. Jack caught sight of Owen tossing a ball and Scully fetching it, so he knew Ava wouldn't be far off.

"Hang with Owen for a minute?" he asked when they both were out of the truck.

Jenna smiled. "Of course."

Jack found Ava in the middle of a row, hair piled on top of her head in a messy bun and pruning shears in her gloved hand. She was hacking away at a branch like it was being punished. He felt bad for the poor vine since he knew it was a substitute for him.

"Hey," he said when he was close enough for her to hear.

She looked up, shears pointed up and open, like she was poised to snip off one of his limbs.

He reached for them. "Maybe put those down for a second," he said in what he hoped was a calming tone.

She narrowed her eyes but relinquished her grip on the tool he didn't want to see turned into a weapon. Jack dropped it to the ground.

"What you have been doing here this past week is amazing. And generous."

Ava shrugged. "Yeah, so?"

A small laugh escaped his lips. He couldn't help it. She was the only one who brought it out of him, and he wished he could think of the right words to let her know that.

"And I don't deserve the help you've been giving me."

She crossed her arms. "No. You don't."

He took a step closer to her, and she didn't retreat—or make a quick grab for the shears to cut his balls off—so he took that as encouragement. "And I was an asshole back at the ranch. I didn't mean to demean what you do."

Her eyes softened, but her expression was still pained.

"Do you think that, though?" she asked, all her anger draining so that the only thing he could hear now was the hurt. "That what I've done with my life doesn't have the same meaning as what you've done with yours?"

His eyes widened. "Jesus, Ava. *No.* Hearing all that shit about how happy my parents were, though?" He shook his head. "In case you haven't noticed, I don't exactly deal well with the unexpected."

That elicited a bitter laugh from her. "I suppose you've

had quite a lot of that thrown at you in less than two weeks. That stuff Jenna said got to you, huh?"

"Yes," he admitted.

"But you don't want to talk about it," she added.

"Not right now."

"I told you I'm not gonna push you, Jack. But I'm also not gonna cut you slack for how you process your repressed emotions, especially if I get caught in the cross fire."

He raised a hesitant hand toward her cheek, and when she gripped his wrist and brought his palm the rest of the way to her skin, he let out a shaky exhale. "I'm sorry," he said softly. "I don't deserve you."

She kissed his palm, then gave him a pointed look. Hell. What had he done now?

"You deserve so much more than you let yourself believe," she said. "But I can't make you see that, Jack. You have to see it for yourself."

Did he deserve another chance with her? Or a chance to prove the father he'd be for Owen was nothing like his own had turned out to be?

She kissed him, and he heard her breath shudder as she did.

She may have hurt him, but he understood why: Her reasons were born out of love. His had come from self-preservation.

The truth was, it was she who deserved *everything*, and he had no clue if he could be the one to give it to her.

CHAPTER SEVENTEEN

After working on the vineyard for the better part of the day, Ava thought she'd relax while Luke and Walker gave Owen a riding lesson. She thought wrong. Instead she watched, heart in her throat, because her son, who she thought was getting so big, was dwarfed atop a giant horse. Walker rode a horse named Bella, one who was only five years old, next to Owen on Cleo, who had belonged to Jack when he was a young teen. Not that he'd ever mentioned her when they'd dated in high school *or* that she was big enough to eat her son.

Horses didn't eat people, though, right?

Luke kept a steady pace on the ground next to Owen, but he was no longer holding the reins or guiding the mare. Her boy was on his own, and damn if he didn't look good on a horse, like she assumed his father did.

Owen grabbed his Dodgers cap by the bill and twirled it in the air like a lasso. "Woohoo! I'm ready to drive some cattle!"

But as soon as the words left his mouth, he lost his balance.

It felt like everything happened in slow motion, but it was over in a blink. Ava burst through the gate, not even thinking about spooking the horses. Her only thought was getting to her son. By the time she did, she couldn't remember how she got from point A to point B—and then there was Owen, upright on the horse again, Luke steadying him back into the saddle.

"Mom!" he cried, a grin spreading from ear to ear. "Did you see that? I almost totally wiped out, and then Luke caught me! And Cleo even stopped, like she knew something was up, and it...was...*awesome*!"

Ava started laughing hysterically as tears sprang from her eyes at the same time. Maybe she wasn't laughing at all, but then again, what did it really matter? Owen was okay. That was the only thing that mattered. Ever.

Walker spun around on Bella and trotted back in their direction while Luke rested a hand on Ava's shoulder.

"I live and breathe this shit, Red," he said. "As long as I'm around when he's on the horse, your boy is in good hands."

Ava had to catch her breath and collect herself before she could respond. By the time she was ready to speak, she knew Luke was right. This was Owen's family, and in the short time they'd known him, they already had his back. And something made her trust that for as long as Owen was in their lives, they would.

"Thank you," she said. "I just—I don't want you to think—it was a knee-jerk reaction, you know?"

Walker and Luke both nodded. "You were protecting your young," Luke said. "No worries. As long as you know now that he's safe on the horse. Safer than any other *Shortstop* I know."

Owen groaned and rolled his eyes, but he was still smiling. He enjoyed the constant ribbing from his uncle, and Ava enjoyed watching it. It was like they really were a family or something. As quickly as the thought made her smile, though, it filled her with guilt.

They had to tell him. She kept rationalizing that she had to know exactly what role Jack would play in Owen's life before telling her son who his father really was. But each second they kept the truth from him was a betrayal of the person she loved most. The ball wasn't only in Jack's court. It had to be in hers, too.

"Jack back yet?" Walker asked, as if he could read her thoughts.

She glanced back to the driveway that was missing his beat-up truck. "Nope."

"He's a man of mystery, huh?" Luke asked.

"More like a closed-off asshole," Walker added, but Ava caught the hint of a smile on his usually sullen face.

"You say 'asshole' a lot," Owen said.

Ava opened her mouth to protest, but then she thought better of it. If adding a few new words to Owen's vocabulary was the price for getting to know the Everetts, so be it.

"He's right, you know," she said with a grin.

Luke tipped his head back and laughed. "Can't argue with the truth."

For a second Walker's jaw tightened, but then his shoulders relaxed. "Well, *asshole*," he said to Luke, "when you're right, you're right."

All four of them laughed now, and Ava forgot *the man of mystery* for a few minutes.

The day's work had gone as planned, right down to learning, thankfully, that the cover crop was doing its job. They wouldn't have to replant, only till—which was still a big job—but it could have been worse.

But Jack had been gone for over an hour now at a meeting in the neighboring city of Pismo Beach. Jenna had already left, and neither Luke nor Walker knew anything about the meeting, either. Jack hadn't bothered to fill anyone in. All they knew was that Jack Senior's lawyer had called and asked to see Jack in person, and he had dropped everything to do it.

The unmistakable sound of tires on gravel broke the laughter and Ava's train of thought.

"Mom!" Owen called as she watched Jack's truck roll up the driveway. "Can I ride for a little longer? I *promise* I'll be careful."

She turned to him, brows raised. "And what about walking your dog?"

Scully, wiped from the day's work, which had included racing Owen up and down the rows of vines, had been passed out on the living room floor when they'd left the house. Ava didn't actually mind walking the dog. She also didn't want to be the mom who said no because, despite knowing Luke and Walker were there, she still worried. It was a prerequisite of mothering, one that seemed to last far beyond the preschool and toddler years.

He looked at her with pleading eyes, so in love with being on that horse. "Ten more minutes? Pleeeaase? Then I'll walk Scully, and I'll even shower without complaining."

She laughed at this, and Luke stared toward the house.

"Go on. I said he was safe, and I don't go around saying shit I don't mean."

Her frantic heartbeat finally slowed. "Twenty minutes," she countered, and Owen's face lit up.

"Thank you!" he cried. "Thank you! Thank you!" He wobbled a bit in his excitement but immediately righted himself. Ava still gasped—and then laughed.

He would be fine. And she? Well, she'd still worry, but then she always would.

* * *

Jack was in the kitchen when she made it back to the house. He sat at the table staring at a business-sized envelope as if he was waiting for it to speak.

"I bet Carnac the Magnificent could tell you what's in there," she said.

His head jerked up, and for a second she thought he might not recognize her.

"What?" he asked, his voice strained.

"Johnny Carson?" she said. "Carnac the Magnificent? It was a bit on his show. My dad has all thirty years on DVD. When Johnny retired, he started over again from the beginning, and when I was old enough to watch with him, I did. It was kind of our thing."

Jack let out a bitter laugh. "Apparently my dad's *thing* is to still keep some sort of twisted hold on me even after he's gone."

Ava worried her upper lip. "You mean the vineyard?"

The line of his jaw flexed and released. "I mean this." He slid the envelope across the table, and Ava moved closer so she could read the words scrawled across it in a jagged script.

For Jackson Everett Junior
    To be read in the event of my death.

"Even when his words were slurred or barely legible, he still managed to get the last one."

She pulled out the chair across from him and sat, resting her palm on top of his.

"So that's why his lawyer called you? To give you the letter?"

Jack nodded. "He had a few other things to go over, but

he wanted to apologize and give me the letter in person. It got lost in a pile of paperwork. He said my father gave it to him days before he passed, like he knew he was at the end. I always thought he was too sauced to even know he was sick."

Ava rubbed her thumb over his knuckles. "You're gonna read it, right?" she asked and felt the veins in his hand tense as he curled it into a fist.

"No," he said flatly. He stood, folded it in half and shoved it in his back pocket. "How's Owen doing with the two knuckleheads?"

He smiled, but she could tell it was forced. She could also tell that the discussion about the letter was over.

For now, she thought.

She slid out of her chair and rose to meet his gaze. "Well, I had a heart attack when he almost fell off of Cleo, but Luke caught him, and Walker was right next to him on Bella."

"Christ," he hissed. "You can tell Luke and Walker to lay off the riding. I didn't invite you here to put your son in danger."

Her breath hitched.

Your son.

He must have realized what he'd said because his eyes widened.

"Jesus, Ava. No. That's not what I meant." He rounded the table so he was in front of her, cupping her face in his hands. "Calling him mine?" he said. "That's a privilege I haven't earned yet."

She got that. Hell, she knew ten years ago he hadn't *wanted* such a privilege. Yet here they were, staying in his home with him. He wanted—*something*. Didn't he?

"Your terms still," he said, a tentative grin taking over

his features. "As far as what happens between you and me while you're here."

If she kissed him now, the subject would be effectively changed. No letter. No talk of them as an "us" instead of a her, a him, and an Owen. But Owen deserved better.

"We're lying to him, Jack. He's out there having the time of his life with his uncles, and I feel like we're playing some huge joke on him. He's a good kid."

"I know," he said softly.

She shook her head. "No. He's a *great* kid. The best, and he deserves the truth. I told myself I wasn't going to give you an ultimatum, but for Owen's sake I have to." He kept talking so much about doing right by her and Owen that she hadn't realized, until today, that they'd missed the mark.

"You're right," he said, his gaze fixed on hers.

Only in his eyes, that storm of blue, could she see his warring emotions—what she guessed was hesitation and fear mixed with his insistence on always doing what was best for everyone else.

"I thought I could wait," she said. "I thought I could let you deal with your dad's death and figure out this vineyard thing, but you're *leaving*. I can't let the month go by only for us to tell him right before you hop on a plane." Owen deserved time with his father *knowing* who his father was.

"Everything this week is your call," he said.

"Okay, then. It should be just the three of us, right?" Not that she had a clue. There was no protocol for something like this, but she figured it should happen without the whole Everett/Ellis entourage. "He has a baseball game Saturday morning. His first of the season. Come to the game, and we'll take him out for lunch after. We'll tell him and take it from there, and whatever happens, the two of you will have at least another week before—"

She didn't want to say what came next, but Jack was good at filling in the blanks.

"Before I move to New York."

She forced a smile, but it felt like her chest was caving in.

They stood there in that heavy silence for several long seconds, the lack of words passing between them saying more than if they'd stated the obvious. Whatever this was with him and her could only ever be temporary unless he gave up his job.

But it was more than a job. It was his career. And it wasn't like he was asking her and Owen to drop everything and come with him to New York. She couldn't, even if he did. She *wouldn't*. Her life—her *future*—was here. So was Owen's.

He reached for her hand and laced his fingers through hers. "I got you something today," he said. "After my meeting."

Her eyes widened, and the change of subject made breathing a little easier.

"It's still in the bed of my truck."

He pulled her toward the door without another word.

When they reached the truck, he lowered the back door and pulled back a small tarp to reveal an easel, a blank canvas, and several tubes of paint.

Ava's hand flew to her mouth.

"I know Owen said the painting wasn't going so great lately, but I thought—I know how much you loved it, and that if things with us had worked out differently, you would have gone to art school ten years ago instead of just applying now. Aaand...I can't tell if you're smiling or crying right now, so if I've messed up again, please tell me. I can take it. I'm apparently on a roll."

Her eyes shone bright. She was sure of it, but not because he'd messed up again. Far from it. So she dropped her hand to reveal a smile. Because despite her and Jack being virtual strangers, he still knew her enough to do something like this.

She threw her arms around him and hugged him close, whispering in his ear, "Thank you." Then she kissed his cheek. "Thank you. Thank you."

He pressed his lips to her neck, and she shuddered. This was exactly what she needed. She'd let her body take over so she could give her brain—and heart—a rest.

"I did good, huh?" he said against her, and it was all she could do not to moan right there.

"You did *really* good," she said, and he peppered her collarbone with more kisses.

This was the language they could speak, one of mutual understanding. And pleasure. They were really good when it came to pleasure.

"Owen and your brothers can probably see us," she said.

He laughed, his warm breath making *her* warm in places he couldn't see. "Nope. They're on the far end of the stable loop. We've got at least three more minutes of being undetected...*unless*..."

He backed her around the side of the truck and up against the driver's side door, which meant they were completely out of sight.

She gasped as he continued where they'd left off, lips trailing to where her cleavage peeked out from her T-shirt. He dipped his tongue between her breasts, and she hummed a soft moan.

"I gotta say," she started, her voice accompanied by small, sharp gasps, "these stolen moments with you are about the sexiest thing ever."

His palms were on her hips, and he slipped his thumbs beneath her T-shirt. Then his hands slowly lifted the cotton up and over her breasts.

"God, I'm glad you don't have neighbors," she admitted, then cried out as he popped the cup of her demi bra down and took her hard peak into his mouth.

"I hate neighbors," he said, his voice rough with what she hoped was a need that matched her own.

She knew they'd have to stop in seconds. Minutes at the most. She wouldn't let Owen and his uncles catch them like this. But hell if she wouldn't take what she could get.

She ran her hands through his golden waves. "Did you have neighbors in San Diego?" she asked.

He nodded, his five o'clock shadow scratching deliciously against her chest.

"Hated 'em," he said before attending to what she hoped wouldn't be a neglected left breast.

She laughed and then cut herself off with a gasp as he flicked his tongue against her nipple.

"You're not capable of hate," she said when she found her voice again.

He lifted his head at this, his gaze studying her for several long seconds. God, she wished she could read what went on behind the storm in those blue eyes.

"They're walking the horses back into the stable," he said. "We should probably—"

She kissed him then, taking her fill in hopes that what he gave her now would tide her over until their next stolen moment. But every kiss made her want another. And she wasn't sure she'd ever truly get enough.

"God, Ava," he said. And he kissed her harder, longer, like he was trying to quench a thirst as deep as a well. "You make me—"

But he didn't finish the thought. He kept kissing her as if this was the last time they'd get to do this.

The hell it was. And hell if she wasn't going to pull some sort of revelation from him, no matter how small.

"What? I make you what?"

He rested his forehead against hers, his chest rising and falling with ragged breaths. "You make me *want*," he finally said.

She sighed and gave him one last soft kiss.

How long had she put herself on the bottom of the list? Owen came first. And that would never change. But maybe it was time to bump herself up a couple of notches. Maybe it was time to let herself want, too.

And hope.

"Well," she whispered softly against his cheek. "I guess that makes two of us."

CHAPTER EIGHTEEN

Jack was happy to give Ava and Owen the guest room, but that meant he'd had to unexpectedly face at least one demon he'd thought he'd avoid—being back in his old room. It wasn't the room so much as climbing that flight of stairs. When he reached the top, he reminded himself that there was no drunk Jack Senior on his arm, fighting off his son's help, but that did nothing to keep the memory at bay. It didn't matter much, just that tonight he'd be more restless than usual. There was also the matter of a chocolate Lab whimpering outside his door. Scully hadn't woken him, only reminded him that it was past midnight and he was still wide awake.

He groaned and rolled out of bed, throwing on the T-shirt and jeans that lay on the floor.

"I'm coming, ya whiny mutt." But really, he was happy for the company of someone who didn't expect any more than to be taken for a walk and maybe play a little fetch with a now tooth-marked baseball. Besides, who could resist a dog named after the Dodgers' former longtime announcer, Vin Scully?

He hadn't confirmed this assumption with Ava or Owen, but he knew there was no other explanation. How had this kid who'd never known him turned out so much like he was when he was young? But if Owen could take after him without the two having ever met, then he could still end up like Jack Senior, couldn't he? There was probably more of a chance after having grown up with the man.

Jack threw open the door, and Scully's whimpers morphed quickly into excited panting and tail wagging.

"You're so full of shit," he told the dog, but gave him a scratch behind the ears anyway.

Luke and Walker's doors were shut, but the master bedroom hung wide open at the other end of the hall. They'd left the room untouched so far—his brothers conveniently too busy to add it to their to-do lists. Luke always had to be somewhere when Jack brought it up, and Walker was usually gone with a six-pack if he was done working the ranch for the day.

Jack knew it was more than just clearing away the last of their father's belongings. After their mother died, Jack Senior held on to *all* of Clare's clothes, her bottle of perfume, and probably even her toothbrush. He'd left all of his wife's earthly possessions exactly as they had been since the day they'd lost her.

He tried to forget about the times he'd successfully gotten a drunk Jack Senior into his own bed for the night, only to find him the next morning still passed out yet clutching one of his mom's old T-shirts like a life preserver. Remembering shit like that tended to stir emotions—like sympathy—that he didn't want stirred. But as he led Scully to the top of the staircase, his stirrings were thwarted as he recalled once again the last time he'd stood on that threshold with his father—and then was knocked violently down the wooden steps—and eventually out of the ranch for good.

"Until now," he said aloud as he gripped the railing much in the way his father had held on to those T-shirts. Like a lifeline.

Scully scampered to the bottom as Jack moved slowly, steadily, holding his breath.

"Damn it," he whispered as he stepped onto solid ground. "Let it go, already," he told himself. But he'd been telling himself that for ten years.

"Come on, boy."

Scully followed him to the front door, where he slid his feet into his boots. The cold night air bit at his flesh, and he shoved his hands into his pockets. The dog ran around the front yard, took a quick piss, and then ran back to Jack's feet, where he stood wagging his tail. He was ready to grab a ball from the back of his truck when someone yelled *"Shit!"* from behind the house.

Instead of a ball, he grabbed a bat and rounded the side of the ranch as stealthily as he could with an excited pooch at his heels. He gripped the bat firmly in one hand, poised to react—until he climbed up on the deck, only to find it littered with crushed beer cans. Luke and Walker had left their lawn chairs abandoned as they poked at something with a stick in the fire pit below.

He dropped the bat onto the ground. "What the hell are you assholes doing?"

He bellied up to the deck rail while Scully leaned down on his front paws, his ass in the air as he still wagged that damned tail.

"Lost a full can in there." Walker stared toward the blaze.

Luke snorted with laughter. "Some shitheads lack the hand-eye coordination needed to open a goddamn can of beer."

Walker pushed his brother good-naturedly, but Luke stumbled too close to the fire for Jack's comfort.

"Consider the can a sacrifice, and get your drunk asses back up here before it explodes or something."

He could see the can. It wasn't exactly in the flames, but retrieving it would be no easy feat, even if sober. He had enough on his plate as it was. He didn't need his drunk brothers ending up in a burn unit on top of it.

Luke and Walker stumbled back up the porch steps, and Scully immediately dropped to his back, tongue dangling out the side of his mouth as he lay in wait for a belly rub. Walker obliged.

"Did I miss the invitation to the party?" Jack asked. "Or is this a nightly routine I'm only now learning about?"

"That depends," Luke said. "Does the party include you filling us in on that meeting you had with Jack Senior's lawyer? I get that you're the most qualified for all that legal speak, but we're not kids. We've been running this place for almost as long as you've been gone, big brother. I think we can probably grasp some of the finer details of what's going on."

Jack found the source of the beer cans—a cooler outside the sliding glass door—and decided he'd rather join his brothers than lecture them, as long as they stayed the hell away from the fire.

"You're right," he said, collapsing onto the bench that ran along the deck's side rail. "I was waiting until I knew how I wanted to proceed, but it's as much your decision as it is mine." He took a long sip of beer and then tilted his head back against the rail ledge. "Thomas—Dad's lawyer—found a buyer for the vineyard."

All three of them were silent for several beats after that. It was Walker who finally spoke up. "Is it a good price?"

Jack nodded. "Best we could hope for, especially without knowing how much crop we'll yield. How to actually turn the grapes into wine. Can we really sit tight and wait for wine to age before even knowing if it's any good? Plus, no tasting room." He scratched the back of his neck. "The deck is stacked against us."

"We could build that tasting room," Walker reminded him. "We get the Callahan brothers involved, and we could get a real good place done for little more than cost."

Jack sighed. "And that would take months more."

"How long we got to decide on the offer?" Luke asked.

Walker stood now and crossed his arms next to his brother. Scully sprang to his feet as well, so he was faced with a line of brotherly and canine interrogators.

"A week," Jack said. "The offer is good for a week."

Walker shook his head and let out a bitter laugh. "And if we sell—I mean *when* we sell because you sure as shit want the hell out of Oak Bluff—you take off to New York, right?"

Jack laughed bitterly. "You act like it's a choice I'm making. I accepted a goddamn partnership. Everything I own that's not in my truck is already in Manhattan." The truth was, the *This is my career* argument was starting to sound less and less convincing even to himself.

"You tell Red about this?" Luke asked.

Jack clenched his jaw and shook his head. "And you won't either. I don't want to tell her anything before I have an answer. She knows about New York, and it's not like me staying was ever on the table."

Because there was that other niggling piece of truth—the one he couldn't admit out loud that had the power to change everything. Ava had never said anything about *wanting* him to stay. Everything had changed since he'd returned, yet at the same time felt like *déjà vu*. She'd pushed him away before because she'd thought it was what he needed, and maybe it was. And maybe it was what he'd thought he needed when he accepted the partnership in New York. But that was before he'd pulled up in front of the Ellis property, before he'd seen his son. Before he'd started falling for the woman he'd never been able to forget.

"I just—I think she and Owen deserve better," he said. Because despite everything that had changed in a matter of weeks, he was still the son of Jackson Everett Senior. He was still the kid who'd put another guy in the hospital when he'd completely lost control. And he was still the man who was terrified of what kind of father he'd truly be when he never intended on being one at all.

Walker scoffed. "Better than what? The son of an abusive drunk?"

Jack rose to his feet so he was eye-to-eye with his accuser. "Yes, Walker. *Hell* yes. They deserve better than the son of an abusive drunk who has no damned clue if he'll be one someday, too. Why is that so hard for you to understand?"

Walker moved closer so their chests almost bumped. Jack knew he was riling Walker up, but hell if he wasn't going to try to make them understand.

"If you're so damn sure you're him, then hit me," Walker said.

Jack's eyes widened. "What the hell are you talking about?"

"Fucking hit me," Walker said again, and this time their chests did bump, forcefully. But Jack knew *he* was standing still.

He placed a hand on his younger brother's shoulder and squeezed. "I think that's one can too many for you. Sleep it off."

Walker sniffed and puffed out his chest. "You think I can't take it? You think I'm not man enough to take what you took on our behalf for five fucking years? I don't need your protection anymore, big brother. I don't need you to waltz in here and take care of everything like you do—and be reminded of how you *took care* of everything when we were kids." He gritted his teeth. "Leave if you're gonna leave, asshole. Be free of this place. But even the score already and just. Fucking. Do it."

Jack pushed him back an arm's length, but he sure as shit wasn't going to let this go any further. "There's no score, Walker. Jesus. You don't *owe* me anything, and I sure as hell don't want to be some twisted Jack Senior surrogate for you so you can deal with whatever it is that's eating you. Do all of us a favor and sleep it *off*." It was like he was eighteen again, trying to coax his father to do the same before getting himself pushed down a flight of wooden stairs.

Walker let out a bitter laugh. "You don't have it in you, even when I deserve it. You stand there, beer in hand, yet other than *one* time—after all the hell you took from him for five years—I've never seen you out of control once in your goddamn life. It ain't my kid or my woman. I'd tell them to run as far away from here as they could if it was. It's *you*, Jack, the one who always kept it together—who took every fist or boot so we didn't have to. So don't tell me they can do better. Don't make that your reason for leaving us—I mean *them*—again."

Walker crumpled his empty can and chucked it forcefully over the railing and into the fire. "Fuck this," he said and stalked off the stairs and toward the open field.

Jack stood there in stunned silence for several long moments.

"He'll be all right," Luke finally said. "He just needs to blow off a little steam."

Jack realized his free hand was balled into a fist, and although he had to force himself to unclench it, he'd never once considered hitting his brother. "You think the same things he does?" he asked. "That you deserve the kind of treatment I tried to keep from you?"

Luke shrugged. "I think it's a hell of a thing for any kid to watch the brother he looks up to most get abused by the one person who was supposed to protect them all."

Luke's ever-present smile was gone, and Jack felt an ache so big it almost rivaled the years of his life he kept trying to forget.

"We all got our demons to dance with, Jack. Walker's still trying to find his way back to the land of the living."

"And you?" he asked.

Luke winked, but it was forced. "Everything I do is living, big bro." He shrugged. "I don't know. I think you gotta do whatever makes living *your* life bearable." He looked around the deck, littered with empty cans. "I'll get this in the morning," he said, then left his brother alone with his thoughts and a confused-looking dog.

Jack crouched so he was eye level with Scully. "That was ten years' worth of unsaid shit that I guess needed saying, huh?"

The dog lapped at his jaw.

"Is that all *you* have to say?" Jack asked him, and he received another slobbery kiss in return. He gave Scully an affectionate pat on the head and stood. Then he started collecting the empty cans, cleaning up the one mess he knew he could.

CHAPTER NINETEEN

Ava backed into the laundry room off the kitchen as soon as she saw her father's name pop up on her phone. She'd done so well avoiding any verbal run-ins with him all week, but now that it was Friday, she knew she couldn't ignore the call and shoot off a quick text. Owen had his first official game the next day, and he'd want to confirm when and where, despite her having emailed her parents the entire season's schedule.

"Hi, Dad," she said softly. Owen was taking a shower, and Jack and his brothers were finishing up in the vineyard. The crop was almost ready to do its thing—or at least try. But it would take the better part of a year to see if the grapes would flourish. They were close enough, though, that they didn't need Ava telling them what to do anymore.

"'*Hi*, Dad?'" he said, the hint of teasing in his tone. "You've been giving your old man the brush-off all week, and all I get is '*Hi*, Dad'?"

He was trying to make light of the situation, but both of them knew what was brewing beneath the surface, so she decided to dive right in.

"This week's been good for him—for Owen. You should

see how well he clicks not only with Jack but with his uncles and his great-aunt Jenna."

He was silent for several beats before saying, "Doesn't mean the Everett boy is good for him. Even if I let slide what happened a decade ago, you can't know a man's character after a couple of weeks."

Ava groaned. "This, Dad. This is why you got the *brush-off* all week. He doesn't deserve your judgment—"

But he cut her off before she could reason with him. "The hell he doesn't, Ava. Who was there for your morning sickness, for monitoring your meals when you got that pregnancy diabetes? Huh? Who was in the delivery room when the epidural wasn't doing its job and you thought those goddamn contractions would tear you apart?"

"Dad," she said, trying not to let her voice tremble.

"If he's such a stand-up guy...If he's *not* someone I should worry about entering the lives of my daughter *and* my grandson, I'm waiting to hear how you've come to this grand conclusion. For *ten* years you hear nothing from him, and the second he waltzes back into town, you take Owen and shack up with this stranger—a stranger with a past full of violence—for a week?"

"Dad!" she cried, and she *was* shaking now, but she didn't care. "How dare you judge him without ever taking a second to look past *one* night—one terrible night—in Jack's life, and how *dare* you judge *me* when everything I've ever done has been for the good of those I loved, including Jack Everett. I'm grateful for what you and Mom did for Owen and me. There is no possible way to ever repay you. But enough is enough. Jack made a mistake when he was a scared, messed-up kid. How long does he have to pay for it?"

"It's more than that," her father said. "I don't care if

Everett knew nothing about his son. *He* walked out of your life and only came back by accident, and we're all supposed to rejoice just so he can leave and hurt you again—hurt the both of you?"

"I gotta go, Dad." She heard the front door open and slam shut, followed by the not-so-distant grumbling of what she knew were three tired, sweaty men. "The game is at eleven in the elementary school baseball field. We'll be there by 10:30. Send my love to Mom."

She ended the call and quickly swiped under her eyes, hoping the three brothers were too exhausted from their longest day of work yet to notice she'd started to cry.

"Something smells good," she heard Walker say.

"Too bad it ain't for you!" Luke answered. "You'll be eating good old-fashioned rodeo fare tonight, my friend."

By the time the three men made it into the kitchen, Ava had a smile painted on her face as bright as the yellow, pink, and orange flowers on the sundress she was wearing.

Jack stopped short as soon as he saw her, and his brothers had to struggle not to plow right into him.

"Whoa," he said. "I thought you were heading back here early so Owen could shower and eat a 'sensible meal' before he was carted off to the rodeo."

She let out a nervous laugh. "He's finishing up in the shower, but I don't care if he stuffs himself full of nachos and hot pretzels tonight. It's a special occasion for him—getting to see Luke compete." Her cheeks grew hot, but she didn't care if they saw her blush. It would hopefully distract from her glassy eyes. "The—uh—sorta sensible meal is for you." She turned toward Jack, who still stood there looking mildly stunned.

Walker pushed ahead of his brothers. "If he's not gonna jump at a home-cooked meal, can I send *him* to the rodeo while I stay here and eat whatever it is you got in that oven?"

Luke smacked his brother on the back of the head. "Forget it, asshole. You and Jenna are on Shortstop duty tonight. Now go shower. You smell worse than the stables."

Walker smacked Luke back, but Ava could tell it was all in good fun. She liked seeing them happy, acting like brothers rather than what she'd overheard the other night. She hadn't been able to make out what the three of them were saying, but sound carried through a house with the windows open and no one or nothing nearby to drown out the noise.

They'd been arguing—all three of them—yet Jack hadn't breathed a word of it to her.

Luke and Walker made their way upstairs to rinse their own hard day's work away. Jack, though, just stared at her.

"What?" she asked, first tightening the halter of her dress and then fidgeting with the long braid that hung over a bare shoulder.

Jack shook his head as if waking himself from a daydream. "Sorry," he said. "You're just—I've never seen anyone so beautiful."

She covered her face with her hands, unable to take such a compliment without going completely crimson.

In seconds she felt his rough hands wrap around hers, pulling them free. She bit her bottom lip as his gaze bore into her, so full of heat and—and something she couldn't name.

Damn it, why was this man so hard to read?

"You made me dinner?" he asked, his voice deep and smooth.

She nodded.

"I thought I was supposed to take you out tonight." He scrubbed a hand across his deliciously stubbled jaw. "I distinctly remember Jenna saying, 'Walker and I are taking Owen to the rodeo so you can take that girl on a proper date. Now don't y'all go and mess it up.'"

She shrugged. "Surprise?"

He grinned. "Was this always the plan?"

She shook her head. "Not until today, actually. But you all worked so hard all week, and I know Jenna had some very specific instructions, but it's our last night here, and I kinda wanted to stay in. With you."

Jack's eyes searched the kitchen and the living room beyond. His Adam's apple bobbed as he swallowed. "I never thought of this place as somewhere to take a girl on a date..."

He trailed off, and Ava's blush changed from one born of flattery to one fueled by utter mortification.

"Shit," she said softly. "Shit. I wasn't thinking. Of course this is a terrible idea. I'll cover the lasagna and leave it for your brothers. I'm sure we can find someplace nice to go without a reservation—"

Jack cut her off with a kiss. Her eyes were still open, wide with the horror of her mistake, until the taste of him registered, until the scent of his sunbaked skin mixed with the musky earth he'd toiled in all day enveloped her, and she sank into this man who could flip off the switch of her worry so that all she could concentrate on was the kiss.

"I need to shower," he said, pulling away.

She nodded. Words weren't exactly possible at the moment.

"And then we are going to have our first date in this house because it's about damn time I make some new memories here. Besides, hell if I'm gonna let Luke and Walker get their hands on a home-cooked meal meant for me."

"There's enough for all of you—"

"Red?"

"Yeah?"

"I'm not sharing the lasagna *or* your company with anyone tonight. Okay?"

She let out a breath and smiled. "Yeah. Okay."

Chaos erupted as Owen and Scully came running from the guest bedroom where Owen had gotten himself dressed after his shower. Walker lumbered down the stairs in a red and white flannel shirt and jeans—just the right amount of California cowboy—followed by Luke in full rodeo gear, including the boots and the hat.

"No stitches tonight," Jack said to his daredevil brother, even though he knew it was a pointless request.

"No promises," Luke countered with a wry grin.

"And *you*..." Jack pointed at Walker. "You are on Shortstop detail. He comes home in one piece without needing to vomit from all the shit you're gonna feed him."

Jenna burst through the front door, and Jack relaxed a little.

"And you're on Walker detail...which means you're backup for Shortstop as well."

Jenna gave him a firm salute. "Sir! Yes sir!"

Jack rolled his eyes but then paused when he noticed a bruise on Jenna's wrist. "Don't tell me the chicks attacked again," he said with concern.

She laughed, but Jack could have sworn the reaction was forced.

"No chicks," she said. "Banged it on a doorknob. Never said I was graceful."

Jack held her chin in his hand, turning her head from left to right as he inspected.

"What in the hell are you doing?" she asked.

He dropped his hand, satisfied for the moment. "Seeing if you've had any other recent *accidents*."

She waved him off. "Who's the guardian here, huh? Me or you?"

"That isn't a clear response, Jenna."

"You didn't ask a question."

"Fine," he said, soft enough that the others—now congregating in the kitchen—couldn't hear. "Here's a question for you: Are you still seeing the egg man, and is he hitting you?" His jaw clenched, and his hand balled into a fist at the thought of anyone laying a hand on his aunt—or anyone he loved.

She scoffed, but he could see it. Something was off.

"We went on a few dates. It didn't work out. So *no*. I'm not seeing him anymore, and he's *not* hitting me."

"Jenna..."

"Jack..."

"Don't play games when it comes to this type of shit," he said. "Because if this guy is hitting you, and I find out who he is..."

"I took care of it," she snapped under her breath. "I have been looking after myself too long to be accused of not knowing how to do it."

Jack opened his mouth to ask her one more question, but the two were bombarded by the whole rodeo posse, ready to get on the road.

Ava bent down to give Owen a hug and kiss. "You have my cell phone number, right?"

Owen recited her number back to her.

"And I have it," Walker said.

"So do I," added Luke.

"Same here," Jenna said.

Ava let out a nervous laugh. "Okay, fine. So I worry when I send my son off to a rodeo that's almost two hours away."

"Ninety minutes," Luke said.

"Eighty if we go at least ten miles over the speed limit," Walker amended.

Jenna groaned. "Which we are *not* going to do since *I'm* driving."

Ava kissed Owen once more on the forehead and stood up. "Well, I guess that's it, then."

Owen looked at his mother, then at Jack. "Are you taking my mom on a date?"

Jack gave the boy a single nod. "With your approval, of course. You all right with it?"

Owen looked him up and down. Then he turned his gaze to Ava. "Are you all right with it?" he asked her.

"Yeah. But your opinion counts, too."

Owen shrugged. "I guess if my dad can't come back to be with us, Jack's pretty cool."

Everyone in the entryway went silent. Ava pressed her thumb to the corner of her eye, and Jack wondered if she was fighting back tears because he felt like he'd been socked in the gut.

But Ava smiled and tousled his hair. "Jack *is* pretty cool, bud. I'm glad you like him."

"So...we should head out," Jenna said, and Jack was grateful for the redirection.

"Okay," Ava said. "Just don't feed him too much junk or let him out of your sight, which I know you won't, but there...I said it. I'm a mom. I can't help it."

Luke pursed his lips. "Actually, I'm worried. Something isn't right."

Ava's eyes widened as Luke slipped out the door and

onto the porch. Seconds later he was back inside with a brown cowboy hat that he plopped on Owen's head.

"Yes!" Owen said, pumping his fist in the air.

Jack laughed, Owen's glee contagious.

"*Now* we're ready to go," Luke said.

"Good luck, Luke!" Ava said as they started to file out the door. "Or is that bad to say? Is it like theater where you have to say *break a leg*? Like, maybe it's *break a hoof*?"

Luke laughed. "Good luck works fine. Now you kids have a good time."

Jack and Ava stood at the window and watched Luke, Walker, Owen, and Jenna trail out and into Jenna's car. Once they were out of sight, he pulled Ava to him and kissed her sweetly on the forehead.

"Tomorrow for sure," he said. "I don't want to keep it from him any longer."

Ava pulled back to look him in the eye. "He's gonna be upset at first," she said. "And he'll want to know how much a part of his life you'll be after this week."

He nodded once, slowly. "What about you? What do *you* want?"

She pressed her lips into a smile and splayed her hand against his chest. "I *don't* want to be at the bottom of my priority list anymore. And I want someone in my life who won't put me there either."

He didn't know what to say. She was the one who was good with words. They'd once made him feel loved when he hadn't felt worthy. But her words had also pushed him away at the one time in his life when something had made him happy. When some*one* made him happy.

Was she saying he could do that for her? She wasn't telling him to go this time, but she also hadn't asked him to stay.

Why wasn't she asking him to stay? And if she did, would he? She hadn't given him a choice before, and maybe that's what this all was—him finally getting to choose. Still, he wanted to know what she wanted, because if she *wanted* him, did New York really hold a candle?

Her brows furrowed.

"What's wrong?" he asked.

She shook her head. "This isn't supposed to be how our first date begins. It's a little heavy-handed, don't you think?"

The corner of his mouth twitched into a hint of a grin. She was changing the subject. And if he wasn't in such dire need of a shower, he'd thank her properly, right here in the entryway.

"How does it go, then?"

She grabbed one of his hands, his calloused palm sandwiched between hers. "Tonight we forget all this complicated grown-up stuff. Instead of me forcing that crease to appear between your eyebrows, let me take care of *you* instead of you worrying about everyone else."

He took a deep breath and let it out. "And who takes care of you?"

She kissed his palm. "Oh, I think if I play my cards right, you'll take care of me just fine."

He backed toward the foot of the stairs, their hands still connecting them. "I'm going to take the fastest shower known to man. Then I'm going to eat that amazing dinner you made. And then?" He dipped his head to give her one soft kiss. "I sure as shit am gonna take care of you right back."

Her mouth fell open, and something akin to a squeak sounded from her throat. He took that as a good sign as he let his eyes take one last look at the beautiful woman before him, before he spun and strode up the stairs.

Ask me to stay, he thought. Because he could be a lawyer anywhere. It wasn't about the partnership. Or money. He realized that now. What mattered most was that she still believed in him like she had all those years ago.

Show me that you're not afraid, that you believe I'll do right by you and our son.

But other than working his ass off on this vineyard and giving Owen some pitching lessons, what the hell else had he done to prove he was up to the task—or to prove to himself that the apple fell far enough from the tree?

Not a damn thing.

Tonight, at least, he could tell her all the things he should have said ten years ago, all the words that were still stuck in his throat today.

And even if he did leave, she'd know why he never could have married anyone else, that it had always, *always* been her.

CHAPTER TWENTY

Ava poured the two final glasses of the Ellis Vineyard zinfandel she'd smuggled from home and met Jack out on the back deck. He stood at the far end, his back to her, gazing out into the distance where the vineyard lay.

"You guys did it," she said. "You and your brothers. Twelve months from now, you'll have a viable crop," she added. He turned to face her and took the glass of wine from her outstretched hand. "You'll get a good return after all that hard work. If you decide to become Crossroads Ranch and Vineyard."

He took a sip of wine and tugged at the belt tied around the waist of her dress. "I thought we were forgetting everything for the night."

"Mmm-hmm," she replied, and he raised his brows, most likely at the hint of accusation in her tone. "Were *you* forgetting everything while staring out toward the vineyard?"

He gave her a crooked grin. "Not even allowed a little silent contemplation, huh?"

She raised her glass to her own lips, letting the warmth of the vintage spread through and embolden her.

She set the glass on the ledge of the deck rail and reached

behind her neck where her halter dress was tied in a bow—
and *un*tied it.

"Depends on what you're contemplating."

The top of her dress fell open, revealing her bare
breasts, her nipples hard merely at the anticipation of his
reaction.

"Christ," he hissed.

She stepped closer and took his free hand in hers, bringing his palm to rest over one of her firm peaks.

"What?" she asked, feigning innocence. "Remember. No
neighbors—unless you count the cows, and I don't think
they care."

He downed the rest of his wine and set his glass next
to hers. Then he pinched her softly between his thumb and
forefinger, and she gasped.

"I guess I'm still reconciling the girl I knew with the
woman you are now."

He took her into his mouth, and she arched her back as
he licked and kissed up her bare flesh until he was nipping
at her neck, her earlobe.

"Same," she said, though she was nearly breathless. She
wasn't even sure how she was still standing because surely
she'd just dissolved into a puddle.

His teeth relinquished her earlobe so he could speak.
"Does this new Ava," he started, his voice so low and
sexy she thought he might simply *talk* her into orgasm,
"still like to make love under the stars?" He kissed her
neck again, then lifted his head. "It's still your call," he
reminded her.

She tipped her head back and glanced at the glorious
night sky sprinkled with tiny, flickering diamonds. She'd
been with Jack before—even slept with him beneath the
night sky. But they had been eighteen. Kids. She'd never

done anything like this in her adult life before, but she'd also never wanted a man like she wanted Jack, so she found herself answering, "Yes."

He lifted her in his arms, and she crossed her legs over his ass—that perfect ass she'd stared at more than once as he'd pruned the vines and tilled the cover crop. For a man who'd spent the past several years in an office behind a desk, he was a natural in the outdoors, strong and capable.

He deposited her onto a pillowed lawn chair, and she couldn't help but writhe in anticipation.

He untied the belt at her waist, then quickly found the zipper that ran down the side of her dress. In seconds the garment was gone, and he hummed with what sounded like satisfaction to see her laid out beneath him in nothing but her white lace panties.

He sat on the side of the chair, silent as he ran a hand from her cheek, down her neck, over her breast, and onto her stomach, where he traced soft circles around her belly button—and then along the faded scar that signified Owen's entrance into their lives.

She wasn't self-conscious. She wanted him to explore every inch of her, and that's exactly what he was doing in his perfect, silent reverence that she felt not only with his touch but with that intense gaze—the one thing about him that hadn't changed.

As he pulled her panties down, each of his hands explored her hips, her thighs, his thumbs rubbing over her sensitive skin.

Goose bumps covered her flesh, but they had nothing to do with the chill of the night air. Every sensation was Jack. All Jack.

Once they reached her ankles, her panties were no more.

His hands skimmed their way back up her legs, stopping only when his thumbs were close enough to tease another sensation from her—one of pure, primal need.

One thumb explored her crease, and he hissed in a breath when he felt how wet she was.

Ava whimpered and squirmed. "Please," she said. "Jack, please."

That same thumb found her swollen center and pressed softly against her.

Words wouldn't come. She could only gasp and hope he understood that what she meant was *More. God. Please. More.*

He slid a finger inside her, then another, and she was sure she was seconds away from coming completely undone. He moved so slowly, with such control, holding her at the edge without letting her teeter over.

He leaned down to kiss her, his lips as gentle and careful as his movements inside her. They'd been virtual strangers for ten years, yet the way he touched her, kissed her, even looked at her—it was as if he knew her better than anyone else.

He was her first love, the father of her child, and the incredible man she'd always known he'd become. And she was falling harder for the man than she'd ever thought possible.

Could he see that, too?

She wanted him, not only like this but with her whole heart.

He pulled back, and she opened her eyes to find him gazing at her, transfixed.

She reached for his face, her thumb stroking the stubble he hadn't shaved, as if he knew how sexy he looked like this.

"You're staring," she said, then gasped as his thumb swirled around her clit.

"You're beautiful," he said matter-of-factly. "So damn beautiful. And *I* get to touch you like this. I get to kiss those perfect pink lips." Then he did. "And I get to look at you bathed in moonlight and stars."

He slid his fingers out, achingly slow as heat coiled in her belly. Then, filling her with the same sweet agony, they sank back inside, pulsing, reaching just the right place until she feared she wouldn't be able to hold out much longer.

She cried out, dropping her hand from his cheek and grabbing the wooden frame of the chair above her head.

"Oh my God!" She bucked against his palm. "You can't"—she gasped for breath—"be all strong and silent"—another gasp—"and then say things like that." She grabbed his wrist to hold his hand still so she could talk. "'Bathed in moonlight and stars'? That's like freaking poetry."

He grinned and tried to peel her fingers from his wrist, but she shook her head. "You make it sound like it's some privilege to touch me."

He tilted his head to the side, his eyes intent on her form again. "Isn't it?" he asked.

She didn't know what to say to that. Because she wanted to read into it and at the same time was afraid it meant nothing more than how he felt right now. In the moment.

"I was supposed to take care of *you* tonight," she said finally.

He shrugged and dipped his head toward the obvious bulge in his jeans. "I think it's safe to say I'm enjoying what I'm doing right now."

His fingers pumped inside her, and she gave his wrist an admonishing squeeze even as she writhed.

"My call. You—you said whatever happened between us here was my call, right?"

"Yep," he said and slowed his movement.

She tugged at his wrist, forcing his hand from her, as much as she hated to do it. "I want to see *you* bathed in moonlight," she told him. "I want to kiss and explore every inch of you, too."

He didn't protest. So she sat up and unbuttoned his flannel shirt, her fingers skimming his shoulders as she pushed it over his arms. She kissed his neck and the dusting of hair on his chest.

"Stand up," she ordered, though her tone was more playful than authoritative.

He obliged, and she got to work unbuttoning his jeans. They'd both been barefoot, so he kicked them off easily. Then she took her time lowering his boxer briefs as he had with her panties, relishing the feel of his skin beneath her own. Her finger ran along the scar on his shin where the bone had been broken and repaired with surgery. They'd been too frenzied that day in the bathroom, when he'd pulled her into the shower, for her to see it. She'd known the scar was there, but time had let her forget. It was only visible on close inspection. And now they were as close as two people could get with the whole night laid before them to explore.

An unexpected tear leaked from the corner of her eye as she imagined the boy he was, what he'd gone through, and why she always knew he'd have to leave.

Then there they were, the two of them bare beneath the moon and stars. Her breath caught in her throat as she stood to meet his gaze. "*You're* beautiful," she said, her voice breaking on that last word.

He pulled her to him, his erection firm against her, and

she buried her face in his chest. "Is this the part where I ask you what's wrong?" He kissed the top of her head, and she could feel him inhale against her hair.

She tilted her head up, not trying to hide the other tears that had sprung free. "You lost so much before I'd even met you," she said. "I need you to understand that I kept Owen from you *not* because I saw you as unfit or unworthy but because I loved you too much to make you stay."

It was the same reason why she thought she couldn't ask him to stay now. He had to want it. He had to want her *and* Owen.

"And when I went to L.A.—I got scared. You had built this life for yourself with someone else. I thought I'd just be taking away what you'd left to find in the first place."

He swiped at her tears with his thumbs, then cradled her face in his palms. "I didn't go through with it," he said.

She nodded.

"It wasn't right between me and her. I could never put my finger on it. She wanted exactly what I wanted—no family—just work. We got along great—"

Ava cleared her throat. "Umm, I know I broke the rules and brought up the past, but I'm not sure I'm *past* the past enough to hear about how great you got along with your ex-fiancée."

And how much you don't want a family.

He laughed softly. "You didn't let me finish. I couldn't put my finger on what was missing *then*." He let out a breath. "Or at least, I wouldn't admit it to myself."

"Jack, you don't have to . . ." Her heart raced.

"I know," he said softly, then kissed her. "But I want to." He kissed her again, soft, sweet nibbles against her lips, teasing not only her body, but her heart. "She wasn't *you*."

She sucked in a sharp breath, then cupped his face in her

palms. "I messed up twice," she admitted. "I should have given you a choice."

"And I should have fought harder for you when you pushed me away. But—" He shook his head. "Shit."

"You didn't have any fight left," she said, finishing his thought. "And I shouldn't have let you leave thinking I was afraid of you. That couldn't have been any further from the truth."

He ran has hands through her hair and down her back. "Okay, Red. Your call."

"Fight for me now," she said, then kissed him. "You can start by making love to me."

In a couple of quick movements, he'd pulled the long pillows from two of the chairs and laid them side-by-side on the floor of the deck. He lowered her down to the makeshift bed, kissing her neck and shoulders as he covered her body with his own.

Then his hand fumbled on the ground toward his jeans.

"We don't need—" she blurted. "I mean, I've been on the pill for a couple of years. I understand, though, if you're worried about . . . you know . . . what happened before."

Not like it mattered. He'd worn a condom when Owen was conceived.

He stopped reaching and stilled above her. "I'm not worried." He said the words with such certainty. "As long as you're sure this is what you want."

She nodded and let her legs part, a silent invitation as she marveled at his long, thick length.

He nudged her slick opening, and she sucked in a breath. Then he sank inside her to the hilt, filling her so completely that she cried out with total and utter abandon. A growl tore from his throat as he slid out and in again, harder and deeper than she'd thought he could go.

Ava hooked her legs around him and arched into his chest. She wanted him closer. She *needed* there to be no more distance. But only Jack could bridge that gap by letting her in.

"I loved you too," he said, echoing her words, and her eyes opened to find him staring intently once again. "But I also hurt you without even knowing I had."

She tried to swallow past the lump in her throat.

"If I could take back what I said to you while you stood there with Owen growing inside you—if I could erase what it must have felt like for you to hear me say I never wanted to be a father—I would."

The muscle in his jaw pulsed, and she leaned up to kiss him.

"You're not your father. No matter what similarities you think you share, you're not *him*."

His movement inside her was slow, controlled. Just like his words. Like everything he seemed to do. But he was opening up to her now more than he ever had, and as much as she ached with what felt like an insatiable need, she didn't want him to stop talking. Not when they were so close to—*something*.

He kissed her softly, rocking into her.

"More," she whispered.

He slid out and back into her with such aching tenderness. How had she been without this for the past decade? How was it possible to want anyone else like she wanted him?

She skimmed her fingers through his already disheveled blond waves. He wanted her, too. She knew he did. Maybe they were done walking the tightrope, done fearing that any second they could lose their delicate balance and fall hard to the unforgiving ground of New York versus California, of will he or won't he be a real presence in Owen's life—or even hers. Maybe she didn't need to protect her heart from Jack Everett. Maybe the pie-in-the-sky fairy tale of school, a career, and her, Jack, and Owen being a family could actually come true.

He kissed her, soft and achingly sweet. "When I left here, I didn't just run from my past. I ran from the best part of my life. *You.*" He cupped her cheek as a tear slid toward his palm. "And Owen, too."

Well, damn it if her vision wasn't completely blurred with tears now. She opened her mouth to respond, but he silenced her with a kiss as he thrust inside her, rocking her to her core. Maybe it was better like this. She wouldn't have to ask him what that meant. Because he could say all that and stay—or he could say it and still leave. Right now, though, as they both teetered on that brink together, she wouldn't be able to form a coherent word even if she tried. But every time she arched against him, she thought the words she wanted to say.

Choose us.

Stay.

I love you.

He'd let this week be her call. She had to let the rest of his life be his. She'd made it clear she wanted him to fight for her. He'd have to decide what that meant because it wasn't her right to ask him to give up something as huge as his career.

At that moment he slid his hand between them, rubbing her wet, swollen center, and even when she called out his name, eyes closed in heartbreaking ecstasy, she still saw stars.

He followed her with his own release, a primal sound tearing from his chest that spoke nothing of the quiet control he wore like a mask for everyone else.

For *her* he had let go.

He collapsed beside her. Still in her. His forehead resting against hers.

She stroked her fingers through his hair. The strands at the nape of his neck were damp with sweat. His eyes were closed, but a soft smile rested on his face. As if he knew she was wondering whether or not he'd fallen asleep, he flexed inside her, and she gasped.

"Sorry," he said, one eye blinking open.

"You are *not*." She retaliated by clenching around his still-solid shaft.

He swore through his teeth, then kissed her hungrily.

"I can't seem to get enough of you," he said.

She knew they'd have to disconnect from one another eventually, but she couldn't bring herself to initiate. Not yet. Instead she hooked her leg over his as he traced lazy circles on her shoulder.

"It might take me some time to explore each and every one of these freckles. Are you sure you and Owen have to go home tomorrow?"

Her heart sank. Their five days were up. But he'd said she was the best part of his life. Owen too. Maybe not wanting them to leave meant he was ready to stay.

"Tomorrow," she said with a nervous smile. "You looking forward to the game?"

He grinned and kissed tenderly along the line of her jaw. "Watching Owen play ball? Hell yes. You know...Jenna and Luke seem to have taken a liking to him as well. I even think Walker tolerates him."

She laughed. "Invite them. Please. It would mean the world to him if you were all there, but after the game..."

"After the game—" He paused and stroked her cheek, then tucked a fallen strand of hair behind her ear.

She shivered.

"You're cold," he said.

"No. I mean yes, but—" There *was* a chill in the night air, and she *was* completely naked. But it was also the anticipation of what tomorrow meant.

He did the unthinkable and slid out of her. She gasped, her sensitive nerves still reacting to him.

"We should probably clean up, put some clothes on. The rodeo doesn't go all night." He kissed her forehead. "There's a towel on the bench if you need it and a sweatshirt of mine on the chair in the office, the room right next to yours. You're welcome to it if you want."

Jack Everett—ever the planner. She chuckled.

"Have you worn this sweatshirt you speak of recently?"

"As a matter of fact, I have."

"So it smells like you?"

He laughed. "I suppose it does."

"Sold. I'm gonna go freshen up and change. We'll put a plan in order for after the game. Then, if it's all right with you, I'm gonna grab those amazing paint supplies you bought and paint that sky."

She felt so light, buoyant. Something had surely shifted between them.

He rolled onto his back, resting his head on his hands. Good *God,* the man was a specimen. Simply looking at him made her want to do what they just did all over again. But he was right. Owen, his brothers, and Jenna would be home soon enough. There'd be another chance for round two. She hoped.

"You know, I never really noticed this sky you speak of before tonight. It's not too bad."

He grinned. He obviously knew she was watching. How could she not? He was beautiful.

* * *

She'd cleaned up and thrown on a tank and yoga pants, then padded into the office for Jack's sweatshirt. It was right where he'd said it would be, hanging over the chair. She held it up for inspection. It was a navy hoodie with UCLA embroidered in yellow and LAW in white.

She brought it to her nose, breathed in—breathed *Jack* in—and smiled. He was *never* getting this sweatshirt back. Tugging it over her head was like having his body wrapped around hers all over again.

She glanced down at the desk, which was maybe a little nosy. He'd been doing double duty all week—working in the vineyard and then catching up on legal work whenever he found spare time. This was his private space.

She should have grabbed the sweatshirt and walked away, but on the top of a pile of folders was one that bore a sticky note that simply read: VINEYARD: OFFER OF SALE.

No more secrets, she'd told him when he'd said he wanted to tell Owen the truth. And he had nodded. He was a man of few words. A nod from Jack Everett was worth a hundred yesses from anyone else.

But here was his final secret. Jack was selling the vineyard.

She'd seen him out there, though. Working with his brothers. He'd enjoyed himself—enjoyed *them.* Hell, he'd gone and told her that she and Owen were the best parts of his life, but now she felt like a loose end. One that would be tied up along with the contract to the vineyard.

Damn him for letting her hope. She'd been all ready to create her own new beginning before he'd forced her straight off the road—and what she thought was her new path in life. Now she was right where she'd been ten years ago—head over heels for a guy about to leave her.

When she made it back to the deck with her easel and supplies, he was already out there, reclining on the chair where he'd almost driven her to orgasm with his hands. Except now Scully was next to him, sitting with his tongue hanging out of his mouth and his tail wagging as Jack scratched behind his ears. He smiled when he saw her, and she forced herself to do the same as she set up and prepared to paint.

"So you know how I applied to Cal Poly?" she asked with forced nonchalance.

"Yeah..." he said, drawing out the word.

She opened and squeezed tubes of paint onto the small pallet, dipping her brush into the inky black. "Well, I'm still missing one small part of my application."

"What part?"

She forced a laugh. "A piece of art. *Meaningful* art. There's an essay component and everything to prove the piece's depth. It's not like I haven't painted anything, but it's been silly stuff like a bowl of fruit...or Scully catching a Frisbee. Nothing worthy of an essay." Oh, she could write plenty now about that portrait of a boy playing catch with his dad, but it might break her in two now that she was sure he was leaving.

He swallowed. "And classes start in August, right?"

"*If* I bring them a piece next week and they approve my application, I start my art degree in the fall session, right in San Luis Obispo like I was supposed to ten years ago."

He sat silent, still petting the dog, for several long beats. Perhaps he was crafting the perfect response. Maybe a way to tell her that he was selling the place they'd all worked so hard to restore. A way to let her down easy after she'd sworn she wouldn't let his short return distract her from what was important—a real future for her and Owen, whether Jack was part of it or not. And knowing that he was getting rid of the vineyard? She was almost positive that meant *not*.

Finally, his eyes met hers.

"I think that's great," he said. "You put your life on hold, not that it wasn't for a good reason, but I'm happy you're doing something for yourself now."

She dropped the paintbrush onto the easel's tray and crossed her arms.

"Are you selling the vineyard?"

His expression barely even changed. There was a hint of shock as his eyes widened a bit, but just as quickly he composed himself. Mr. Control.

"Maybe," he said simply.

"Maybe?" She dropped her hands to her sides, balling them into fists. "I told myself I wasn't going to fall for you because I knew we were moving in different directions. But being here with you—with Owen and you together—made me think we were moving toward something real. What was this whole week? If the big thing that was holding you back was this deep-seeded fear of what kind of father you'd be, how have you not realized by now what I've always known—that you are a *good* man, Jack Everett? And good men make good fathers. But I'm part of that equation, too. It's more than Owen who deserves honesty. I do, too."

He swung his feet off the chair and planted them on the ground. Then he ran a hand through hair that still looked freshly fucked. Except now *she* felt fucked in a whole different way.

"I'm not keeping anything from you, Ava. But I didn't think there was a point in telling you until I'd made a decision. It's not like we're—"

Her eyes widened.

"Shit," he said. "*Shit.* I didn't mean it like that. I've spent the past ten years living on no one else's terms but my own. This?" He stood and motioned between them. "My decisions affecting someone else? That's brand-fucking-new."

She huffed out a breath. "I know. But...but how can we do what we just did? How can you say what you said about us being the best parts of your life while you're planning on selling off one of the biggest reasons for you to stay?" She was pushing him now. Damn it. She'd sworn she wouldn't. But she'd messed up with him more than once by saying nothing. This time she had to lay it all out on the table.

"What happened to you giving me the choice I didn't have a decade ago?"

He didn't mean it like that. She knew he didn't, but the words still stung. She *hadn't* given him a choice before, and now she was pushing him to make the one *she* wanted. Well, she guessed there was no going back now.

"What would happen if I asked you to stay and build a life with us here?" she asked.

"What would happen if I asked you and Owen to come to New York with me?"

Her mouth opened and then closed.

"You don't want to give up your life," he said. "And I wouldn't ask you to."

She threw her hands in the air. "But *my* life makes me happy, Jack. I have Owen, the vineyard. I'm going back to school. I have everything I want—except *you*."

He stepped toward her, and she took a step back. If he kissed her, she'd let her physical need take over, and she needed a clear head now.

"Ava—you and Owen make me happy. I *want* to be the dad he deserves, and maybe if we all start fresh..."

His voice was so gentle, so earnest, that it broke her heart even though he hadn't left yet.

"My life is here. Tell me that New York is going to make you happier than what I've seen these past two weeks with you and your brothers."

He scrubbed a hand across his jaw. "I've been thinking a lot about happiness this week—and how you and Owen have shown me that maybe it is a possibility for me. But every time I think of giving up this partnership, I think about how selfish that decision would be. New York means that Luke and Walker won't go bankrupt if the ranch falls out of the black. New York means that you and Owen will never want for anything."

She groaned, her hands fisted at her sides. "Owen doesn't need money. He needs a father. And I need someone who's going to put us first and not take the easy way out. If New York is truly what you *want*, then go. But if it's another escape—"

"You say I'm not my father," he interrupted, "but how do you know that I'm good enough for him *or* you? Everything your father is afraid of could be true. *I* didn't know I was capable of what I did to Derek until I did it. And when I saw a bruise tonight on Jenna's wrist?" His chest was heaving. "She swore to me that whatever was going on with that damn egg guy was over, but hell, Ava. If you knew the scenario that played out in my head when I thought about someone laying a hand on her…Maybe I'm protecting you like your father is."

Her breath hitched and she started to form the words, but was interrupted by the unmistakable sound of tires rolling over gravel in the front of the house, followed by the loud hoots and hollers coming from Jenna's apparently open windows.

Scully sprang to his feet and started running in circles in front of the sliding door.

Jack held her gaze for a few seconds more, but she didn't know what else to say.

"What does it matter if I believe in you if you don't believe in yourself?" She shook her head. "You keep choosing the past," she said. "And I'm standing right here offering to be your future." She stroked his cheek. "Owen only has a few months left of school. We'll plan a trip to New York this summer so you can see him. I'll make a long-distance relationship between you and him work, but I'm not up for it in terms of us." She'd end this before her heart broke again because it was the only chance at reclaiming her life.

He wrapped his hand around her wrist, and she felt his jaw pulse beneath her palm. But he said nothing.

She forced a smile. "Maybe you should go make sure Luke survived the night without a trip to the ER."

Then she pulled free of his hold, opened the door, and followed the dog inside.

CHAPTER TWENTY-ONE

The whole lot of them—well, everyone but Jenna, who'd gone home last night—sat around the kitchen table eating breakfast as Owen recounted his night at the rodeo.

"Jack, did you know that Luke can ride a horse while he hangs upside down on its side? And that he can stand on two horses at once... while they're *moving*?" Owen shoved a spoonful of Cheerios into his mouth.

"It's called Roman riding, Shortstop, and your buddy Jack has actually *never* seen me do it."

Ava's eyes darted to Jack's, but he had already hidden his expression behind a coffee mug as he took a slow sip.

"Never?" Owen said. "But, like, he won two hundred dollars last night. That's how good he is!"

Luke shrugged. "But not the belt." He winked at Owen. "I'm good, but I wanna be the best."

Jack set his mug down and looked from Luke to Walker. He hadn't just missed the first nine years of Owen's life. He'd missed much of his brothers' lives, too. Now he was traveling across the country to miss the rest of it, and it all felt—wrong.

What *if* he stayed? He could practice law here as well as he could there. Would Luke and Walker really want that after all that he'd missed? Could Ava forgive him for letting logic make his choices when he should maybe start listening to his goddamn heart?

"Jack!" Owen said after swallowing his food. "You *have* to come next time. And Mom, too. You could do a date at the rodeo, right?"

Ava was the one to look away this time. He hated this tension between them, especially after last night. Damn it, *nothing* had ever shaken him to his core—utterly changing how he looked at his life, his future, the possibilities—like the way he felt when he was inside her.

He should have told her about selling the vineyard. But she terrified him. Because up until last night he'd convinced himself that what was brewing between them was nothing more than residual chemistry from when they were eighteen. That he could live without it like he had for the past ten years. But Ava wasn't the girl he remembered. She was a strong woman now, someone who'd put her own future on hold to raise an amazing kid. She was beautiful, and sexy, and full of so much passion that she couldn't keep it bottled up if she tried. It made him wonder if what he'd been doing since he left had really been living at all.

"So are we gonna watch some baseball or what?" Walker asked, pushing his chair from the table.

He had been sober last night when they'd returned home from the rodeo, Walker carrying a sleeping Owen in his arms. And this morning proved the same. Ava and Owen's presence seemed to be affecting all of them for the better. So why couldn't he pull the goddamn trigger and decide to stay?

"Are *all* of you really coming?" Owen asked. "That's so awesome," he said, not waiting for an answer. "Walker, can you show my friends the pictures you took of Luke on your phone? I'm gonna learn how to trick ride someday. You'll teach me, right?"

His eyes shifted from Walker to Luke. Ava coughed on her sip of coffee, and Jack just watched everything play out before him.

"I'll teach you whatever you want to know, Shortstop," Luke said.

"If you ever take a breath and stop *talking*," Walker added, but he winked at the kid.

Was this what it would be like if he gave up a future in New York for a life he hadn't realized he'd ever want? Family breakfasts, Walker sober, and Luke teaching his son how to ride?

Every puzzle piece fit—except for Ava's trust in him not having any more secrets—and his trust in himself that he and his father shared nothing more than a name.

Ava, silent through it all, finally looked at her phone and spoke. "We should go," she said. "I need to drop Scully at home before we head to the field. We'll meet you all there."

At the sound of his name, Scully sprang up and started spinning in circles, and whatever invisible thread had held them all together in that makeshift family moment snapped.

Everyone was up and moving. Jack piled cereal bowls and coffee mugs into the sink, knowing he'd be the one to take care of them later. Because that's what he did. He took care of things so others wouldn't have to.

He'd sent money to his brothers when he'd finally started earning more than he needed to live on. He'd only allowed himself the barest of necessities. He didn't need any more, and he certainly never let himself want. That was his penance for leaving.

Because he'd *wanted* to leave. That was his one luxury. Ava was right. He'd escaped the life that had tried to break him, taking care of his brothers from a distance instead. It was the only way he knew how to show them what they meant to him without having to be in a place where he'd lost all of his good memories.

But look at what they'd done in only a couple of weeks. They'd created new ones, and with one tiny omission about the vineyard, he'd possibly destroyed that.

They deserved more. Ava and Owen deserved more.

The screen door banged shut a few times as people—and a dog—exited. An engine revved in the driveway, and he guessed it was Luke starting up the truck. But Jack remained in the kitchen—separate, where he was safe. He might have been ten years older, but it seemed not much had changed. Even after a couple of weeks in this house, he still couldn't let the past go.

"You coming?"

He turned from the sink to see Ava lingering in the hallway leading to the front door.

"Yeah. Why would you—?" *Damn.* "Did you think after how we ended things last night that I was just going to cut my losses? I messed up by not telling you about the vineyard, but I'm in over my head here. I don't know how to be the guy you think you see in me, Ava. I've spent ten years convincing myself that everyone was better off if I kept them at arm's length. I don't know how to see myself any other way."

She shrugged. "And I don't know how to want anything less than the world for Owen." She forced a smile. "And for myself."

He watched as a single tear slid down her cheek. Then he remembered Walker begging Jack to hit him. As much as Ava and Owen seemed to bring out the best in everyone around them, his presence had upset the balance of so many lives. The thought of hurting his son, though? It tore at something deep inside him, making it hard to breathe.

"You don't want to tell him," Jack said. It wasn't a question.

She shook her head. "That's no longer the issue. You *are* his father. You have as much right to his life as I do. I'm just asking you to be sure about one thing—that no matter where you are, you'll be an active presence in his life and not simply a signature on a check." She let out a shaky breath. "I have no right to put this kind of pressure on you when I'm the one who created this situation, but he has fantasized about you his whole life."

"And you don't think I'll live up to the fantasy," he interrupted.

She worried her bottom lip between her teeth before she spoke. "Actually," she said, "you'll probably surpass it, which will make it that much harder when you leave."

She blew out a breath and plastered on a smile. The mask she wore for her son. How often did she have to do that? And how much of that was because of him?

"Time to go. Don't want to be late for warm-ups with the team. I'll see you and your brothers there. Is Jenna coming?"

"She texted," Jack said. "She said she had something to take care of but that she'd be there before the game ended." He stuck his hands in the front pockets of his jeans. "I never wanted to hurt you," he said. "Not then. And not now."

"I know," she said. "We kind of messed it up together, though. Didn't we?"

He strode toward her, stopping when he was close enough to hear her breathe. He skimmed his fingers through her hair, and she squeezed her eyes shut, forcing another tear to fall.

He kissed her wet lashes. Then his lips found hers, and she melted into his touch. Were ten years too much to repair when having her this close made everything else fade away?

"Why is *this* so easy for us?" she asked when they paused to catch their breath. "But everything else is so hard?"

He kissed her forehead and then pulled her close, and she buried her face in his chest.

"Because I have a messed-up past that won't seem to let go," he said softly. "And there's no way in hell I'm letting that get in the way of your future."

She pulled back and cupped his face in her palms. "*You* can let go, Jack. You are stronger than anything he ever did to you."

She didn't let him respond. She simply kissed him as if it was the last time she ever would. And he let her. Her fingers tangled in his hair as she parted her lips and invited him inside. He savored the taste of her, her scent, the feel of her skin against his. He held her tight, afraid to let go because this couldn't be it. It couldn't be good-bye.

She pulled away first, and his gaze never faltered as he watched her walk down the hallway and then out the door. He turned to grab his Dodgers cap from the counter and noticed her easel still standing outside on the deck.

He ran to the door to catch her, but she, Owen, and Scully were already pulling out of the driveway and onto the main road.

"What's the holdup, asshole?" Walker called out from where he stood, his back leaning against Jack's truck.

"I'll be right there," he said. And he jogged back toward the sliding glass door to grab Ava's canvas from the deck.

He stopped short once he was out there, eyes transfixed

on what he'd thought would be the unfinished painting she'd abandoned during their argument last night. But she must have come back outside after getting Owen to bed because what stood before him was a replica of the sky under which they'd made love last night. This painting would get her into Cal Poly in a heartbeat. But she'd have taken it if that's what she wanted.

Ava had shown him beauty in a place where he'd only ever found pain.

But that wasn't the whole truth. Was it?

Yes. His last years in Oak Bluff had wiped out any good memories of the place. But there *had* been good here at one point. The realization of it had crept up when he wasn't looking, whether it was Jenna recounting his parents' courtship or the revelation of what they'd built together, not just in that damned spare room but in the ranch as a whole.

Then there were these past two weeks working on the vineyard with his brothers and the only woman who'd ever been able to break through his carefully constructed walls. He'd made new memories in a place he'd thought it impossible to do so.

He'd always thought his past would be trampled to dust the day Jack Senior was laid to rest. But Ava was right. His father was gone, but he was still hanging on to the pain. *He* needed to be the one to let go.

"How?" he asked aloud. "Someone tell me how, and I'll do it."

But no one was there to answer. So he grabbed the painting and brought it inside. But he didn't bring it to his truck.

Convincing himself she'd left it on purpose, he decided to keep it—his best new memory, and the hope that it wasn't his last. New York might be on the other side of the country, but he wouldn't stay away like he had before. He didn't need to anymore.

"So, Red's parents seem nice," Luke said sarcastically as they approached the Ellis clan sitting on the bleachers behind first base. "You piss in their rosebushes or something?"

Jack rolled his eyes. "More like I got their daughter pregnant and then disappeared for ten years."

"Shit," Walker said. "'Not like that's on you. You didn't have a fucking clue."

Jack shrugged. "I'd rather they take issue with me than make Ava's life hell." He side-eyed both his brothers. "Just—don't be a dick," he said before they were close enough for anyone to hear.

"Which one of us?" Luke asked.

But they were within spitting distance of Ava and her parents now, which meant he couldn't give Luke a proper, brotherly response.

"Mr. and Mrs. Ellis," he said in a professional tone. "I'm not sure you ever met my brothers, Luke and Walker."

Luke extended a hand to shake, but Walker simply crossed his arms.

"It's nice to meet you," Mrs. Ellis said with a genuine smile. Mr. Ellis did *not* reciprocate the gesture.

"Luke is pretty big in the local rodeo circuit," Ava said. "And Owen got to have his first rodeo experience last night."

Mr. Ellis narrowed his eyes at his daughter. "You brought my grandson to a rodeo?"

Luke cleared his throat. "Actually, sir, we took Owen on our own so your daughter and Jack could have a night to themselves."

Christ. Smacking his brother on the back of the head

would only fuel the fire. He opened his mouth to play defense, but Ava beat him to the punch.

"Jack worked all day and well into the early evening in the vineyard," she said. "I wanted to give him a home-cooked meal as a thank-you."

Walker scoffed. "Yeah, while we had to eat nachos and hot pretzels."

Mrs. Ellis laughed, but Ava's father didn't even crack a smile.

"Rumor has it you got a pretty nice offer on that broke-down vineyard of yours," he said.

"You told him?" Jack asked Ava, but she shook her head, her eyes wide.

"Dad," she said, her voice shaky, "do you have something to do with that offer?"

He didn't have a chance to respond as Owen ran off the pitcher's mound where he'd been warming up.

"Grandma, Grandpa, did you guys see that curveball? Jack taught me that. Did you know he was a pitcher?" He squinted past them toward the parking lot. "Hey, isn't that Jenna? It's so cool you all came to my game."

Jack turned to see Jenna standing on the curb next to the driver's side of a car stopped on the wrong side of the street, idling behind a stop sign. He didn't recognize the vehicle or the driver. He was about to turn away and give her privacy, realizing it was probably a man she'd spent the night with. But then he saw the guy grab her wrist . . . and Jenna try unsuccessfully to pull away.

"Shit," he said. She hadn't ended it, and the piece of shit had laid his hands on her again.

Jack ran across the short expanse of grass to the idling vehicle, ripping the guy's hand from Jenna's arm before even saying a word.

Jenna gasped and turned to face him, and Jack fucking lost it when he saw the fresh, purpling bruise on her cheek.

He pushed Jenna out of the way and yanked the car door open, tearing the asshole from his seat. He dragged him around the front of the car, slamming him down on the hood before raising his fist to the man who'd raised his own to Jenna.

"Jack! Don't!"

Ava's voice cut straight through to him. He had one hand around the guy's throat and the other pulled back into a fist poised to beat him bloody. But he turned toward her voice to see all of them crowded in front of the car—Jenna, Luke, and Walker. Then Ava with Owen at her side, the boy staring at him in horror, exactly like his mother had ten years ago.

Ava's parents seemed to appear out of nowhere, her father bellowing as he stepped in front of his daughter and grandson, as if to shield them from what he was about to do. "This!" he cried. "This is why you'll never be good enough for my daughter and why you'll never be the father that boy deserves. You're just like your old man. And I'll be damned if I let you do to Ava and Owen what you did to Derek Wilkes...and what your father did to you."

Jack looked at his fist raised in the air, then at the man beneath his outstretched hand whose lips were turning blue. He let go and stumbled back. "Somebody call the cops," he said, barely recognizing his own voice.

"I'm on it," Luke said, pulling his phone from his pocket.

Only then did it register what Ava's father had done.

He turned toward the gathered crowd and saw Ava with her hand cupped over her mouth and Owen's disbelieving stare volleying from her to him.

"You're—my dad?" Owen asked, the hurt in his eyes more devastating than anything Jack could have imagined.

"He didn't know," Ava said, taking a step toward her son, but Owen only backed away.

Jack's eyes were fixed on Owen, whose own were red as tears streamed down his cheeks. The boy was getting dangerously close to the curb.

"Mom?" He was sobbing now. "You"—he hiccupped, trying to catch his breath—"you always knew? This whole time we were at J—at his house, and—and you didn't tell me?"

Not another step, Jack thought as he watched Owen retreat farther, and the boy stopped as if he could read his mind. Jack straightened and let out a breath as Owen turned his gaze to him.

"Do you...Do you not want me? Is that why you didn't say anything?"

Ava reached for her son, but he shook his head and took another step back, not realizing he was stepping off the curb.

It all happened in seconds. Owen stumbled several extra steps to keep himself from falling and Jack eyed the car around the corner making a left-hand turn right toward his son.

The driver wasn't looking.

Ava screamed.

Jack's only reaction was to run.

Owen was in his arms before he heard the sound of tires screeching, before he smelled the burnt rubber. But it was too late.

CHAPTER TWENTY-TWO

Owen sat, quiet and stoic, as the emergency room doctor cleaned and stitched up the gash in his chin. He didn't speak in the ambulance, either. He simply cried softly. But Ava knew the tears had nothing to do with physical injury.

He walked away from the accident with five stitches. *Five* stitches when it could have been—

Ava choked back a sob. If it hadn't been for Jack...

She cleared her throat. "Excuse me, Dr. Bennett, but have you heard anything else about Jack Everett's condition?"

The woman finished tying off Owen's suture and then straightened to face Ava. "I'm sorry, Ms. Ellis. But last I heard, he was still in surgery. And please, call me Dr. Chloe."

The young doctor pushed her glasses up onto her head and brought her attention back to her patient. "That ought to do it, Owen. And can I just say, you are one of the bravest patients I've ever had."

He pressed his lips into a small smile. "Thanks."

She stood and reached into the pocket of her white coat and produced a raspberry Tootsie Roll pop. Ava was sure this would get a more Owen-like response, but he simply held out his hand when she offered it to him and then set it on the hospital bed beside him.

She pulled her dark brown ponytail tighter and stuck Owen's chart under her arm. "I'll hand this off to the nurse who'll get started on your release paperwork."

She offered her hand for Ava to shake, and she did so, albeit absentmindedly. Now that Ava knew Owen was okay, her thoughts traveled elsewhere. "I'll have someone notify you when Mr. Everett is out of surgery. In the meantime, there's a coffee machine in the waiting room, or I can have someone show you all to the cafeteria."

Ava shook her head. "I don't want to miss any news. But thank you, Dr. Chloe."

The woman smiled and ducked behind the curtain that was their illusion of privacy.

Owen sat with his legs dangling over the side of the bed, head hanging low as he stared at the knees of his still-white baseball pants. Not a mark on them. The only part of Owen that had hit the asphalt was his chin. The rest of him had been cocooned inside Jack's solid frame.

Ava took a chance and sat down next to her son, nudging his knee with her own.

"You still not talking to me?" she asked.

He shrugged but didn't say anything. Still, she took the gesture as permission to continue.

"I met Jack when I was eighteen," she said softly. "He and his brothers moved to our area after the winter holidays, so they were new to school second semester. I was the one chosen to show Jack where his first-period class was, and you want to know what?"

She held her breath, waiting, *hoping*, for a response. Anything to show her that he wanted to know their history—the history of how he came to be—because that wanting meant they were one tiny step closer to forgiveness.

The seconds stretched out before them, and Ava felt the tears pricking at her eyes when Owen finally let out a breath and asked softly, "What?"

She laughed nervously. "He was this beautiful, golden-haired boy with eyes as blue as the ocean. And I think I fell for him right on the spot." She rested her hand on Owen's cheek and urged him, gently, to make eye contact.

He did.

"His eyes were just like yours," she continued. "*Are* just like yours."

"The same blue?" he asked.

She nodded. "And the same sadness." She dipped her head to plant a kiss in Owen's auburn waves. "I know you heard your grandpa say some stuff about Jack's daddy."

Owen chewed on his lip. "His dad hurt him?"

She kissed the top of his head. "Yeah, bud. He did. It's not my place to tell you everything that happened to Jack before I met him. That he'll have to tell you himself. But all I can say is that I would have done *anything* to take away his hurt, just like I would do for you right now. And back then, it meant not telling him about you because he had to leave. That was the only way I knew how to protect him—by letting him go."

"So he never knew about me?"

She shook her head. "I was so young when I had you and so scared that if I told him, he would have stayed. Because that's the kind of guy your dad is. But I didn't want to be the one to keep him in a place that caused him so much pain, so I did what I thought was right back then."

She grabbed a tissue from the box on the counter and wiped at Owen's eyes.

"Did you love him?" Owen asked.

"So much."

He leaned his head against her shoulder, and she let out a shuddering breath. She knew they had a long road ahead of them, but her son would forgive her. Eventually, time would help repair what she'd broken.

"Do you—love him now?" he asked, and Ava let out something between laughter and a sob.

"So, so much," she admitted. "I don't think I ever stopped." She wrapped her arm around him and squeezed him close. "We were going to tell you. After the game. We just wanted you to have some normalcy before we turned your world upside down."

He straightened to look at her. "He—he wants to be my dad?"

Her tears flowed freely now, but she didn't care. Even though she knew Jack was moving to New York, one thing was certain. "Yes, sweetheart. God, yes. He wants to be your dad."

"And Luke and Walker? They want to be my uncles?"

She nodded. "And Jenna is dying to let you know she's your great-aunt."

The hint of a smile fell from Owen's face. "That man hurt Jenna. The one Jack almost hit."

It wasn't a question. He knew.

Ava skimmed her fingers through her son's hair. Yesterday, his biggest worry in the world had been keeping his cowboy hat from falling over his eyes at the rodeo. Today he'd learned that people hurt others—some intentionally, and some who thought they were protecting the ones they loved from greater pain.

"Yeah. He did. But she filed a report with the police after the accident. That man won't hurt Jenna anymore."

Ava remembered the look in Jack's eyes when she'd screamed for him to stop—as he listened to her dad confirm everything Jack feared—that he was a replica of his own father. She'd never be able to erase that moment for him.

The curtain slid open and a nurse walked into their small space with a clipboard. "Just a few signatures for you, Ms. Ellis, and some post-op instructions, and you two are free to go!"

Dr. Chloe popped her head in as well. "Wanted to let you know that Mr. Everett is out of surgery and in recovery. The information desk should have a room number for you within the next hour." She grinned. "It was a clean break where he'd broken the leg before, and the surgery was a success. He'll be up and about in no time."

Ava released a shaky exhale, and, without even thinking, sprang from the bed to hug Dr. Chloe. "Thank you!" she said. "Thank you. Thank you."

Her grateful smile fell when she let go of the doctor and saw her parents striding toward her from the nurses' station.

"They said Owen was being released, and damn it, I want to see my grandson." Her father was storming toward them now, but Ava stepped in front of Dr. Chloe to cut them off.

"Mom...Dad...I asked you to wait in the waiting room. There isn't room back here for all of us."

Her father made like he was about to take a step forward, but Ava shook her head.

"Do you...have this under control, Ms. Ellis?" Dr. Chloe asked.

"Yes," she said and dipped her head back around the curtain. "Back in a sec, bud, okay?" she asked Owen.

He nodded and opened up his Tootsie Pop. She smiled. He'd be okay. She and Owen would be okay.

Ava led her parents back in the direction they'd come from until all of them were in the waiting area and out of earshot of Owen's room.

"Ava." Her mom spoke first. "We're *so* sorry everything happened like this. We just want to make sure Owen is okay."

"He will be," she said. "He's got more than a cut on his chin that needs healing, but he'll get there. What about Jack? I don't see you storming through the surgical wing making sure *he's* okay."

Her father's face paled, and he collapsed into a chair. "He could have killed that man. I saw it in his eyes."

"A man that was *hurting* his aunt... like Derek was hurting me. Just because I walked away from that party with only a few bruises shouldn't have meant that Derek was exonerated in your eyes."

Her father's shoulders sagged.

"You were so horrible to him, Dad," Ava said. "You made him believe in his worst fear when he proved today that he's a better father than most, and he's only known his son exists for two weeks."

Her voice grew stronger with each word she spoke, with what she should have said to defend Jack not only ten years ago but when he'd shown up on the day his father was laid to rest.

"You *knew* what happened to him back then. But did you know he took every beating so his brothers didn't have to? Some kids grow up to be just like their parents. Sometimes that's good, and sometimes not. Deputy Wilkes was a good man as far as I knew, but his son *assaulted* me. If Jack hadn't shown up when he did... Yes, things got out of hand, but try to remember what might have happened if he came looking for me five minutes later."

Bradford Ellis, a man who'd always seemed such a hulking presence, crumpled as his face fell into his hands. It was Ava's mother who spoke.

"He was afraid he'd turn out like his father if he ever had kids. And then today—he saved his son's life," she said.

Ava nodded and her mother pulled her close.

"I couldn't tell him about Owen," Ava said, her face buried in her mother's neck. "I couldn't tell him when the only thing he knew about fatherhood was that his own dad had almost killed him, and he swore he'd never put a child of his own in that same position."

She pulled away from her mother so she could speak to both her parents. "Jack made a mistake ten years ago, but today he is the *only* one who is blameless in this mess. And if you need some sort of proof that he is *nothing* like his father, I think the fact he didn't lay a hand on that guy *and* put his own life in front of Owen's should be evidence enough." She sniffled and straightened her shoulders. "He has a new life waiting for him in New York," she added. "Across the damned country. I gave him the choice I should have given him ten years ago—to decide what part he wants to play in Owen's life. And *mine*. And you, Dad, setting up the buyer for their vineyard and then everything you said? He'll be on his way out of here—and probably out of both our lives—the minute he gets released."

Her father ran a hand through his thick gray hair and slumped farther down in his chair. "I'm—I'm sorry," he said. "You're a mother now. You understand what a parent would do to protect his child..." He trailed off, his eyes darting toward her mother, no longer able to hold his daughter's gaze.

"I get it, Dad. God, you know I do. But I also get that we can be so blinded by this need to protect the people we love that we end up hurting them anyway."

He stood, a once-towering presence now humbled by his own daughter's words. "I never wanted to hurt you."

She pressed her lips into a smile she knew didn't reach her eyes. "I know. And I never wanted to hurt Owen. Or Jack. But guess what?" She shrugged. "I did. I hurt the two people I love most, and I can't undo that. We can't undo any of the damage that's been done."

"Then what can I do to make things right?"

She'd give anything to have the right answer, if there even was one.

"I'm going to go and get Owen. You and Mom can take him to the cafeteria, the gift shop, whatever. Get him anything he wants. And when I get the thumbs-up from the doctor to do so, bring him upstairs to see his father."

"Okay," both her parents said in unison.

She hadn't lost her son. Now she had to make sure that no matter where Jack Everett went from here, she wouldn't lose him completely.

The future she wanted included art school, independence, and finally wanting something for herself. That hadn't changed. But it wasn't enough anymore. Jack had shown her that. And even if it was too late for the two of them, she wouldn't pretend anymore.

If he left, at least he'd know the truth. He was more than the father of her child. He was the boy she fell for when she was only eighteen—and the man she'd loved for ten years.

And that would never change.

CHAPTER TWENTY-THREE

Jack opened his eyes, yet he was sure he was still sleeping, stuck in one hell of a nightmare. Either that or his life had just rewound ten years to the night Jack Senior had pushed him down that flight of stairs.

He glanced around the familiar-looking hospital room and then down to where his leg extended in front of him, wrapped in plaster from the knee down. His bed was only partially reclined, so he was practically sitting up and able to take in his surroundings without struggle. Even Jenna was there, head slumped and eyes closed as she dozed in the chair beside him. Everything was the same.

The only thing off was the livid bruise on Jenna's cheek.

The accident.

Owen.

The asshole who'd been hitting Jenna.

He struggled to sit up but then hissed through clenched teeth.

"Shit!" His arm flew to his side as he tried to catch his breath.

"Hey," Jenna said soothingly as she straightened in her chair. "Careful there, tough guy. You've got a few bruised ribs, but luckily none are broken."

He swallowed with difficulty, his throat raw, and the sense of *déjà vu* continued as he remembered the same sensation following the surgery to repair his broken tibia more than a decade ago.

"But I rebroke the leg," he said, and Jenna nodded. "Owen," he added, growing anxious. "What about Owen?"

All the pieces were falling into place. Why hadn't she mentioned Owen yet?

"Oh, you know," Jenna said, a soft smile spreading across her face. "You were just the heroic dad who put his life ahead of his son's. He got a nasty gash on his chin, but he's all stitched up and hanging with his grandparents in the cafeteria."

Jack exhaled a shuddering breath and let his head fall back against his pillow.

"I knew something wasn't right with you," he said, staring straight ahead. "I knew, and yet I let you go back to him to get hurt again."

"Don't," Jenna said, moving forward in her chair, and he finally met her gaze. "You had enough on your plate, and I thought I had it under control. The only reason I met with him this morning was to end it for good. The other two times—the lip and the bruise on my wrist? He was drunk. I thought if I ended things when he was sober that he would react differently."

Her eyes shone with the threat of tears, and Jack grabbed her hand that rested on the side of his bed.

"Instead he fucking *hit* you."

She squeezed his hand. "I filed a police report, something I should have done after the first incident. But I was embarrassed."

"What the hell are you talking about?" he asked.

She shrugged. "I seem to have this radar that homes in

on guys with serious issues. I thought for once I'd found a good one, you know? He was so sweet, and the first time it happened I made myself believe it was an accident, that he'd had a little too much to drink. I swear, the night of the rodeo, I *had* ended it. But then he called, told me he was getting sober, and Jesus, Jack. After what happened to y'all with your daddy, I should have known better."

He tugged on her arm, and she slid close enough so he could pull her into a hug and kiss the top of her head.

"I spent five years hiding what Jack Senior was doing to us, trying to see the good in a man who'd lost his way until I forgot there ever *was* good in him. Let yourself off the hook. But promise me something."

She straightened to look at him. "What?"

"You, me, Luke, and Walker—we're the only family we've got. You took care of us when you should have been living your life. Now it's time you let us take care of you."

She nodded. "You're wrong about one thing, though," she said, standing.

"What's that?"

"We're not the only family you've got." She pulled open the door and popped her head outside, but Jack could still hear her. "He's awake now."

The door swung wider as Jenna waved and headed into the hall. Before it shut, Ava slipped quietly into the room, barely past the door, leaning against it as it closed behind her.

"Hey," she said tentatively.

"Hey," he answered. "Jenna said Owen's okay."

"Five stitches in his chin, which he sat through like a champ." Ava smiled. "He really wants to see you—when you're up for it."

He scrubbed a hand over his face. "He's not pissed at me for not telling him the truth?"

She laughed softly, but it wasn't a true Ava Ellis smile. He knew those well enough, and it hurt more than his broken body to see what the past two weeks—hell, the past ten years—had done to make that smile harder to find.

"He was upset but more because he thought you left because you didn't want him. So I told him everything I could. No details about your dad, but he knows things were bad for you, and he knows you never knew about him. And—and all those awful things my father said, he knows they aren't true. We all do. Because you could have chosen to walk down that path today. You could have hit that guy and made yourself believe that you were *exactly* like Jack Senior, even though we all know you'd have just been protecting your own. But you didn't do it."

One small tear escaped down her cheek, and it killed him that he couldn't go to her. Then the floodgates were open. She stood there against the door, the tears falling faster than she could brush them away.

"And I promise, my father knows he was wrong, that he went over the line. After what you did today?" She shook her head, her hand flying to her mouth.

Jack wanted to pull her to him, to end this damned cycle of grief and guilt that had kept them apart for so long.

"Come here," he said.

She nodded and took slow, hesitant steps to the side of his bed.

"Sit." He patted the spot next to his uninjured leg, and she lowered herself gingerly beside him.

"You chose Owen," she said. "You chose to save your son rather than hit that man, and I know in my heart that you would always choose to protect him rather than hurt him."

Jack threaded his fingers through hers, and she squeezed his hand.

"It wasn't always the alcohol," he said softly, and Ava's brows drew together. "That night he knocked me down the stairs, yeah. He was drunk. I was trying to get him to bed, and he was trying to push me away, claiming he didn't need help. It *was* an accident."

He blew out a breath as his heart hammered in his chest. It was easier to blame his father's behavior on a combination of grief and booze. But the truth was, drunk or sober, the man who'd existed before his mother's death was never the same man after.

"There were those few times when he was sober and I could tell Luke or Walker was riling him up before he even got to his first drink, and I'd push him to the brink. I'd say whatever I could so he'd lash out at me instead. And then I'd lie to protect him."

He shook his head and squeezed his eyes shut.

"Because he was your dad."

He nodded. "I could have killed that guy today," he said, remembering the rage he'd felt at realizing what that man had done to Jenna.

"But you didn't. You could have ignored everything else around you and let loose on him, but you stayed in control. You stayed in control and you saved your *son*."

She didn't bring up Derek Wilkes, but she didn't have to. He'd let loose on that guy ten years ago, and it scared the shit out of him to think of what would have happened if Derek's buddies hadn't pulled Jack away. But maybe he wasn't that messed-up kid anymore. He still had a lot of issues to deal with, but he was at the wheel now—driving the demons out instead of driving himself to the brink.

She reached her free hand for his cheek, and he felt her

thumb swipe at something wet at the corner of his eye. "I *love* you, Jack Everett. I loved the boy I met when I was only eighteen, and I love the man you are today." She leaned forward and kissed him, and he tasted the salt of her tears. "You've had my heart for ten years."

He pulled her hand to his lips and pressed a soft kiss to her palm. "I love you so damn much," he said. "Both of you, and I think that scared the shit out of me even more than stepping foot back in that house. Losing you once almost broke me, and the thought of losing you again—*and* Owen? How the hell does a man live with that kind of fear?"

His voice shook with the words, but he let go of that measured control. For Ava and Owen he could finally do that.

She kissed him again. "You won't lose us. Even when you go to New York. We'll figure it out. I don't know how, but we will."

He cupped her face in his hands, which was no easy feat with one tethered to an IV, and tilted her head so her mouth was a breath from his. "Ask me to stay," he said softly, and her breathing hitched.

"But you said—"

"Ask me to stay, Red."

"Stay," she whispered.

"Okay," he whispered back. "But only because I'm in love with you and our son, because I can be a lawyer anywhere—and because the Crossroads Vineyard doesn't stand a chance without your expertise."

She laughed through her tears. "*Our* son. You said *our*."

He grinned and brushed his lips against hers. "Yeah. I guess I did." And then he claimed her mouth with his, sealing the deal and letting go of their past.

The door flew open as Luke and Walker barreled their way through.

"Don't mind us," Luke said. "Ain't nothing we haven't seen before."

"Speak for yourself," Walker said. "Just because they're all happy and shit doesn't mean I have to watch."

"Nurse said you were awake," Luke added. "So here we are with all our brotherly support." He held out his hands as if to say *Ta da!*

Jack cleared his throat, and Ava laughed.

"Hey, assholes," he said, his voice hoarse and throat still raw. "This is actually a private room. You ever heard of knocking?"

But both brothers were already lost in exploring a box of baked goods on a table across from Jack's bed.

"Help yourself, by the way," he added.

Luke read a small card that was tucked under the twine that had tied the box together. "Lily Green sent these over?" he asked.

Jack struggled to sit up straighter, then winced, forgetting the whole bruised rib situation.

"Sorry," Ava said. She kissed him and crawled out of the bed. "I'm probably not helping." She handed Jack the small remote that controlled the bed.

"Actually," he said, narrowing his eyes at his brothers, "you're the only one who was."

Walker plucked a black and white cookie from the box. "And here I thought your buddy's wife only did barbeque," he said to Luke. "You really missed the boat with that one."

Luke shoulder-checked his younger brother a little more forcefully than usual, but Jack decided not to push that envelope any further. Because for a man who'd thought for so many years that he was better off on his own—that his absence was protecting those he loved—he was damned happy to have all this commotion for once. Not that he'd admit it.

That was when he glanced to the left and realized the door hadn't ever shut. Lingering in the doorway was a hesitant Owen, chewing nervously on his top lip like his mother so often did, and staring up at the ceiling in quiet contemplation—just like his dad.

Walker took a healthy bite of his cookie and then turned to where Jack was staring at his son. "Oh yeah," he said. "Shortstop here has been sitting on the floor outside your door ever since his grandparents brought him up."

Ava backed away from the bed, motioning for her son to come closer. He approached slowly, stopping short of leaning against the mattress.

"Hey there," Jack said.

"Hey," Owen said. "Are you—okay?" he asked, his voice soft and unsure.

"I will be," Jack said. "Heard you got some stitches."

Owen lifted his head so Jack could see the underside of his chin.

"That's a badass gash," Luke said.

Walker smacked his brother on the back of his head, and Ava groaned. All of it—the sheer normalcy of it—made Jack grin.

"Your uncle's right, you know. Your friends are gonna think you're pretty tough."

"I didn't even cry when the doctor stitched me up."

Jack laughed softly. "But you know, it would be okay if you did."

He thought of all he'd kept hidden, years of pain he'd bottled up, thinking he was safe if he just got far enough away. But safe was being who you were in front of the people you loved—and having them love you anyway.

"I know," Owen said.

"Hey," Jack added. "I've been meaning to ask you something. You name that dog of yours for Vin Scully, the former announcer for the Dodgers?"

Owen nodded.

"Did you know that he was with the Dodgers longer than any other announcer was with a single team?"

The corner of Owen's mouth turned up. "Sixty-seven seasons," he said.

Jack grinned. "You ever been to a game?"

"Just once. Mom, Grandma, and Grandpa took me after my eighth birthday. New season hasn't started yet this year."

Jack scrubbed a hand across his jaw, thinking of all the birthdays he'd missed. He couldn't dwell on that, though. He couldn't change the past, and he got that now. But he could change how things went from here on out.

"You had a birthday before I got here. Didn't you?"

Owen's eyes brightened. "End of February."

Jack grinned. "You think I could maybe take you to your second game? I hear they got this great new pitcher."

Owen nodded, but then he swiped at an almost imperceptible tear under his eye. "Thank you, by the way, for saving my life. I'm sorry you got hurt."

Jack swallowed back the knot in his throat. "Do you know why I did it?"

Owen shrugged. "Because you love my mom."

Jack glanced up at Ava. "I do. I love your mom. But that's not why I ran in front of that car."

His chest tightened. This was the moment of truth, and as much as it was in his nature to do so, for once Jack wasn't holding back.

Owen looked at him expectantly, and Jack told him the only thing he could—the truth.

"I ran in front of that car because you're my son, and I love you. And I would do anything, Owen, *anything* to protect you."

Owen's eyes widened, and Jack watched as the boy's shoulders relaxed and he let the first tear fall. He threw himself at Jack, wrapping his arms around his neck and burying his face into his shoulder.

"I love you, Ja—I mean—Dad." Owen's voice broke on the last word, and the weight that had pressed itself into Jack's chest for half his life finally lifted.

He squeezed his son close and let out a shaky breath. "I love you, too, Shortstop."

They stayed like that for several long moments before Owen finally straightened. Jack's eyes met Luke's and then Walker's.

"We're not selling the vineyard," he said. "And I'm not taking the job in New York."

Walker laughed, then said quietly, "Fucking grapes."

"Yeah," Jack said with a grin. "Fucking grapes."

CHAPTER TWENTY-FOUR

Thanks to the titanium rod in his leg, Jack didn't need to use his crutches. Despite the doctor's orders to only walk in the cast when absolutely necessary, though, he paced the office floor, the sealed white envelope in his hand.

"There is no way you're going to put your shit behind you if you don't read it," he said aloud. Then he laughed because he was alone. Talking to himself. Afraid of a stupid piece of paper.

He paused mid-pace when he heard a dog's bark. Then he lifted the shade to see Owen and Scully running past the side of the house toward the back. That meant Ava wasn't far behind.

They were early, and there was no way he would be able to do what he planned to do without reading the goddamn letter first.

"Like a Band-Aid," he said under his breath. "Just rip it off."

So he did. He tore open the envelope and pulled from it a single piece of plain white paper.

The lines were crooked, and the handwriting a barely legible scrawl, but Jack could make out the words well enough to let Jack Senior have the last one and then be done with it.

He could have sat in the plush leather office chair. He probably should have, given his physical and mental state. But even if no one saw him, he had one thing left to prove to his father and himself: no matter what that letter said, and no matter what his father had done, he was still standing.

Well, shit. It took him 'til now to realize it? *No matter what the letter said...*

He didn't need to know what was in the envelope. He'd already closed the door on that part of his past. Now it was time to think about his future.

He tore the letter in half without reading farther than his name on the first line. Then he tore it again and again until it was practically confetti and tossed it in the trash.

A soft knock sounded on the door.

Jack cleared his throat. "Yeah, I'm coming."

"It's me," Ava said. "Owen's out back with your brothers and Jenna. Can I come in?"

Jack's eyes fell to the shreds of his father's words in the garbage can.

"Door's open," he finally said.

"Jenna said you've been hiding out in here for almost a half hour," she said, striding through the door. She stopped short when she saw him, crossing her arms and narrowing her eyes. "You are *right* next to a chair. You know you're only supposed to put weight on your leg if you need to—" Her expression softened, and she took a few steps closer, resting her palm on his chest. "Hey. What's wrong?"

He didn't say anything, just pulled her to him and kissed her until he felt like he could breathe again.

"Hey," she said again softly, her lips still moving against his. "Are you okay?"

His lips lingered on hers for several seconds more until he finally backed away. "I am now."

She glanced at the trash can next to his feet. "Was that the letter?"

"Leave it to Jack Senior to have the last word even from the grave."

"You read it?" she asked.

"Nope. I realized I don't need to. I've already moved on."

His leg started to throb, so he decided now was a good time to sit and collapsed into the chair.

She said nothing at first, then just climbed into his lap, wrapping her arms around his neck. She hugged him tight and he buried his face in her hair, breathing in the scent of her, the woman who grounded him and brought him back to the present when he'd been stuck for so long in the past.

"I don't know if I can ever forgive him," he said. "But I can move on."

She lifted her head and gave it a soft shake. "You don't have to forgive him today. But maybe someday. With more time."

His mom would like that. Wouldn't she? Some sort of peace between them. Maybe. All he had was time, now.

"And I made the decision to stay because I can be a lawyer anywhere. But you and Owen are home."

She swallowed and bit her lower lip, her green eyes shining.

"I can't justify what my mother's death did to him, but I get it." He cradled her face in his hands. "If I lost you like that?" He couldn't finish the thought, so he kissed her again.

"You won't," she told him, an unmistakable quaver in her voice. "Not if I have anything to say about it. But if you did?" She skimmed her fingers through his hair, her palm resting on his cheek. "If by some horrible twist of fate you did, you'd be strong enough for you and Owen to get through it, just like you were for your brothers."

He wrapped his hand around her wrist and pressed a soft kiss to her palm. Then he exhaled a shaky breath, and with it he let go of the fear that had kept him from this woman for ten long years.

"Come on," he said, straightening in the chair. "I have something to show you."

Ava glanced at Jack in the passenger seat of her Jeep and grinned.

"It's killing you not to drive, isn't it?"

"Maybe." His head thudded against the back of his seat, and Scully rewarded him with a sloppy kiss on his ear.

"Owen," Ava said, swatting at the Lab and pushing him back toward her son. "You're supposed to keep an eye on your dog when we're in the car."

Owen laughed. "I watched him slobber all over Dad. That's keeping an eye on him, right?"

Ava's breath hitched at how easily Owen had transitioned from calling Jack by his name to calling him *Dad*. It had only been a week since the accident. But they'd spent every day visiting Jack in the hospital after school. Some nights they brought him dinner, while others Jack took Owen to the hospital cafeteria for junk food and some one-on-one bonding time. She wasn't sure what the two of them did while she waited patiently in Jack's room. All she knew was that the two of them always came back smiling, and Jack brought her back something chocolate each time.

"Anyway," she said, cutting off her own thoughts before she got all teary-eyed, "this is supposed to be your welcome home family dinner." She glanced at Jack in her peripheral vision. "What do you need to show me at the vineyard that can't wait until daylight?"

Jack turned toward the back seat. "What do you think, Shortstop? Should we tell her?"

Owen giggled. "Not yet."

Jack turned his gaze to her as she pulled to a stop alongside the rows of grapevines. "Sorry, Red." He leaned toward her and kissed her on the cheek. "Not yet."

She rolled her eyes, put the car in park, and hopped out of the vehicle so she could speed to Jack's side of the car. But he was already standing on the road by the time she got there, Owen and Scully at his side.

"Did you even bring your crutches?" she asked, angry that she hadn't checked before they left.

Jack shook his head. "We're not going far."

"I hope not," she said. "It's getting dark." She tilted her head toward the sky. "At least it's a clear night."

"Come on," he said, taking her hand. "Shortstop, you got the supplies?"

Owen nodded and opened the back door of the Jeep. "Scully and I are right behind you."

"Supplies?" Ava said as Jack pulled her onto the grass toward the first row of vines. She tugged at the hem of her UCLA LAW sweatshirt—because *yes,* it was hers now— and her hand fidgeted in Jack's grasp. "What's going on?"

Jack stopped at the first plant in the row, the one they'd started on together that first day she'd come to Crossroads. Seconds later Owen was there with a plaid blanket over one arm and an excited Labrador by his side.

"Supplies," he said with a knowing grin.

Jack helped their son lay the blanket down flat—and then redo it after Scully ran back and forth across it.

"Sit, Scully," Owen said, and the dog obeyed, tail wagging and tongue dangling out of his open mouth.

"You too," Jack said to her. "Please."

She sat, but her heart raced. She was already teetering on an emotional edge listening to Jack and Owen talk like they'd been father and son for Owen's whole life. Jack was so good with him already, and her heart threatened to burst each time she saw him simply ruffle Owen's hair. She wasn't sure she could take much more.

Jack gingerly lowered himself beside her, but not completely. He stopped at his knees. No. Scratch that. He stopped at *one* knee while his good foot stayed planted on the ground.

"What—what are you doing?" she asked, but Owen answered instead of Jack.

"He wants to ask you something," he said.

Jack grinned. "It's kind of a question for all three of you."

Ava's eyes burned, and she let out something between a laugh and a sob.

"You know I never even noticed the sky—how you can see the stars out here at night—until you showed me." He almost lost his balance, and she rose on her knees to grab those strong shoulders that carried so much weight for all those years, and steadied him. He laughed. "You showed me that there is something good where I couldn't find it before."

He grabbed Owen's hand and patted his knee, and Scully moved to his side.

"This place doesn't haunt me anymore," he said. "Not if it's the place where you are. *Both* of you."

Scully barked, and Jack laughed. "I meant all *three* of you." He scratched behind Scully's ear. "Hey, Red? You think you can fix Scully's collar before he knocks me over?"

Ava's brows drew together, and she squinted in the waning light to try and figure out what was wrong with the dog's collar, when something sparkled and caught her eye.

She gasped as her hand flew to her mouth. "How did you—? You just got released this morning."

He smiled, then got to work unbuckling the dog's collar so he could remove the ring she was too stunned to touch.

"Actually," he said, pinching the silver band between his thumb and forefinger, "your father called in a favor to a jeweler friend of his."

Her eyes widened. "You talked to my father?"

Jack nodded. "He stopped by after you left to pick Owen up from school last Monday."

She wanted to ask more questions. She wanted him to tell her everything she'd missed when she wasn't at his bedside. But he was kneeling in front of her—on a broken leg, no less—with a diamond ring in his hand and their son standing beside them, grinning.

"And *you* were in on this?" she asked.

Owen laughed and shrugged. "Maybe."

"Ava," Jack said, and she tried to focus, but her head was swimming.

"Yeah?" Her voice shook.

"I know it's only been three weeks..." He smiled. "Well, ten years and three weeks, but I was wondering if you all wanted to marry me."

Scully barked. *His* mind was made up.

Owen stifled another laugh.

And Jack just looked at her expectantly, his blue eyes no longer the storm they'd been all those years ago when they'd met, or when he'd forced her off a country road a few short weeks ago.

"Just to clarify," he said, when she hadn't yet been able to formulate a coherent sound, "in case you need convincing, I love you, Ava. Pretty sure I have since the first day I met you in the school office, even though falling for someone was the furthest thing from my mind." He tucked her hair behind her ear. "You are so strong."

She smiled.

"And stubborn."

She narrowed her eyes at this.

"In a *good* way," he said. "I was convinced that there was nothing good in my life other than my brothers and Jenna. But then you pushed past every wall I tried to put up. You made me feel like I was worthy of someone else's love." She opened her mouth to say something, but he interrupted her. "I'm not done yet."

She bit her lip and waited.

"I love the girl you were when I met you and the amazing woman and mother you've become. I'm a better man for knowing you. For *loving* you."

Tears fell from her eyes and she shook her head. "I hate that you ever thought you weren't good enough. That I made you believe that when I pushed you away," she said with a sniffle. "You were *always* a good man. And you're already an amazing father."

They both looked at Owen, who beamed back at them.

"I'm just following your lead," Jack said. "You were a single mom raising this spectacular kid. I couldn't ask for more but to learn from the best."

"Mom," Owen said. "Are you gonna answer him?"

Ava laughed. And cried. And nodded. Because he

wasn't simply staying. After everything, he wanted her—
them—all of it.

"Yes!" He slid the ring onto her finger. "Yes," she said
again, placing her palms on his cheeks. "I love you." She
kissed him. "I have only ever loved *you.*"

"Yes!" Owen yelped, and he and Scully ran up and down
the aisle of vines.

"I was kind of hoping you'd say that," Jack said softly
as he lowered himself to the ground and pulled her into his
lap. "I wouldn't mind hearing it again."

"Which part? Yes, I'll marry you?" She laughed. Then
she kissed him for breaking his heart all those years ago,
for all the time they'd missed, and for all the years ahead.
And in his kiss she felt the long-empty corners of her
heart fill.

"I like that part," he said. "But I was kind of referring to
what came after."

She smiled and let her forehead fall against his. "I love
you, Jack Everett."

"That's the part I'm talking about." He kissed her one
more time. "And I love you, Red."

They entered the ranch to whistles and hollers from Luke
and Walker and a teary-eyed Jenna, who pulled Ava into a
warm hug.

"Thank you," she whispered.

"For what?" Ava asked.

Jenna backed up to meet her with a watery gaze. "For
helping bring him back from a place none of us could
grasp." Ava opened her mouth to speak, but Jenna kept
going. "I don't mean San Diego or New York," she said.
"From the moment I found him in that hospital a decade
ago, he was beyond my reach."

"And then I pushed him away," Ava said shakily.

Jenna shook her head. "He needed to leave in order to re-alize that one day he could come home again. I'm just sorry it took him so long to get here."

The two women embraced again, and Ava could feel the shared pain lift from where it had been hovering in the air. She looked at Owen and Luke wrestling with Scully, at Walker sipping a beer, shaking his head at his nephew and brother, and at Jack leaning against the kitchen counter, grinning and taking it all in.

She went to him, pressed her palms to his chest and her lips to his.

"You look happy," she said.

He laughed. "I'm not sure if you heard, but I asked this amazing woman to marry me, and she said yes."

She bit back a smile. "Is that so?"

"Yeah, but I wanted to ask her *one* more thing."

She tilted her head, her eyes narrowing. "You sure do ask a lot of questions."

He laughed. "I know Owen has school tomorrow," he said, "and that you'll have to head home after dinner."

"Mmm-hmm," she said, brows raised.

"Well, it being my first night home from the hospital, I was thinking I probably shouldn't sleep alone."

"Luke or Walker didn't volunteer for the job?" she asked. "I bet Walker is a closet spooner."

He crossed his arms and leaned back, giving her a pointed look. Her hand flew to her mouth, and she stifled a laugh.

"I was wondering if maybe you'd take me home with *you* tonight. But if you think one of my brothers could bet-ter care for a man just home from the hospital..."

She swatted him on the shoulder, but all at once the joke

was over. She bit her lip, not sure if the tears would start again once she tried to speak.

"No," she said, head shaking. "I *don't* think they could do a better job. I almost lost you last week," she added. "If you think I'm letting you out of my sight now that you're home—"

He kissed her before the reality of what she'd said had a chance to sink in any further.

"Good," he said softly against her. "A sleepover it is."

CHAPTER TWENTY-FIVE

Jack watched from the doorway as Ava sat on the side of Owen's bed and bent to kiss him on the forehead.

"You want me to sing?" she asked, and their ritual made him smile. He knew his son was still a boy, but he was maturing, and the events of the past few weeks had probably sped up the process. Still, a warmth spread through him to see that for these two people he loved, some things hadn't changed.

Owen's brows drew together as he chewed on his upper lip.

"He gets that from you, you know," Jack said.

Ava turned to look at him from over her shoulder. Not wanting to interrupt a part of their life he didn't quite fit into, he hadn't announced his presence.

Scully pushed past him and made his way into the room where he hopped onto the foot of the bed and curled up at Owen's feet.

"I think I tired him out," Jack said.

She'd left the man and the dog in the backyard when she'd finally put an end to the evening's activities by announcing that it was, in fact, a school night, and Owen had to get ready for bed. Jack had said he and Scully would follow them in soon, but he was stalling, unsure of his role in what had become, to Ava and Owen, routine.

"Mom?" Owen asked, and she turned her attention back to her son.

"Yeah, bud?"

"Could—could Dad maybe tuck me in tonight? I mean, if it's okay with you." He looked up at Jack. "And only if you want."

Owen's tentative tone made something in Jack ache—that Owen could think for one second he'd say *no*.

"I was kind of hoping you'd ask," Jack said, striding toward the bed. Okay, so it was more like *limping* toward the bed, but he still felt steady on his feet. He could do this.

He lowered himself on the other side of the mattress and reached for her hand. She grabbed it and gave him a reassuring squeeze before she rose.

"I'll let you two have some man time," she said with a grin.

Jack raised his brows. "Fair warning, Shortstop. I don't really do the singing thing."

Owen shrugged as Ava pulled the door shut behind her. "That's okay," he said. "It's kind of Mom's thing anyway. Maybe we could think of something that's just ours?"

Jack grinned, eying his son's bookshelf where he saw everything from Harry Potter to a baseball card price guide. "How about we read?"

He waited until Owen dozed off against his arm—and then he waited a few minutes more. Finally, after assuring himself he'd get to do this again, he slid quietly from the room in search of his fiancée.

He found her in the extra bedroom, where close to a

dozen finished canvases lined the floor against the far wall. He glanced at the one she was working on and winced.

"That is one hell of an ugly tree," he said. "You ever think about getting rid of the one out back? It doesn't look like it's fruit-bearing...or olive-bearing. Is an olive a fruit?"

Ava sighed. "I've been trying to paint that stupid tree for the better part of a decade. I thought if I could paint it, that it would be the one and only piece of art worthy of admission to Cal Poly. I thought I had to prove something to myself with a stupid tree."

"But now you don't?"

She shook her head. "I already got in, didn't I? With the portrait of you and Owen playing catch that I painted before it even happened."

"Because you knew," he said.

"I hoped," she admitted.

She crossed her arms, paintbrush still in hand. She was wearing nothing but an oversized white T-shirt he guessed was her regular uniform when she worked on her art. The paint-splattered garment slid down her left shoulder, exposing her pale, freckled skin.

Jack kissed it, then smiled as he felt her shiver.

"You boys have a good time?"

He nodded. "I didn't sing, if that's what you're asking. We did some bedtime reading instead."

"Oh yeah?" she asked. "What book?"

Jack gave her a wry grin, and she shook her head. "You read baseball stuff, didn't you? I'm going to be left out of conversations now if I don't know the Dodgers' batting order. I've basically lost my son to his father and vice versa."

She swiped the paintbrush across his cheek, but he grabbed it from her before she got the other.

He raised his brows. "Tell me about the tree," he said softly. "Or I retaliate."

She shrugged. "I have more brushes."

"And I'm not going anywhere. So talk to me, Red." She reached for the brush, but he was too quick, hiding it behind his back. "I'm not *leaving*," he said.

Without the brush to occupy her fidgeting hands, she wrapped her arms around her midsection and blew out a long breath. "I bought this house *because* of that ugly tree."

His brow furrowed. "Why the hell would you do that?"

"Because the last time I saw you—when I told you I wasn't in love with you—" Her voice shook.

He reached for her, but she held out her hand, staving him off for just a bit more. "I have to say this. And you can forgive me or not for all I've kept from you. But in order to move forward from this, I need you *not* to make it easier for me."

It killed him to do it, but he took a step back. For her.

"That's where we met," she continued. "Under that ugly tree across the street from the school. I called you there to tell you about Owen, but instead I pushed you as far away as I could because I knew—after the party and then what happened with Walker—that you wouldn't survive here if you stayed. So I hurt you more than you were already hurting, and now you're here, and you gave me this ring, and you want to *marry* me." She shrugged. "I've been telling you since the moment you got here to face *your* past, but the truth is, I guess a part of me is still stuck under that tree."

He dropped the brush onto the table next to her easel and closed the distance between them. His eyes searched hers for the girl who couldn't let go. "Tell me now," he said, his voice gentle. "Tell me now what you wanted to tell me then."

He swallowed past the years of separation, and he was eighteen again. Eighteen and lost until *she'd* found him.

She glanced out the window toward an innocent tree that had no idea the role it played in her torment.

"Hey, Red. It's okay. Pretend we're there."

She rested both of her hands on her flat belly. "I'm pregnant," she simply said.

Without hesitation, he covered her hands with his own. "I'm gonna be a father."

She nodded. "A really good one. I think it's a boy."

He smiled. "Who'll love baseball, and Vin Scully, and have an excellent pitching arm."

She laughed. "I'd like to name him after your mom." Her voice caught on that last word, and he watched her struggle to hold it together. For him.

"That means more to me than you will ever know." He realized he'd never thanked her for making Owen his, even when he wasn't here.

He kissed her then, and as their lips met, he felt her finally let go.

He scooped her into his arms, her bare legs warm against his hands, and carried her from the room. She narrowed her eyes, and he knew she wanted to give him hell for putting the extra weight on his leg, but he gave her a quiet "Shhh," warning her that if she said anything now, she'd wake Owen. Besides, he was so quick, she was on her back on top of her unmade bed in a matter of seconds.

Jack returned to the door to gently close it, and she rose onto her elbows. "You are terrible at following the doctor's instructions," she said.

He shrugged. "Doc didn't know I was making love to my future wife tonight."

She sucked in a breath, and he shook his head. "No more tears."

"But these are happy ones."

He stood above her and she tugged at the belt loop on his jeans. "Come here," she said.

He obeyed, climbing over her, but she shook her head and pushed him to his side so they were facing each other.

"I get that in the hospital you were hooked up to machines, which didn't leave you much of a choice. But part of this deal"—she motioned between them—"is that you don't get to be an island anymore. You put everyone else ahead of *your* needs. And I love that about you. But you've got people to take care of you now, and you better let them do it."

He tilted his head toward hers, the warmth of their breaths mingling between them. "Are *you* one of these people who want to take care of me?"

She rested her palm on his cheek. "For as long as you'll let me."

He kissed her, long and slow and sweet—at first. But when she parted her lips, his tongue slipped between them and he grew hungry with need.

"I missed you," he said as he came up for air.

Her leg slid between his, and her hand snaked around his back. "I know. A week is too long."

He kissed along the line of her jaw, nipped at her earlobe, and smiled when she gasped. "Not just this week." He rose on his elbow, and with his free hand gripped the hem of her paint-spattered T-shirt and tugged it over her head. *He* was the one who was short of breath now. Because there she was, in nothing but a pair of black panties—and the diamond he'd placed on her finger. He helped her out of the former as quickly as he had the shirt.

"I *missed* you," he said again, his voice rough, and the look in her green eyes was one of complete understanding.

She pulled his face to hers. "I know." She gave him a quick, chaste kiss. "But there's one thing wrong here." She looked him up and down.

"What's that?"

She raised her brows. "You're wearing entirely too many clothes."

He barked out a laugh, only to be shushed by the beautiful, naked woman beneath him. He was out of his own shirt in seconds, but the jeans over the cast were another story. Together, though, they made it work, and soon he was bare before the woman he couldn't get enough of.

"See?" she said. "That's how it works. Letting someone take care of you."

Without warning, she pushed him down on his back and sank over his erection, burying him to the hilt in her slick heat.

A low growl rumbled in his chest. He pulsed inside her, eliciting soft, short breaths that let him know that even injured he could still get the job done.

She squeezed her knees against his hips, tightened her muscles, and slid up and down his length so slowly he thought he might lose his mind.

"This," she said, lowering her head to his so she could kiss him. "This is me taking care of you for the next hour or so."

He raised his brows. "An hour? You think very highly of a man who hasn't been inside you for a week." And who felt like he might lose control in a matter of minutes. But that didn't worry him anymore—letting go with her. He wanted every part of this woman—body, heart, and soul. And he knew without a doubt she'd given all of that to him.

What surprised him now was, after all these years of distancing himself from that kind of connection, it was so easy to give back to her.

She rocked against him, her movement slow and controlled. "We'll just have to do it more than once, then. To work up our staying power."

He laughed, then wrapped his arms around her so the whole length of her body was flush against his. "I love you," he said, his hands gripping the backs of her thighs.

She gasped as he tilted his pelvis toward hers. "I love you, too," she said.

"I always thought I couldn't be happy here—coming back to this place. But you and Owen changed that."

She smiled. "You're really happy?"

She arched her back, and one of his hands snuck between the place where they joined. She cried out as he pressed a finger against her aching center.

"I'm happier than I ever thought possible," he said. Because he never could have dreamed this—a second chance with the only girl he ever could have loved.

"Promise?" she asked.

He kissed her, and her body melted against his.

"Cross my heart, Red. I'm finally home."

ABOUT THE AUTHOR

A librarian for teens by day and *USA Today* bestselling romance writer by night, **A.J. Pine** can't seem to escape the world of fiction, and she wouldn't have it any other way. When she finds that twenty-fifth hour in the day, she might indulge in a tiny bit of TV to nourish her undying love of vampires, superheroes, and a certain high-functioning sociopath detective. She hails from the far-off galaxy of the Chicago suburbs.

You can learn more at:

Website: AJPine.com
Twitter @AJ_Pine
Facebook.com/AJPineAuthor
Instagram @AJ_Pine

**For a bonus story from another
author that you'll love,
please turn the page to read**
Rocky Mountain Wedding
by Sara Richardson.

If anyone had told Ruby James she'd be marrying the man
of her dreams after starting over at the Walker Mountain
Ranch, she'd have keeled over laughing. Yet here she is:
ready to marry her soul mate, Sawyer Hawkins—and make
the adoption of their sweet foster daughter official. But just
before the event that will make their family complete, a
miraculous little wrinkle appears in her plans...

ROCKY MOUNTAIN WEDDING

SARA RICHARDSON

To Grandma Richardson

Every family should have an Elsie to love them no matter what

CHAPTER ONE

Whoever coined the term blushing bride had it all wrong.

Ruby James studied herself in the full-length mirror that hung over the door in her friend Avery Walker's bedroom. In front of an audience that included her bridesmaids, Avery and Julia; her soon-to-be aunt-in-law, Elsie Walker; and her matron of honor, Paige, Ruby'd been attempting to squeeze herself into her wedding dress for the last ten minutes. It was supposed to be a prewedding tea, one more girls' celebration before she officially became Mrs. Hawkins.

But now her hair, which had been neatly piled on top of her head, had broken free, frizzing around her face as if she'd just spent an hour out in the humidity. Speaking of her face...her forehead looked like it might pop a vein.

Blushing bride? More like gasping, heaving, red-faced bride.

"Come on," Paige said, clutching either side of the gaping zipper. "Suck it in, Ruby. We can do this." If anyone could do it, Paige could. The woman actually had biceps. As a mountain guide, she'd climbed most of the cliffs within a thirty-mile radius of Aspen. You'd never know it just looking at her on the street, what with her petite frame, gleaming hazel eyes, and wavy streaked hair, but Paige was pretty much a badass. "Suck it in," she commanded.

"I *am* sucking it in," Ruby wheezed. Lordy! She'd been sucking it in for the last decade. Not that she was overweight, just a bit curvy, which her faithful fiancé, Sawyer, insisted he loved. *Don't you dare lose a pound*, he'd say when she'd mention a diet she might like to try. *You're perfect.* Then he'd grab her ass and tell her he liked having something to hold on to. She directed her gaze to the mirror again and ran it down her body in a critical assessment. Lately, though, it seemed like he'd had a whole lot more to hold on to. Obviously. The wedding was four days away and her dress didn't fit.

Grunting, Paige yanked on the fabric. "Okay, on the count of three you'll inhale and clench that stomach," she instructed. "Then I'll jerk up that damn zipper before it knows what hit it."

"Good idea," Paige's sister-in-law, Julia, chimed in, wheeling her chair closer to the spectacle like she wanted a front-row seat. Julia had recently gotten back from her own wedding in Tahiti, where she'd married her childhood sweetheart, Isaac. And wow, the woman looked good—the tanned and glowing new bride. Her long dark hair was sun-streaked and lovely, and those exotic brown eyes of hers seemed to glisten in a way they hadn't before.

Ruby would bet that the woman hadn't had any problem fitting into *her* wedding dress.

Then there were Avery and Elsie. They'd probably *never* sucked it in. Though she had a seven-month-old,

Avery had one of those naturally lean bodies. Along with her blond hair and ice-blue eyes, she could still walk the runway somewhere. Elsie may have been a bit plump, but she was still petite and graceful—the typical grandma-to-everyone.

Cheeks puffed out in a sigh, Ruby checked herself in the mirror again. "I don't know what I'm going to do." It was Thursday. The wedding was on Sunday. "I'll have to find a new dress." Which would break her heart. After she'd bought this dress, she'd had Elsie make a matching dress for Brookie. In just a few short months, she and Sawyer would be officially adopting the sweet foster girl they'd both come to love and they'd wanted to make sure she was an integral part of the ceremony.

"Like hell you will," Paige grunted. She'd always had a slight competitive streak, and this dress had just become her nemesis.

"We'll get it this time, dear," Elsie soothed. "Don't you worry."

"It'll fit fine," Avery agreed, but concern rounded her eyes and Ruby could practically see her thinking through a plan b.

"Here goes," Paige said, getting a tighter grip on the material. "One, two, three."

Straightening, Ruby inhaled and held her breath, cinching her ribs so tight she swore they touched her spine.

Behind her, Paige cursed with the passion of a sailor and jerked the two edges of the satiny material together.

Blood pounded in Ruby's head. Her fingertips tingled.

"Come on!" Paige groaned. "Avery, pull up the zipper!"

Avery jumped into action and tugged.

Ruby's body jolted. She swayed. Whoa...she was going

to pass out. The air whooshed from her mouth with hurricane force. Her body slumped forward. "God, I feel like I'm going to break a rib!"

Paige stood behind her, eyeing that zipper. "I'm sweating," her friend complained. "I'm actually sweating right now."

The others looked at Ruby with varying degrees of concern.

She turned back to the mirror, shifting to the side to study the profile view. It was such a beautiful dress. Satin with a sheer layer over it, fitted across the bodice and down over the curve of her hips with a slight fan in the skirt. "It fit me perfectly when I bought it," she wailed. It had made her feel exactly like a princess. Now she felt like a hog ready for spring.

How could she have gained that much weight in three weeks?

Elsie knelt on the floor in front of her and gathered one of the seams in her hand, inspecting it closely. "Oh, I can fix this," she murmured. "It'll be nothing for me to take it out a bit. There's plenty of room in the seams."

"Thanks, Elsie." She patted the older woman's hand. "But that doesn't fix the problem. I don't understand how I could've outgrown a dress in three weeks." Sure she was a baker at the ranch, but she never sampled more than one of everything. Of course, all of the stress lately had fooled her into believing she was hungry most of the time. But she still watched what she ate...

"Don't worry about it," Paige said, falling back to a leather chaise like she was spent. "That last month before my wedding, I stress-ate everything in sight."

"But you didn't have to have your dress altered days before," she pointed out.

"No, but the dress didn't stay on long, I'll tell you that much." Paige laughed, elbowing Avery.

"Can we not hear the story about what you and my brother did in the limo again?" Julia begged. "Please?"

Paige grinned at her sister-in-law. "I'm just trying to make the point that the dress doesn't matter all that much." She stood and threw an arm around Ruby. "Sawyer loves *you*."

"I know." But she still wanted to be beautiful for him...

"Oh!" Avery popped up and jogged to the dresser. "I have the perfect thing!" She dug through the top drawer and snatched out some nude-colored elasticy thing. "Spanx!"

She tossed it to Ruby.

A laugh tumbled out. She'd heard about these things but didn't realize they actually existed. Holding it up, she inspected the contraption. "Is this supposed to fit around my arm?" she asked. Actually, it might be too tight for her arm...

"No one wants to wear those things." Julia snatched the Spanx out of her hand and tossed it aside. "Maybe you're just bloated. Are you PMSing?"

"Not that I know of." She slumped to the bed, suddenly feeling like she could sleep for a year. "My period is all over the place. No idea when it'll hit next."

"Oh my God." Avery clapped a hand over her mouth. "When's the last time you *had* your period?"

"Oh...well..." Her mind jogged back through the months. When nothing turned up, her thoughts evolved to a frantic sprint. "I'm not sure." She didn't like the way everyone's eyes grew rounder and rounder. They all knew well and good she'd likely never have children. "It's never been regular. I have endometriosis," she reminded them.

"That doesn't mean it's impossible for you to get pregnant, right?" Julia asked.

Her ribs cranked tight. "I ... don't know." She'd always tried not to think about it—to let that possibility remain in her heart. Over the years, she'd scrubbed out all of that hope.

She couldn't be pregnant. She just couldn't be.

"Have you and Sawyer done the deed?" Julia demanded to know. Seeing as how she'd seen the woman only a couple of times in the last six months, they hadn't had the sex discussion.

"Excuse me?" Heat boiled inside, rising to her face.

"You know, have you made love, had a quickie in the shower, taken a roll in the hay?"

Yes. To all of those. But Elsie—*Sawyer's aunt*—was sitting right there!

"Of course they've had sex," Paige answered for her. "This isn't 1950."

Elsie chuckled. "Oh, please. As if we weren't having sex in the fifties. You girls talk like I'm a prude!"

Ruby fanned herself. "No, it's just weird for me to discuss how many times your nephew and I have made love." Not to mention the manner in which they'd made love ...

The woman smiled. "It only takes once, dear."

Sure. For women with healthy, functioning reproductive systems. But she'd given up on that dream a long time ago ...

Avery clamped a hand onto her knee and peered into her eyes like she was trying to make a diagnosis. "Have you been more emotional lately?"

"Uh ..." Did crying at a particularly sentimental toilet paper commercial count? That sweet mama bear and her little cub ... she teared up just thinking about it.

"Bloated?" Avery asked before she could expand.

"Well…" She rested a hand on the pouch that had formed low on her stomach.

"Overly hungry?" Avery fired off, as if taking that as a yes.

"Oh my God." She'd been famished. All the time. Sometimes she'd wake up at two thirty in the morning and find herself wandering to the kitchen…

The answer was met with chatters and squeals and flapping arms.

"I knew you were glowing!" Elsie chirped. "I just knew it!"

Her heart seemed to strike her ribs. "I'm not glowing. I'm not…" *Pregnant.* That was ridiculous! "It's just the wedding. Bringing Brookie home. The stress of all the changes."

A knowing gleam lit Avery's blue eyes. "Have you been peeing a lot?"

Now that she mentioned it…Ruby crossed her legs.

"What about your breasts? Any tenderness?" Her friend reached over and honked the left one.

"Ow!" A stab of pain radiated and she flinched, swatting Avery's hand away.

A collective gasp hushed the room.

"Yep. Preggers," Paige confirmed with a nod.

"I'm not pregnant!" She couldn't be. It wasn't possible. The tiniest seed of hope burrowed deep, but she mentally tried to pluck it out. Hot tears zigzagged down her cheeks. A laugh sputtered out. *Damn it!*

"I have a pregnancy test left over!" Avery squealed as she bounded out of the room.

She rushed back in and thrust the box into Ruby's hands.

"Go!" Julia said, nudging her off the bed. "Come on.

What are you waiting for? If you take the test, you'll know for sure."

Her hands clasped the box tight. She stared down at it. What if she was pregnant? How would that affect Brookie? They'd only just brought her home...

"Move it, woman." Paige grabbed her hand and yanked her to her feet.

Swallowing the bubbles her stomach had churned into her throat, Ruby slogged toward the bathroom, legs teetering the whole way.

"We'll be right here," Paige said, squeezing her shoulder.

"Make sure you follow the instructions," Avery advised.

"Oh, this is so exciting!" Elsie sang.

"Hurry, go," Julia said, prodding her to the bathroom door.

Her hand felt like ice as she turned the knob. Once inside, she shimmied off her dress and left it in a puddle on the floor. Carefully, she read the instructions, then completed each step as detached as possible so she could distance herself from the hope that hammered in her heart.

A knock sounded on the door. "How's it going in there?"

Not caring that she wore only her skimpy slip, Ruby opened it. She couldn't do this alone.

Her friends all crowded in, huddling around the small stick that lay on the countertop. Seconds dragged into eons as she stared at the tiny plastic window.

"I think that's two lines," Paige announced. "Has it been two minutes?"

"It's only been thirty seconds," Julia said, eyes focused on the stick. "But that's definitely two lines."

Breaths stuttering in and out of her withering lungs, Ruby picked it up. Two lines. Two very distinct pink lines.

"Lordy. Oh, Lordy," she choked out, with a sob between the words. Who would've thought that two tiny lines could change her life forever? She swayed. Hands steadied her, but she couldn't see whose. Someone guided her back to the bed and sat her down.

"I can't believe I'm pregnant." The words started a fresh round of sobs. Gasping breaths burned her lungs. Tears flooded her eyes. "I can't be pregnant."

Elsie scooted in next to her, gathering her into a hug. "There, now. It's a bit of a shock, but it's wonderful news."

"What about Brookie?" she blubbered. "She just came home." She was still adjusting to a new life. A new school. She'd already had some issues with the other kids at school accepting her. How would she deal with this news?

Elsie took her shoulders in her hands and steadied Ruby with that loving gaze of hers. "You listen to me, dear one," she said with that perfect blend of authority and compassion. "Sawyer and Brookie will be thrilled. This is *good* news, Ruby. Let the joy in."

"Yes!" Julia agreed, squeezing her hands. "This is so exciting! You're having a baby!"

"We have to celebrate," Paige added.

"Great idea!" Avery clapped her hands and led the way to the kitchen. "Let's get out the ice cream."

Ruby followed behind them, resting a hand on her stomach. There was a life in there, growing and beating and becoming a little person.

Let the joy in. Sighing out every hesitation, she did. She closed her eyes, inhaled deeply, and let herself fall in love with this baby.

Oh God, she was having a baby! Happiness flooded in and carried away every fear and doubt.

She and Sawyer were going to have the family they'd always dreamed about. She'd never been so happy. Not in her whole life.

She only hoped Brookie would feel the same way.

CHAPTER TWO

I hate shopping." Sawyer detoured to a bench in front of the sixth jewelry store he'd let his groomsmen drag him into. After looking through glass case after glass case he'd started to see double.

Scrubbing the blur out of his eyes, he slumped down to the cold wrought iron, groaning. Shopping was right up there with going to the dentist.

"You grew up with two sisters," his cousin Bryce Walker reminded him. "How could you hate shopping?"

"They always turned it into a marathon." Exactly how it felt right now. He'd only wanted to find the perfect wedding gift for Ruby and Brookie. Never thought it would be like searching for the ninth wonder of the world. They must've trudged through every store in downtown Aspen and he'd come up empty-handed. *Damn.* He hadn't been this exhausted after he'd run that half marathon through the backcountry last year.

The innocent victims he'd taken along on this mission gathered around him—Bryce, cousin and best man; Ben Noble, the cowboy who'd married Paige; and Ben's brother-in-law, Isaac. They were the best friends he'd ever had—the only ones he'd ever want to have his back, but even they couldn't come up with the perfect idea.

"The tennis bracelet would've been great," Ben said in that optimistic tenor that'd made him a good congressman in his previous life.

"Ruby doesn't care about jewelry." Sawyer zipped up his coat. The sun had settled low in the sky, barely peeking over the peaks beyond, encasing the streets of downtown Aspen in chilled shadows. It was almost five o'clock and most of the friendly storefront windows were starting to go dark. November happened to be the shoulder season between the leaf-peeping and ski seasons. The town was dead. "I need a gift that means something." Their wedding was only a few days away and this was the start of a whole new life for both of them.

In the last couple of months, they'd overcome so much—Ruby had worked hard to reclaim her strength after living as the victim of domestic violence, and he'd finally grieved for the son he'd lost with his first wife.

And then there was Brookie. In her eight years of life, she'd been moved from foster home to foster home. Now they were adopting her. The three of them were coming together as a family. This day wasn't just about getting married. It was about starting over. Embracing a new beginning.

From the silence surrounding him, he knew they all got it. They understood what he was thinking. And no one seemed to have a solution.

"We need some inspiration," Bryce finally said.

Isaac nodded with a grin. "Burgers and beer."

"Now, there's the first good idea I've heard in three hours," Ben agreed. "Let's hit my in-laws' café."

Sawyer pushed off the bench. They'd already paraded

through the majority of the stores anyway. They were out of options. "Sounds good." He never turned down the chance to eat at the High Altitude Café. Paige's parents had owned it for years, and even though the place was a dive, they served the best burgers in Aspen.

Hands shoved into his pockets, Sawyer followed the others down the block, and for the first time since they'd walked into the cigar shop a shot of energy zipped into his step. They should've stayed there for an hour and a half enjoying the expensive Cubans.

"You sure you have time for dinner?" Bryce asked, pausing to wait for him.

"Yeah. Ruby's busy with last-minute wedding stuff." At least that's what she'd told him on the phone. She'd also said Aunt Elsie was picking up Brookie from school and taking her to get a manicure and pedicure. Which meant he had more time to come up with an idea for the perfect gift.

But the three blocks to the café didn't expand his creativity. He followed Bryce past the restaurant's shoddy hand-painted sign.

If it hadn't earned the reputation for serving up the best meat in town, everyone would pass right on by the High Altitude Café. The red bricks were old and crumbling, and the whole building seemed to lean slightly to the left. But once you got past the dingy windows and the ancient facade, you didn't worry so much about the walls falling in. You were too busy cleaning your plate.

"Man, I love the smell of charred meat." Ben held open the door.

Sawyer sauntered past him, stomach already growling. He had to admit, a burger and beer were exactly what he needed right now.

The place sat empty, seeing as how it was too early for

the dinner rush. He followed Ben to a large round booth in the center of the room, which happened to be red vinyl. Because what small-town café was complete without a red vinyl booth?

"Well, well, well." Pete Harper, Ben's father-in-law, sauntered out from the back. He and Ben had gotten off to a rocky start, but once Ben had put that ring on Paige's finger, he'd suddenly turned into the son the Harpers had never had. Except for their other two.

"Sorry, boys, this table's reserved for paying customers," Pete boomed, ornery as ever.

"Hey, Pops." Ben greeted the man with a firm handshake and half a hug. "We're payin'. You know I'm good for it."

The older man waved him off. "Like hell you are. What can I getcha?"

One by one they all slid into the booth.

"Bring us a round of the IPA. Coke for Bryce," Ben answered for everyone. This wasn't their first rodeo at the High Altitude Café.

"You got it, kid." Pete Senior lumbered past the bar and disappeared into the kitchen.

Ben handed out menus.

"Bet that guy scared the shit out of you when you first started dating Paige," Isaac said, nodding toward the kitchen door.

Sawyer laughed. That was an understatement. "I don't remember you really *dating* Paige."

"Yeah. As far I remember, there weren't many dates involved," Bryce agreed.

"What can I say?" Ben shot back. "She was totally into me."

"That's not what Julia said," Isaac threw in. "I believe she described you as one hundred percent whipped."

"Can you blame me? My wife is hot," he insisted. Not that Sawyer could think of Paige that way. Too much like his little sis. Which meant he'd best change the subject before Ben started in on how good she was in bed.

"You'd think one of you married guys could help me come up with a gift for my fiancée." They should be better at this than him. "What'd you get Paige for a wedding present?" he asked Ben.

"A horse," he answered, as though it were a no-brainer.

Yeah, that wouldn't work. He glanced at Bryce.

His cousin shrugged. "A new baseball bat." If Sawyer hadn't known how much Avery loved baseball, he might've been gawking at him the way Isaac was right now.

"A baseball bat? Why, so she could keep you in line?"

"Nah, she doesn't need any help with that," he admitted. Talk about one hundred percent whipped. "It's for our team with the town league. And she loved it. Trust me."

Sawyer had no doubt; he'd seen her hit a grand slam with that bat. But a bat wouldn't mean much to Ruby. "Isaac, tell me you've got something better than a horse and a baseball bat."

He shrugged like he couldn't make any promises. "I booked Julia a spa day while we were in Tahiti."

"There ya go." Ben clapped him on the back. "What woman wouldn't want a spa day?"

"A spa day doesn't last." He could do that for her birthday. Or even for Mother's Day. But this was their wedding. This was the start of their life together. "It has to be something memorable. Something she can hold on to."

Silence settled again as they all traded clueless stares.

"First round is on me, boys," Pete Senior called, balancing the bottles on a tray like he'd been waiting on people his whole life. He lumbered over to the table. "Next one's on my son-in-law."

Everyone laughed as he set the bottles in front of them.

"Hey, Dad." Ben took a swig. "What'd you get Mom for a wedding present?"

Pete Senior sipped his own beer. "A grill. Not one of the fancy numbers, either. It was charcoal." He leaned in. "Then I cooked her a steak. Best roll in the hay we've ever had, that night was. I still remember it like it was yesterday."

"Thanks for that," Ben muttered, then guzzled more beer as though trying to chase away the mental picture.

His father-in-law guffawed. "You asked." He left his beer sitting on the table like he planned to come back and join them. "Now, what can I getcha to eat?"

"I might not be hungry anymore," Ben said.

"Well, I'll take the Heart Attack Burger," Sawyer countered. After the day he'd had, he deserved it.

"Sounds good to me," Bryce said.

"I'll do the Blue Cheese Burger," Isaac added, handing the menu back.

"I'll bring you a Hot and Spicy, kid," Pete said to Ben before plodding away.

"So I don't think Ruby would appreciate a grill." She got in enough kitchen time with her job as the baker at the Walker Mountain Ranch. Sawyer kneaded his forehead. Who would've thought this would be so hard?

"What about a honeymoon?" Isaac asked. "That was really all Julia wanted. Time away. A beach..."

"We're not going on the honeymoon until February. Want to give Brookie a chance to get more settled before we take off for a week. It's already booked. Besides—"

The door opened and a rush of cold wind fluttered the checkered curtains that draped the windows. In walked Paige, followed by Julia, Avery, and ... "Ruby."

Every time he saw her, his heart sighed with a warm rush of longing. He still couldn't believe he'd found someone like Ruby. Someone so compassionate and warmhearted. Not to mention stunning, with that long reddish hair and her sweet heart-shaped face. Those luminous green eyes that hinted at a deep tenderness.

"What're you ladies doing here?" Ben asked, rising to give his wife a hearty kiss on the lips.

"We got hungry," Julia answered for Paige as she wheeled herself to the open end of the booth. "You gentlemen aren't the only ones who can eat meat."

No lie there. He's seen Julia put down a burger before. Girl could eat. She'd grown up on a cattle ranch.

Avery wedged herself in next to Bryce, but Ruby hung back by the door. Why didn't she come and sit next to him? His eyes questioned her, but she quickly looked away.

A cold stone dropped straight to the pit of his stomach. Something was up.

"We figured we'd find you guys here," Avery said, stealing a sip of her husband's beer. "Didn't last very long out in the shops, huh?"

"What do you mean?" Bryce demanded as though he took exception to that. "We were out there for at least an hour and a half. That might be a record for me."

"What were you shopping for, anyway?" Paige broke in. "I mean, the last time Ben went shopping, he called me from the store in a panic because he didn't know which credit card to use."

Sawyer tuned out the razzing comments from the rest of

the wives and tried to analyze that bewildered expression on Ruby's face. She'd edged closer to the group, but still clung to the outskirts...

"It's no secret shopping isn't our thing," Isaac said. He threw an arm around Julia and gathered her to his side. "Is that why you came? To rescue us?"

Sawyer's gaze still held Ruby. Her face had lowered and she was staring at the floor.

A cold dread seeped in and spread all through him. Was she angry? Upset? Having second thoughts about the wedding?

The rest of her friends traded awkward glances.

"Um. We...were hungry," Paige said, seeming to widen her eyes in Ruby's direction. Giving her a silent cue?

What the hell was going on?

"Really hungry," Julia added.

Avery turned to peer at Sawyer, her blue eyes wider than normal. "Maybe you and Ruby should get your own table, though," she suggested with a counterfeit innocence, obviously trying to disguise an agenda.

"Uh." His heart picked up. He looked at Ruby for reassurance, but she wouldn't let her gaze connect with his. "Okay."

A heaviness weighted his body as he scooted out of the booth and headed toward Ruby. She quickly turned away from him and ducked into a booth in the corner. He slid in across from her, his heart feeling exactly like a punching bag in a boxer's gym. "What's going on?" He could hardly squeeze the words past the fear that constricted his throat. *Please don't say you're having second thoughts about the wedding...*

Tears reddened the rims of her eyes. "There's something I have to tell you, Sawyer."

The possibilities flickered in his mind. Had she cheated on him?

No. This was Ruby. He'd been betrayed before, but he refused to let that color his life now. As a cop he'd been trained to think through worst-case scenarios, but it didn't matter. Whatever she said would not rip their happiness away. He wouldn't let it. "It's okay." Instinctively he reached for her hands, gripping them tightly in his over the table. "Whatever it is, we can make it okay." She'd been through hell, but that was over for her. He'd make sure. Whatever was wrong—whatever had her so upset—he'd fix it. He'd protect her from it. No matter what.

Her eyes finally rose to his, but they didn't seem sad. Somehow the tears made them seem brighter, more alive. "My wedding dress doesn't fit me anymore," she uttered, her voice barely stronger than a whisper.

Relief rushed in, purging the fear. "What'd you mean?" He tried not to smile. While Ruby had been complaining about her weight for the last month, she'd never looked more beautiful. Sure, her body may have been a little softer, but he loved her that way.

"I've gained weight, Sawyer," she insisted.

"No you haven't." He squeezed her hands again. "You've never looked sexier." He was pretty sure he'd proved that to her yesterday when he'd stopped by her place for lunch. And couldn't keep his hands off of her. Never got around to eating, but he hadn't missed it a bit. Now that Brookie lived with Ruby full-time they had to be creative and steal time alone when they could get it.

According to the slight dimple in her cheek, she did recall the afternoon as fondly as he did. "Trust me, Sawyer. I've put on a couple pounds."

He let go of her hands and caressed her cheek in his

palm. "You can buy a new dress. Maybe the sizing was off," he said, thinking how much better she would look once he got her out of that dress, anyway. Maybe wearing the new lingerie he'd gotten her. "Who needs a dress?" he murmured so the others wouldn't hear.

"It's not the dress," Ruby whispered, and the somberness in her gaze snagged his attention back from drifting toward thoughts of their wedding night.

"I'm pregnant."

The room dimmed and then everything seemed to get brighter. "What?" His head shook. He must not have heard her right. She'd already told him it'd be hard for her to get pregnant. She had that condition...

But she was smiling at him, this big, happy, beautiful smile with tears spilling from of her eyes.

God. Oh God. Hope clamored for release from his heart, but he kept it caged because she couldn't be pregnant. "What, Ruby?" he gasped. Suddenly it was hard to breathe.

This time she took his hand in hers, squeezing it tightly, forging that connection they'd developed until he felt it spark in his gut. "We're going to have a baby."

A baby. Letting that word—that life-changing word—sink in, he eased in a measured breath, then let it sigh out. Elation rose up and overpowered him, made his head dizzy. He couldn't speak, couldn't say one damn thing. He could only stare back at his fiancée with this ridiculous open-mouthed grin, letting that news shine all through him.

"I took a pregnancy test." Ruby went on cautiously, like she wasn't sure how he was taking everything. "And we stopped by the clinic on the way here. The doctor said he thinks I'm about eighteen weeks along."

"Eighteen weeks?" he choked out. That was almost halfway...

"Everything looks fine. The doctor's not concerned," rushed out, as though she was worried about him.

Because she knew. She knew about Matthew. That he and his ex-wife had lost a baby right around this same time...

"I'm scheduled for an ultrasound next week."

An ultrasound. A baby. They were having a baby. In less than five months!

Finally, sense came back to him, and he was not the same man he had been two minutes ago. Not even close. Her words had changed everything. The life and light inside of her had changed everything.

"I know this isn't the best place to tell you," Ruby whispered, tears cascading again. "But I didn't want to wait. Oh, Sawyer, I'm so worried about how Brookie will feel..."

"No." He pushed out of his chair. He would not let her worry, her fear, steal this moment from her. From them. Easing to his knees in front of her, he placed his hands on the softness of her stomach—that place that would protect him or her, that would nurture their baby into life. "There can't be any worrying, Ruby," he said, peering up into her emerald eyes. "This is a gift. And we'll accept it. And we'll let ourselves enjoy it." No matter what happened. They'd both lost so much, and this new life inside of her was their restoration. "Brookie will be ecstatic." They'd never wanted her to be an only child. They'd wanted their house filled with chatter and laughter and the stampeding of little feet. "She will love this baby," he said, nodding until Ruby started to nod with him. "And so will we." Hell, he already did. He loved Brookie and this baby and Ruby more than he ever thought he could love.

On the outskirts of his vision, he became aware that everything else had stopped. All the conversation and laughter from across the room. He glanced over, and sure enough, everyone stared at him and Ruby.

He shot to his feet and pulled Ruby up, bringing her in against him, holding her, letting his own tears free. "We're having a baby," he hollered like a fool, laughing and crying.

The room broke into a concert of squeals and congratulations.

"We need a bottle of champagne, Pops!" Ben called to his father-in-law.

Ruby clung to him. "I don't think we should tell Brookie until after the wedding," she whispered in his ear. "Maybe after the ultrasound."

"Okay, but I can't wait too long." Brookie would be excited. It would be a lot of change, but they would get her through it. Together. "Everything will be fine. Amazing. We'll prove to her that she's the daughter we've always wanted. Both of our kids are what we've always wanted." Ever since they'd gotten engaged, this was what they'd talked about, planned for. A family.

After everything they'd been through, this was their new beginning.

CHAPTER THREE

She hadn't known it would feel like this. Being a mom.

A *mom*. Love the likes of which she'd never felt pierced Ruby's heart until warmth bled all through her, until the all-too-familiar tears saturated her eyes.

From her car, she watched children spill out the doors of Aspen Elementary School, their voices and giggles a sweet melody that made her belly glow with a fervent longing, as if she could actually feel the baby growing, second by second, cell by cell. She rested her hand there, watching for Brookie to come skipping toward her, backpack askew, that dark, curly hair she'd pulled into a ponytail this morning in beautiful disarray. Sawyer was right. Brookie was everything they'd ever wanted. And now this new baby would knit the four of them together as a family. Brookie and her sibling would always have each other. Always. Even after Ruby and Sawyer were gone.

The thought, the blessing of that knowledge, filled the cracks in her confidence. She'd been so worried since Brookie had come to live with her as they waited to formalize the adoption. Technically, right now, she was only the girl's foster mom—not according to her heart, but according to the state. Everything had been an adjustment for both of them. But Sawyer was right. This was good news. And ever since she'd dropped her off at school earlier that morning, Ruby couldn't wait to share it with Brookie.

She straightened, eagerly straining to see over the bobbing heads of the kids that bounded toward the crowded parking lot.

There she was! The sight of her daughter sent her heart soaring, but as the girl neared the car, the scowl on her face spiraled it into a crash. While all of the other kids walked in small groups, grinning and giggling, Brookie walked alone. She'd been at the school for only a month, and she wasn't having an easy time.

Attempting to cleanse the worry from her expression, Ruby inched the car forward in the carpool line. Brookie looked up and saw the car, but she didn't smile and her eyes didn't light. Every once in a while they would, and Ruby would see a glimpse of hope, but bringing a foster child to live with you didn't result in a sudden happy fairy-tale ending.

It was hard. There were so many kinks to work out. And there were days Ruby wondered if she was enough. If she could love enough. If she could give enough. But then she would stare into Brookie's dark, innocent, thick-lashed eyes and she would decide she would be enough. She would do whatever it took to be what this girl needed.

The car door opened and Brookie scooted in, head hanging so low her chin grazed her collarbone. Though she only wanted to gather the girl against her chest and hug away whatever had upset her, the cars behind her impatiently inched forward, and Ruby knew she had to drive out of the parking lot.

A weighted silence pressurized the car. She glanced in the rearview mirror. "How was school today, honey?"

"I hate it," Brookie uttered, voice teetering on tears. "I'm not going back to school. Ever." Anger provided a feeble covering for deep sadness, Ruby knew. She remembered. She'd felt that so often when she was trying to survive her own foster home experiences. It was almost like if you kept everyone out, you couldn't get hurt.

But now she understood hurt was crucial. You couldn't know love if you didn't know pain.

She slowed the car, looking for Brookie in the rearview mirror again. "What happened?"

The girl said nothing, only stared out the side window, her face tightened into a hard mask of anger.

"Remember what we talked about Brookie?" she said softly, attempting to draw the girl's gaze to her own. "You can tell me anything. You don't have to deal with everything by yourself anymore."

That was maybe the hardest thing for a foster child to learn. To share their burden with someone. To trust someone with it. Ruby stepped on the brakes, pausing at a stop sign. "Maybe I can help. If you tell me what's bothering you."

The mask melted and tears ran down her cheeks. "Today at recess Charlotte asked why my own mom didn't want me."

The words struck her, quick and fast and white-hot, like a lightning bolt.

"Then she said you won't want me either." Brookie sniffled fearfully. "Because I'm not your real kid. And since you're getting married, you and Dad will have your own real kids someday." The words seemed to break open the dam of emotion she'd been trying so hard to hold back.

They broke Ruby, too. They were cruel, but they weren't the real source of Brookie's insecurity. No. That came from years of being moved around, at first with relatives after her mother was put in jail and then into the homes of strangers.

Choking back her own tears, Ruby swerved to the side of the road and put the car in park, not giving a damn that the car behind her honked.

After waiting for the SUV to pass, she climbed into the backseat next to Brookie and held out her arms. "Come here." There was nothing she could say to undo those words, those doubts. She could only show her again and again that she was wanted, that she was valuable and cherished. "Your dad and I love you very much," she whispered into the girl's hair. "We chose you, Brookie. We chose you to be our little girl, and now you will always belong with us." She smoothed her hand down Brookie's back, gathering her in closer, feeling like she could put her back together with all of the love that lived in her heart. "Nothing will ever change that." She had said those same words before, as many times as she could, and yet each time the power of them seemed to grow. Brookie clung to her like Ruby was lifting her out of a flood, face buried against her chest, warm against her breast. Arms secured unyielding around her waist.

Ruby gently peeled back her head and searched her eyes. "Do you believe me?"

Brookie's lip still trembled with uncertainty, but she nodded.

Blotting tears with her shirtsleeve, Ruby reached forward between the seats and dug a hand into her purse. "Your dad and I got you something to remind you. So you'll never forget that you belong to us." They'd planned to wait until the wedding ceremony to give her the necklace, but she needed it now. Sawyer would understand.

She lifted out the small package that was wrapped in delicate flowered paper. "Open it," she said, holding it out to Brookie.

The girl's eyes widened. "What is it?"

"You'll see."

She ripped at the paper until it lay in shreds on their laps. The small velvet box creaked as she popped it open.

Brookie gasped and studied the heart-shaped locket. "Always," she read. That was the inscription they'd chosen for the heart.

Ruby helped her open it to reveal a picture of the three of them. A grin broke through Brookie's sadness and erased the tremble from her lip. "Always," she said again, sounding sure and hopeful.

"Now you won't forget," Ruby said as she carefully removed the necklace and clasped it around her daughter's neck. "And next time Charlotte says something like that, you show her this."

Brookie swung her arms around Ruby and squeezed the breath clean out of her. "Thanks for choosing me."

She hugged her back. "We'll always choose you, Brookie." After what she'd been through herself, Ruby would make sure her children grew up knowing that they were loved and wanted. She would remind them every day. She and Sawyer would always choose Brookie and the baby.

But the sight of the girl's still-teary eyes kept the secret locked away. When the time was right, she would tell Brookie she was going to be a big sister.

But not today. She was still too fragile. Right now Brookie couldn't handle one more change.

* * *

"So you ready for all this?" Bryce asked in that direct way he had.

"Yes." Sawyer didn't even hesitate. He was ready. *They* were ready. To him the actual wedding was simply a necessary activity. It was every day after that mattered most.

"Avery and I are so happy for you." Bryce tossed his hammer back into the toolbox. They were out installing the arched garden arbor they'd built for the ceremony on the ranch's back patio. As long as the weather held, they'd planned to do the whole thing out here at sunset, hemmed in by the towering pine trees with a perfect view of the snow-studded peaks on the horizon.

"Thanks." Sawyer admired the view. "This is the perfect spot." He stood back to inspect their work. The morning of the wedding, the florist would decorate the arch with Ruby's favorite flower—mountain lilies—though she didn't know it yet. That was one of many surprises he'd planned for her.

"Guess we'd better get cleaned up," Bryce said, latching the toolbox. "See if Mom needs help getting things ready for tonight."

"Sounds good." Sawyer checked his watch. Almost four. Ruby would've just picked up Brookie from school. After a couple of errands they'd meet him here before the party started at six.

"Your mom didn't have to do another party," he said, following Bryce up the steps toward the lodge.

His cousin just laughed. "You do know who you're talking about, right?"

"Oh, yes. I know." If there was one thing Aunt Elsie loved, it was planning parties. She'd already thrown

Ruby a massive wedding shower, and she'd insisted on inviting the whole wedding party over tonight for yet another celebration before the celebration. By the time the wedding rolled around, they'd be all partied out. Not that he didn't appreciate it. "I'm just ready to move past all of the events." Settle down, move in with Ruby and Brookie for good...

"I hear ya," Bryce said, holding open the door for him. "You couldn't pay me to have another wedding. It's exhaust—"

"Sawyer!"

Just inside the dining room, he jolted to a stop. There, sitting at the table, were Mom and Dad, along with Thomas and Aunt Elsie. He blinked. His parents weren't supposed to be back from their European tour until tomorrow. Not that he wasn't thrilled to see them, that they'd cut their trip short for the wedding, but he'd had it all planned out. He'd wanted to introduce Ruby and Brookie at a quiet dinner at his place. Not at a huge gathering at the ranch. Mom and Dad could be slightly overwhelming, especially for someone who didn't have a family of their own...

"Come here and give us a hug!" Mom cried out in her weepy voice. "Oh my God. I can't believe I haven't seen my baby boy for six months." She popped out of her chair and hurried toward him, fanning her face with her hand as though trying to dry her tears.

"Hey there," he said, catching his mom in a hug. She was as petite as Aunt Elsie—the two of them obviously shared genetics. But Mom had always been more sophisticated somehow. Probably because she'd married a corporate lawyer in Aspen while Aunt Elsie had married a ranch hand. Still, the two of them looked like they could be twins, barely ten months apart. Only difference was his mom kept her hair short and styled and dressed like she'd just stepped off a geriatric runway in Paris.

"Sawyer." She shook her head, looking him over as though she couldn't believe he was standing there. "Look at you. My handsome boy. I've missed you so much!"

"Marybeth, stop smothering him." His father nudged her out of the way. "Good to see you, son." He caught his hand in a firm shake, the way he'd always done. Though the man had somehow miraculously gotten a tan, he still looked the same—tall and broad, sturdy jaw, the same blue eyes as his own.

"Good to see you, too, Dad." It was. He'd missed his parents. He just hadn't expected to be reunited with them here, the evening of the party, the evening when there would be chaos and crowds. God, he hoped his sisters weren't coming up early. He didn't need them fussing over him, too.

"And, Bryce." His mother clucked. "I just can't wait to meet my little great-niece."

"She can't wait to meet you, either," Bryce said dutifully, leaning in to give her a quick hug before shaking Dad's hand. "I should actually run home and see if Lily's awake. I'll bring her by if she is."

"Please do," Mom gushed, waving as he headed out the door.

"We should get moving, too." Behind his parents, Aunt Elsie scurried around, collecting teacups. "We have a whole heap of work to do yet in the kitchen, don't we, Thomas?"

Thomas muttered an agreement, and Sawyer couldn't help but feel that she was giving him a moment alone with his parents for some reason. Unease spread through him, dimming the anticipation of the upcoming wedding. What had they been talking about when he walked in?

Before he could ask, Aunt Elsie and Thomas slipped into the kitchen.

"So..." His mother started right in, taking his hand and leading him to the table like she used to when she wanted to give him a firm talking to. "When do we get to meet your fiancée?"

He sat across from his parents. Why did it suddenly seem like they were facing off? "Her name is Ruby." Which they knew well and good. She was all he'd talked about on the phone with them.

"Yes." His mother waved her hand in a dismissive gesture. "When do we get to meet Ruby?"

He glanced at the clock on the wall. "She and Brookie should be here soon."

"Wonderful." But she didn't smile when she said it. Instead, his mother and father shared a look. "That gives us a chance to chat, then."

He heaved a sigh. When his mother said "chat," it usually meant she did a whole lot of talking and everyone else listened. "Chat about what?" he asked. He wasn't as good at catering to the bullshit as he'd once been.

Mom handed the floor to Dad with a decided tilt of her head, and he had a flashback to being eight years old, when he'd gotten busted for sneaking out the ATV without asking.

"Well, son," Dad bellowed in his courtroom voice. "We have some concerns."

Of course they did. His parents were nothing if not overprotective. Which had meant he'd grown up in a stable, loving home, so he wouldn't complain about it. Especially knowing the alternative—seeing it in both Brookie's and Ruby's lives. "Let me guess." He shot them both a wry smile. "You think it's too fast. That we haven't known each other long enough."

"Exactly," his mother said through a relieved sigh.

"Six months isn't enough time to know if you want to marry someone," his father insisted. "I courted your mother for two years."

Yeah, yeah, yeah. He'd heard the story many times. Trying to maintain a grip on his slipping patience, he looked at them directly. He wasn't a child anymore. No matter how much they wanted to forget that. "Kaylee and I dated for years before we got married," he reminded them. "And look how that turned out." Their marriage had gone down in flames.

"Do you think you might on the rebound?" his mother asked, nodding as though trying to convince him.

"Ruby is not a rebound." She was his best friend. His favorite person in the entire world. She'd helped him grieve the loss of his son. She made him want to be a better person. "This is right." He simply knew. "I don't need more time."

"Son, you're about to have yourself an instant family," Dad said, as if he didn't realize that. "A wife, a daughter. Parenting is hard enough without being newly married. It's best to take things like this slow and ease into it."

His temper flared. Did they think he didn't realize how hard this would be? "I'm not looking for something easy." He wanted something real, something lasting. That's what he and Ruby had worked so hard to build these last few months. They weren't going into this blind. They'd done the counseling, the parenting classes. They'd shared their fears; they'd worked through their problems. The work wasn't done, but they were both committed to it. Problem was, his parents had spent the last eight months wandering through Europe. So they wouldn't know any of that, even though he'd mentioned it in their weekly conversations. They hadn't *seen* it.

"What's the rush?" Dad asked, hands raised as though addressing a jury.

"Maybe you should take a little more time," his mother suggested, her eyebrows arched into hopefulness. "We don't want to see you get hurt again."

His jaw tightened. "I don't need time." He knew everything he needed to know. They were committed to each other and to Brookie. Not to mention...they would have this incredible miracle to make their family complete. "With the baby coming—" *Shit.* Nope. Hadn't meant to share that tidbit with them yet.

"Baby?" his father repeated.

"Baby?" his mother echoed.

No use denying it, pretending. Every time he thought of the baby, that grin snuck out. How was he supposed to keep that kind of thing a secret? He couldn't. Didn't want to. He wanted to tell everyone he loved so they could share in the joy of it. "Ruby's pregnant," he said, and yep, he was grinning like a fool again.

"But you never said a word on the phone!" Mom accused, as though he'd kept it from her on purpose.

"We didn't know. She just found out. But the doctor thinks she's nearly eighteen weeks along."

Dad cleared his throat and sat straighter. "You're sure the baby is yours?"

"God, Dad. Really?" He called him out with a look. His father had never been an asshole. Now was not the time to start.

"Sorry," the man said, straightening his suit coat. "This is a lot to take in."

"Two kids," his mother breathed in disbelief. "You're going into a marriage with two kids."

"And I can't wait." Anticipation warded off the irritation

with his parents. "I'm ready for this. And I need you both to be happy for me and to celebrate and to treat Ruby like one of your daughters," he said firmly. "She has no one else. No one. We are her family."

His mother lowered her gaze into a look of blatant repentance. "Right. You're right. I'm sorry, son. Of course we'll celebrate. Of course we'll love Ruby."

For Ruby's sake, he hoped she meant it.

CHAPTER FOUR

The room had started to spin. Ever since she and Brookie had walked into the Walker Mountain Ranch's kitchen, Ruby felt like she'd just stepped off of a merry-go-round. No matter how many times she blinked, she couldn't seem to steady herself. And the scents she usually loved—cinnamon and the sugary fragrance of delectable baked goods—had her stomach clenching with repulsion.

Was it the pregnancy? A stomach bug? She had no idea. She'd never bothered to learn anything about being pregnant. Never thought she'd need to. She'd heard of morning sickness, but what about late afternoon?

She would've asked Elsie, but the woman stood on the other side of the island helping Brookie frost a cake for the evening's festivities.

Easing in a shaky breath, Ruby attempted to squelch the nausea that swelled in her stomach. Her empty stomach. She hadn't eaten a thing since breakfast. Hadn't had the time. Not with all the running around, last-minute wedding errands. Two more days of this craziness. She couldn't get sick. Not now. The party started in an hour, and she was supposed to be a guest of honor.

"That's it, Brookie," Elsie said, with an encouraging nod. "What a beautiful flower. You're a natural. Just like your mom."

"This'll be the best cake ever," Brookie sang, dolloping the thing with another heaping spoonful of frosting.

Ruby's stomach heaved. God, she had to get away from that rich smell before she threw up. "I think I need some air," she managed to say, already heading for the door to the dining room. Maybe a few minutes of sitting in the crisp fall air on the beautiful patio would remedy her sudden aversion to smells.

"Of course, dear. We'll finish up here." Elsie waved her away. "Take all the time you need. Don't come back until you have some color in your face."

"Thanks." She pushed through the door and escaped into the dining room. Such a lovely room. Windows lined the entire back wall, letting in enough of the early-evening sun to warm the space. Small tables were scattered around the perimeter, while a large one anchored the center. She hurried past it, running her hand along the chair backs to balance herself. The scent of fresh evergreens filled her senses, but she didn't fare much better with that than she had with the cake. Wrapping an arm around her churning stomach, she stumbled toward the patio doors.

"Ruby." Sawyer jogged around the fireplace and caught up to her. "You're here," he murmured, leaning in for a kiss.

She turned it into a quick peck before backing away. "I need to step outside. I think I need some—"

"There's something I have to tell you," he interrupted with a worried frown.

That didn't help her stomach any. She swallowed against the volcano rising in her throat. "What is it?"

"My parents are here."

"What?" Nerves swirled, intensifying the chaos in her stomach. The Hawkins weren't supposed to be back until tomorrow. She'd already been nervous about meeting them—the quintessential model parents. She needed time to prepare...

Sawyer eased an arm around her waist and pulled her closer. "They got in earl—"

"Sawyer!" A woman's voice echoed in the vaulted room.

Marybeth Hawkins bustled past the fireplace, followed by a man dressed in crisp khaki pants and a starched polo shirt. James Hawkins. She recognized him from the pictures Sawyer had shown her.

"Is this *Ruby*?" the woman demanded to know.

She tried to smile, really tried, but moving, even engaging one more muscle seemed to hurt her stomach more. She had to lie down...

"Yes." Her fiancé's shoulders seemed to tense. "Mom, Dad, I'd like you to meet Ruby."

"Wonderful to finally meet you," his mother said through a tight-lipped smile. "I'm Marybeth."

While the words were polite, they weren't warm. Neither was her gaze. She reminded Ruby of one of those women you'd see in a Viagra commercial—refined elegance with her white hair cut in a stylish crop, just the right touch of eye shadow and mascara, dressed in a chic flowy tunic with leggings and boots. Marybeth Hawkins might've looked like her sister—the same plump lips and glowing cheeks. But her sharp blue eyes were assessing instead of warm and peaceful like Elsie's.

Didn't she like her? Ruby's stomach roiled. Heat gathered in her throat. "Um, it's nice to meet you, too," she almost whispered. Air. She desperately needed cold, clean air.

"This is my dad, James Hawkins." Sawyer gestured to the man with his same facial structure, his same thick wavy hair, though his father's was graying.

"It's a pleasure, Ruby," he said in a formal tone.

But she could only nod. The nausea had gained momentum and was now crowding into her throat. *No. Not now. Not here.* She couldn't throw up in front of her in-laws!

"Please excuse me," she choked out, clutching her stomach and making a break for the patio doors. A cold sweat blanketed her neck and she knew there was no way she'd make it in time. Instead, she stooped to her knees and threw up in the potted evergreen plant two feet away from the doors.

"Ruby . . ." Sawyer knelt by her side before she could inhale a breath. "Honey, what's wrong?"

"I don't know," she cried. "Oh, I'm so sorry. I don't know what's wrong with me." Humiliation pulsed in her cheeks. Instead of making a good impression on Sawyer's parents, she'd thrown up in front of them.

Marybeth stood over her, a hand pressed against her chest as though she were in shock.

Tears mingled with the perspiration on Ruby's cheeks.

"Hey." Sawyer rubbed a hand against her back. "It's okay." He glared up at his mother.

"Of course it's okay," she said quickly. "It's not your fault. You poor thing. I had morning sickness constantly when I was pregnant. I'm sure it's just the baby," the woman murmured.

"What baby?"

Brookie. Still on her knees, Ruby spun.

Their daughter stood near the kitchen door.

Oh no. Ruby closed her eyes. This wasn't how she'd wanted Brookie to find out about the baby.

An awkward silence crowded the room. Sawyer's parents seemed to look at him for direction.

With a squeeze on her hand, he promised her everything would be okay. Then he stood. "Hi there, sweet girl." He held out his arms for a hug, but Brookie stood stationary, staring at them, eyes narrowed into slits of suspicion.

"What is she talking about?" the girl asked, a tremor running through the words. "What baby? Who's pregnant?"

Marybeth's mouth gaped as though she'd just realized her mistake. "Oh. Um. Well..." She shot her son a desperate look.

His jaw tightened. "Mom, Dad, maybe you should help Aunt Elsie in the kitchen."

"Great idea," his father said, already halfway to the door.

"I'm sure she has so much to do," his mother added, scurrying behind him. "We'll see you all in a little while."

While they made a quick escape, Ruby slid her hand into Sawyer's and he pulled her to her feet. Her legs shook, but she couldn't tell if it was from throwing up or from the way Brookie looked at them. Like she knew they were hiding something from her.

Sawyer's hand didn't let go of hers. Somehow his strength, his warmth always seemed to give her the courage she needed. "Brookie, we need to talk to you," she said, glancing into Sawyer's kind, calming eyes. The love she saw there never failed to reassure her. This wasn't the best time to tell her about the baby, but they couldn't lie. They'd worked too hard to build her trust. If they didn't tell her now, they'd have to start all over.

"Let's get you into a chair first, babe," Sawyer said, nestling her under his arm and leading her around the fireplace until they'd made it to the leather sofa in the sitting room.

Brookie followed at a distance, still eyeing Ruby with that heartbreaking mistrust.

Sawyer waved her over and patted the seat between them. "There's something we want to tell you," he said carefully, glancing at Ruby as though he didn't know quite how to put it.

After a brief hesitation, Brookie crept over and wedged herself between them.

Hope gathered, crowding Ruby's heart. Who cared what that horrible little girl at school had said? Brookie knew they loved her. She knew they wanted her. A baby wasn't going to change that.

She turned to look into the girl's dark vivid eyes, still seeing so much of her younger self there. "I'm expecting a baby," she said, heart flipping. "Which means you're going to have a brother or a sister."

She waited for the ecstatic openmouthed grin that had taken over Brookie's face when she'd given her the locket. Instead, the girl scooted to the edge of the couch, head tucked, shoulders slumped. "Why do you need a baby? I thought you wanted me."

"We do want you," she assured her, the hope steeling into something harder—determination. It fortified her against the fear. "This doesn't change anything, Brookie." She smoothed a finger over the heart-shaped locket that dangled around the girl's neck. "Remember? You'll always be our daughter no matter what."

"We promise," Sawyer added. "No matter what. Forever."

She nodded, but her eyes were still cast down, and she wouldn't look at either one of them.

"It'll be great having a brother or a sister," Sawyer insisted, taking her hands in his like he hoped his excitement would rub off on her. "That means you'll always have a best friend. Someone to play with. And you can always watch out for each other."

Despite the nausea lingering in her stomach, Ruby smiled at him. Love bloomed in her heart yet again for this man. Sitting with him and hearing the love overflowing in his voice as he talked to their daughter made her heart feel whole. It was the same feeling she had to believe Brookie would experience one day. The girl still had so much to overcome—the mistrust, the fear, the insecurity. But she couldn't have found a better dad than Sawyer. And Ruby might not be the perfect mother, but her love for these two children of hers knew no limits.

Whatever it took for Brookie to find wholeness and happiness, they would get her through this together.

* * *

"I propose a toast!" Dad raised his glass.

Everyone around the dinner table quieted—Bryce and Avery, Ben and Paige, Isaac and Julia, Elsie and Thomas. Brookie had been pretty quiet since the great revealing of the pregnancy, but at least her smile was starting to come back.

"To my son and his beautiful new wife," his father said. "May you find the same happiness your mother and I have."

A blush intensified Ruby's natural coloring, making her face radiant as everyone cheered and clinked their glasses together.

Sawyer couldn't help but smile. Had to hand it to Dad. The man was making a heroic effort to atone for the disaster earlier. Come to think of it, Mom wasn't doing such a bad job either. Before dinner she'd made sure there was a proper introduction and she'd rearranged the seating so Brookie got to sit by her. She'd even insisted that the girl start calling her Grammy, just like all of her other grandchildren. During dinner, Mom had entertained Brookie with stories about him growing up—God knew she had plenty of material.

"To Ruby and Sawyer!" everyone chorused. A jovial tone took over the room as they clanged their glasses again.

"May you two kids have a long and happy marriage," Thomas added, stretching his arm around Aunt Elsie and nestling her in against his side.

Color rose to her face, too. In typical Aunt Elsie fashion, she scooted some distance between them. Though Thomas had become a fixture around the ranch as of late, Aunt Elsie insisted they weren't dating.

"To the babies!" Paige blurted, then slapped a hand over her mouth.

"Babies? As in plural?" Sawyer asked, jaw suspended in disbelief. Did she know something he didn't?

Paige turned to Ben's sister, Julia. "Sorry! I'm just so excited that I'm gonna be an auntie!"

"What?" Aunt Elsie gasped.

Isaac and Julia both grinned. "We didn't want to steal Sawyer and Ruby's thunder with the wedding coming up and everything," Isaac said.

"But yes," Julia continued. "We're expecting a baby, too. Next spring."

"Oh my God!" Ruby shot out of her chair and threw her arms around Julia. "Are you kidding? This is the best news!"

Sawyer followed her to the other side of the table and

shook Isaac's hand. "Congratulations, man." Those two deserved it. After everything Julia had been through with her accident and with Isaac in the navy, they'd finally reconnected at Ben and Paige's wedding. Now here they were, starting a family of their own.

"Maybe the babies will share a birthday!" Avery cried, bouncing Lily on her lap. "Think of the parties we'll have. It'll be so much fun!" She pressed a kiss against her daughter's temple. "You're going to have little cousins to play with, sweetie."

Sawyer cringed. He knew Avery hadn't meant anything by it, but Lily already had a cousin. He looked over at his daughter, and sure enough, Brookie's smiled had thinned into a worried expression.

A hurricane-force sadness beat against his chest. No matter how many times they told her they loved her, that they wanted her, she still doubted. She still doubted her place here with them, with their extended family.

Bryce happened to be sitting across the table from Brooklyn. His cousin shot him a look of understanding before he reached over and patted her hand. "And all of the babies will have the best older, wiser cousin in the world," Bryce told her. "They're gonna want to be just like you."

"Of course they will," Avery agreed quickly, her face flushed. "You're such a good cousin to Lily," she went on.

Murmurs of agreement hummed around the room while all of the adults exchanged concerned glances. They knew Brookie's struggle. They'd seen it over the last month.

Ruby looked at Sawyer with sadness muting her eyes. This was what she'd worried about. Why she hadn't wanted to tell her about the baby yet. They hadn't been able to make the adoption official, and he had a feeling Brookie wouldn't feel secure until they did. That was the worst part about it. Damn. He had to call the social worker again. See if they could move things up. He didn't know what to say anymore...

"To Brookie!" Mom said, raising her glass and saving the whole mood of the party. She squeezed the girl's hand. "We're so happy you're part of our family now."

A shadow of a smile crept across Brookie's lips as everyone raised their glasses.

"To Brookie!"

Sawyer silently thanked his mother with a smile. Brookie might doubt now, but someday she would know. She would feel connected, and her whole identity would be rooted in something bigger.

As long as they had this community—this family—they could make it through anything.

CHAPTER FIVE

Y ou don't have to stay, you know," Ruby said, fully aware that the comfort of snuggling up with Sawyer on the couch robbed the words of any real conviction. The yawn that broke through clearly revealed she never wanted him to leave. "Shouldn't you be out partying to celebrate your last weekend of bachelorhood?"

"Screw bachelorhood," Sawyer said, massaging her shoulder. "This is where I want to be."

Yes. Her, too. They were sitting in her living room— the living room that would be officially *theirs* in just two more days. And it was so cozy and lovely. Almost indulgent. Something out of a dream. After they'd put Brookie to bed, Sawyer had built a fire. It crackled inside the charming brick hearth, painting the room with a tranquil glow that somehow caressed away the tension from the scene at dinner. Ruby burrowed even closer to Sawyer's solid shoulder, though it was difficult to scooch her lower body right up against his, what with Nellie the wonder dog wedged between them.

"Thanks for driving us home." After everything that had happened at dinner, Sawyer had wanted to get

Brookie tucked in so he could make sure she was okay. The poor girl had been so quiet on the ride home. So withdrawn. Though they'd tried to coax out her feelings with the questions they'd learned in their training, she kept insisting that she was simply tired and wanted to go to bed.

Ruby hoped that was the case. It sure hadn't taken Brookie long to fall asleep.

"Oh, by the way, I'm staying all night," Sawyer said in his *don't argue* tone. "Need to keep an eye on you. You weren't feeling good earlier."

As if she needed a reminder. She squeezed her eyes shut, trying to block out the memory of that special meeting with his parents. "I can't believe I threw up in front of James and Marybeth Hawkins." They were the picture of sophistication and class.

"They've already forgotten all about it," he insisted.

She laughed. "Right. They'll never forget that introduction." She sure wouldn't.

"They love you," he murmured in her ear. "Because I love you."

She rested her head against his chest, feeling his heart beat right into hers. "I love you, too." That was what grounded her now, what kept her steady. Love. She prayed it was enough. For him. For Brookie. For the baby. She might not be able to fix everything in their lives, but she wanted to love them all well.

Still, if the scene at dinner was any indication, this was going to be a long road with Brookie.

Fatigue pulled at her eyelids. "Are we crazy, Sawyer?"

He stretched his neck to peer down at her, those blue eyes focused and intense. "What'd you mean?"

"I mean jumping into all of this so fast. We'll have two

kids." The thought was so foreign. Six months ago, she never thought she'd even have one child...

"We're not crazy," he said, pulling her in tighter. "We're brave."

That's what he'd taught her. How to be brave. And as long as they were together, she could do it—anything, whatever it took. She held her breath, wanting to feel only the solidness of his body against hers. The strength. The love. That was real. That bond was real.

Sawyer touched his lips to the ridge of her ear, prying a soft sigh from her mouth. Goose bumps spread across her right side, pricking her body with that delicious anticipation only he could tease out of her.

"This is what life is about, Ruby. This is what matters." His warm breath grazed her eardrum. "You and Brookie and the baby are what matter to me."

His lips slipped down her neck, to the base of her jaw, where his tongue grazed her skin, and she should've been prepared, but every time he kissed her that way—all passionate and indulgent—it hit like a shock, causing a wave of pleasure to ripple down her stomach, then back up again until she wanted nothing more than to be pressed against him, clinging to him while they made love...

With a disgruntled sniff, Nellie stood and shook herself, sighing as if to say *not again*.

Ruby laughed. The dog was like a teenager who got grossed out every time Mom and Dad started to get frisky.

Without a glance back, Nellie pranced down the hall, presumably heading for the princess doggy bed Brookie had moved into her room.

"Come on." Sawyer scooted himself off the couch and took her hand in his, pulling her up against his body, his strong hands massaging her shoulders in the most sensual, inviting way. "After the day you've had, I think you could use a back rub."

She could use more than a back rub, but she didn't need to tell him that. He knew her. Everything. Over the last couple of months, she'd held nothing back from him. And now, even the thought of his hands on her body was enough to send sparks of hunger dancing through her.

"It *was* a pretty tough day," she agreed, following him to the bedroom. She hadn't felt so sick in a long time, but after she'd eaten something, all of a sudden, her stomach seemed to settle.

With a wicked grin, Sawyer turned and locked the bedroom door. "Which means you deserve some special treatment." He slipped behind her and unzipped her dress, working his hands beneath the fabric to caress the tension from that vise grip that had claimed her spine.

Her head fell forward as his hands worked her weary muscles over, digging in and kneading.

With each touch, everything in her—all of the worry and tension softened into peace. She was still standing, but she might as well have been floating.

Leaning close, Sawyer kissed her neck while his fingers unclasped her bra. Then he spread his hands over her skin, cleverly brushing her dress and bra straps over her shoulders so that her clothes fell away from her body.

"Feeling better now?" he murmured against her neck while his hands skimmed her lower back, climbing their way down to her underwear.

"So much better," she whispered, shuddering in rapture at the way his hands knew her body.

"God, I never thought you could get any sexier," Sawyer said, tugging down her silk undies. "Then you got pregnant." He slipped in front of her and ran his hands over the small swell of her belly, circling his fingers around her belly button. "I love you so much, baby." His hands moved to her bare hips and tugged her closer, which gave her the perfect opportunity to start undoing the buttons on his shirt.

"I love you, too, Officer Hawkins," she teased, continuing her way down the buttons until she could tear the thing off of his shoulders. His chest. Oh, mercy, his chest. Tossing the shirt aside, she pressed her palms against the hard muscles, moving them over the dents and bends.

Heavy breaths broadened his shoulders, and she loved seeing that look on his face, the one that proved she could seduce him, too. She loved the hard beat of his heart beneath her palm, the feel of his erection pressing against his jeans.

"I love your body," she said, in case she hadn't already made that clear. Lifting her lips to his neck, she climbed her way up to his ear. "You know what else I love?" she murmured, undoing his pants and shoving them down.

His breath hitched. "What?"

"Making love to you." She slipped her hand into his and pulled him toward the bed.

He stepped out of his pants and left them behind. "You're amazing," he breathed against her lips. Then he tilted up her chin and kissed her mouth in a teasing preview. The heat of his tongue, the strong grip of his hands against the back of her head, anchored her in that moment, stilling her in the sea of stress and worries that'd had her floundering all day. The intimate connection carried her away from everything else until it was only the two of them breathing, kissing, touching.

"How long has it been?" he whispered in her ear before

nipping his way down her neck and over her breasts, grazing his tongue across her skin. "It feels like forever since I kissed these."

A titillating shiver overtook her. She threaded her fingers into that beautiful mess of thick dark hair. "I believe it's been..." Her lungs caught. *Ohhhh*... She swore his tongue possessed some sort of magic. "Two days since you came over for lunch."

He grinned, hugging her against him. "That was the best lunch ever."

"The best until the next lunch," she promised, pushing him down to the mattress. He caught her hand and pulled her with him.

They hit the bed, bodies tangled together, and he rolled onto his side next to her, sliding his hand up her thigh, then higher until her entire lower half was clenched with want. His fingers danced over her hip bones in long, teasing strokes.

She let her head fall to the pillow, feeling that anticipation mount into a seductive pressure that pulsed through her. "I need you," she breathed. "God, Sawyer, I need you."

His wet mouth kissed her neck while the heel of his hand parted her legs until his fingers stretched into her. She moaned as he fingered her center, unleashing the sensations that made her hands grab at the sheets.

"Mmmm," he murmured, obviously fascinated by watching her lose herself in the ecstasy of his touch. But as much as he enjoyed turning her on, she had other plans. Shifting, she turned on her side and swung her leg over his waist so she could stroke him.

"Oh," he sighed, shoulders going limp as she thoroughly rubbed both hands up and down the length of his stretched flesh. He convulsed against her, straining his hips closer.

"Come here," he growled, his hands gripping her hips and guiding her over his body.

She straddled him, clasped their hands together, and pinned his against the mattress, leaning over to kiss him. And maybe to torture him just a little.

He groaned, lifting his head to kiss her breasts. But that wasn't enough. Not even close. He'd already pulled her body taut—pushing her right to the edge—and there was only one thing that could finish her, that could satisfy the craving he'd stirred up inside of her.

Moving her body down onto his, she hitched her hips and his thrust met hers. The feel of him sliding so deep into her released a cry of pleasure from her lips. Eyes wide, she pressed a hand over her mouth. Unlike their little lunchtime rendezvous, they had to be quiet.

"I love that sound," Sawyer whispered, lifting his hips until she rode him, each thrust so hard and fast that the friction heated her core. She bit down on her lip to keep quiet, but a moan of pleasure snuck out. She couldn't help it. Sawyer made it very, very, very hard to stay quiet.

His hands clasped hers as he kept their rhythm, the one they'd found together. The one that made her heart pound and her lungs burn and her body let go.

Oh God, she loved how he made her let go.

Thrusting her body higher, he grunted her name, and that was it; she couldn't hold on. She arched her back, pressing into him at an angle that broke her apart. Pleasure surged, wave after wave, rendering the rest of her body useless. She collapsed over Sawyer and buried her face in a pillow so she could cry out the way her release demanded.

He came right behind her, locking her tight in his arms, body thrashing beneath hers, a low moan radiating from his throat.

She tried to move, to let him breathe, but her body had been encased in a lovely, lazy warmth that made everything too heavy.

He shimmied to his side and settled her against him, kissing her temple, then wrapping his arms all the way around her so that his hands met at her belly.

"You'll always be enough for me, Ruby," he said, resting his cheek against hers. She snuggled in closer, believing again that everything would work out, that they could manage whatever came their way.

They would always be enough together.

* * *

Someone was screaming.

Sawyer bolted upright in bed, heart tumbling like a boulder down a rock wall. Was it a dream? He held his breath.

"Sawyer! Oh God!" Ruby screamed from someplace distant and muffled.

Not a dream. The sound of her fear gripped him. He shot off the bed and tore out of the room, nearly colliding with Ruby in the doorway.

"She's gone," she wheezed, then bent over as though she'd been running. "Brookie is gone."

"No." That was crazy. She wasn't gone. She couldn't be gone. He'd checked on her at one o'clock this morning and she'd been peacefully sleeping in her bed. He took Ruby's shoulders in his hands to settle her. Getting worked up like this couldn't be good for the baby. "She's here somewhere," he said, choking back his panic. She had to be here. "She probably went next door to Aunt Elsie's for doughnuts."

But Ruby's head shook. Tears streaked her cheeks. Her

body shuddered. "I just called. Elsie hasn't seen her this morning."

His field of vision shrank. All he could see was Ruby's face, pale and terrified. "She took Nellie for a walk, then," he wheezed. Panic throbbed in his heart.

"I found Nellie curled up by the front door," she sobbed. "It was unlocked, Sawyer. And her coat is gone."

The room turned into a narrow tunnel. He stumbled around Ruby and jogged to Brookie's bedroom. Everything was neat and girly. The frilly white bedspread. The purple paint and flowery curtains she and Ruby had picked out one month ago.

He walked around, noting the details. Her pajamas were piled neatly on the bed. The coat that usually hung in her closet was gone. His pulse screamed in his ears as he ran back to the living room, passing Ruby and charging out the front door. Her bike had been propped up against the front porch last night...

Gripping the railing, he tripped down the steps, unable to find his footing.

It was gone. Which meant no one had come in and taken her. She'd left on her own.

"Ruby! Sawyer!" Aunt Elsie ran toward him, still in her bathrobe. "Did you find Brookie? Is she okay?"

"She ran away," he said, the shock of it rooting him to the ground. He couldn't move, couldn't turn back to face the brokenness on Ruby's face. How could she walk away from them?

"It's because of the baby," she sniffled. "I knew she wasn't ready. She needed more time to adjust..." The words dissolved into a cry of agony.

Sawyer inhaled deeply enough to stop his own torment. *Think like a cop.* He had to think like a cop right now and take action. Every second that passed meant she got farther away from them, and he knew the statistics. The more time that passed the less chance they had of finding her.

He sprinted up the porch steps, an adrenaline-fueled fire burning through him. "We need pictures of her." He caught Ruby's hand in his and tugged her back into the house. "Recent pictures. Print some out."

"I'll help you," Aunt Elsie said, rushing to Ruby's side while he took off to the bedroom to pull on a sweatshirt and snatch his cell phone off the bedside table. When he came back out into the living room, Ruby was slumped on the couch holding her face in her hands.

Aunt Elsie stood nearby, talking on the phone. Had to be Thomas, from the sound of things.

"Hey." He knelt in front of his fiancée, searching for her eyes, attempting to fill her with the hope and confidence he was so desperately trying to grasp.

"We have to find her," she moaned. "We have to find her right now. We don't even know how long she's been gone..."

"I'll find her," he promised. He would fucking mobilize everyone he knew. Every person he'd ever had a conversation with in this town. He'd beg for their help until they had an army out searching. He shot to his feet and snatched his keys off the coffee table.

Ruby clawed at his shirt. "Where are you going?"

"I'm gonna call the station and start searching. They can get the word out." They could organize and set up perimeters and call out the search and rescue dogs. But he had to get out there now.

Ruby flailed to her feet. "I'm coming with you." She started to fly past him, but he caught her in a bear hug.

"No." He gazed down into her eyes. "Ruby, honey, I need you to stay here."

She fought his grip. "I can't! I have to come with you. I have to find her...Oh God, our sweet girl..."

"She might come back on her own." *God, please let her come back.* "If she does, you need to be here for her." He steered her to the couch. "And you need to think about the baby. Too much stress isn't good." She already looked weak and sick. He felt it, too, a raw fear taunting at the back of his mind, pounding through his pulse points. But he couldn't let it take over.

"I have to go." He nodded toward Elsie. His aunt would have to keep Ruby here and do her best to keep her calm.

"Come on, dear," Elsie said, taking her hand. "Let me make you some tea. Everything will be fine. They'll find her," she reassured in that wise, comforting way. "Thomas is already on his way to the station, too."

Ruby allowed herself to be led a few steps, then stopped abruptly. "Oh God. Oh my God." Sobs racked her upper body until she bent over. "I can't believe she's gone." The expression on her face gutted him. Her eyes were wide and hollow, her mouth twisted with pain. "So many things could've happened to her." She gripped his shirt in her fist. "We can't lose her, Sawyer," she gasped, swaying as though she was about to faint.

"We're not gonna lose her," he said firmly, holding her up, letting her sob against his chest.

"Okay, honey. Everything will be okay." He lifted her into his arms and lowered her to the couch, smoothing his hand over her hair until she raised her eyes to his. "I need you to have faith in me, Ruby," he said, his own raking fear taking his voice low. "I'll find her. Trust me." He rested his hand on her belly. "Take care of our little peanut. That's your job right now. To wait for Brookie to come home and take care of this baby."

Leaving her in Aunt Elsie's capable hands, Sawyer sprinted out the front door and called dispatch to report a runaway. God, a runaway. He'd heard too many stories about the terrible things that happened to girls who ran away. Traffickers picked them up. Or they got hurt. She was on her bike. Crossing streets...

Shutting it all out, he climbed into his truck and peeled down the driveway, straining his eyes to see through the early-morning haze. Nothing. He saw nothing but deserted streets that were just as empty and dark as his heart. God, where was she? He didn't know. He had no idea where to start looking, but he would find her. He would walk every square mile of this town until he got her back.

They couldn't lose the daughter they'd only just found.

CHAPTER SIX

Ruby had experienced terrifying nightmares before—dreams where she'd felt the fingers of darkness curl around her neck, suffocating her with fear. She'd wake, heart racked with convulsions, pearls of sweat rolling down her temples. Though stuck in a state of chaos, all she had to do was inhale the familiar reality of her new life—the laundry-fresh scent of her comforter, the melon candle she kept on the nightstand. Then she could exhale the terror. But now every breath she took in, every breath that left her lips, kept her suspended in a cold and complete darkness.

On the outskirts of everything, she was vaguely aware of the concerned whispers rebounding between Paige, Avery, Julia, and Elsie, but she couldn't seem to bring the world into focus so she could hear what they were saying. She could only picture Brookie's sweet face, those bright innocent eyes, the curious quirk to her mouth.

My God. Ruby thought she had already been through hell—the victim of neglect in the foster system growing up, coming out of it only to find herself tangled in an abusive relationship. But she didn't know it was possible for her heart to hurt like this.

Their little girl had walked away...

"Ruby, sweetie..." Paige wedged herself next to her on the couch. "Can you try to eat something? Please?" She held up a plate. "Elsie made scrambled eggs and bacon. You need the protein."

The salty scent made her stomach clench with a nauseating shudder. She pressed her fingers against her lips, shaking her head slowly back and forth, that small movement making her dizzy. "I can't," she whispered. Her body—her heart—felt completely empty, but she couldn't fill it with anything besides the joy of holding Brookie in her arms again.

"You need energy," Avery said gently. She sat on the coffee table across from Ruby, knees touching hers, bouncing a squirming Lily on her lap. "And so does the baby."

Looking right through them, she searched the other side of the room for Elsie. "Has Sawyer called?" she asked, wringing her hands to alleviate the strain in her heart.

"Not yet," the woman murmured. "But he's only been gone for a half hour, dear. They're likely still getting organized."

A half hour? Was that all? It seemed more like a year the way the minutes had stretched out, tormenting her with their never-ending silence. Each one gave her mind cause to wander farther and farther into the realm of ugly possibilities. "What if she went into the mountains?" Brookie was so small, so vulnerable, and she had no one to protect her out there...

"Then Sawyer will find her," Julia insisted, wheeling herself over. "Along with Isaac and Ben and Bryce. They're all out there searching. They won't stop until they find her." She said it with such confidence, such unwavering hope, that it buoyed her, giving her a better grasp on her waning strength.

"I should be out there, too." They were all out searching for her daughter while she sat here helpless. She was so sick of feeling helpless. There was a time in her life when she'd let weakness take her over, when she'd believed she didn't have the power to change things. But she thought she'd left that scared woman behind.

"You need to rest," Avery insisted, settling Lily on the floor.

"Rest?" The wisp of strength sparked anger and built within her until it fortified every cell. "I'm not dying of cancer. I'm pregnant," she spat. Why had Sawyer made her stay at the house? Why the hell weren't they out there searching together?

I need you to have faith in me.

She didn't know how. She didn't know how to hold on to that faith when a chunk of her heart was missing.

"How about some tea?" Elsie set a steaming mug in front of her. "It's chamomile. Your favorite."

Though the anger boiled, she tried to force herself to smile and say thank you. These women had been with her through the worst of everything. Through the time when she'd gone back to confront her abusive ex-fiancé, through the months of counseling and dealing with the lingering pain after. They had befriended her when she had no one else in the world. They'd become her family. They'd made her strong enough to face anything.

Even this.

Hands trembling, she lifted the mug and sipped. The warmth blazed a trail down her throat, warding off the cold fear that had encased her heart. Inhaling, she straightened, stacking her shoulders, even under the unbearable weight.

She'd had to dig deeply to find her courage before, and now she was braver and stronger than Sawyer was giving her credit for.

After another sip of tea, she plunked down the mug on the coffee table. "I can't sit here and wait." She started to stand, but Paige tugged her back down.

"Whoa, chica. We all know you're Superwoman, but right now you have to think about the baby."

"I am thinking about the baby," she shot back, not caring that her voice had risen. "I'm thinking about my entire family, damn it." Things wouldn't always be easy. There would be battles, moments of darkness and despair. Life had already taught her that. And she refused to hide from them. She refused to let Sawyer take this on by himself.

Shaking off Paige's grip, she pushed to her feet. "My little girl needs me." She stared them down, focusing her glare mainly on Avery, who'd pulled her toddler back into her lap. "What would you do if you were me?"

The woman's gaze dropped to the ground. She got it.

"I'm going to look for her." And no one could stop her. Not her friends and not Sawyer. Something had happened to Ruby when she became a mother. When she'd made the decision to adopt Brookie—to make the girl hers forever— her whole focus had shifted. And the only thing that mattered to her in the world was making sure her daughter was safe.

Taking their silence as a victory, she stalked across the room, ripped open the closet door, and pulled out a coat. "Elsie and Julia, will you wait here in case she comes back?"

"Well, of course, dear, but shouldn't you eat some—"

"Thank you." She cut off Elsie before glancing at Paige,

then Avery. "Are you two coming with me? Or am I doing this alone?"

They exchanged a concerned look, but both stood, and Avery handed Lily off to her grandma.

"Of course we're coming with you," Paige grumbled. "But you're telling Sawyer we did everything in our power to try to stop you. Understand?"

"Yes." She would happily tell him she defied his orders to be part of the search party that was looking for Brookie. He didn't get to take that away from her. He didn't get to treat her like a child. Sawyer should know her well enough to know she didn't need to be protected all the time. This was supposed to be a partnership, only he wasn't giving her the chance to carry her part of the burden.

He didn't think she could handle it, but she would prove him wrong.

* * *

A frigid wind blew straight through her as Ruby got out of the car.

Heavy gray clouds sagged over the mountains, shrouding the peaks in a gloomy haze. She'd always thought they were so beautiful—the towering granite spikes that loomed at a distance, but now they looked dangerous. Cold. Brookie could be out there somewhere, wandering alone in the unforgiving wilderness.

They hadn't found her yet.

On the way over, Paige had called Ben to get an update, and he'd told her everyone was gathering in the park. They'd already had the police search the airport and bus stops, and they'd set up perimeters on the highway at both ends of town, he'd said. But they hadn't found her. The next step was launching a foot search.

Paige came around the car and gathered her in a half hug. "Look at this! Half the town must be here."

Staggering under the weight of it all, Ruby turned, taking in her first view of the park. It had always been one of her favorite spots in Aspen—a small manicured gem in the center of town. Green grass, a small playground, and a bandstand where they put on summer concerts. She and Sawyer and Brookie had had a picnic there just last week, enjoying the last of the Indian summer they'd experienced through October.

Now, instead of kids playing and dogs chasing Frisbees, the park swarmed with orderly activity. A massive crowd had gathered around the bandstand. Police buzzed among them, handing out flyers, directing them.

There had to be a hundred people here. All searching for Brookie. "Wow," she whispered, hope percolating once again.

"Look at all of these people," Avery said, pulling on a wool cap. "We'll find her for sure."

The sight of so many people here to help made Ruby believe it. "Come on." She linked her arms through Paige's and Avery's, and the three of them made their way across the street. It wasn't hard to find Sawyer. He stood in the center of the chaos, head ducked in to talk with one of the other officers on the scene. When he saw her approach, his jaw locked. "Thanks, Sommers. Keep me posted," he said, dismissing the other man.

Ruby's heart ached with the need to be wrapped in his arms, to feel his solid body against hers to quiet the storm inside of her. But his stony expression slowed her steps. She wriggled away from her friends and stopped, studying him from a distance.

Stress lined his mouth and eyes. His gaze wouldn't quite meet hers. He marched over. "What're you doing here?" His fatherly tone set her on edge. It almost sounded like he didn't want her here.

"I came to search for Brookie," she ground out. "You can't expect me to sit around and do nothing." All she'd done was imagine the worst possible things that could've happened to her. At least if she was out here, moving, searching, she would be *doing* something.

"Go back to the house, Ruby," Sawyer said with an uncharacteristic coldness. He looked at Paige. "Take her home."

"Excuse me?" His sharp tone delivered a blow to her heart. "This is not your decision," she informed him. "I'm staying. I'm going to search along with everyone else and you're not going to stop me."

His cheeks seemed to hollow, like he'd aged ten years in a matter of minutes.

"Um, we'll just wait over there," Paige murmured, dragging Avery toward a table where someone had set up a coffee station.

"What's the plan?" Ruby demanded before he could start lecturing her about taking it easy again.

Sawyer stared at something over her shoulder. "Bryce and I are taking the ATVs up Aspen Mountain."

"You think she went up the mountain?"

"I don't know," he snapped, turning his back to her. "I don't know where she is."

She watched him stalk away, swallowing back tears. Why was he acting so distant? Sawyer never talked to her this way. He never raised his voice and dismissed her.

She caught up with him and grabbed his arm. "I'm coming with you."

He jerked away. "There's no way in hell I'm letting you come with us." His head shook. "On an ATV, Ruby? Are you out of your mind?"

She fought the sting the words caused. "I want to help."

He finally looked at her, straight into her eyes. She waited for him to pull her close, to stroke her cheek the way he so often did. Instead his face hardened. "You shouldn't even be out here. The stress isn't good for the baby."

"The baby is fine," she nearly yelled. Pressing her eyes closed, she tried to regain control. "But Brookie isn't. She's alone, Sawyer. And I sure as hell am not going to sit on my ass at home while she's out here somewhere." This time she turned her back on him. He'd shut her out. He'd pushed her away when she needed him. When he needed her. "I'm staying," she called over her shoulder. "So deal with it." By the time she'd made it to Avery, Bryce, Paige, and Ben, the trembling in her hands had spread to her shoulders.

Sawyer stood where she left him, upper body slumped, staring at the ground. An overwhelming sadness tempted her to run back to him, but he'd made it clear he didn't want her around. Grinding her jaw against the tears, she latched herself onto her friends again. "Come on," she said, tugging them toward the street. "We're going to start searching the town." She would knock on every door they passed until she found someone who'd seen Brookie.

"Is Sawyer okay with that?" Avery asked uncertainly.

"It doesn't matter." He wasn't even acting like Sawyer. It was like he'd become someone else.

"He's scared," Paige said, linking her arm through Ruby's. "I've never seen him so scared."

Ruby kept walking. "He's not acting scared. He's acting angry." At her. As if he blamed her for the whole thing.

Avery slipped in front of her, cutting off Ruby's steps.

"Think of how this feels for him, sweetie. He's used to being in control, solving people's problems. But right now he feels as helpless as we do."

"Then why won't he say that?" Instead of pushing her away? Instead of talking to her like she was five years old?

"He's in cop mode," Paige said. "Trust me. I've seen it before. When he's on a case, he doesn't break his focus for anything. Especially not for emotions."

"But that's not fair. You can't do that in a relationship." She didn't want him to hide that part of himself from her. That was real. He'd seen her cry so many times. He'd seen her at her worst. He didn't always have to be the hero. He could hurt, too. He could be lost. Then she could help him find himself again just like he'd done for her. That was what a marriage had to be. They had to be in it together. "I want to be there for him. I want him to *let* me be there."

"Maybe that's what he needs to hear." Paige nudged her back toward the park.

Her shoulders slumped. Her friends were right. Sawyer had shown her nothing but patience, especially when she hadn't been willing to let him in all those months ago. He deserved that same patience from her.

She glanced at the crowd milling around the park. "I should find him." They had to start over, align themselves on the same side.

Leaving her friends on the sidewalk, she rushed back to the bandstand, pushing her way through the crowd, searching the blurred faces for him.

"Ruby." Thomas snagged her sleeve. "How're you holding up?" He gave her a hug, and she let herself steal an extra few seconds in his comforting, fatherly arms.

"Okay," she whispered. But she wasn't. She was aching for Sawyer, aching for Brookie, aching for their little family. "Have you seen Sawyer?" she asked Thomas, forcing herself upright. "He was just here..."

"He went off with Bryce, Isaac, and Ben. They're headed up the mountain."

A crushing disappointment bore down on her.

"Anything I can do for you?" Thomas asked.

"No. Thank you." No one but Sawyer could soothe that pain inside of her. He was the only one who could reassure her that they would be all right. That no matter what else happened, their love for each other would sustain them and bring them through. No one but Sawyer could steady her.

And he was already gone.

CHAPTER SEVEN

Sawyer gunned the ATV up an embankment and jerked on the brakes. Standing, he tried to get a look at the trail above. Nothing but the massive trees and boulders, the endless wilderness stretching out in all directions. No sign of Brooklyn. Not a trace. She could be anywhere in the hundreds of thousands of acres surrounding them.

A cold fury boiled inside of him, fueling him to crank the throttle.

The machine tore up the trail, jostling his body, charging him with a surge of adrenaline, but he couldn't move fast enough. Couldn't change anything. Couldn't rewind the day back into the night.

How had he slept through the sound of the front door unlocking and opening? Why hadn't he woken up? Why hadn't he made absolutely sure Brookie was okay after the shock of hearing about the baby?

He could've been more aware. Picked up on the fact that she wasn't happy. He should've. This was on him. Ruby had been right to be concerned about her, yet he'd brushed it aside.

A tree appeared in front of him. He jerked the handlebars and squeezed the brakes again, jolting the thing to a stop. Heavy breaths pressed into his ribs, echoing in his helmet.

A cold wind boiled the murky clouds above him, blowing against him or maybe through him. Though sweat glazed his skin beneath his helmet and fleece, he shivered. God, where was Brookie?

Shadows passed in front of his vision—the what-ifs building into a nightmare that threatened to take over.

"Hawkins!"

Bryce's shout shattered the images.

His cousin eased his ATV up next to him. "Damn. Slow down. You're gonna kill yourself."

"I can't slow down." It felt like he was already dying. Like some unbearable weight was slowly crushing his heart. "I can't stop. Not until I find her." Because if he did—if he stopped and sat still, he wouldn't be able to climb out of the darkness.

"Hey." Bryce reached over and planted a hearty grip on his shoulder. "*We'll* find her. It's not up to you. You don't have to do it alone."

The reminder grated against the years of training and experience on the job. He always fixed things on his own. That was part of the job description. He solved problems, brought justice to hopeless situations. He should be enough. He should be able to do it for his own family.

With a jerk of his hand, he gunned the ATV's engine, ready to put it in drive. But before he could release the brakes, Bryce steered in front of him.

"Quit being such an ass."

"Excuse me?" He ripped off his helmet to release the heat that built against his skin. "My daughter is *gone*."

"No shit," Bryce said, ripping off his own helmet and cutting the engine. "And we love her, too. So stop acting like you're the only one who cares. I know you've already lost a baby, but—"

"Oh, so now we're gonna have a counseling session on the side of a damn mountain?" Screw that. "I don't have time for this."

"You're gonna fucking make time," Bryce shot back. "I saw what you did to Ruby down there."

"What the hell are you talking about?" What about what Ruby had done to him? Completely disregarding what he'd asked her to do. Putting herself and the baby in danger?

"I'm talking about shutting her out." Bryce glared at him the way only a cousin who was more like a brother could. "I'm talking about how you tried to make her stay home while you ran out to be the hero again. I'm talking about how you just pushed her away in the park. That kind of thing doesn't work in a marriage."

His hands fisted. He'd never hit Bryce. Well, not in anger, anyway, but he was this damn close. "She has to think about the baby," he growled. "This is too much for her."

"You're not gonna lose the baby," his cousin said, backing down. "I know you're worried because of what you went through with Matthew. But you won't lose this baby, Sawyer."

How the hell did he know that? Ruby had had problems in the past. She wasn't even supposed to be pregnant. Yesterday it had seemed like all of their dreams were coming true, and now everything was falling apart, piece by piece. And he couldn't stop it.

A crushing sorrow gripped his windpipe. "What if she

does? What if she loses the baby? And what if we don't find Brookie?" That was it, what he feared the most. The one fear he couldn't face. Losing these children who already owned his heart.

"We'll find her," his cousin said again. "But only together. All of us. And you and Ruby fighting on the same side."

Guilt wormed through him, tunneling through the walls he'd built around his heart to protect it from this kind of pain. Bryce was right. He never should've shut her out. The memory of her broken, sad eyes came back to haunt him.

"You're about to get married," his cousin reminded him. "You don't get to take things on your own anymore. You're a team. No matter what. Especially when life sucks."

"I wanted to protect her." Ruby had survived so much already. He wanted to give her a happy life, a life where she didn't have to suffer anymore.

"She doesn't need you to protect her," Bryce said, pulling his helmet back on. "She needs you to love her."

He did. He loved her more than he loved his own life. That's what he should've told her. Regret pounded through him as he gazed down at the town below. Where was she? "I should go back." He had to apologize. He had to let her in.

"I'll let Ben and Isaac know we're heading down," Bryce said before he peeled out.

Just as Sawyer went to slip his helmet back on, the radio clipped to his belt crackled.

"Hawkins? This is Officer Gonzales."

His heart stopped. He let the helmet fall to the ground

and ripped the radio off his belt. "This is Hawkins. Go ahead."

"Need you to meet me at the gas station over on Maroon Bells Road. I think we might have a lead."

* * *

Wind. Oh, that cold fall wind. It bit at Ruby's cheeks, chilling them until they tingled. A warm fire burned inside of her, fueling her to keep walking, to keep looking, to keep herself upright and moving. Brookie would freeze if they didn't find her soon. The temperature couldn't have been more than thirty degrees with the wind chill. And a billowing gray haze had replaced the friendly blue sky. Aspen had yet to see its first snowfall of the season, but it didn't look to be too far off.

Yanking up the zipper on her fleece, Ruby kept her head down and fought the wind's invisible force.

"You need to take a break," Paige insisted from behind her. Her friend jogged up next to her and yanked on her arm. Yeah, like that was enough to make her stop and sit down.

"I'm not taking a break," she said for the fifth time in an hour. And the way Paige and Avery were hounding her, it wouldn't be the last either. Yes, she knew her body had weakened considerably since they'd started out two hours ago. But she'd managed to block it all out—how Sawyer had been so cold to her earlier, the hunger, the thirst, the clouds descending on her head. She would keep blocking out everything until she saw Brookie. That's how she would make it through this. She could picture that moment when she would hold Brookie against her heart. She could smell the sweet scent of that strawberry shampoo they used on her hair . . .

Warmth flooded her. That's the picture she would keep in her mind, the one she would hold on to.

Leaving Avery and Paige a few steps behind, she chugged up the sidewalk to yet another house. The three of them had stood on so many front stoops—had knocked on so many front doors—that they didn't even look different anymore. As she raised her hand to knock, she vaguely noticed the red front door, the pot of silk flowers sitting on a wooden bench.

A small dog yipped from the other side of the stained wood. The dead bolt clanged, and it opened.

Ruby staggered back a step. This girl. This young girl with bouncing blond curls, glistening blue eyes, and dimples in her cheeks. It took only a second to place her. Charlotte. This was the girl in Brookie's class. Brookie had pointed her out when Ruby had volunteered a couple weeks ago. Charlotte was one who'd made things so hard on her. The one who'd planted the idea that Ruby and Sawyer wouldn't want her after they had their own child...

"My mom doesn't want to buy anything today," the girl announced with the practiced apathy of a preteen. She went to close the door, but Ruby braced a hand against it.

"Wait," she gasped. An ache gripped her belly and unleashed turmoil inside of her. The shaking anger shuddered through her until she couldn't hold her hands steady. Instead of befriending a girl who desperately needed someone to reach out to her, this girl had picked on her daughter...

"Who's at the door, sweetie?" A woman appeared behind Charlotte. She had the same hair, the same eyes, but a friendly way about her smile. "Can I help you?" she asked politely.

If Ruby had met her on the street, she would think this

woman was kind and approachable. So different from her daughter.

"I'm Ruby Hawkins." Or at least she was supposed to be. Tomorrow. "I'm Brooklyn's foster mom. She goes to school with your daughter Charlotte."

"Oh," the woman chirped. "So nice to meet you, Ruby. I'm Stephanie Taylor." She stuck out her hand and shook Ruby's, her warm skin providing a brief reprieve from the cold. "I've heard so many wonderful things about Brooklyn. Charlotte just adores her." She glanced down at her daughter, but Charlotte's face had paled and her eyes were as wide as Brookie's got when she was caught in a lie.

Yes. She was definitely caught, but Ruby hadn't come here to tell this woman all of the terrible things Charlotte had said. "Brookie is missing," she choked out, keeping her gaze firmly on the girl's face. "She ran away this morning."

"Oh my God," Stephanie gasped. "How awful." She stepped out onto the porch, her expression genuinely horrified. "What can we do? How can we help?"

Charlotte seemed frozen in place.

Ruby held out a flyer they'd been distributing at the park. Anger still thundered through her, churning her stomach, tightening her chest. "We're going door to door to ask if anyone has seen her. Or heard from her."

Stephanie took the flyer and glanced at it. Tears glossed the woman's eyes. "Oh, this is awful. I'm so, so, sorry. I can't even imagine..." She sank to her knees in front of her daughter. "Do you know anything, Char? Anything at all that will help them find Brooklyn?"

Ruby saw the girl swallow. She shook her head, eyes fallen. "No. I don't know anything. I swear. I haven't seen her."

The fear in her eyes disclosed the fact that she knew exactly why Brookie had run away.

Stephanie stood. "We'll help you search. Do you have extra flyers? We can knock on doors, too. That way you can cover more ground."

"Yes. Thank you," Ruby said, her throat hot with the gathering tears. How could such a wonderful woman have such a cruel child?

"I'll go get our coats." She squeezed her daughter's shoulder as she retreated down the small hallway, obviously thinking that Charlotte's sullen silence had something to do with worry over her friend.

After her mother was out of earshot, the girl started to cry. "Brookie's really gone?" She sniffled.

"Yes." And it didn't appear that she had to remind the girl why.

"I can't believe it," Charlotte whispered, wiping away her tears as though she was afraid her mother would see them. "Did she...say why? Did she leave a note?"

A pain radiated low across her stomach. Ruby placed a hand there, massaging and poking, but it wouldn't go away. "She didn't leave a note," she said. "But I know she was afraid we didn't want her." The pain deepened into a stabbing sensation that cut across her entire abdomen. Wrapping an arm around her stomach, she hunched and tried to lessen the sudden pressure.

"I'm so sorry," Charlotte cried softly. "I didn't mean to hurt her feelings. I shouldn't have said those things to her..."

"What things?" Stephanie asked. She rushed back to the front door. "What things did you say to Brooklyn?"

Charlotte glanced up at Ruby, but she couldn't stand straight anymore. She couldn't think past the terrible cramping that squeezed her stomach. *Oh God*. Was something wrong? She turned slightly, so she could lean her back against the brick wall.

"I told Brookie her mom and dad wouldn't want her if they had their own baby," the girl confessed.

"Charlotte!" Stephanie gaped at her daughter. "Why on earth would you say something like that?"

"I don't know!" she wailed. "I don't know. Sometimes foster parents aren't very nice. Like in *Anne of Green Gables*. But I didn't know she would run away!"

Ruby closed her eyes, the pain taking her over. It wasn't the stress. Wasn't the emotions. It was the baby. Something was wrong...

"Oh my God, I'm so sorry," Stephanie said, stepping closer. "I'm horrified. I can't believe Charlotte's behavior."

Ruby tried to answer, but her heart rate had spiked and her lungs couldn't keep up.

The woman placed a sympathetic hand on her shoulder. "Are you all right? We're going to do everything we can to help you find her," she assured her.

Ruby clamped her hand on to the woman's wrist. "My friends," she murmured. "I need you to find my friends." She couldn't stand anymore. It hurt so much. Slowly, she sank to the sidewalk.

"Oh no." Stephanie sank with her. "Are you sick?"

"I'm pregnant." A fresh batch of tears welled. *God, please let the baby be okay.* She couldn't lose this baby. Sawyer couldn't lose this baby. "My friends should be around somewhere. They were going to the neighbors' houses."

Stephanie glanced up at her daughter. "Go find her friends."

"Paige and Avery," she called as the girl hurried away.

"Do you want me to call your husband?" the woman asked.

"No." She shook her head. "No. Please. He has to keep searching for Brookie." If they called him, he would come. And Brookie needed him more than she did. Panting against the waves of pain, she pulled her knees into her chest.

"Oh, honey," the woman murmured. "Should I call an ambulance?"

"No." God, no. Paige and Avery could get her to the ER. "I'll be fine. Maybe just some water." She was so thirsty. When was the last time she'd even had anything to drink?

"Of course." Stephanie shot to her feet and disappeared right as Paige and Avery sprinted up the walkway.

"What happened?" Avery cried, dropping to her knees next to Ruby.

"Are you okay?" Paige shrieked, panic rising in her eyes.

"Cramps," Ruby managed. She slung an arm around her belly.

"Oh no," Avery whispered.

"Is that bad?" she asked her friend, the cold fear she'd felt all morning icing her over again.

"No," Paige insisted, glaring at Avery. "Everything's fine. The baby's fine."

"I'll call Bryce and have him find Sawyer," Avery said, already going for her phone.

"No," Ruby nearly shouted. "He can't stop searching. Not now. Not until they find her."

"But…don't you want him with you?" Avery demanded.

Yes. More than anything. She always wanted Sawyer with her. But once he heard about the baby, all he would want to do is be by her side, and their daughter needed him more right now. "I have you two," she said, trying to smile.

"That'll do." Until they knew what they were dealing with. "Like you said, everything is fine." She glanced at Paige for a shot of the woman's confident encouragement. Lord knew she needed it right now.

"That's right," Paige declared with a definitive nod. "Everything will be fine."

That's what Ruby was counting on.

CHAPTER EIGHT

Sawyer tried not to glare at the gas station owner, but that was quite the challenge. "So you're telling me a little girl came in here at six this morning—*alone*—and bought a package of powdered doughnuts and you didn't think it was strange?"

"She told me her parents were waiting outside," he shot back, standing at full height as though telling Sawyer to back off. He was a big guy, tall and bulky, skin inked like a badass, but Sawyer had adrenaline on his side.

"And you didn't think to glance outside and check?" He stepped up to the guy, fully knowing his anger was misplaced but not caring enough to harness it.

"What'd you want from me? This is Aspen. Not Denver."

Exactly. Things like this shouldn't happen here. To a family that was just starting out, to parents who've waited so long for children.

"Enough, Sawyer." Bryce pulled him away.

"Thanks for the info," Ben said to the gas station owner. "We appreciate it."

His friends formed a barrier around him, giving him no

choice but to go outside. In front of the glass, he paced, try-ing to relieve the pressure. If Brookie had been here at six, that meant she'd already been gone an hour and a half by the time they'd discovered she was missing. The gas sta-tion sat on the very western edge of the town, which meant she'd either continued on down the highway or headed up into the mountains. Neither scenario calmed him.

While he paced, his friends stood in a circle, trading the-ories.

"Wouldn't she go somewhere she was familiar with? Somewhere comfortable?" Isaac asked.

That stopped Sawyer cold.

"I mean, she's only eight. If they didn't find her at the airport or the bus station trying to get out of town, maybe she went someplace she knows."

Someplace she knew. Someplace comfortable. "The ranch." God, why hadn't he thought to search there in the first place? He looked at Bryce. "Did you see anything be-fore you took off this morning? Her bike?"

A look of sudden understanding dawned on his cousin's face. "I didn't see anything, but I couldn't find Moose be-fore we left. We were in a hurry, so I didn't worry too much about it…"

Moose, Bryce's massive Bernese mountain dog was missing. Brookie was missing. And those two loved each other.

Sawyer took off running for his SUV. "We have to search the ranch." It wouldn't have taken long for Brookie to get there after the gas station. It wasn't more than three miles up the road.

They all climbed into the car, huffing and out of breath.

"I should've looked around before we left," Bryce said. "I didn't think she could get all the way to the ranch by herself."

Sawyer jammed the key into the ignition and started the engine. "You'd be surprised what she can do when she's determined." The girl had learned how to fend for herself. That would be her greatest strength someday, but it could also hurt her. She had to learn to let people in, to let people help her. She had to learn how to depend on other people just like he did.

Flicking on the lights and siren, he tore out of the gas station parking lot.

"When we get there, Isaac and I'll search the lodge," Ben offered. "You two know the grounds much better."

"And I'll text Thomas and tell him to bring the search party to the ranch," Bryce added.

"Thanks." Hope soared through him for the first time in what felt like a dark eternity. "I should call Ruby," he said, digging out his phone. He hit the speed dial and braced it against his ear, maneuvering around the cars that pulled over.

It rang until finally her voice mail picked up.

"Can you try Avery?" he asked his cousin. He had to tell her they'd found a real lead, that they were getting closer.

Bryce called his wife and clicked on the speaker. "Hey, babe. You know where Ruby is?"

There was a long pause.

"Um. Yeah. I'm with her," she finally said.

"Tell her we've got a lead," Bryce said. "We're heading out to search the ranch. We think she might be there somewhere. That she might be with Moose."

"Oh. Good. That's great," Avery answered in an uncharacteristic monotone.

Sawyer and Bryce exchanged a look. She should've been ecstatic.

"Everything all right?" Bryce asked her.

"Yep!" Now Sawyer detected too much enthusiasm.

Something wasn't right. Sawyer held out his hand. "Let me talk to Ruby."

"Um. Now's not a good time."

"What?" Sawyer demanded. What the hell did that mean? He snatched the phone away and took it off speaker. "Look, Avery. I need to talk to Ruby. Put her on the phone. Please," he added before she hung up on him.

"S-he...um...well...c-can't talk right now," Avery stuttered.

"Why the hell not?" Sawyer was done being polite. Their daughter was missing and she couldn't talk to him right now?

"She's...in the restroom."

"Oh." Why hadn't she told him that in the first place? "Have her call me, then. The second she can."

"Of course," Avery said quickly. "I have to go. She'll call soon." The phone clicked. He tossed it back to Bryce.

"Everything okay?" Isaac asked, leaning between the seats.

"That was weird," he said. He couldn't get Avery's shaky tone out of his head. "Something's up. She was acting strange."

"Yeah, she didn't sound normal," Bryce agreed.

"Want me to call Paige?" Ben asked.

"Nah. Ruby'll tell me what's going on when she calls me back." She wasn't the kind of person to keep things from him. Back when they'd first met, she'd kept everything from him, but since then he'd earned her trust. He may have royally screwed up earlier, but he would make it up to her. Gunning the engine, he raced to the ranch's driveway.

"Let's go find our little girl."

* * *

"Bryce called me," Avery announced as she barged into the closet-like ER exam room.

Ruby shifted, trying to get herself comfortable. Once they'd found out she was pregnant, they'd whisked her to a room faster than a hot knife could cut through butter. Since then nurses had been in and out, fussing over her, forcing her to change into one of those hospital gowns.

Generous, the term "gown." It was more like a small square of cotton that flapped open in the back every time she moved.

She smoothed the blanket over her legs, grateful for the extra coverage. "You didn't tell him anything, did you?"

"Of course not. But I'm such a bad liar. He has to know something's up."

That was true. The woman told her husband everything. Every. Thing. She should've told Avery not to answer her phone.

Avery crossed the room and sat in the chair next to the gurney. "They said they have a lead on Brookie, though."

A bolt of hope struck her chest. "What? Where? Where is she?"

"They think she might be somewhere around the ranch."

"The ranch?" Could she have been eight miles away from home this whole time?

"We couldn't find Moose before we left," Avery explained. "I let him out at five when I woke up with Lily. But then we all went back to bed until Elsie called."

"You think Moose is with her?" Huge tears bubbled up and spilled over. That meant Brookie wasn't alone. Moose would protect her. He would watch out for her. "Oh my God." She let her head fall back against the pillow. "That's such good news. So they're there now? Looking for her?"

"That's where they were headed when he called." Avery breathed out a sigh. "I really think you need to tell Sawyer what's going on," she said quietly. "He deserves to know. And I told him you would call him back."

"No." She rested a hand on her belly, massaging gently, trying to quiet the ache. "I'm not telling him yet. We don't even know what we're dealing with." But she refused to consider the possibility that the baby was in trouble. The nurse had already come in to interview her; then she'd taken her vitals and found the baby's heartbeat. Oh, that sound! It was the pounding of life and hope, and it had beaten into her own body, strengthening her heart. She had yet to see the doctor, but that sound—that soft little pulsing had stayed with her, replaying over and over. The music of life. Everything would be okay. The baby was healthy. Sawyer was about to find Brookie. She had to believe that.

"My God, trying to find coffee around this joint is like searching for the Holy Grail," Paige complained on her way back into the room. She must've been gone for twenty minutes on her quest for a caffeine fix.

"So what'd I miss?" She plopped down on the bed next to Ruby.

"They think Brookie is at the ranch." She squirmed again, breathing shallowly through another hollow pounding in her abdomen. "They're there looking for her." She should be out there, too. The ranch had thousands of acres. They'd need a whole search party to help...

"Really?" Paige leaned in and hugged her neck. "That's great news. Oh God. I hope she's there."

"I talked to Bryce," Avery informed Paige. "And I'm pretty sure he could tell there's a crisis."

"You let her talk to Bryce?" Her friend whapped her shoulder. "Are you kidding? The woman who can't keep a secret to save her life?"

"I didn't know who was on the phone when she stepped out to answer it." Otherwise, you can bet she would've stolen the damn thing and thrown it out the window. The last thing Sawyer needed was something to divert his focus when they were so close to finding Brookie.

"I'm not good at keeping things from my husband, okay?" Avery gave them her best glare, but Ruby could still see the shadow of her friendly smile. "You act like that's a bad thi—"

The door busted open. In charged Elsie, followed by Julia, who was giving Lily a ride on her wheelchair.

"Ruby!" Elsie gushed, scurrying right for the gurney. "Oh, my dear girl. I can't believe this. Are you in pain?"

"I'm okay." Instead of sharp, shooting pains, the discomfort had eased into more of an intermittent cramping. Still uncomfortable, but getting better.

"Well, what is it? What's wrong?" Elsie demanded, her gaze bouncing first to Ruby, then to Avery, then to Paige.

"No doctor yet," Paige answered for her.

"What?" The woman pinned her hands to her hips, which somehow made her seem taller. "Whyever not?"

"ERs are notorious for taking forever," Julia said, spinning her chair in circles to make Lily giggle.

But Elsie looked downright offended. "Well, that's ridiculous. You're expecting a baby, for heaven's sakes! They need to get on this." She stalked to the door. "Don't you worry, dear. I'll take care of this right now."

"That's okay. I—"

But Elsie left the room in a cloud of obvious disgust. The

woman's tenacity made her smile. She should know better. Never try to stop Elsie when she's on a mission.

"So now that they have a lead on Brookie, is Sawyer on his way?" Julia asked, wheeling herself closer to the bed.

"No. He doesn't know." Ruby extended her arms, and Julia helped Lily climb up onto the mattress. Ruby pulled the girl in close, inhaling that powdery, baby-fresh scent. "And no one's going to tell him, either." She shot Paige and Avery a look. "Not until Brookie is found."

"Understood." Julia slipped her hand into Ruby's and squeezed. "From what I hear, they're gonna find her real soon."

Her throat started to close up again, so she simply nodded and buried her nose in Lily's soft hair. God, she couldn't wait to hold Brookie. Couldn't wait to hold her and Sawyer's sweet baby in her arms.

"Not to worry, dear." Elsie paraded back into the room, the beaming smile on her face indicating that she'd accomplished her mission. "I've found the best doctor in the business."

Meg Carlson, a longtime friend of the Walker family, followed Elsie into the room. Ruby had met her a handful of times at various events, but she'd never really talked to her.

"So I hear I'm late," Meg said with her friendly smile.

Ruby's face heated. "No. I mean, *I* wasn't complaining."

"Don't worry about it." The woman rolled over a stool and sat. "We're always late around here. But I did take time to read through your chart." She held up a clipboard.

Ruby braced herself. "Do you know why I would be cramping?"

"Not yet," she said, but she quickly reinstated her smile. "It could be a variety of different things." Her eyes scanned

Ruby's check-in papers again. "During pregnancy, your body is undergoing a ton of changes. So it could be muscle related. Everything is stretching out a bit. Your body's trying to make room." She flipped the chart to the next page. "And I see the nurse wrote down that you haven't had anything to eat or drink yet today."

"No. I haven't been able to..." Instead of explaining the situation again, she let the words trail off.

"Elsie filled me in," Meg said sympathetically. "I'm so sorry. I can't imagine what you're going through."

"Thanks." Ruby glanced at the clock over her shoulder. Almost noon. Brookie had been gone at least five hours...

"So the problem with not eating or drinking during pregnancy is that dehydration can also cause cramping. It's important to take care of yourself. That's the best way to take care of the baby."

"So that's all it is, then?" Elsie asked, hands clasped hopefully in front of her chest. "Dehydration?"

"Hopefully." Meg stood. "But with your history, I'm concerned enough to run some tests. I'd like to start with some blood work. And I'll call your OB and see if he'd like us to do an ultrasound."

Ruby nodded. "Yes. Anything." Anything to make sure this baby was completely healthy.

"I'll put in the orders and we'll take a look at the lab results, then go from there."

"Okay." Relief pulled the knots out of her shoulders. She relaxed against the pillows, suddenly so exhausted.

Elsie squeezed her hand. "It's all precautionary, dear. Just to make sure. Isn't that right, Meg?"

"Yes. We want to make absolutely certain that the baby is one hundred percent healthy." She backed toward the door. "Do you want me to call Sawyer?"

"No." It came out fast and harsh. "I mean, not yet."

Meg glanced at Elsie, then back at her. "You might want him here, Ruby. Especially when we get the test results back." There was a hint of a warning in her tone. And Ruby got it. The woman had to prepare people for bad news all the time.

"He's still out searching for Brookie. I don't want him to know. Not until she's safe." She snuggled Lily again. "Besides, I have plenty of support." All of her best friends were crowding her with their love.

Meg smiled again. "Okay. That's your decision. Let me know if you change your mind. I'd be happy to call him and ease his concerns, if that would help."

"Thank you," she murmured. But a conversation with a doctor would not be enough to ease his concerns. He'd already lost a baby once. If he found out she was here, he would come.

"All right, then. I'll check back in after we get the labs." With a wave good-bye, she trotted out the door.

"All good news," Elsie insisted, stealing Lily from the bed. "Soon we'll have answers. And Brookie will be home. And we'll all be gathered tomorrow for your beautiful wedding."

Ruby closed her eyes and held on to that word.

Soon.

CHAPTER NINE

The Walker Mountain Ranch had always been Sawyer's second home. A refuge of family and comfort and safety. He'd spent so much time there growing up that he knew the land, the steep slopes, the rocky cliffs that loomed above the lodge. Now the mountains beyond the log structure seemed cold and treacherous. There were so many places to slip and fall. There were the resident bear and mountain lions. As a kid he'd never given the dangers of this land a second thought, but the knowledge that Brookie might be out there—a tiny needle in the haystack of thousands of acres—made his lungs fill with sand.

"Still can't find Moose," Bryce said, trotting up to him. "He's gotta be with Brookie. He wanders, but he always comes when he hears the whistle."

Why hadn't the dog heard it? Because he was too far away? Because he wouldn't leave Brookie's side and she wasn't able to walk? He shoved the thought out of his mind and faced his cousin. "I called Thomas. They're headed over." The four of them wouldn't be able to search the acreage alone. Ben and Isaac were already scouring the cabins and the interior of the lodge. He and Bryce had swept the land that lined either side of the driveway, but there'd been no sign of her. No sign that she'd been here. Maybe they were wrong…

Bryce clamped a hand onto his shoulder. "She's gotta be here. With Moose. We'll find her."

Sawyer scanned the acreage spread out all around them. Hope waned. They had so much ground to cover. "Thomas also said he called out search and rescue. They're hoping the weather clears so they can get the chopper up."

From the look of the clouds building above them, he wasn't too optimistic. Which meant they'd better get going. "We can search the back of the property while we wait for everyone else to get here," he said.

"Sounds good," his cousin agreed. "I'll take the stables."

"I'll check out the maintenance barn, then head on up to the north." Sawyer jogged in the opposite direction, trying to peer into the shadows between the evergreens while he made his way to the back side of the lodge.

"Brookie!" he shouted, the smallness of his voice mocking him. Like she'd ever be able to hear him out there.

He sprinted past the woodpile and along the north side of the lodge, but the back patio sat vacant. Passing the swimming pool, he skidded down the small dirt embankment to where the trees grew thicker, darkening his vision, hemming him in, unearthing a memory.

He'd been lost in the forest once. The summer after he'd turned six his dad had taken him on his first backpacking trip. While his father was setting up the tent, Sawyer had wandered. He hadn't meant to go far, but he'd heard a hawk crying out somewhere nearby so he'd tried to follow the sound. Next thing he knew, he stood in a valley instead of on the swell of land where they'd decided to make camp. When he'd glanced around, he'd realized everything looked the same. The trees and the rocks and the carpeted forest floor. He couldn't even see the peaks; the trees were too tall and too thick. That's when panic had spurted through him.

If you're lost, you stay where you are. Don't move, he'd been told his whole life. So he'd sat underneath a pine tree, huddled and terrified, sure his dad would never find him— that he'd have to learn to hunt and live off the land, build his own shelter and figure out how to start a fire. There was no better feeling he could ever remember than that moment when his father had rescued him from the spreading darkness.

According to his dad, he was missing for only about twenty minutes and he was only a quarter of a mile from where they'd pitched the tent. But he remembered how the stark loneliness had hollowed him. He'd never felt so alone. Until now. The moment he'd realized Brookie was gone, he'd shut out everything else, isolating himself in a wilderness of emotion he couldn't express. Even to Ruby. The one who'd reached out to him such a short time ago and reminded him that he wasn't alone.

Hunger pains stabbed his gut. He wished she was with him now, holding his hand while they searched for Brookie together. He needed her. God, he needed her. But she hadn't even called him back. Probably because he'd been such as ass to her.

Outside of the maintenance shed, he stopped and dug out his phone. He had to hear her voice. Had to beg for forgiveness for trying to keep her out. After ripping off his glove, he dialed her number, holding his breath until the line clicked and she answered.

"Sawyer? Did you find her? Did you find Brookie?"

He let her voice fill him, let it seep into those cracks in

his heart. "No. Not yet," he murmured. "But I think we're close." They had to be close.

"Okay," she whimpered. "Okay. I know you'll find her."

"I'm so sorry I tried to keep you out," he said, closing his eyes against a sting of emotion. "I want you with me, Ruby. I need you." The confession broke him free. "Can you come?"

"I want to." There was a catch in her voice, as though it were on the verge of breaking. "I want to so much. But I can't."

Can't. The word stunned him into silence.

"You were right," she almost whispered. "The stress. It's too much."

The wilderness seemed to close in on him. "Are you okay? Is the baby okay?"

"Yes," she said with a fortifying strength. "Everything's fine. I just need to rest a while." In the pause, he thought he heard something in the background. A radio? "I'll let you go so you can look for her," Ruby said quickly. "I love you, Sawyer."

"I love you, too," he managed before the line clicked. A thread of worry stitched his chest tight. Earlier she hadn't cared how tired she'd been. She'd stormed the streets driven by the same conviction that had enabled her to overcome so much in her life. But now she wouldn't come. No. She said she *couldn't* come. And Avery had been acting so weird on the phone earlier...

"Hey!" Bryce's shout snapped up his head. "You find anything yet?" his cousin called from the other side of the shed.

"No." He tried to clear his head. Ruby had said the baby was okay...

"We need the ATVs to search the hills." Bryce swiped

sweat from his forehead and shed his coat. He must've sprinted all the way from the stables. "Just heard they're calling for snow tonight. Up to a foot."

Urgency pounded through Sawyer. Snow meant freezing temperatures. Hypothermia. "Okay. The ATVs. Yeah. You can take one out to the west and I'll go—"

Woof!

"—north." Sawyer choked on the word. Bryce's head lifted, and he scanned the trees. Neither of them spoke. Sawyer couldn't. He swore that was Moose's low bark. Swore it.

"Moose!" Bryce's shout echoed back to them. His stuck his fingers in his lips and whistled.

Woof!

He hadn't imagined it. That was Moose barking. Not close, but not miles away, either. He strained his ears.

"I think it's coming from this way." Bryce yanked on his arm and they raced around the maintenance barn, hoofing it down the narrow path that skipped over a small brook and ended at the trailhead to the waterfall. The secret Walker Mountain Ranch oasis, where Ruby had placed a memorial to his unborn son, Matthew.

Woof! Moose bounded out of the woods, ears flapping, tail lashing the trees.

"Good boy, Moose!" Bryce called, clapping his hands. Both of them shot up the trail while Moose ran circles around them.

"She's at the waterfall. She has to be." Brookie knew it well. They'd hiked there so many times this fall to visit her brother's memorial...

His cousin halted. "I'll go back and get the ATV. Meet you up there." He shot down an embankment and disappeared.

Sawyer flew over the packed dirt, unsure how his legs were even moving. At the top of the first incline, he spotted Brookie's pink bike stashed in a bush. She couldn't have ridden it all the way to the waterfall. It was too steep.

"Where is she, Moose?" Sawyer gagged out, still afraid to believe. So close. This whole time she'd been so close.

The dog leaped and spun in another circle, barking like he'd lost his mind. Then he tore up the trail and out of sight.

Sawyer's lungs burned. His quads pinched, but he sprinted hard up the switchbacks, seeing nothing but the trail and his boots until the trees cleared and it was right there—the falls, the pool, the bench.

Brookie. Curled up on the bench. Sleeping.

A surge of joy he'd never before experienced caught him up and pushed him to her, heart reeling from the relief of waking from this nightmare. Colors flooded his vision again, where everything had gone gray. His lungs unlocked and let in the sweet mountain air.

Moose beat him to the bench and licked the girl's face until she stirred. Her head lifted and she saw him.

"Daddy."

He would always remember the way she said it. That look of pure wonderment on her face. He knew that feeling. The one where you were being rescued, pulled out of a lonely dark place when you thought maybe you would have to live there forever.

"You're here," his daughter sighed, her dark eyes drooped and groggy.

Sawyer caught her in his arms, not caring that he might be crushing her. "My princess," he breathed. "Oh God, my little princess."

He held her that way for as long as it took for his heart

to stop thrashing his ribs, feeling her warmth, her soft cries against his shoulder.

"We were so worried, Brookie. We missed you so much."

"I'm sorry," she sobbed, tearing herself away from him, peering up at him with a look that broke him. "I couldn't sleep anymore. And I wanted to be with Matthew."

"You could have woken me up. I would've come with you." Tears mingled with the sweat that ran down his face. "I'd go anywhere with you. Anytime."

"I didn't want to bother you." In between sniffles she hiccupped. "Now you have a baby coming..."

His hands cupped her cheeks and guided her gaze to his. "You are just as much my child as the baby is." He knew she might not believe him now. But he would prove it to her every day. Eventually his love for her, Ruby's love for her, would undo the damage her heart had sustained over the years.

"I'm sorry," she said again. "I'm so sorry, Daddy."

"I know. It's okay, baby." He hugged her. "We have to call Mom. She's so worried. We've been searching everywhere for you."

He dug out his phone and dialed, then held the phone between him and Brookie.

The speaker crackled. "Hello? Sawyer, dear, is that you?" Aunt Elsie. Why was Aunt Elsie answering Ruby's phone?

"Yeah. It's me. And Brookie." Those hot tears singed his eyes. "We found her. Where's Ruby?" He couldn't wait to tell her, couldn't wait to hear the same relief he felt in her voice.

There was a long pause. "Ruby is in with the doctor right now," Aunt Elsie said quietly. "We had to take her to the hospital."

"Mom's in the hospital?" Brookie cried, tears clouding her eyes again. "Because of me?"

"No," he assured her as he clicked off the speaker and brought the phone to his ear. He clenched his hands into fists so Brookie wouldn't see him shaking.

"What happened?" he asked his aunt, bracing himself against the fear that tried to claw through his happiness.

"She's had some pain and cramping. She didn't want you to worry, dear. She wanted you out searching for Brookie."

Pain and cramping. That was exactly what his ex-wife had experienced before she'd miscarried...

"The doctor is running some tests. I'm sure it's nothing to worry about, but I know she'd love to have you here."

Nothing to worry about? His jaw locked. "Yes. I'm coming. We're coming," he sputtered, body already in motion. He whisked Brookie into his arms so he could run down the trail and meet Bryce. "Tell her I'm on my way."

CHAPTER TEN

Ruby had never cared much for doctors. The few she'd seen in her unsettled life had been formal and indifferent. But Meg had this easy way about her. Maybe it was the freckles and the cropped blond hair. She could've been a teacher or a perky barista at the local coffee shop. If it weren't for the white coat and scrubs, you'd never know she'd spent the better part of her life in school.

"So the blood work looks okay," Meg informed her, rolling the stool closer to the gurney.

"That's good, right?" Paige asked. She was the only one who'd stayed in the room when Meg had come back. Elsie, Julia, and Avery had wanted to give them some space, Ruby suspected, though they'd claimed they needed to use the bathroom.

"Yes. That's good news." The doctor scanned a chart. "Your iron levels are low, so I'd like you to start taking a supplement."

A supplement. Ruby let out a steady breath. That sounded easy enough. "Of course. I only found out about the pregnancy a few days ago, so I haven't had time to pick up a vitamin."

Meg nodded in that friendly, understanding way. But then her face tightened into a more serious expression.

Ruby felt Paige's hand on her shoulder.

"You're also measuring significantly small for how far along you are," Meg said.

The tenor of concern in her voice kicked up Ruby's pulse. "Small."

"It could be the way you're carrying, but I called your OB, and he definitely wants an ultrasound so we can check on the baby's growth."

Ruby met Meg's eyes, searching for something to steady the rush of fear that swooped in and dropped her stomach. "Why wouldn't the baby be growing?"

"Sometimes there's an issue with the cord or the placenta," Meg said carefully. "Or maybe the baby is really petite. We won't know until—"

The door crashed open and Elsie rushed in, followed by Avery, Julia, and Thomas. "They found her! Oh, Ruby, they found Brookie!"

"What," she gasped, clutching at the sheets to pull herself upright.

"She was at the waterfall," Elsie sang. "Can you believe it?"

"Moose led Bryce and Sawyer there," Thomas added. "She'd fallen asleep on Matthew's bench."

"Thank God." Meg scooted her stool out of the way so everyone could crowd the bed.

They all closed in, cheering and hugging and sniffling. But Ruby felt frozen in place. The strength she'd amassed to carry her through started to crumble. And now she could let it go. She didn't have to be strong anymore because Brookie was home. Emotion whirled—joy and fear and relief and anguish—churning her into a whirlpool that took over the last bits of strength until she was hunched over and weeping into her hands.

"Oh, honey." Paige leaned down and held on to her.

"They're on their way here right now," Elsie soothed.

"I'll give you all a minute," Meg said, squeezing Ruby's shoulder. "The ultrasound tech should be here soon."

Ruby couldn't even nod. The tears and heartbreak flowed out of her and she felt so weak. But it was okay. Because the people around her were strong. And they would hold her up.

They did, comforting her with hugs and murmurs of love.

"Ruby." It was the only voice that could've lifted her head. She couldn't see through the blur of tears, but she could feel Sawyer in the room. Her body responded with a good hard squeeze, and she swung her legs over the side of the bed. But before she could run to him, to Brookie, they were there. Brookie threw herself into Ruby's arms, and it suddenly felt as though the world had miraculously been made right. That connection with her daughter surged, pumping joy into the limbs that had been lifeless and weary.

"I'm sorry, Mom. I'm so sorry," Brookie whimpered against her shoulder.

The room quieted, everyone else filing out, leaving only her and Sawyer and Brookie, a huddled mass crying on the bed. Sawyer had managed to get those strong, powerful arms around them both, as though he were holding their little family together.

"Oh, Brookie." She stroked the girl's soft curls. Love doubled the size of her heart. "I'm not mad. Not at all. I just missed you." Her voice had gone soggy, but it couldn't be helped. "I can't imagine my life without you, sweet girl. I love you so much."

"I love you, too." Though she and Sawyer had said those words to Brookie many times, the girl had never said them back until right then.

"I won't leave again. I promise. Not without asking," Brookie cried, clinging to Ruby. "I didn't mean to scare you. I didn't mean to hurt the baby. Will it be okay?"

Ruby looked into Sawyer's eyes. His were searching, almost pleading with her to say yes. She slipped her hand into his. "They're doing tests to check on the baby. But I think *he* or *she* will be okay." She leaned down to plant a kiss on the girl's forehead. "And it wasn't your fault. Not at all. The doctor said this kind of thing happens sometimes."

"Okay." Brookie sighed. "Okay."

The door opened, popping that protective bubble that held them in. Elsie practically dragged in a poor scrub-clad woman. "This is Lisa. The ultrasound tech," she announced, as though it were her place to introduce everyone and make sure they were doing their jobs. "I found her in the hallway."

The woman greeted them with a warm smile, despite being ordered around by an elderly woman. "Nice to meet you all," she said, pushing over her cart.

"Hi there." Ruby wiped the tears from her face. But she didn't let go of Brookie. God, she might never be able to let go.

"Are we ready to get started?" the tech asked.

She and Sawyer shared a look. On the off chance something was wrong, she didn't want Brookie to be there to hear about it.

"Actually," Elsie broke in, "Thomas and I were hoping to take Brookie upstairs to the cafeteria for a doughnut."

The girl's eyes sparked. "I *am* pretty hungry."

Ruby pried her arm off the girl's shoulders. "Okay." She pulled her in for one more hug. "But hurry back."

"We'll have her back in no time," Thomas assured her. Smooshing Brookie in between them as though promising they wouldn't let her out of their sight, they left the room.

"So it sounds like we're going to do some measurements," the tech said, guiding Ruby to lie on her back.

"Yes. That's what the doctor said."

Sawyer eased onto the mattress and threaded his arm around her, stroking her hair in the most comforting way. "What are you looking for?" he asked. And Ruby felt the tremble in his forearm.

"Meg said my waist is measuring smaller than it should be for how far along I am," Ruby answered. "She just wanted to make sure the baby is growing."

Sawyer's brows knit tightly together. "Why wouldn't the baby be growing?"

While Ruby explained the possibilities Meg had gone over, the tech focused on pressing some buttons on the machine. Then she lifted Ruby's hospital gown.

"This'll be cold," she warned before squirting goo on her belly.

It was. Slimy and cold.

She pressed the wand into Ruby's skin. "This'll help warm it up."

A heartbeat pitter-pattered on the small speaker.

Sawyer's breath caught. "That's the baby?"

Ruby nodded, watching the screen where a small form was taking shape.

"Found the head," the tech murmured, clicking the keyboard a couple of times. "See the eyes? The nose?"

"Yes," she whispered. The power of it knocked out her breath. "Wow. I can't believe there's a tiny little person in there."

Tears slipped down Sawyer's cheeks. He held her hand tightly in both of his. "Does it look okay? Is the baby big enough?"

"I'll let the doctor go over the results with you," the tech said, gliding the wand lower on her belly. Then she winked. "But so far so good."

Sawyer blew out a breath.

Ruby squeezed his hands.

The tech paused the wand right underneath Ruby's belly button. "Do you want to know the gender?"

Sawyer leaned closer to study the monitor. "That's a boy. Definitely a boy."

"Good eye," the tech confirmed.

"A boy," Ruby repeated. "We're having a baby boy." God. She'd never thought she would say those words. Never thought she would feel the signs of life growing inside of her. They both watched, captivated as the tech moved the wand and clicked the keyboard, showing them the tiny hands, the sweet little feet.

"That's about all," she finally said, wiping the wand with a paper towel. "Like I said, the doctor will go over the full report with you." She glanced around as though wanting to make sure no one would hear. "But in my professional opinion, this is a very healthy baby."

"I knew it," Sawyer said with a wide grin.

The tech waved a quick good-bye and pushed the cart out of the room, leaving them alone for the first time in too long.

"Ruby." She loved when he said her name like that, all low and tortured, like he needed her. He climbed onto the bed, stretching his beautiful body out next to her and gathering her into his arms.

His body never failed to wrap hers in a luxurious warmth. Even on a gurney. Even in the hospital...

"I screwed up." His cheek rested against hers, the stubble sending a cascade of tingles down her right side. "I didn't mean to shut you out. I just wanted to fix everything for you."

She peered at him sideways. "You *do* have quite the hero complex."

He grinned, traced her cheek with his finger. "Can't help it. I never want you to hurt again. I want to give you the perfect life."

"Perfect doesn't exist." Life was joy but also pain. Fear and courage. Suffering and triumph. And love. Love is what made all of it—even the sadness and scary moments—worthwhile. She turned to him, so they were face-to-face, chest-to-his glorious chest. Then she wrapped a leg over him for good measure. "We'll never have a perfect life or a perfect family, Sawyer."

"I know." The frost that had held his face so still and cold earlier that morning had melted away, revealing the friendly creases that lined his mouth, the crinkles that softened the corners of his eyes. "I'll stop shooting for perfect and aim for happy instead," he teased, placing his hands on her hips and hitching her closer to him.

"It's not your job to make the rest of us happy," she reminded him. "We work on it together. We choose it. All of us. Together."

"Together," he repeated; then pressed his lips against hers.

* * *

Most of the time Sawyer loved the loud chaos of family. Most of the time. But not when it interrupted him making out with his soon-to-be-wife. The two of them could've used a few more minutes alone, but the crowd paraded in anyway—all of the people who knew him and Ruby the best filling the room until it was stuffy and loud.

Brookie launched herself onto the bed between them, cuddling up against her mom, then closing her eyes and sighing as though she'd never been more at peace.

Tears brightened his fiancée's eyes again as she wrapped the girl in her arms.

"Oh, just look at you." Aunt Elsie sniffled. "Such a beautiful family."

Sawyer peered at his daughter, grinning at the sight of chocolate smeared under her chin. She looked so whole and happy. So healthy. Their little girl. And now they'd have a boy, too.

Paige elbowed her way through the crowd until she stood at the edge of the gurney. "You guys are killing me! What'd the doctor say?"

Sawyer shared a look with Ruby. "We haven't seen the doctor again yet, but the tech said the baby seems to be very healthy."

"Oh, thank God," Avery gasped, leaning her head on Bryce's chest.

With a slight nod and a big smile, Ruby prodded Sawyer to continue.

Good thing, because he wouldn't be able to keep this next bit of news a secret for long. "And it's a boy. We're having a boy."

Brookie gasped. "A brother! I'm getting a brother!" She leaped to her knees and started to bounce on the bed, swinging her arms around Sawyer's neck and hugging him tight.

He caught her and stood, twirling her around while she giggled and squealed. Everyone else closed in, too.

"Congratulations." Bryce whacked him on the back while Avery hugged Ruby.

"Such great news!" Julia wheeled herself over and squeezed his hand. Isaac scrubbed Brookie's hair. "You'll make a great big sister," he said, earning another open-mouthed grin.

Paige threw her arms around both him and Brookie, squeezing so tight he almost gagged. "You two can call me to babysit anytime," she said with a wink at Brookie. "I'll let you do whatever you want."

The girl giggled.

"We'll keep that in mind," Sawyer said with a roll of his eyes.

"Don't worry. I'll be there to supervise. Make sure she doesn't spoil them too much," Ben added with a playful tug on his wife's hair.

Sawyer laughed. Something told him Ben would spoil Brookie just as much as his wife did. And that was fine by him. The more people she had loving on her, the better off she'd be.

Aunt Elsie and Thomas pushed their way past Ben and Paige. The older man shook his hand. "You deserve this, Sawyer. You'll make a great dad."

"Thanks." He would do his best. And when he didn't know what to do or how to fix things, he'd hit up one of the other dads. He had a lot of good examples to choose from.

"Sawyer, dear," Aunt Elsie murmured sweetly. "Why don't you help me find Meg so we can break Ruby out of here?" She obviously had some hidden agenda, given the direct gaze that halted his argument. Even though he was pretty sure Meg didn't need to be bossed around, he followed his aunt out into the quietness of the hallway.

Before he could ask her what was going on, she handed him an envelope. "This is the deed to the duplex," she said. "I want you and Ruby to have it. For your family."

"What?" He shook his head. He couldn't accept this. He and Ruby had planned to rent the duplex until they'd saved enough to buy a home of their own. "We're not taking your house. We can't—"

"Of course you can," she interrupted. "You're going to need more space now with that baby coming. I'll move out after the wedding so you can get started on renovations right away."

He shook his head. Was she being serious? "But...where will you go?"

She shrugged. "I'll stay at the ranch for a while. Until I find a new place. I want something smaller anyway. Less to take care of."

Sawyer steadied a hand against the wall. "You have to let me buy it from you. It's worth a lot of money. I won't just take—"

"Yes, you will. Because it's a *gift*," she emphasized. "I don't need the money. Don't even want it, if you want to know the truth." She said it like they were talking about twenty bucks instead of hundreds of thousands of dollars. "It will be the perfect family home for the four of you."

Perfect. It was the perfect gift, exactly what he'd been looking for. A home of their own, where they could build happy memories. A refuge. A place for their family.

The stubborn ox in him wanted to argue, to wear her down until she agreed to accept something in return. But it would be useless. Aunt Elsie's generous heart knew no limits. She'd never had any practical boundaries. When she wanted to give, she gave big, no matter what it cost her.

And now so would he. He would live as generously as possible to honor her sacrifice.

"Thank you," he said, tucking the envelope into his pocket. "You'll never know how much this means to us."

But the happy twinkle in her eyes said she did.

CHAPTER ELEVEN

As a little girl, Ruby had dreamed about her wedding day.

In the midst of the ugliness and fear that had filled her world, she would imagine that someday everything would change. She'd pictured it happening the same way it had for Cinderella—the white horse and carriage, the prince, the castle so lovely and enchanted and the entire town celebrating.

What she saw in front of her was even more beautiful than a fairy tale like that. Because it was real. From her place on the top tier of the ranch's back patio, she gazed out on the powdered mountain peaks glowing in the soft pink light of the setting sun. She saw the evergreens— their branches laden with last night's snowfall—sheltering the perimeter of the beautiful stone patio below, where all of her favorite people in the world had gathered near the wooden arch Sawyer had built himself.

Tiki torches lined the edges, adding to the glow of warmth and happiness, despite forty-degree temperatures. They'd known it would be cold, so they'd decided to keep the ceremony short, but she could stand up here for hours, watching their few bundled guests mingle in hushed excitement—Sawyer's parents; Elsie and Thomas, who had agreed to marry them; a couple of the ranch hands and guides; a whole crew of Sawyer's colleagues, dressed in their starched uniforms.

The harpist they'd hired started to play, delicate notes floating on the calm mountain breeze. As if on cue, the door to the pool house north of the patio opened and Sawyer emerged, looking so tall and strong, so handsome in a crisp white shirt and pressed khakis. The groomsmen followed him—Bryce and Ben and Isaac—all of them tugging on their bow ties as though they were being strangled.

Ruby couldn't help but laugh. At least she hadn't made them wear tuxes. They probably would've staged a revolt.

"Ready?" Paige asked, bouncing up and down like she couldn't wait anymore.

Ruby reached over and grabbed Brookie's hand. They were going to walk down the aisle together, but they had to go last.

"After you." Ruby stepped aside so Paige and Avery and Julia could start the parade. They moved down the center of the crowd in a slow processional, even Paige, which was a miracle given how fast that woman usually liked to go.

"Mom?" Brookie tugged on the skirt of her dress.

She leaned down. "What is it, sweet girl?"

"I'm so nervous," her daughter whispered. "There's a lot of people down there."

She knelt. "Don't focus on the people, honey." She smoothed Brookie's lovely hair. "This is about you and Dad and me. That's all. Focus on the three of us. On our family."

Biting her lip, Brookie nodded.

"And just think, as soon as we get this part over with,

there'll be cake," she added, knowing that their shared love of baked confections would calm her.

Sure enough, Brookie grinned. "Triple chocolate cake!"

The music changed, and that was their cue. Taking her own advice, Ruby focused solely on Sawyer—on her husband—as she made her way to him, holding tightly to their daughter's hand.

She'd never seen anything as beautiful as the sight of him grinning through his tears. This was exactly why she hadn't worn any mascara.

Underneath the arch, Thomas stood tall, looking so debonair in his best Western shirt and jeans, the light-colored cowboy hat tilted on his head. As soon as she and Brookie stopped at the very edge of the center aisle, he cleared his throat.

"Thank you all for being here to celebrate this family today." His deep tenor carried, bringing a hush over the crowd. "These sacred vows are not just between Ruby and Sawyer, because you will not only be a new couple, but you will be a new family. So, Brookie, will you please join us now for the special family rites of this wedding."

Still holding tightly to Ruby's hand, Brookie walked forward, looking at her father, only at her father and nothing else, leading Ruby to the archway. With her back to the crowd, Brookie took both of their hands and joined them together as a family.

Thomas handed Sawyer the passage to read.

"Brookie," he started, then paused, inhaling deeply as though attempting to keep his composure. "Thank you for loving us and for allowing us to love you with all of our hearts," he said. "We weren't there when you took your first steps, but we promise that now we will love and support you in every step that you take in your life."

Brookie sniffled loudly, tears streaking down her soft skin.

As though he couldn't stand it, Sawyer knelt and gazed into their daughter's eyes. "We love you, Brookie, and we are devoted to making your life full of happiness and accomplishments, nurturing your creativity, encouraging your independence, and making sure you always know what a gift you are to this world."

Ruby wiped away tears, then joined him on her knees, holding on to the joy that radiated from Brookie's beautiful face. She wasn't sure she'd be able to speak, but she would try. "We are devoted to ensuring that you thrive to your fullest potential," she read. "And that while you reach for the sky, you remain grounded by the love of our family and our home," she murmured, silently willing Brookie to always remember those words.

Thomas gave his throat a hearty clearing, as though he was having as hard a time with the tears as they were. "Brookie, do you have the rings?" he asked, his usually gruff voice soft.

The three of them stood and Brookie nodded, holding up the small box they'd decorated together.

Facing the audience, Thomas positioned himself between them and joined their hands together. "Brookie, please hand the ring to your dad."

She carefully opened the box and held the delicate band between her fingers. With a wide smile she offered it to Sawyer.

"Sawyer, place this ring on Ruby's finger and hold it there as you repeat after me: I give you my promise to be by your side forevermore. I promise to love, to honor, and to listen as you tell me of your thoughts, your hopes, your fears, and your dreams. I promise to love you deeply and truly because it is your heart that moves me, your head that challenges me, your humor that delights me, and your hands I wish to hold until the end of my days."

Sliding the ring onto her finger, Sawyer made his vow to her, the sincerity in his eyes, the gravity of his deep voice making her believe. In love. In them. In the gift of their family.

Thomas shifted to look at her. "Brookie, please give the ring to your mom."

The girl carefully plucked it from the box, as though she feared she might drop it. She opened her hand and Ruby took the gold band between her fingers.

"Ruby, place this ring on Sawyer's finger and hold it there as you repeat after me."

Nearly breathless, she slipped the ring onto his finger and held it there against his wonderfully warm skin, whispering the words. They filled her heart with an unbending joy and conviction that bound her to this incredible man. Forever. The whole world changed with that one word. That commitment. For the first time in her life, she wasn't alone. She wasn't on her own. She belonged to Sawyer and he belonged to her and that made them stronger.

Thomas rested a hand on each of their shoulders. "Ruby and Sawyer, may all your days be filled with joy and happiness. It is with honor and great pleasure that by the power vested in me by the state of Colorado I now pronounce you husband and wife."

"Kiss her!" Paige yelled before Thomas could deliver the famous last line.

Ruby saw Ben nudge his wife with a grin.

"What?" Paige demanded. "Come on, Sawyer. Let's get this party started!"

"Yes," Sawyer agreed, taking her into his arms and dipping her low. "Let's get this party started."

The heat from his lips melted her heart and she no longer heard the hearty cheers and whoops that surrounded them. She only heard the echoes of his promise beating all through her.

* * *

The Walkers had always known how to throw a party. Ruby leaned against the couch cushion, wondering how she'd stay awake for the ride home.

Most of the guests had already gone. The presents had been opened; wrapping paper littered the floor. And now it was just the Walkers and Thomas, the Harpers, the Nashes, and James and Marybeth sitting around the fireplace, sipping wine while they chatted and laughed and simply enjoyed the peace of being together.

"You haven't opened our present yet," Marybeth said suddenly, scurrying behind the couch and coming back with a large box. She waved at her husband until he set down his wine and retrieved another box.

"Some of our favorite memories are from family dinners," the woman said warmly. While they'd gotten off to a rocky start, Marybeth was friendly and kind and Ruby was sure they'd get along well.

"We hope your family will build those same memories together," she said, nudging the box closer to Ruby.

Carefully, she tugged on all of the corners until she could lift the paper away. "Oh, wow." The boxes held a set of the most beautiful china she'd ever seen. White plates with a delicate gold band circling the edges.

"Those were Grandma's," Sawyer said, inspecting the box.

"And it was her mother's before that." Marybeth beamed, and Ruby saw how much this offering meant to her. It meant Marybeth accepted her as a daughter, that she wanted her as part of their family.

"It's so beautiful." She opened the box and took out a plate, running her fingers over the smooth surface. She'd never had anything so lovely. "We'll think of you every time we use it." Every time she set the table for a special occasion, she would feel that connection to family.

Sawyer shifted next to her, stretching out his legs. "I guess this is a good time to give you my present."

Brookie, who had been leaning her head against her father's shoulder barely able to keep her eyes open, perked up. "A present?"

"Yes." He stood and snatched a large manila envelope off the mantel. "It's actually from Aunt Elsie and me."

Ruby took the envelope from his hand.

Brookie scooted to the floor and peered over her shoulder. "What is it?"

"I'm not sure," Ruby said, carefully breaking the seal. She pulled out the papers inside. "Floor plans?" She flipped through. The last one was a drawing. Of Elsie's duplex. Or...what would've been the duplex. Except in the drawing it had been converted to a single-family home. Mouth gaping, she peered up at Sawyer.

"Aunt Elsie wants us to have it. It's ours," he said simply.

Ours. Her eyes burned with the flood of tears. She turned to look at Elsie, this woman who'd given her hope and a family and a place to belong. This woman who'd already offered her so much. "This is too much," she whispered. "We can't take your home."

"It's not my home any longer," Elsie said in her kind motherly way. "You two will make it yours."

Ruby looked down at the plans again.

Sawyer lowered himself to the ground beside her. "See? That'll be the new living room, open to the kitchen." He pointed to the room at the back of the house. "And this'll be Brookie's new room. I'm thinking we'll add in a bathroom all for her."

"Really?" Brookie gasped. "My own bathroom?"

"Really," he repeated.

"And the baby's room will be right next door to yours, Brookie." He pointed to the other square, but Ruby could hardly see past the tears.

"You're going to do all the work?" she asked, amazed that he had planned all of this.

"My crew and I," he said, hiking his thumb toward Bryce and Ben.

Isaac grinned. "Damn. Too bad we have to head back to Dallas. Hate to miss out on the manual labor."

"I'm sure you can come back and visit," Ben shot back.

"Pass the plans over here," Paige said, holding out her hand. "I gotta see how much work this is gonna be."

Ruby handed them over, and Avery and Paige *ooh*ed and *ahh*ed.

After everyone had gotten a good look at the plans, Thomas cleared his throat as though he had an announcement to make.

He slipped off his cowboy hat and gazed at Elsie. "Don't you think this is a good time to tell them our news?"

"What news?" Bryce demanded, his head pitched forward like he was sizing up Thomas.

"Well . . ." Thomas fidgeted with his hat, turning it in circles with his hands. "Elsie and I are dating," he said firmly.

"Pshaw, Thomas," Elsie squawked, whapping his shoulder. "We go to dinner once in a while, but we are *not* dating. Don't be ridiculous."

Ruby raised her hand to hide her smile. Elsie's face was redder than a scalding-hot oven burner.

Thomas seemed to ignore the desperate look that Ruby was sure was meant to shut him up.

"Damn it all, Elsie," he said, tossing his hat aside. It landed in the middle of the scattered wrapping paper. "I'm tired of just going to dinner once in a while."

The room went so silent, you could've heard a mouse cough. Ruby glanced at Sawyer, who didn't bother to hide his amused smile.

"Now, I've loved you for a long time," the man went on, as though he didn't want to give her another opportunity to interrupt. "After Judy passed, I didn't think I'd love anyone else. Ever. But I was wrong."

Sawyer moved in closer to Ruby. He slipped his arms around her waist and held her, and she knew it was because they'd both been given the impossible. They'd felt the same way Thomas had. That they'd never find love again, and yet here they were, surrounded by more than they ever could've dreamed of.

"Thomas...oh, my dear Thomas," Elsie breathed, tilting her head, gazing at him in that affectionate way older women have.

He pushed off the couch and stooped to one knee. "Elsie Walker, you are the loveliest woman in this world. And I would move heaven and earth to make you happy. Would you do me the honor of becoming my wife?"

Ruby looked around the room. Everyone seemed to be on the verge of crying or whooping or doing *something*, but they were frozen, waiting for Elsie.

"Oh my. Oh dear. Oh my dear." Her hands were stuck to her cheeks as she peered down at Thomas.

He waited patiently, gentleman that he was, not rushing the moment, not speaking another word. But Ruby had to tighten her jaw to keep from yelling out "Yes!" for Elsie, because she was not that polite.

Finally, Elsie simply held up one finger, as though telling him to wait. She popped off the couch and hurried over to Ruby, untying her Walker Mountain Ranch apron and slipping it over her head. "Here you go, dear." She placed it into Ruby's hands reverently, as if it were the Lincoln Bible. "You're ready to manage your own kitchen now." She looked back at her beloved Thomas, whose knee had to have been going numb. "And I'm ready to start a new life with the man I love."

The chorus of celebration did start then, Brookie squealing, laughter bubbling, everyone hugging.

Ruby watched Sawyer dance a silly waltz with Brookie. Resting her hand on her belly, she teared up again. Elsie's words branded her heart. A new life. That's what she'd learned at the Walker Mountain Ranch.

Love brings new life wherever it goes.

ACKNOWLEDGMENTS

It's hard to believe it's time to say good-bye to everyone at the Walker Mountain Ranch! I fell in love with these characters and am so grateful to everyone who helped me bring them to life.

I absolutely love working with the whole team at Forever. Megha Parekh, you are such a brilliant editor. Thank you for pushing me to create authentic characters. I so appreciate your hard work and creative insight. Marissa Sangiacomo, thank you for helping me get the word out about the Heart of the Rockies series. It's so fun to work with you! And to all of the incredible people behind the scenes in sales and marketing and design—thank you, thank you, thank you for doing all of the things I would never be able to do on my own.

Thank you to my agent, Suzie Townsend, for working out the details for this project. I'm so blessed to be able to work with you!

While writing the wedding scene in this book, I searched everywhere for inspiration on blended-family vows. Thank you, Shyamala Littlefield of *Ceremonies for Sacred Days,* for letting me borrow your beautiful phrasing.

To my husband, Will, thank you for being by my side

for every adventure, every joy, every disappointment, every moment no matter what. I love you. AJ and Kaleb, there is no greater gift than watching you grow and make your mark on the world. You are funny and smart and creative, generous and compassionate. I am one lucky mama.

ABOUT THE AUTHOR

Sara Richardson grew up chasing adventure in Colorado's rugged mountains. She's climbed to the top of a fourteen-thousand-foot peak at midnight, swum through Class IV rapids, completed her wilderness first-aid certification, and spent seven days at a time tromping through the wilderness with a thirty-pound backpack strapped to her shoulders.

Eventually Sara did the responsible thing and got an education in writing and journalism. After a brief stint in the corporate writing world, she stopped ignoring the voices in her head and started writing fiction. Now she uses her experience as a mountain adventure guide to write stories that incorporate adventure with romance. Still indulging her adventurous spirit, Sara lives and plays in Colorado with her saint of a husband and two young sons.

Learn more at:
SaraRichardson.com
Twitter, @SaraR_Books
Facebook.com/SaraRichardsonBooks

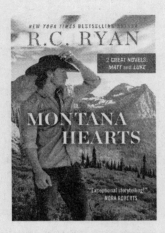

MONTANA HEARTS (2-IN-1 EDITION)
by R.C. Ryan

Fall in love with two heart-pounding Western romances in the Malloys of Montana series. In *Matt*, a raging storm traps together a rugged cowboy and a big-city lawyer who can't stop butting heads. But when one steamy kiss leads to another, will differences keep them from the love of a lifetime? In *Luke*, a stubborn rancher thrown from his horse is forced to accept the help of a beautiful stranger. But as they begin to feel sparks, will secrets from the past threaten their newfound feelings?

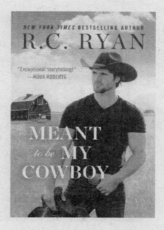

MEANT TO BE MY COWBOY
by R.C. Ryan

Fresh off a bad breakup, Annie Dempsey has rules for her new life in Devil's Door, Wyoming: no romance, no drama, and steer clear of the Merrick clan—her family's sworn enemies. But when a charming stranger steps in to protect Annie from a sudden threat, rules fly out the door. Because her mystery hero is...Jonah Merrick. As she hides from a dangerous pursuer at Jonah's ranch, they can't deny the chemistry pulling them closer together. But can they put their family rivalry aside to make room for love instead?

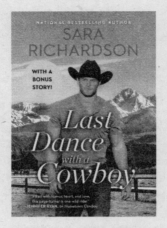

LAST DANCE WITH A COWBOY
by Sara Richardson

Leila Valentino will do anything to keep her grandparents' Colorado winery afloat. Even partner with August Harding, the first—and last—man to break her heart. The cowboy's investment offer could save the business, but her grandparents have no idea how close they are to going under. So Leila insists that August pretend he's back in town for her. When their faux relationship starts feeling for real, a second chance seems possible—but can August convince Leila that this time he's not walking away? With a bonus story by Carolyn Brown!